THE BOY WHO CRIED BEAR

THE BOY WHO CRIED BEAR

A Haven's Rock Novel

KELLEY ARMSTRONG

MINOTAUR BOOKS
NEW YORK

First published in the United States by Minotaur Books, an imprint of St. Martin's Publishing Group

THE BOY WHO CRIED BEAR. Copyright © 2024 by KLA Fricke Inc. All rights reserved. Printed in the United States of America. For information, address St. Martin's Publishing Group, 120 Broadway, New York, NY 10271.

www.minotaurbooks.com

Library of Congress Cataloging-in-Publication Data

Names: Armstrong, Kelley, author.
Title: The boy who cried bear / Kelley Armstrong.
Description: First edition. | New York: Minotaur Books, 2024. |
    Series: Haven's Rock; 2
Identifiers: LCCN 2023036198 | ISBN 9781250865441 (hardcover) |
    ISBN 9781250341310 (Canadian) | ISBN 9781250865458 (ebook)
Subjects: LCGFT: Detective and mystery fiction. | Novels.
Classification: LCC PR9199.4.A8777 B69 2024 | DDC 813/.6—
    dc23/eng/20230816
LC record available at https://lccn.loc.gov/2023036198

Our books may be purchased in bulk for promotional, educational, or business use. Please contact your local bookseller or the Macmillan Corporate and Premium Sales Department at 1-800-221-7945, extension 5442, or by email at MacmillanSpecialMarkets@macmillan.com.

First Edition: 2024
First International Edition: 2024

10 9 8 7 6 5 4 3 2 1

For Jeff

THE BOY WHO CRIED BEAR

PROLOGUE

Max

"We're being stalked," Max whispers to his big brother. "I think it's a bear."

Carson scowls and waves for Max to be quiet.

"I'm serious," Max whispers, loud enough to attract the attention of Kendra, leading the group hike.

"Everything okay back there, buddy?" Kendra calls over her shoulder.

"It'll be better when you turn around and take us back to civilization," Carson says. "This is even more boring than last week's hike."

Kendra raises her middle finger, and Max can't suppress a smile. Mom says Kendra is a social worker, but Carson says that she's too cool for that. Max thinks Mom's right, though. They've mostly only had social workers who are, well, kinda boring. Kendra's fun, and she knows how to handle thirteen-year-olds like Carson when they're being jerks.

Carson might respect Kendra, but that doesn't keep him

from grumbling and kicking the dirt the moment she turns away. Max knows his brother doesn't want to be here. Carson hates the forest. He's scared of it, though he'd never admit that. Max wishes he'd admit it. He wishes Carson would admit all the things that scare him, because then Max could admit them, too.

Carson is scared that the bad men will find them here. Max shouldn't call them "bad men." That makes Carson roll his eyes. Max is ten, and "bad men" is little-kid talk, which was fine when they *were* little kids, and Mom and Dad explained about the bad men and why they had to play a hiding game. Witness protection—Max knows the proper words now.

Their parents saw something bad, and they'd done the right thing by telling the police. The "bad man" went to jail, only he had friends who were angry, and that meant witness protection.

Max didn't used to be afraid of these people. His family always had their "Captain America shield," as Dad called witness protection. Then the shield broke. Now Dad is dead, and Mom is injured, and they're hiding in the wilderness and Carson is so mad. Mad and scared, and being scared only makes him more mad.

These days, Carson hates everything. Mom calls it "a phase." She also says he has a reason to be angry, and he needs to "work through his trauma." Carson's seeing Mathias for that. Mathias is a psychiatrist and also the town butcher, just like Kendra is a social worker but also the town plumber and the hike leader. Max is doing therapy, too, only he talks to Isabel, who's a psychologist but also runs the town bar, which everyone calls the saloon, like in the Wild West, which is really cool.

To Max, everything about Haven's Rock is cool. It's like being at summer camp, except it's for grown-ups, and he and Carson are the only kids, and that's kinda awesome.

"Stupid hikes," Carson mutters, kicking his feet. "I don't know why you like them so much. There's nothing to see but trees."

Max could point out what Carson is missing. So many things that he'd run out of breath listing them. *Look at that orange mushroom—it's edible, but that one's old and will taste bitter. Over there is fox scat—it's pointy at the end and has fur in it. See that ground squirrel—when they hibernate, their bodies go below freezing.*

He could say all that. He *has* said all that and more, and Carson only grumbles that he's starting to sound like Sheriff Eric, which Max considers a compliment—the sheriff knows *everything* about the forest—but Carson doesn't mean it that way.

Max also doesn't say that Carson could have stayed behind. Mom insists Carson come on the hikes to look after Max. She can't because of her bad leg, after she was shot by the men who killed their father.

Max is allowed to go on his own with Sheriff Eric or Detective Casey, but Mom thinks Kendra is "a bit young" to look after Max. Kendra is twenty-three, which is older than Max's last teacher, but he knows not to say that. Just like he knows not to speak to Carson until he has to.

If there's a predator stalking them, he has to say something.

"I really do think it's a bear," Max whispers.

"Good. A bear attack might be the only thing that'll make this hike interesting."

Max scowls at him.

"There's no bear, Max. Don't do this again. You embarrassed us enough the last time."

Carson stalks off ahead.

Max glances to the left. There's nothing there now, but he'd definitely heard an animal earlier. A big animal.

Ever since Max told Isabel he had nightmares about people

sneaking up on him, Sheriff Eric has been teaching him how to track sounds in the forest. One day, after a really bad nightmare, they'd sat in the woods all morning, listening for animals.

The crack of a twig. The rustle of undergrowth. A grouse, startled from its hiding place. And sometimes, there's no sound at all, which says there's a predator nearby.

Earlier, there'd been three noises. A crackle. A rustle. Another crackle. Each had come at least thirty seconds after the last, meaning the creature is following them.

Stalking them.

It's big, too. Sheriff Eric taught him how to guess the size of a creature by the size of the noise. This isn't a rabbit.

Arctic hare, he corrects. They have hares here, not rabbits. While hares usually have longer hind legs and ears, Arctic hares have shorter ones. Unlike rabbits, they live alone or in pairs, but when it gets really cold, they've been known to huddle with others for warmth. Right now—late summer back home and early fall here—the hares are starting to turn white for winter camouflage. There'd been a lot of them this year, which Sheriff Eric says means there'll be more lynx and fox—and maybe even wolves—next year because more food means more of their kits and cubs will survive.

Max hurries to catch up with Carson, wanting to tell him about Arctic hares, but the look on his brother's face warns him not to. He'll tell Mom instead. She likes to hear everything he's learning, even on the days when the pain is so bad she has to stay in bed. Sometimes, if he listens at the door, he hears her crying. He's never sure if it's because of the pain, though, or because Dad's gone.

Max keeps peeking to the side, trying to see what's stalking them. Three months ago, he'd have been so scared he'd have run and told Kendra right away. He knows better now. There are six of them on the hike. Kendra is up front, leading the way. Behind her is a man whose name Max doesn't know yet. He's new, and he's gawking around like he's never seen a tree before. Then there's Lynn, who came with her husband, but Max hears them fighting all the time. Next come Carson and Max. Gunnar brings up the rear.

Kendra carries a gun. Gunnar does not, which is funny, because of his name. But Gunnar *does* have bear spray. So does Kendra. With one gun, two cans of bear spray, and six people, they shouldn't need to worry about bears. Whatever is following them is just curious. Still, Max should tell Kendra. That's what Sheriff Eric would say. But the last time they were out for a walk, Max thought he saw a bear following them, and he'd told Kendra . . . and there'd been no bear.

Carson had said Max was imagining things, but Kendra and Sheriff Eric and Detective Casey believed Max. Kendra and Sheriff Eric had searched for tracks or fur or broken branches. Detective Casey brought Storm to sniff around.

No one found any sign of a bear. They'd all been really nice about it—*better safe than sorry*—but Max had wanted to curl up in embarrassment. He'd felt like a little kid with everyone humoring him.

So now, even though Max should tell Kendra, he can't. Not without proof.

"Can you just listen?" Max whispers to Carson. "Tell me if you hear what I hear."

"I don't hear anything except you."

Max stops talking, in hopes that Carson means "Be quiet so I can listen." But Carson keeps walking with that look on his face, the one that says he doesn't want to see or hear anything.

"Just listen," Max says. "Please."

"I don't hear it."

"You're not listening."

"Would you stop this?" Carson hisses. "You're embarrassing yourself. Do you want Eric to stop giving you those lessons?"

"*Sheriff* Eric."

Carson rolls his dark eyes. "He's not a real sheriff."

"Yes, he is. He has a hat and a gun. Detective Casey says they used to have horses, in the other town. Just like a real sheriff."

"You're such a baby. If you keep this up, Mom's going to decide those lessons with Eric are freaking you out. She might even decide you shouldn't go into the forest if you can't stop jumping at every noise."

"I'm not jumping. I'm being aware of my surroundings."

Another eye roll. "Now you even sound like him."

"Hey, kid," Gunnar calls. "Is your brother being an asshole again?"

"Yes," Carson says.

"I wasn't talking to you, asshole."

Lynn looks back sharply, her eyes wide. "Did you just call Carson an—?" She mouths the word.

"Course not," Gunnar says. "That would be wrong."

As soon as Lynn turns away, Gunnar mouths *Asshole* to Carson, who flips him the bird. Gunnar only grins.

"Come back here, kid," Gunnar says to Max. "Your brother needs a time-out."

"Finally," Carson says, and walks on ahead.

Max slows to let Gunnar catch up. Gunnar is older than Kendra—he'd turned twenty-eight last month and the bakers made him a cake. So Carson shouldn't need to come along when Gunnar's there, right? Max tried saying that to his mom, but she wouldn't listen. Like it didn't matter how old Gunnar was, she still didn't trust him with her son.

If she'd been really worried, she wouldn't have let Max near

Gunnar. But when Gunnar is around Max, Mom watches him, the way she might watch a dog she didn't quite trust. The dog might seem friendly, but something about it put her on guard.

"You okay?" Gunnar asks when they fall in step together.

Max shrugs.

"Something up?"

Max is about to shrug again. Then he pauses and thinks.

Gunnar seems friendly. No, not *seems*. Max has met plenty of people who act that way but they aren't. Gunnar *is* friendly. But there's something else there, too.

Gunnar reminds Max of a stray cat that lived in their old neighborhood. A big ol' tom, Mom called it. It even kinda looked like Gunnar—shaggy yellow hair and lots of muscles. It was always prowling around, but it'd come out to see Max and even let him scratch its ears. Max knew it wasn't a pet, but it also wasn't dangerous. At least, not to him.

Should he lie to Gunnar and say nothing's wrong?

No, he really needs to tell someone, and he trusts Gunnar to know what to do with the information.

"I heard something in the forest," Max whispers. "An animal. I wanted Carson to listen for it, but he thinks I'm imagining things, like the last time."

"No one said you were imagining it the last time, kid. They just didn't find whatever you saw. Tell me what I'm listening for."

"Anything. A rustle of leaves. A crack of a twig. I've heard both. A few times."

"Which side?"

Max jerks his chin left.

"Okay, let's take a listen."

Gunnar doesn't seem like the type to humor kids, but he must be. Still, would Max rather Gunnar made fun of him for worrying, like Carson does? Or brushed him off, like grown-ups sometimes do, acting as if every fear is just a monster under the bed?

It doesn't matter. Max has told an adult, as he's supposed to, and Gunnar isn't making a big deal out of it, which Kendra might have. If Gunnar doesn't hear anything—

"Kid?" Gunnar leans sideways toward him. "Keep looking straight ahead."

"Okay . . ."

"When I count to three, fall back a couple of steps. Just a couple. Then look over your left shoulder. There's a dried-up stream over there."

"I know."

"Look on the other side of it. I think I see something big and brown."

"Okay."

"Count of three. Fall behind but only two steps. Stay close enough to run back to me."

"Okay."

Did Gunnar really see something? He might not seem the type to humor a kid, but he *is* the type to humor himself. Play along with Max because he's bored.

Does Max trust Gunnar not to make fun of him? That's the big question, because amusing yourself by playing along is something bullies do.

Does Gunnar seem like a bully? Max isn't sure, but there's no audience here to amuse. That's what bullies do. They play along, and then you fall for it, and everyone laughs.

That's one good thing about being in a town of grown-ups. No one's going to laugh if Gunnar plays a mean joke on a ten-year-old.

"Kid?" Gunnar says. "You with me?"

Max nods. "Count of three. Fall back two steps. Look over my left shoulder, across the creek."

"You got it. Now, three . . . two . . . one."

As Max falls behind, he gets a granola bar out of his left pocket, acting like it's stuck and that's why he's slowing down. Then the bar pops out, and he looks over his left shoulder. Way over it at first, like he's just realized he's at the back of his group. His gaze swivels forward, slowly, just gazing at the forest as he turns around.

Something moves, a blur of brown disappearing behind bushes.

Was that a bear?

It must have been. It was at least as tall as Gunnar. A bear on its hind legs.

Could it have been a tree stump? Or a bush?

Not unless stumps and bushes can move.

Whatever it was, it's behind the bushes now, and when Max peers, he can still see the top of its brown head above the branches.

"I'm not seeing things, right?" Gunnar says right beside him, making Max jump. "There's something behind those bushes. Right—" Gunnar swears as the top of that brown head disappears.

"It dropped to all fours," Max says. "They only stand up on two legs to look around or scare other predators."

"By 'they' you mean bears."

Max nods.

"Couldn't be a moose?" Gunnar asks. "No antlers, so maybe a doe?"

Max considers. Moose *are* as tall as a man. He calls up the mental image of what he'd just seen. A round furry head with what looked like ears.

Max shakes his head.

"Shit." Gunnar takes a deep breath. "If it's following us, we need to tell Kendra. Come on. Stay right beside me."

Gunnar takes his bear spray from its holster and picks up speed. Max has to jog to keep up. He looks ahead and realizes they've fallen behind. The others are up around the bend, and they can't see them. Max's heart starts to pound.

They shouldn't have fallen so far behind. That means they're separated from the group. Just two of them, with no gun. If the bear is stalking them, and it realizes that two people have fallen back—one of them just a little kid . . .

Max glances left again and—

Something's there.

Something's right there.

"Gunnar?" That's what Max tries to say, but the word won't come out. There's something in the woods beside them, moving behind the thick bushes.

There's a break in the bushes, and Max sees fur. Brown fur and then a massive paw with long, curving claws.

"Gunnar?"

It comes out as a squeak, and Gunnar doesn't hear him, and there's a bear, right there. A bear moving fast, still on its hind legs.

That's not how it works. They can't move like that on two legs. But this one is, and it's right on the other side of the bushes and then the bushes drop low and the bear looks over and its eyes meet Max's and they aren't bear eyes at all.

They're human.

CHAPTER ONE

Casey

"Bigfoot," Anders whispers at my ear. "I can't believe we're searching for Bigfoot. This is so cool."

I glare at our deputy. Anders only grins back and waggles his brows.

"I'm joking," he says, his voice still low enough for only me to hear. "I wouldn't say that in front of anyone else. Poor kid's been through hell. If I were him, I'd be too damn scared to go into the forest at all. Hell, sometimes I *am* too damn scared, and I've been living out here for six years."

Looking at Will Anders, it'd be hard to believe anything could frighten him. He's over six feet tall and built like a quarterback. An army tattoo on his biceps speaks to an early career in the military police. But, yes, despite his years in Rockton, he's not entirely comfortable in the forest, as evidenced by the big .45 at his hip. Dalton and I carry smaller guns and accept that we aren't likely to stop a grizzly. Anders hedges his bets in any way he can.

An hour ago, ten-year-old Max saw something on a hike. It seems to have been a grizzly. Max described a tall brown-furred creature, which is also what Gunnar saw. But Max swears when the beast looked at him, it had human eyes. So, yes, that naturally leads to jokes about Bigfoot. Jokes that I know Anders would never make in front of other residents. Jokes that we need to ensure other residents don't start making themselves, in case Max overhears. He'd already admitted he'd been reluctant to report hearing something after a similar incident turned up nothing.

Max is a smart kid. He's also a kid suffering from PTSD. Being smart *and* traumatized means he's aware that he might be jumpy, and he doesn't want to be the boy who cried bear. But worrying about that led to a situation where a group of hikers had been stalked by a grizzly, and the only one who noticed had second-guessed himself until it was almost too late.

"Fuck."

I follow the curse to the guy standing off to my left. Sheriff Eric Dalton. My partner in . . . well, everything. Husband, colleague, best friend, co-founder of Haven's Rock, our tiny sanctuary town in the Yukon.

The curse makes me smile. He's been trying to cut back on profanity, particularly his affinity for every variation on that particular word. I'm mostly just amused by his efforts.

Dalton strides over with brown hairs pinched between his thumb and forefinger.

"Moose, right?" I say, half joking, half hoping.

He shakes his head. That curse told me what I needed to know. It's grizzly fur.

"Storm was right then," I say, patting our Newfoundland. She's our tracking dog, or that was the excuse Dalton used for buying me my dream-breed puppy. We *have* trained her in tracking, though, and her reaction earlier told me we weren't dealing with a moose. She smelled bear.

"Any prints?" Anders asks.

"Ground's too dry. Found a couple of scuff marks, but all I can tell from them is that they're big and they aren't hoofprints. Got a few broken branches. Bit of trampled undergrowth. And this"—he lifts the fur—"four feet off the ground."

"Shit." Anders casts an anxious glance around. "That's a problem, right? A grizzly stalking a group of six. It should know better."

"We're lucky Max noticed it," I say.

"Yeah, it's good he noticed, but I'm not sure they were in real danger. Bear was looking for an opportunity. Would it have attacked if Gunnar and Max fell behind for longer? Or was it just getting closer for a better look?" Dalton shrugs. "Hard to say. The fact it fled is a good sign."

"It's still a concern," I say.

"Hell, yeah. The question is how to play it. In Rockton, I'd have leaned in hard. Possible man-eating grizzly on the loose. No one takes a single step outside town until we've dealt with it. Scare the shit out of people."

"But we have children in town now, children who've already been traumatized."

"Yep, and I don't know shit about dealing with that. We're going to need to consult with the experts."

"Isabel and Mathias."

"Get their take on it. How do we properly convey the magnitude of danger while not giving the kids an extra helping of nightmare fuel."

Anders looks around again. "And the magnitude of danger is?"

"High for anyone who wanders into the forest on their own.

A healthy bear isn't going to stalk a group of six humans. But we *are* heading into hibernation season."

"It could be an old bear," I say. "Old or sick. If it's not fat enough to hibernate, it'll get desperate."

"Yep. We gotta find that bear and put it down."

"And the part where Max says he saw human eyes?" Anders asks. "What do we make of that?"

"I don't know," Dalton says. "Gunnar saw a bear. Even Max says he saw a bear except for the eyes. I hate to say it, but I think Max just . . ." He shrugs again. "Got spooked. Can't blame him."

"We should run that by Mathias and Isabel, too," I say. "My Psych 101 interpretation would be that it was some kind of traumatic hallucination. All the bogeymen in that poor kid's life have been human."

"He sees the bear, gets spooked, and flashes back to the shooting," Anders says. "He thinks he sees human eyes. That makes sense."

"Except for one thing," I say. "It *wasn't* just the eyes. He said the bear was moving fast on two legs." I look at Dalton. "That's not possible, right?"

Dalton tilts his head. "Bears rear up to look, sniff, or intimidate. They can walk on their hind legs, but not well and not fast. I have seen one approach on two legs. It reared up and kept coming like that because it was facing off against a human. It moved at what I'd call walking speed, and it wasn't far—maybe ten feet?"

"So, not normal behavior, but not impossible either, right?"

"Yep. I'd like to keep looking. Then we'll head back to town and come up with a plan."

★　★　★

Dalton finds two more pieces of evidence. One is a very clear impression of a bear's front paw, in a softer section of the dried-up streambed. The other is more fur caught high above ground level.

We have a grizzly less than a mile from Haven's Rock, and it's stalking our residents. That's a problem. A huge one. But our hidden, off-the-grid town is deep in the Yukon wilderness, hundreds of miles from the nearest community. Wildlife is going to be a concern, just as the environment itself can be, and if that's all we face up here, we'll count ourselves lucky.

Haven's Rock is our Rockton 2.0. The first version had been around since the fifties, when it'd been intended as a sanctuary for those fleeing political persecution. It morphed into a town for anyone in need, anyone who needed to escape something down south, get away for a few years, recalibrate and let the threat die down before they returned.

Obviously, one class of people who need to escape are criminals. Rockton wasn't for that. Not on paper anyway. Okay, fine, yes, they'd admit to letting in white-collar criminals who paid dearly for the privilege. That seemed fair. Those people had stolen money, so let them repay it by financing the residencies of real victims. Only the board in charge of Rockton hadn't stopped there. They'd let in violent criminals, and when things went wrong—whether with the criminals or the regular residents— they'd blocked every solution that might cut into their profits. A sanctuary for the persecuted became an investment for the rich.

When we pushed too hard for changes, they dismantled Rockton. So we built Haven's Rock. Yes, there's still an outside investor, but she's one of the earliest Rockton board members and the only one who'd been on our side. She doesn't need money—she's an elderly billionaire—so we trust her as much as we can trust anyone.

The only problem Émilie poses is that she's a little *too* invested in Haven's Rock, in an ideological way. We'd planned to spend the first year with our own crew, acclimatizing to the new area and preparing the town for residents. But we'd put Émilie in charge of finding and vetting arrivals, and we discovered she's too damn good at it.

Building hadn't even finished before she had an urgent case—a couple and their teenage daughter. In the end, that fell through, but by then we'd agreed to admit a few others—since we were already opening early—and we couldn't change our minds. That was this past spring. We now have twenty-four residents, including Max's family.

Rockton didn't allow children or couples. We wanted to change that. We still believe in our decision, but we are quickly seeing how much easier it was when every newcomer was a lone adult, a stranger among strangers. Easier for *us,* that is. But they're the ones who matter, so we're the ones who need to adjust.

When we return after looking for the bear, we consult with Isabel about Max and Carson. Mathias is there, but Mathias being Mathias, his advice is less than stellar.

"Tell them whatever you like," he says in his French-Canadian accent. "It will not matter. If the children wish to go into the forest, they will go into the forest. If they are traumatized by what they encounter there?" He shrugs. "It will teach them not to go back into the forest."

I glare at him.

He throws up his hands. "You asked for my advice."

"I asked for your professional opinion. As a psychiatrist. Not as a serial killer."

He waggles a finger at me. "Nothing has been proven, and if I did kill anyone, they deserved it."

Mathias's response may suggest that we're doing this "fresh

start" thing all wrong. But if you took our core staff and re-moved those who have committed murder, we wouldn't have enough people to run Haven's Rock. That includes me.

At nineteen, I took a gun to confront a guy whose actions had put me in a coma. I just wanted to scare him. He wasn't scared, and he blamed me for the beating that put me into that coma. So I pulled the trigger. While I hadn't gone to prison, I'd sentenced myself to a mental one for a very long time, unable to get past the guilt. I won't say I'm past it now, but I've come to terms with the mistake I made, and I hope what I've done with my life compensates in some way. That's what Rockton—and Haven's Rock—was really about for some of us. Not escaping our past but confronting it and doing better.

"Doing better" really isn't Mathias's thing. He was a crim-inal psychiatrist who killed criminals in creatively appropriate ways. He's not a textbook serial killer, driven to murder. He just doesn't mind killing when he thinks it's warranted. He's also a good psychiatrist and a really good butcher, so we let him join us in Haven's Rock. And because no one dared tell him no.

We also have a diagnosed sociopath in town. Twenty-one-year-old Sebastian, who murdered his parents at the age of eleven and spent the next seven years in jail. In jail and in therapy, which doesn't always work for sociopaths. Sebastian learned to accept his diagnosis and, under Mathias's mentorship, might be the resident least likely to commit murder. Unless they really need murdering, and then he might be the most likely. Right now, though, he's back near Rockton with Mathias's dog, Raoul, and his girlfriend, Felicity. That's Sebastian's girlfriend, not the dog's.

I look from Mathias to Isabel, our former psychologist turned bar owner. We're having this meeting in the Roc—a reincar-nation of our former bar, which now also serves as a coffee shop during the day. It's late afternoon, and we closed the coffee shop early for our meeting, which consists of me, Dalton, Anders, Mathias, and Isabel.

Isabel taps her manicured nails on the wooden table. In this kind of town, no one should be able to keep their nails like that. Isabel manages to maintain an aura of glamour even in hiking boots.

"Mathias has a point about the impossibility of keeping the boys out of the forest," she says. "Which doesn't mean we shouldn't try. Will? You should speak to their mother. Dana is most comfortable with you. We don't want to put them on house arrest. Particularly Carson, who might have no interest in the forest but will go there just because we forbid it." She glances at Mathias. "Agreed?"

"Agreed," Mathias says. "The boy is exceptionally angry. I want to teach him to throw knives."

I look at him.

"You do not think I am serious? He needs an outlet for his anger. I am struggling to convince his mother of that. She wants him to do nothing violent . . . and he only wants to do things that are violent. Knife-throwing is more cathartic than marksmanship or archery."

"So I should speak to Dana," Anders says. "About the bear thing, not the knives. Explain the danger and discuss ways to keep the boys inside the town limits without Carson rebelling. What if I suggested Carson join me on patrols?"

"*Non,*" Mathias says. "He will see through that and know you are humoring him. I will deal with Carson. Isabel will deal with Max. You will deal with the town patrols. Casey and Eric will deal with the bear."

CHAPTER TWO

It's too late to start a serious hunt for the bear—already five o'clock, with the sun setting in a few hours. Dalton and I will head out for a while after the town meeting, mostly just to scout for signs of the bear getting near town. Tomorrow the hunt will begin in earnest. Both times, we'll leave Kendra behind. She's our best shot—and has experience with bears—so we want her here, along with Kenny and Anders, the three of them on rotating two-person patrols.

We've returned home to prepare for the town meeting. Our house is a tiny two-story chalet—all dwellings must be small out here, partly for heat efficiency and partly for camouflage.

We need to minimize our town's footprint. It's already about half the size of Rockton. The world has changed, and keeping a place like this hidden, even in the Yukon, is becoming near impossible. I used to marvel at how Rockton managed to avoid exposure threats. Now I know there *were* exposure threats. They were just handled. And Émilie was the person handling them—yet another reason we need her on our team.

As soon as I get home, I head for the bathroom. As we'd

been walking home, I thought I felt something I've been waiting for, but I discover I'm mistaken.

My period hasn't come.

It's a week late.

And I'm trying not to panic.

When I'd been beaten into a coma at nineteen, I'd lost a few things. My ability to trust a man in my life. My ability to run properly, after permanent muscle damage in my leg. And my ability to have children.

At the time, the last had been least important. I was nineteen, in police college, not sure I even wanted kids and pretty damn sure I was never going to find anyone to have them with.

When the doctors said I would likely never be able to bear children, I'd barely listened. I was focused on the endless rehab in my future. They'd suggested the damage meant I could conceive but probably not carry a baby to term, and yet I hadn't asked enough questions even to be sure of that. There'd been too many other concerns, all more critical at the time.

A few years ago, with Dalton in my life, it became a question we had to consider, and so we had, at deep and endless and anxious length. Did we want kids? Soon? Someday? Never?

In the end, we agreed on this, as we did on most things. We weren't ready for kids yet, but we probably would be in the future. When the time came, we would investigate our options. I would find out exactly what the medical concerns were. If the problem would be carrying a baby to term, Dalton wanted more concrete details, and if I was in any danger, we'd move straight to adoption or surrogacy. But we'd figure that out if and when the time came.

The time is *not* now. Now is the worst possible moment.

I tell myself I'm not pregnant. How can I be? I'm on birth control.

Except . . .

I screwed up. I'd been using an implant, which seemed the best choice for up here. A few months ago, it gave me some trouble, so I went on the pill instead. Only I haven't taken daily medication in years. When residents started arriving and the town wasn't completely ready, I reached a point where I barely remembered my own name. And I did not remember to take the pill.

It was only a few days. April—my sister and the town doctor—said not to worry. Well, she actually said "It's too late to worry about that now, isn't it?" in her very typical April way. I should just get back on the pill and not mess up again until I can go south and see a gynecologist and find out for certain what the issue is—conceiving or carrying—because I should have done that years ago and what the hell am I doing taking chances with my health. She even said "hell," which told me just how angry she was.

I hadn't mentioned the missed pills to Dalton. He didn't need one more thing to worry about, and as April said, it was too late to do anything anyway.

My time had rolled around, and I'd had cramping, so all was well, right?

That's all I'd had. A bit of cramping.

It's stress, that's all. When I get a chance, I'll talk to April and take a test to be sure, but I don't want to tell Dalton that I'm late. I'm certain it's nothing, and telling him could lead to . . .

Hope?

Is that what I'm afraid of? That he'll hear I could be pregnant and at first freak out because it really is the worst possible time, but then the idea will settle and he might start to hope I *am* pregnant? To realize he's ready for kids, and the timing could not be worse, but it wasn't as if we'd chosen this. A happy accident.

Is that how I'd feel?

I honestly don't know.

We cannot afford time out for a baby now. I wouldn't even raise the subject for at least a year, probably two. We're run ragged with the new town, and that won't end anytime soon.

But what if . . . ? What if I didn't "accidentally" forget to take the pill? What if I'm ready for kids and I subconsciously sabotaged myself?

That's ridiculous. I know it is. I would never take that choice from Dalton. We make every decision together, and this is the most important decision of all.

But what if, subconsciously . . .

No. The mind doesn't work that way. The problem is that I'm not sure how I feel about the possibility I could be pregnant, and a tiny part of me whispers it might not be the worst thing ever.

That's why I'm making up nonsense about subconscious sabotage. If part of me would be okay with this, that sets me spiraling into "Ack! What if I somehow forgot those pills on purpose!" as if maternal instinct and my fertility countdown clock conspired against me.

We had the chance for a baby once, when we found an infant in the forest and had to decide what we'd do if we couldn't locate her parents. We'd concluded that we'd keep her. When we did find her parents, the pang I felt made me acknowledge it was time to consider "the baby" question. If we had been willing to keep her, did that mean we wanted to start a family? The answer was no. We were too early in our relationship, too "selfish" as we'd put it, wanting the other person all to ourselves for a little while longer.

That's what this is. A possibility. If I feel that I might be okay with it, then we need to have that conversation again after I take the test and confirm I'm not pregnant.

Have the conversation. Decide on a timeline. Then get to a damn gynecologist for answers on the state of my reproductive organs.

When I come downstairs after checking in the bathroom, Dalton looks up from the couch, where he's settled in with a novel to wait. He studies my face, and I try to school my features, but it's too late.

"What's wrong?" he asks.

The word "nothing" pushes up, but I keep my mouth shut against it. He'll know I'm lying, and we don't do that. We don't lie about how we're feeling, and we don't make excuses when we aren't ready to talk about it. Oh, we've done both in the past, but we've realized that we need as much honesty as possible. Respect each other's privacy and respect each other. That means I don't require an excuse.

"Just something I'm working through," I say. "I'll talk about it when I'm ready."

There. Simple honesty. He nods, and there's no sign that he's hurt. We need that space, and we need to give it to each other.

Someone pounds on our front door, and Dalton glares in that direction.

"Remind me why we didn't build our place a mile from town?" he says.

"Because the folks in charge can't *be* a mile from town?"

"Sure they can. They shouldn't be, but they *can* be. That's why we're in charge. So we can make shitty choices that benefit no one except ourselves."

I put out a hand. "Don't get up. I'll answer it."

"Wasn't getting up," he says. "Because I wasn't answering it."

I shake my head. I understand his point, and I secretly agree. We did build our chalet outside town. There are woods between it and Haven's Rock. A privacy buffer for a guy who really would rather live in the forest and for a couple who'd really rather live too far from town for anyone to come wandering by.

That strip of forest *does* help. Residents aren't allowed into the woods, which they know includes crossing that strip. It's just not safe, you see. If they need us, they can find one of the other staff and pass along a message.

Most of the staff also won't traverse that strip for anything other than an emergency or a planned social visit. There are a few exceptions, and I have a pretty good idea who has breached the border this time. The one person who doesn't see a border.

I open the door to a woman just under a decade older than me. Curly black hair clipped back. Skin a few shades darker than mine. Brown eyes flashing in annoyance, which if I'm feeling grumbly I'll say is her usual expression. This is Yolanda, Émilie's granddaughter.

Yolanda was the woman in charge of building Haven's Rock— she runs her own construction company. The town is done except for a few small things that we're working on ourselves. So why is she still here? Because she wants to be. She's decided she's staying, and there's not much anyone can do about that.

When I first met Yolanda, I couldn't wait to get her out of Haven's Rock. The more I got to know her, the more I admired and respected her, and the more I thought we could even be friends. That hasn't happened. No one gets close to Yolanda. She's brilliant and driven and prickly as hell. I still admire her. Still respect her. And I still kinda can't wait to get her out of

Haven's Rock . . . at least when she's standing in my door, glaring like I short-sheeted her bed.

"Hello, Yolanda," I say. "Come to walk us to town for the meeting?"

"Come to talk about the meeting. The one I missed."

I frown.

"You, Eric, Will, and the shrinks," she says. "Deciding what to do about this bear. I should have been there."

I try not to sigh. At least not out loud. Yolanda has declared herself Émilie's representative in Haven's Rock, here to look after her grandmother's interests and make sure we aren't running a con game on an old woman. Except that's entirely a self-appointed role. Émilie's role is advisory—she's made it clear that she's available if we need help, in addition to finding residents, but otherwise, this is our town to do with as we like.

As far as Émilie knows, Yolanda is just here enjoying some time to herself while supervising final construction. If we told her that Yolanda insists on acting as her representative—taking on a leadership position—she'd put Yolanda on the first flight out. But there's another reason Yolanda is here. She has early-onset Parkinson's, and she's dealing with that, while avoiding telling Émilie, whose husband died of it.

So Yolanda has a good reason for staying. Also, she more than pulls her weight. She might be a billionaire's granddaughter—and an extremely successful entrepreneur herself—but she lives in the dorm-style housing for residents, insists on taking her turn at even the worst jobs, and doesn't demand anything . . . except this: that she be treated as her grandmother's representative.

"Phil wasn't at the meeting either," I say. "He's the town manager, the closest thing to a mayor we have, and if he wasn't there—"

"His girlfriend was. She'll tell him what he needs to know."

True. Also, if Phil wanted to be there, he could have been, but with Isabel in attendance, he hadn't bothered.

"We weren't discussing what to do about the bear," Dalton says as he comes up behind me. "We were discussing how to convey the threat to the residents, now that we have kids in town. That's why Isabel and Mathias were there. As the boys' therapists."

"And Will?"

Dalton opens his mouth. He's going to say that Anders was there as head of the militia, in charge of patrols. And as soon as his mouth opens, he shuts it, because he sees the trap.

Claim Anders was there as militia, and it supports Yolanda's claim that the meeting was about dealing with the bear. It wasn't. Anders was there because that's how we run things. Administration is loosely structured, as it was in Rockton. Anders had been with us checking for signs of a bear, so he might as well join the meeting. Yolanda was not, so we didn't inform her.

"We have a fucking grizzly bear," Dalton says. "A potentially desperate predator who may be willing to try its luck with human prey. It was urgent. If you heard we were meeting at the Roc, you could have joined us. We have no idea what you do and do not want to be called in on, so we're going to handle it the way we handle every crisis. The crisis itself comes first. We bring in everyone who needs to be consulted. You are entitled to answers before a town meeting. You are entitled to give your opinion. You are not entitled to an engraved invitation."

"I can patrol with Will, Kenny, and Kendra," she says. "I have a gun, and I might not be a hunter, but I can also shoot a rifle."

I swear I can hear Dalton grinding his teeth. This is how Yolanda ends arguments. Instead of acknowledging his point, she moves on. By dropping the matter, she's saying he's right.

He just wishes she'd admit it. Personally, I don't care, as long as we *do* move on.

"Fine," Dalton says. "Talk to Will. Right now, we have a meeting to run." He starts to say more, and I'm sure it's something like "Do you need an invitation to that, too?" but he decides against it and heads to get his boots.

CHAPTER THREE

In Rockton, I instituted the practice of town meetings, for which Dalton may never forgive me. His way of handling communications was, well, not to handle them at all. That's why he has Anders. Which left his deputy passing information to a few key people, who'd tell more people, who'd tell a few more people . . .

One can imagine how well *that* system worked. Anders ended up spending more time correcting misheard accounts than he had spreading the initial news. To Dalton, the problem was that people felt they were owed information when they were not. They should trust that his team had the situation under control.

I saw the chaos that created, so I convinced Dalton to let me run town meetings when we had information that we—okay, *I*—thought needed to be shared with residents.

In theory, it's an obvious solution that should have been instituted years ago. We're a democracy, damn it. People have a right to know things that affect them.

Except . . . we're *not* a democracy. We can't be. I may have grumbled about Rockton being a police state, but it was more like a factory. There were people in charge, who were not elected to those positions, and whose word was law on the factory floor. And, like the average factory, the people on the floor got screwed while those in charge reeled in the profits.

Haven's Rock is more like a not-for-profit organization. There are still people in charge, though, and they are not elected. We're like a board of directors that is fiscally responsible to the organization, which includes the residents. Everyone in that organization should be treated well and fairly. Entitled to a say in the running of the organization, though? No.

And while town meetings sound good in theory, in practice there are days when I kinda wish we just went back to Dalton's way. Because the more information you give people, the more they feel empowered and, again, technically that's a good thing, but it's like a new hire wanting to conduct a forensic accounting on the company's books. We're running a complex system here, and having newcomers constantly questioning our choices only slows things down.

Haven's Rock is also proving different because of the new dynamics. We allow couples and families. Again, in theory, that is an excellent move. Early Rockton *did* allow couples— Émilie and her husband went there fleeing political persecution. But when you're dealing with family units, it changes the town dynamics, and I see that as I get up on the podium. I don't look out on a community of individuals, united by happenstance. I look out on clusters of couples and separate individuals.

In Rockton, people like Anders and Kenny had put a lot of effort into community building. They'd made newcomers feel welcome with a vast array of activities. We need to do more of that here, and we haven't had the chance. Of forty townspeople, over a dozen are staff, and we're a tight-knit group. Among the residents, we have one family—Dana, Carson, and Max—and four couples. That leaves a group of singles drifting about, mostly keeping to themselves, not sure where they fit in.

I start with my usual welcoming preamble. In a regular meeting, there'd be community updates. Today, I get straight to business.

"Some of you may have heard there was a disturbance on today's hike," I say. "A brown bear was spotted in the forest."

Notice how I say "brown bear" rather than "grizzly"? Same creature, but one term is more loaded than the other.

"It came too close to the hikers for comfort," I say. "The bear did not attempt to engage with them and fled at the first loud noise, which is good. But we are heading into hibernation season, where older or sick bears may become desperate for sustenance to get them through to spring."

Desperate for "sustenance" is so much better than "might eat people," but a ripple still goes through the residents. It's even more pronounced with the staff who've been in the Yukon long enough to know this is a real concern.

"So we are taking this very seriously," I continue. "All forest forays will be canceled until this is dealt with. If you were scheduled for the upcoming berry gathering or logging shifts, please speak to Phil, who will reassign you. The next hike is canceled, as is the fishing expedition."

"What?" Grant says. "Why?"

His wife—Lynn—had been on the hike, and she leans over to hiss, "It's a *bear*."

"So? They have guns. There's no reason to cancel the fishing trip."

Dalton steps forward. I hesitate, and then back away. Sometimes, that's just better.

"We don't need fish," Dalton says.

"We've had this trip planned for weeks and—"

"We don't need fish."

"You keep saying that," Grant mutters.

"Yeah, in hopes you'll finally hear it. There is a grizzly bear in the woods. It followed our hikers, including your wife. Ask her if she wants you going on that fishing expedition."

Lynn takes Grant's arm and tries to whisper to him, but he throws her off. He might not like another man shutting him down, but that goes double for women, including his wife.

"Don't be stupid," a voice says.

Grant wheels to find himself looking at thirteen-year-old Carson. When Grant puffs himself up, Carson rolls his eyes in a way only teenagers can.

"Seconding that," Gunnar says from the rear. "Only I'll change it to 'don't be an ass.' There's a grizzly. I saw it, and I'm not going in the forest again until Eric and Casey drag a new bearskin rug back to town."

"Bearskin rug?" says one of the new residents, his voice rising. "You're going to kill it?"

"No, he's going to ask it to come back and lie down on the floor," Gunnar says.

That gets a few chuckles, which makes the other guy's cheeks heat.

"You can't kill it," the guy says. "It hasn't done anything."

"It stalked us," Kendra says. "That makes it a threat. It's unfortunate, but there it is. We'll make good use out of it. I know a mean recipe for bear sausage, if Mathias lets me help with the butchering."

The guy gapes at her. "You're . . . you're Indigenous. You're supposed to protect nature."

Her brows shoot up. "What do you think we do, sit around chanting for dangerous bears to go away? We hunt them down and use as much as we can. That's respect."

"It's not right," the guy says. "The grizzly is a majestic creature. A symbol of the north. An apex predator."

"Yep, an apex predator who can kill you with one swipe of its claws."

I clear my throat and take the podium back. "We will hunt down the bear. That's the only way to end the threat."

"It's not right," the man mutters, and a few others nod and make noises of agreement. We have two vegetarians in town, and neither of them says a word. The ones complaining will probably also be first in line for that bear sausage.

I can snark, but I also might have been uncomfortable with this when I arrived. I'd have wanted more proof that the bear is dangerous, which works with regular northern communities, but not in one where people haven't seen an actual grizzly outside photos.

"I want in," someone says. I follow the voice to one of our first residents. I don't know much about Louie. The only person in town who knows everyone's backstory is Dalton. That's for their privacy. Dalton keeps those secrets unless there's a reason someone else needs them.

Louie arrived in late spring. He's in his forties, bull-chested and balding. Whatever he did for a living down south, it doesn't apply up here, where a dental hygienist is far more useful than a lawyer. If your skills can't be utilized, you go into the general rotation right now—we don't have enough residents to assign permanent jobs.

"You want in . . . ?" I say.

"On the hunt. Big game is my specialty."

I shake my head. "That won't be necessary. Sheriff Dalton and I are handling it. But thank you for your—"

"How about a little friendly wager?" Louie shows his teeth in a smile. "If I can outshoot you, I can go in your place."

Louie glances at Dalton for his reaction, but Dalton just stands there, arms crossed, like Louie hasn't finished speaking. It's Anders and Kendra who react, both laughing.

"You might want to see Casey shoot first," Kendra says.

"No," I say. "We aren't having a 'friendly wager.' That isn't how we do things here."

"Afraid you'll lose?"

"Casey can outshoot *me*," Dalton drawls. "But oddly, she's the one you're challenging."

"Then just take me along. I'm a dead shot."

"Good to know," Dalton says. "We can always use hunters. Don't recall seeing that on your application form, though."

"Because I don't want to hunt rabbits. I want a grizzly."

Dalton rocks forward.

"We don't do trophy hunting up here," I cut in. "But after you leave, I'm sure we could recommend an outfit to take you out. Okay, so Eric and I will handle the bear hunt. Kendra, Will, Kenny, and Yolanda will patrol the town, taking shifts for around-the-clock coverage. Everyone else will stay within the borders. If you hear something, notify one of the staff, who will alert whoever is on patrol."

I look out at the group. A few—including Louie and the anti-bear-hunt guy—lean forward like racehorses champing at the bit. They're waiting for the magic words: Does anyone have any questions?

"Thank you all for your time," I say. "We hope to have an update tomorrow. If you have concerns, talk to Phil."

From the back of the crowd, Phil gives me a sour look. I only smile. Then I get the hell out of there.

CHAPTER FOUR

After the meeting, we still have a couple of hours of daylight left, time to grab a sandwich and head out for a look.

We take Storm. She knows what she's sniffing for—we have a sample of bear fur that we can use to tell her to be especially alert for that particular creature. She does find a track, but it's black bear, and the beast stayed well away from town.

We're not concerned about the black bear. Nor about wolves or even wolverines. At one time, I'd have freaked out about any of them being close to town. Then Dalton told me that they're *all* close to town. That's the northern wilderness. People would come to Rockton hoping to see a moose or a bear, and go home without a single sighting. Yet moose and bear were all around, staying out of sight. That's the important part—they stay out of sight.

Any predator that makes itself known is a potential threat. The rest are just going about their daily lives and want to be left to it. This black bear is doing exactly that, and it's only a danger if someone surprises it. Even then, if it has an exit route, it'll almost certainly take it, as fast as it can.

"I haven't heard the wolves in a while," I say. "Think we could have spooked the pack?"

"Not us," Dalton says. "The miners."

I make a face. We spent months finding this perfect piece of pristine wilderness. Okay, no wilderness is "pristine" in the sense of being empty. We hadn't been overly shocked to find there was someone living out here in a well-camouflaged cabin that had escaped our notice. She calls herself Lilith, and she's a wilderness photographer with a pet wolf—having rescued and raised him from puphood. That's all I know about her, and except for the wolf, I can't guarantee any of it's true.

As far as we can tell, Lilith isn't a threat. She wants what everyone up here wants. Peace, quiet, and privacy. We've opened some basic trade with her, mostly to keep on her good side.

Then the miners came. A lone miner discovered gold in a stream here and sold his claim to a company, which set up camp. We know nothing about them. No, scratch that. We know they make us very nervous, because they aren't a couple of guys with a small mining operation. They have armed security, and they've made it very clear that the only thing they want from Haven's Rock is for us to stay the hell away. Which we have, gladly.

While they're about four miles from Haven's Rock, we have heard them when we're out hiking or hunting. The wolves would hear them from even farther away. We built Haven's Rock to intrude as little as possible on the landscape. This isn't our land, in any sense of the word. We want to minimize our footprint and disturbance. Part of that's about not being caught squatting and part is about respecting whose land this actually is.

Does the mining camp have a permit to build out here? Émilie says no. If such a thing were possible, she'd have found a way to obtain one for us.

Whoever runs that camp doesn't care about disturbing nature *and* they don't care about trespassing. That makes us nervous.

"You okay?" Dalton asks.

I shrug.

He puts his fingers under my chin, lifting it and lowering his mouth in a kiss. I let myself fall into that kiss, rolling out from under all my anxieties. When he goes still, my heart does a double thump.

He pulls back, finger going to his lips as his gaze slides to the left.

Whatever's there, it's downwind, meaning Storm only growls *after* she senses Dalton's tension. Her gaze swings in the same direction. She must see something, though, because the hair on her back rises as the growl vibrates through her flanks.

I squint. It's still daylight, but we're in the forest, where dusk comes early. I can't see anything, and Dalton's gaze is still moving, meaning he doesn't either.

I tap his arm and motion at Storm.

He nods and follows her gaze. His squint says he doesn't see anything either. Then a silent curse tells me he does. I catch it then. A tall shadow in the forest.

Dalton reaches for his bear spray as my hand lowers to my gun. Then Dalton hesitates, his head tilting. A moment's more hesitation, and he's striding forward.

"You think I can't see you?" he says. "Get the fuck out here—"

The figure runs, crashing through the forest like a bull moose.

"You know what I hate doing?" Dalton mutters as he takes off.

"Chasing assholes through the forest?"

No answer, though I'm sure he gave one. He's just too far away for me to hear it.

I slap my thigh for Storm, and we give chase. Between my bad leg and her bulky build, neither of us is a sprinter. Dalton takes that role. We're just here for backup.

As Dalton runs, I catch a glimpse of his target. It's definitely human. Did he know that for sure? Either way, the guy is on the run, and from what I can see, it *is* a guy—a man, tall and stocky, and no more of a sprinter than Storm.

That's when I spot the second figure.

It's off to my left. Dalton doesn't notice. He's running after his target, and the second figure is to his rear. The figure's arm swings up, pointing something toward Dalton and the runner.

"Stop!" I shout as I spin, my own gun rising.

"Whoa!" a familiar voice says, hands shooting up. "It's me. Gunnar."

"Put down your weapon," I say.

"What weapon?" He flaps his hands over his head.

"You were pointing something at Eric."

"My *finger*. I was pointing my finger at *Louie,* the guy you're chasing. I was telling you he went that way."

I eye his hands, which are indeed empty. Then I lower my gun and say, "Get in front of me."

"What?"

"Get in front of me. I'm Eric's backup, and I'm not letting you out of my sight. Now run."

"Shit? Really?" Gunnar says. "My hip still hurts from, you know, getting *shot* a few months ago."

"If it's bothering you, you should catch the next plane home. Now, run."

"It's just Louie."

"*Run.*"

He does, still grumbling.

"Eric!" I shout. "It's Louie." Then I say, to Gunnar's back, "How do you know that?"

"'Cause I followed him. I was up in my perch, and I saw him leave, so I came to warn you guys."

We'll deal with this later. Gunnar shouldn't have come into the forest after we forbade it. In fact, at the meeting he said he wasn't going back in the forest until we killed the bear.

The last time he followed someone in, he got shot, which apparently didn't teach him a lesson. He should have told Anders what he saw and let Anders find us. But Gunnar is a grown man who knows the risk he's taking. How much do I want to argue about him coming to warn us instead of taking time to find Anders first?

I'll need to think about that. For now, judging by the shouts and snarls, Dalton has run Louie to ground.

"Get off me, asshole," Louie is saying.

"I'm pinning you down because you have a goddamn butcher knife in your hand."

"It's not a butcher knife. It's a hunting knife."

As we catch up, Dalton starts to spin, gun rising, and I realize I forgot an important piece of information.

"Gunnar's with me," I quickly call. "He followed Louie."

"Holy shit, that is *not* a hunting knife," Gunnar says. "That belongs to Mathias."

"It's for hunting," Louie says. "For field-dressing game."

"You actually took one of Mathias's knives?" Gunnar says as I pluck it from Louie's fingers. "Hoo, boy. No need to punish him, guys. Just make him take that back to Mathias and admit what he did."

Louie snorts. "The guy is a gray-haired old shrink. I'm not concerned."

"Then you, my friend, are an epically shitty judge of character. How do you think he got so good at butchering?" Gunnar leans down toward Louie, prone on the ground under Dalton's boot. "Disposing of his victims."

Louie twists his head toward us and rolls his eyes.

"Enough," I say. "Yes, that is Mathias's knife, and yes, you are telling him you took it, but that is secondary to the real issue."

"Wanna tell us what you're doing out here?" Dalton says.

"Let me up, and I will," Louie says.

"Talk, and I will. Maybe."

"You don't scare me any more than that French guy. I'd like to see how tough you are without that gun."

Dalton cocks his head. "Really?"

Gunnar snickers. "Nah, I don't think you do. You weren't here last month, when we held wrestling matches. Will Anders won, obviously. I thought I'd get second place. I didn't even get third."

"I'm guessing the point of this story is to tell me that the sheriff came in second. And third?"

Gunnar hooks a thumb at me.

"We're not wrestling so you can decide whether I deserve your respect," Dalton says. "As tempting as it would be to kick your ass right now, I'm told that's wrong." He slants a look at me. "Yes?"

"Sorry," I say.

Dalton says to Louie, "I deserve your respect because you got on that plane and came out here and handed it to me, along with a fair number of your personal freedoms. It's a trade. I protect you, because you agreed to let me do that. So you respect my authority. Whether you respect *me* or not is another matter, and I don't give a shit about that. I just need you to listen to what I say, and if I say stay out of the fucking forest? You stay out of the fucking forest."

"Please tell me you weren't going after a grizzly with a knife," I say.

When Louie doesn't answer, Dalton nudges him with his boot. "You were out here looking for that bear, right?"

"What else?"

Dalton and I exchange a look. What else indeed.

"You said you're a big-game hunter," Dalton says.

"I am."

"You wanted to test your marksmanship against Casey."

Louie doesn't answer. We exchange another look.

"Get up," Dalton says.

Louie takes his time. He knows something is up.

Dalton holsters his sidearm and removes the shotgun from his back. "You're going to shoot this. You make one move to swing it in our direction, and I will fire."

"You'll shoot me?" Louie says, his voice rising in equal parts concern and outrage.

"Yeah." Dalton holds up the can of bear spray. "With this. Now, take the gun."

Louie does. Then he looks down at it. "What kind of rifle is this?"

"It's a shotgun," Gunnar says. "Even I know that."

Louie hands it back. "I can't shoot that." He waves at me. "Give me what she's got. *That's* a rifle."

I look at Dalton. Obviously, we hadn't expected to test Louie's marksmanship with a shotgun, but the fact that he didn't recognize it casts some doubts on his big-game-hunter story.

When Dalton nods, I hand over the hunting rifle. Louie starts positioning it awkwardly.

"You're going to need the magazine," Dalton says.

Louie blinks at him.

"We don't carry them loaded when we're not actively hunting," Dalton drawls as I hand over the magazine.

Louie fusses with the rifle and magazine, frowning and obviously having no clue how to put them together.

"It's not the sort I've used," he says, a touch of a whine in his voice. "You've got some really shitty gear out here."

"Shitty for what?" Dalton says. "Taking down an elephant?"

"If it'll take down an elephant, it'll take down a grizzly."

"When's the last time you went hunting?"

Louie bristles. "Last winter. Up in Alaska hunting wolves."

Now I'm the one bristling, I can't help it. I glance at Dalton. His mouth is set in a firm line.

"From a plane," Dalton says.

"Got two."

"From a *plane*." Dalton's lip curls now, contempt rolling off him.

"Wow," Gunnar says. "People actually do that?"

"If they can afford it, they do," Louie says. "Not that any of you would know about that." He hands me back the rifle and magazine. "Screw this. I'm done."

I look at Dalton. We can't force Louie to prove his shooting skills. Dalton had asked because neither of us likes Louie's story, and now we like it even less.

In a close encounter with a bear, a knife would be better than a rifle, but we're not looking for a close encounter. If Louie was, that'd mark him as a macho idiot. But he just admitted to hunting wolves from a plane, and his confusion over our guns suggests he only shoots them after someone else has set them up and handed them to him. Even then he's shooting from a distance. A very long distance in a very safe environment.

Is he refusing to fire the rifle because he isn't accustomed to the type and afraid he'll do badly? Or is he lying about all of it, knowing we aren't going to have the kind of high-powered distance rifle he claims to use?

If he's not a hunter, why insist on joining the bear hunt? Did he only challenge me to a shooting contest knowing no one would allow that? Claiming credentials without needing to prove them?

Dalton's shoulders drop, just a fraction, which tells me he doesn't see any point in pursuing this. He glances my way. I nod. Pushing Louie to shoot won't resolve anything. If he does poorly, he'll blame the gun.

Better to let this ride.

Better to let him think he got away with it.

"Anything else?" Dalton says to me.

I shake my head.

He turns to Louie. "You're not hunting this bear. It's extermination, not trophy gathering. You'll return the knife to Mathias and then report to Phil in the morning. Tell him you're on shit duty for a week."

"Shit duty? What's that?"

"Exactly what it sounds like. Cleaning up the shit."

CHAPTER FIVE

Dalton takes Louie to town while I walk back with Gunnar. I've decided I'm not going to comment on him breaking the rules. If he were a resident, I'd have to. His safety would be my primary concern, above any other rights. But Gunnar is . . . Well, Gunnar is special. In many ways, as Anders would say.

Gunnar was part of the construction crew. After he "helped" us when two coworkers went missing, he declared he'd earned a spot on the smaller crew that would stay until construction was complete. Then, after everyone except Yolanda and Kendra left, he wrangled a spot on staff.

There's an element of blackmail in that. Gunnar had seen things he shouldn't have, and he manipulated his way onto the staff because manipulation is what Gunnar does best. He's not even subtle about it and, oddly, that makes it harder to refuse him.

Gunnar plays his cards faceup. He's also a good worker. So we didn't fight to send him home. That doesn't mean we trust him. There must be a reason why he was so eager to stay. But Gunnar's open honesty applies only to his actions. His past is a closed book. No, his past is—as far as Émilie's private investi-gator can tell—an *empty* book. Devoid of anything suspicious. Which makes me even more suspicious.

For now, Gunnar is on the staff because at least then I can keep an eye on him. If he chooses to go into the forest knowing there's a grizzly, that's on him. At least if he gets eaten, I won't need to waste more time puzzling over his motives for staying in Haven's Rock.

We get to bed at a reasonable hour, meaning "before midnight." We want to be up at dawn for the hunt, and we manage to not only do that but slip off without anyone delaying our departure. It helps, of course, that dawn comes before six and, as fall settles in, early-morning temperatures aren't much above freezing. When we leave, the town is dark and silent.

We start where yesterday's hike had abruptly ended. From that spot—where Max and Gunnar saw the grizzly—we attempt to follow the bear's trail. We'd tried that yesterday, but neither Storm nor Dalton had been able to follow it far. The trail was easy where the bear had bolted, crashing through undergrowth. But that segment only lasts about twenty feet. Then the visible signs vanish, as if the beast calmed down and ambled off.

Either Dalton or Storm *should* still be able to find something. They don't. The bear headed into a rocky area, and they lost the trail there yesterday. We try again today with the same results.

When we can't go forward, we go backward. Max said he'd first seen the bear across the dried-up streambed, and Dalton finds signs of it near there. We pick up that end of the trail, with the same results: we can follow the trail for about a quarter mile before it disappears, having looped from that same rocky stretch it returned to later.

The rocky stretch suggests the bear came from the mountain nearest to Haven's Rock. On earlier forays, we've spotted bears up there. That isn't surprising—mountains are prime grizzly habitat.

The problem is that we presume there's more than a single grizzly on the mountain, meaning we can't shoot the first one we see. That's why we'd wanted the trail. Without that certainty, we aren't shooting.

We spent the next few hours scouting the mountainside and spotting only a moose and a few mountain goats.

"I want to try the trail again," Dalton says. "It bugs me that we're losing it like that. Rocky ground means I'm less likely to see signs of disturbance, but Storm should be able to follow the scent."

Storm's ears tilt back, as if she's catching her name and thinking the tone means she's done something wrong.

I pat her head. "Let's take a play break first. We have plenty of time and—"

Storm's head rises, a growl vibrating through her.

"We are approaching!" a voice calls. "Our weapons are lowered, and we expect the same from you!"

"That depends," Dalton calls back. "Who the hell are you?"

"Your friendly neighbors," the voice says.

It's not Lilith, unfortunately. It's a man's voice, strong and confident and vaguely familiar, that familiarity raising the hairs on my neck.

"The miners," I mutter under my breath.

Dalton's grunt says he'd also figured that out.

The man appears. The first time I saw him, he'd looked like what Louie claims to be—a wealthy trophy hunter. He's a silver-haired, impeccably groomed man wearing a small fortune in outdoor gear. One would think that after three months in the bush he'd look a little less impeccable. He doesn't. This isn't a guy out there getting his hands dirty. He doesn't even carry a gun. That job falls to the two men flanking him, both stone faced and wearing sunglasses despite the overcast day. Their boss also wears them. Not protection against the sun so much as partially obscuring their faces.

"You're trespassing," Dalton says.

The man's silver brows shoot over his sunglasses frames. "Am I?"

"You know you are. You set the boundaries. We've honored them."

"So have we . . . except today, when I crossed to come speak to you, having no other method of communication. Fortunately, you saved us most of the trip by being out here"—he glances between the rifle and shotgun on our backs—"hunting. I do hope you haven't lost another person from your little hamlet in the woods."

Neither of us answers. Nor do we ask what he wants or whether there's a problem. He'll get to it, and nothing about our encounters with this man have inclined us to be friendly or helpful. Oh, he's friendly himself, but in a way that makes those hairs on my neck prickle.

"It seems we have ourselves a situation," the man says.

Again, we know that anything we say can be used against us. Ask whether he means the grizzly, and if he knows nothing about it, he can use that as an excuse to come on our side of the invisible wall—to "help" us hunt it. Ask *what* he means, and if it *is* the grizzly, then we'll seem inept—unaware of a threat on our land. And if it's not the grizzly? Then chances are, he's about to accuse us of something.

"A wild man of the woods," the guy says.

"A what?" Dalton says.

"We have ourselves a situation, and that situation is an intruder, and that intruder appears to be a wild man of the woods. A hermit. A homesteader. Call it what you will. Someone who has abandoned society to live out in these woods for so long that he's gone a little feral himself."

Dalton's shoulders tighten almost imperceptibly. I'm sure mine do, too. We're thinking the same thing.

Hostiles.

But that was Rockton, and it's a situation we resolved.

"Go on," Dalton says.

"One of my men spotted a wild human," he says. "He reported it to me. I am reporting it to you."

Dalton and I exchange a look. When Dalton gives a slight nod, I say, "Are you certain it was a man and not a bear?"

"I believe my men know the difference."

"Can you give us any details?"

The man unzips his jacket and removes a manila envelope. He holds it out to me. "Everything you need will be in here."

I take the envelope and struggle not to look confused. "I appreciate you bringing this to our attention. We'll read through this and be on the lookout. If we spot anything, do you want us to let you know?"

"I don't think you understand. I'm not warning you. I'm telling you to deal with this."

"Deal with it?" Dalton says. "You think this man has something to do with us?"

"No, but I believe in professionals."

The man pauses. I'm beginning to understand this particular speech technique. He makes some vague comment, and we're supposed to say "What?" and he can smugly explain, making us look and feel stupid.

So we say nothing.

"Leave professional work to professional people," he continues after a moment. "I get the sense that finding people is a specialty of yours." He raises his hands, as if we were going to protest. "I'm not asking for details. What you do in your little hamlet is your own business. Just as mining is my business. But dealing with wild people in the forest is definitely *not* my business, and you both strike me as people who are better equipped for that sort of thing."

"Uh-huh," Dalton says.

"Not that I expect you to do it for free." The man flashes his teeth. "Whatever's going on in that little hamlet of yours, it doesn't seem terribly profitable."

Again, there's no answer to this. Tell him it's not about profit, and that narrows down the possibilities of what Haven's Rock could be. Lie and say he's mistaken, and he just might take a bigger interest in our "little hamlet."

"If you're offering to pay us," Dalton says, "I don't think you'd like our price."

The man's brows shoot up. "Well, well. I do appreciate a man with a good understanding of his own value. Never sell yourself short, boy. I admitted I lack your particular skills, and so you are, rightly, going to make me pay dearly for them."

Dalton doesn't react to the man's patronizing bullshit. He only says, "I am."

"Name your price."

"The mountain."

I bite my tongue against a laugh. Dalton's throwing the guy's game back at him. Say something seemingly nonsensical and make him ask what Dalton means.

"You want . . . the mountain?" the man says.

"I do."

A false laugh. "You do ask for a lot. Mountain-sized, in fact. I'm presuming there's a joke here I'm not understanding. Local humor?"

"No humor at all. We have established a border between our two settlements, complete with a strip of no-man's-land. The problem is that we have not established a north and south boundary. Are we not allowed to head west at any latitude? Or is there a boundary? I'm going to suggest we make it easy. We each have two miles of the stretch between us. We should have the same distance to the north and south. Beyond that, it's open to either group."

"Reasonable."

"The problem is the mountain. That'll put it mostly on our side, but a little into yours. We'll be hunting that mountain, and if our game heads into your territory?" Dalton shrugs. "It's a problem."

"So you want the mountain."

"I do."

"All right. Solve this little mystery and it's yours."

"Solve it?" I say. "Or *resolve* it?"

I'm pleased that it takes him a moment to work that out.

"Ah," he says. "Do I want you to take care of this mountain man? That would be entirely up to you. Either you get rid of him—in any way that suits you—or you bring us what we need to track and get rid of him—in the way that will suit *us*."

He could cast a glance at his two armed men. He doesn't need to. I have zero doubt that "get rid of" means a permanent solution.

"You can deal with him if you'd prefer," the man says. "As

long as we don't encounter him again, I don't care how it's handled."

I open the envelope.

"May I presume we can take our leave?" the man says.

"Not until we see what you gave us," Dalton says. "And decide whether we want the job."

I skim the pages. There are two. One is a handwritten report and the other a map showing where this "wild man" was sighted.

"Is this it?" I say, waving the pages.

"It is."

"I have questions. I'm going to need to speak to—"

"No."

"You want us to investigate?" Dalton says, taking the pages from my hand and holding them out. "We need to be able to interview the witness."

"Ask me your questions. I'll answer if I can and relay answers if I can't."

Dalton's jaw sets. "That's not—"

"What if this were reversed? If one of your people saw something, and you needed me to help. Would you let me speak to your person?"

It's not the same. Our people are refugees, promised privacy. His are employees. But if we say it's different, we give him valuable information.

"That would depend on the situation," Dalton drawls. "If we deemed it urgent, we'd let you speak to them. Is this urgent?"

"I don't know. Is it urgent to you? Seems to me this problem affects both of our settlements, and I might argue it's more urgent for yours than mine. You have women. We do not. We are a town of men chosen for their fortitude. This mountain man clearly didn't want to tangle with our person. Would he think the same about all of yours?"

"I'd rather tangle with one of your boys than with . . ." Dalton nods my way. "But I will take the point that this threat affects us all, and I'll grant you your privacy as much as I can." He looks my way. "Does this work?"

I make a face. "Not ideal. But, sure. If I can ask some questions, that'll have to be enough."

CHAPTER SIX

After I question the man, Dalton and I are off, tramping through the woods in silence. After about a kilometer, we pull off the path and find a log to sit on.

"Well?" I say. "What do you think?"

Dalton scratches his stubble. "Not sure *what* to think."

I take out the pages, along with the notes I made. "Could this be Max's Bigfoot?"

"Seems likely."

According to the report, the miner had been working the claim when he'd walked away for the main reason anyone leaves a wilderness path or campsite—to take a piss. While he was doing that, he'd heard something, thought it was one of his coworkers playing a joke, and turned around sharply to, well, to spray the prankster. There are aspects of male humor I will never quite get, and from the way Dalton cocks an eyebrow at that part, there are aspects he'll never get either.

Anyway, our miner wheeled to spray his prankster and found himself looking at a guy dressed in skins. A big, brawny man—well over six feet, according to the miner—with scraggly hair, a long brown beard, and wild eyes. He'd lunged at the miner with what looked like a homemade blade. The miner shouted, and the man took off through the forest.

My questions had been about exactly how the guy was dressed. All the report said was that he was wearing "skins." People up here often wear tanned hides and furs, and there's a huge difference between a person wearing homemade buckskins and boots and a wild man draped in the raw hides of dead animals. Apparently, whoever took the report failed to realize that, and when we asked, the answer was clear—this was not tanned and sewn clothing. It was hides. More specifically, bear hides . . . or at least one bear hide, worn in a very significant way.

The figure had been draped in a bearskin, like some kind of Viking berserker. The hide still had the skin of the head attached, which the man wore on his own head. He had the forelegs apparently tied over his own arms, with the paws—and claws—intact. Why they decided this wasn't report-worthy, I'll never know. Maybe they thought "wild man of the woods" covered "wearing a bearskin like a Halloween costume."

Does this match what Max saw? Yes. Gunnar and Max had both seen ears and paws, which is explained by the costuming. Max saw human eyes. Gunnar had only seen a brown-furred face. A man with a long brown beard and hair wearing a bear-head hood would explain both.

We'd found fur and large indistinct prints. The costume explains the fur, and the large man explains the prints, with the bearlike one being from the hide.

"It also explains the behavior," Dalton says. "Max and Gunnar saw it moving on two legs, further and faster than we'd expect from a bear. And getting close to humans isn't normal bear behavior."

"It *is* normal human behavior."

He nods and looks out over the forest with frustration and worry.

"We scouted before we built," I say. "Multiple times."

"Not well enough, apparently."

I shake my head. "We'd never have found Lilith's cabin unless we walked into it. The miners arrived after us—that's just bad luck. As for a guy living in the woods?" I shrug. "I'm hoping he's just passing through. It's fall, and everything in the forest is settling in for the winter. If he's nomadic, like Jacob, that's what he's doing. Passing through looking for a good spot."

Dalton's brother, Jacob, lives out here, just as their parents had. Jacob is now with one of Rockton's former residents, Nicole, and they have a baby boy. When winter comes, they'll be moving into Haven's Rock, at least until little Stephen is older. There's also a former sheriff of Rockton—Tyrone Cypher—living out here along with his Rockton girlfriend, Jen. And they are far from the only people in these woods.

When Dalton doesn't comment, I say, "With any luck, having seen multiple groups of people, he's already moved on. This won't be where he wants to spend his winter."

Dalton only nods.

I reach to scratch behind Storm's ears. "You're thinking of the hostiles."

He grunts. Then he shakes his head. "Can't be them. They're gone, and we're too far away."

"Which means it's unlikely, but not impossible. If it is a hostile, that actually makes this easier. We can call in Émilie to get him down south for help."

The hostiles had been Rockton's "wild people of the woods." Dalton grew up thinking they were just a fact of life, like bears and wolves. There were wild people in the forest, dangerous people, and you avoided them.

The story was that they were exactly what the miners think this guy is—someone who retreated into the forest and lost his human self, reverting to something feral. That might be the *Lord of the Flies* narrative, but people don't usually do that unless there's an underlying mental issue. For a whole *group* to do that . . . ? I hadn't bought the story. We'd investigated and solved the mystery, and the hostiles have been taken south for treatment.

Could there be one remaining? Absolutely. Could he have wandered this way? Sure—Jacob and others move much farther in their seasonal travels. Could we have coincidentally ended up in the same area as the lone hostile holdout? That's unlikely, but not impossible.

It's more likely that this is just an ordinary resident of the deep Yukon wilderness. One who has gone a little more "mountain man" than most. The bearskin is almost certainly an affectation. Something he saw once in a movie and thought it looked cool.

It's also possible he's mentally ill, and Dalton and I discuss that. I'd hesitate saying it in front of others, because for many people "mentally ill" means dangerous, when all I mean is that he could have any number of issues that might lead him to a lone life in the forest, and only a subset of those render him an actual threat.

He did apparently threaten the miner with a knife. But we're still unclear on whether it constituted an actual attack. Out here, it's not unusual for encounters to involve threat displays, whether you're dealing with humans or animals.

We often approach a stranger with our gun in hand, not raised, but being clear we are armed. I'd like to know exactly how serious this "attack" had been, but for that, I'd need to interview the witness, and that's not happening.

"We should stop by Lilith's cabin," I say. "See if she's seen anything . . . and warn her if she hasn't."

Lilith lives at the foot of the mountain. As I said, we'd never have spotted her cabin unless we stumbled over it. Even following her trail here in the spring, I didn't see it. Dalton had, his gaze being better attuned to irregularities in the landscape.

I've never been inside her tiny cabin, but I know there's a darkroom, so I'm presuming the rest is like a studio apartment. Up here, economy of size is an absolute must for winter. Our chalet is about a thousand square feet, and that's positively palatial. It's only possible with top-notch insulating—sixteen-inch-thick walls and quadruple-paned windows. People living in the forest don't have those options, so their cabins are minuscule, which also helps Lilith's place disappear.

Even now, approaching it and squinting, I struggle to see the shape against the forest. She's avoided sharp and regular angles, and the roof is low and sloping. When I do see it, I smile, as if I've spotted the last item in a hidden-object game. I also smile at the cabin itself. It looks like a witch's hut, with the sod roof and vines and forest critters. The critters are fake—painted on—but no less charming for it.

I'm walking toward the cabin, about to call a welcome, when Dalton grabs my arm. I don't even have time to look over before a snarling gray wolf erupts from the forest. Dalton yanks me behind him. Even Storm falters. She'd been ambling along, smelling the wolf up ahead but unconcerned. It's just Nero, her friend. The two don't exactly gambol together—the way Storm does with Mathias's wolf-dog, Raoul—but they enjoy each other's company. The canine equivalent of adult friends rather than childhood playmates.

When Nero bursts out, snarling, Storm only stares. Her nostrils flare, as if checking that this is indeed the wolf she knows, because he certainly isn't acting like calm, dignified Nero.

When he lunges at her, any hesitation evaporates, and she snaps and snarls, her front legs digging in as her head lowers.

"Back up," Dalton murmurs, his eyes never leaving the wolf.

"Nero," I say as calmly as I can. "We're going to back up now."

Yes, I know the wolf can't understand me. It's the tone I want to convey, calm and nonthreatening.

We take three steps backward. Storm holds her ground, snarling, until I call her, and then she awkwardly backs up, not wanting to turn away from him.

"Lilith?" I call.

No answer.

Nero stays where he is, near the edge of the cabin. He's stopped growling and just stands there, guarding his person and her home.

"Lilith!" I call louder.

Dalton gives it a try. Still no response.

Nero very clearly doesn't want us coming near the cabin, and I'm not sure what to make of that. The first time we met Nero, he was guarding something for Lilith. He'd been firm about wanting us to keep our distance, but it'd been a very polite firmness. Since then, I've only ever seen him with Lilith. He's never been like this. On the other hand, it's not as if we've seen him a hundred times.

We both try calling Lilith again. When no answer comes, I say, "I don't think she's at home."

Dalton grunts.

"But I also don't think she'd go into the woods and leave him here." I raise my voice. "Lilith? If you're inside and busy—or just don't want visitors—can you say something? Otherwise, we'll be worried."

Lilith isn't some reclusive and paranoid forest dweller. Put her on a TV show, living in this cabin and dressed in her hide clothing with her wolf companion, and she'd seem laughably miscast. She'd look more at home in a power suit walking down Bay Street.

She's not the most sociable person, but if she were inside, she'd come out and tell us she wasn't in the mood for visitors. There's zero chance she's hiding while waiting for us to go away.

I turn back to Nero. He looks more like himself now, standing there calmly but firmly blocking our route.

"I'd like to check the cabin and make sure Lilith is okay," I say to Dalton. "Can you hold Storm back while I see if he'll let me approach alone?"

There's a pause. Dalton wants to say no. At the very least, he wants to go in my stead. But of the three of us, I'll pose the least threat in Nero's eyes.

Finally, Dalton grunts, which is as close to assent as I'll get.

I lift my hands and keep my gaze on Nero, just below his eyes. Not overly submissive, but not a challenge either. I step forward. The wolf growls. I stop.

"Nero? I just want to be sure she's okay."

Another step. Another growl. It is a polite warning, but a warning nonetheless.

I'd have been concerned if he kept lunging at me, even if rabies and distemper aren't an issue in the Yukon. Yet after the initial outburst, he's reverted to his usual self. He just doesn't want us near the cabin, and I have no way of knowing whether that could mean Lilith is soundly asleep inside or . . . ?

It's the "or" that worries me. She wouldn't hunt without Nero. She wouldn't leave him behind to go gathering fall berries or photographing the landscape or fishing or hiking. None of those things would be more difficult with Nero, and all would be safer with him.

"Nero, I just want—"

His fur rises as I step forward, and his lip curls.

"That's a no, Butler," Dalton says. "You are not getting to the door."

"I'm worried."

"I know."

"I'm especially worried because there's a bearskin-wearing wild man in the forest."

"I know."

"So . . . ?"

"Leave a note, and we'll come back when we can. Yeah, I know that's not what you want to hear, but I don't see any other answer."

I grumble, but he's right. I back up to Dalton and Storm, and take off my backpack to start a note.

CHAPTER SEVEN

Max

"Life sucks."

Max startles from his reverie in the middle of kicking a rock. He looks up sharply to see Gunnar falling in step beside him.

"Life sucks," Gunnar says again. "It's a lesson everyone learns eventually, but some of us learn earlier than others."

Mom would say you aren't supposed to talk to children like that. Carson would grumble that Gunnar's being weird—again. He's right. Gunnar is weird. But when it comes to grown-ups, there are two kinds of weird. Creepy weird and just plain weird. Creepy weird was the crossing guard who always wanted to talk about video games, and there was nothing wrong with *that*, but Max's gut had said the guy was creepy weird, and then he started inviting Max over to his place to play games "but don't tell your mom, 'cause they're rated M" wink-wink. Gunnar wasn't that kind of weird. He was just ordinary weird.

"I don't want to talk about it," Max says.

"You don't want to talk about what you saw in the forest."

Max glances up, frowning.

"Oh, you thought I meant the other stuff. Nah, I wouldn't ask you about that. That's none of my business. If you *wanted* to talk about it, I'm a good listener, but I'd never ask. I mean about what's currently sticking in your craw. The fact that everyone's out looking for a bear when you said that's not what you saw."

Max lowers his head and resumes walking. That *is* what he's mad about. Oh, they'd all been nice about it. Never questioned what he saw. That made it worse, like he was a scared little kid who had to be humored.

You saw a monster under the bed? Describe the monster please. I'll take notes.

He kicks another rock.

"You pissed off because I didn't back you up?" Gunnar says.

Max shrugs. Kind of? Except he knows that's not fair because Gunnar never contradicted Max's story. He just said he didn't see the eyes.

"You embarrassed about saying you saw human eyes?" Gunnar asks.

Max stiffens. He *is* embarrassed. He's partly upset because they treated him like a baby, and partly mad because they didn't take him seriously. But he's also embarrassed that he might have made a mistake. Only grown-ups don't usually ask if you're embarrassed, because it might make a kid think that they *should* be embarrassed. They stick to words like "upset" and "angry."

"They should have warned you what they were going to say before that meeting," Gunnar says. "I get it. The sheriff and Casey don't have kids, so they aren't quite sure how to deal with you. They're good people, and they didn't mean to hurt you. They just didn't think."

Max nods and blinks back tears prickling his eyes.

"You want me to leave you alone?" Gunnar asks.

Max shakes his head. Gunnar might be weird—and he might say things grown-ups aren't supposed to say to kids—but Max likes that. He's spent all day being in a bad mood after hearing about the bear hunt.

He tried talking to Carson, but his brother told him to stop whining. He tried talking to Mom, but she did that thing both his parents did, where they never doubted Max's experience, even if they didn't think it happened that way. That made him mad sometimes. It was like Sheriff Eric and Detective Casey not just coming out and saying they thought he saw a regular bear. Mom wouldn't either. She accepted what he thought he'd seen, which he guessed was better than denying it, but still . . . His mom had focused on praising him for doing the right thing by reporting it, before the creature—man or bear—hurt anyone.

"You wanna come up to my perch?" Gunnar says. "See if we can spot it out there?"

When Max hesitates, Gunnar glances down at him. "You can say no, kid. It's always okay to say no to an adult who asks you to go somewhere, especially if your gut does that twisty thing. Listen to your gut. And if you do want to come up, then I'm going to suggest you go first and get out on the edge, where people can see you. Then I'll come up."

Max shakes his head. "We can both go up together."

"No," Gunnar says, his voice oddly firm. "You're saying that so you don't make me feel bad. Fuck that shit. You don't know me well enough to trust me, and so you shouldn't, not when I'm inviting you to a private spot. You go up. You get on the ledge. Then I'll come up."

Yep, Gunnar is definitely weird.

Max nods and starts walking. Gunnar's perch is in a storage building that isn't completely done yet. The main level is full of stuff, but there's a loft, too, and the front part is open. That's where Gunnar sits. Max once heard Gunnar and Yolanda arguing about it, in that not-really-angry way people sometimes argue. Bickering, Mom calls it when Max does it with Carson.

"You going to finish closing that loft up?" Yolanda said.

"Hmm, that makes it sound like a choice," Gunnar said. "If it's a choice, then no."

"Close it up, Gunnar. Before winter, or everything in there's going to freeze."

"Maybe we should make it cold storage then."

"It's winter in the Yukon. Everything will be cold storage."

Max figures they've all decided to humor Gunnar. If he likes sitting up there, then they aren't going to make him seal it up until it has to be sealed up.

Max knows the way. He's been there before, with Carson. He goes up the ladder and through the loft to the front part, where the roof slopes on either side. Gunnar has what Carson called "a sweet setup" there—blankets, a cooler with beer, some snacks. It's a little weird, if Max is being honest. It looks like something Max would do—a place to hide from the grown-ups. Except Gunnar *is* a grown-up. Supposedly.

Max sits near the edge. He doesn't dangle his legs. If he did, someone would definitely see him and maybe tell his mom, and if Mom saw him with Gunnar, she'd come running. If he stays near the edge, he's not hiding—anyone can look up and see him—but he's not making it easy either.

Max looks out, spots Gunnar, and lifts a hand. Gunnar jogs around to the door. A couple of minutes later, he plunks down a few feet from Max and leans back against a post.

"You get cold, grab a blanket," Gunnar says. "You get thirsty, don't grab a beer."

Max shakes his head, and they sit there, looking out over the town. It's late afternoon and everyone's finishing up work or trying to get to the coffee shop before it closes.

He plays a memory game, where he tries to remember everybody's name. It's easy for people like Kendra and Dr. April, who he sees all the time. But then there are new residents he's never spoken to. They're like teachers in other grades, where they're just faces that pass in the halls and he only knows that they're teachers.

He can name all but two of the people below, so that's good. Then he turns his attention to the forest. Mom keeps saying how beautiful it is up here, but she can't really see it when she's stuck in the town surrounded by trees, with the mountains just peeking over the top. From up here, the forest seems to go on forever, and Max can make out the lake just past the town, and then the mountains in the background. It's like something out of a painting.

Seeing those endless trees scares Carson. Oh, he pretends he thinks the forest is boring, but Max can tell it scares him. It scares Max a little, but in a good way, if that makes sense.

The men who broke into their house, killed their dad, and shot their mom were the worst kind of scary. A Halloween haunted corn maze is fun and scary. This is more like riding his bike down Devil's Curve, as fast as he can. It feels scary and good at the same time. The forest is full of adventure, but who knows what lurks out there. That can be bad, but it's also interesting.

"You want to compare stories?" Gunnar asks.

Max pulls from his thoughts. They've been up in the loft long enough that people are all heading back to the residences or to the saloon.

"Compare stories about what?" Max asks.

"That thing in the woods. I'm not sure it's a bear. I said that, but I think Casey just figured I was being nice to you. Which is bullshit. I'm never nice."

Gunnar flashes a grin, but Max only rolls his eyes. Sometimes Gunnar really seems like he's Max's age. Right now, he's that kid who doesn't want to be "nice," thinks it's not cool, except he is nice, in his way. Not that he's *all* nice, but he can be, more than he probably likes.

"Something about that critter was wrong," Gunnar says. "The way it moved. It wasn't like a bear."

"You've seen bears?"

"Nah, which is the problem, right? I can't tell Sheriff Nature Boy that it moved wrong based on stuff I've seen on TV."

"You don't like Sheriff Eric much, do you?"

Gunnar shrugs. "Don't know him well enough to like him. Don't particularly want to know him better either. He's not my type of guy, and I'm not his type, so whatever. About the bear-man, though, I've been thinking—"

A voice from below calls up, "Max? You letting Gunnar lure you up to his lair with candy? Better watch out, or he'll talk your ear off."

It's Yolanda. Max likes Yolanda more than most people here do. She doesn't take anyone's shit, as Carson would say.

Max waves to Yolanda, and she smiles, and it's her real smile, not one of the tight-lipped ones she gives to others.

"Get your butt down here, Gunnar," she says. "You were supposed to help Kendra with those bolts at five."

"You mean she wants my biceps," he calls back. "It's not about me. It's about my body. I feel so used."

Yolanda starts to say something, and then glances at Max and stops, which only makes him *really* want to know what she was going to say.

"I'm borrowing your tree-house buddy for ten minutes,

Max," she says. "If you want to hang up there a little longer, I'll have him bring you back a blackmail cookie."

"Blackmail cookie?" Gunnar says to Max as he stands.

Max only smiles. It's a secret between him and Yolanda. Detective Casey really likes cookies, but so does everyone else, and sometimes, Detective Casey is too busy to pick up cookies before they sell out. Devon always puts some aside for her at the bakery. Yolanda found out, and Devon—like most people in town—is kinda scared of Yolanda, so if she wants some of Detective Casey's private stash, he gives her a couple.

Max once saw Yolanda eating them and figured out they were Detective Casey's, so now if he's around, she gives him one to keep him quiet. That's why they're blackmail cookies. Not that Max would ever have tattled on Yolanda. It's a private joke between them, and he likes that.

Gunnar leaves, and Max stays where he is, looking out over the town. After he's sure Gunnar's gone, he peeks into the cooler and checks the beer. He wouldn't take one—he's just looking, and maybe trying to see whether there's enough in there that he could take one sometime and not be noticed. He would give it to Carson. That might make his brother happy. Or it might make him scowl and call Max a little kid who thinks beer is cool.

There are only three bottles in there anyway. Gunnar would notice one missing.

Max is walking back to his spot when he sees something in the forest. Something brown, walking on two legs.

He freezes, as if the creature could spot him. Then he peers out, shading his eyes against the sun.

Is that his bear-man? He can't tell from here. It's definitely walking on two legs, though, which bears don't do. It's brown, like a grizzly, but it could just be someone in a brown jacket with the hood up. He can't see whether there are ears.

It's not Sheriff Eric or Detective Casey. Sheriff Eric's coat today was black, and Casey's was blue. It's not Deputy Will or Kenny on patrol either—Max spotted them walking the other way. Kendra must be back from patrol if Gunnar needed to help her. The brown figure is deeper in the woods.

Max takes one last look and then barrels through the loft. He's down the stairs so fast he almost trips. Once outside, he pauses. There's a spot where he could sneak into the forest without being seen. He wants a better look. He also knows he shouldn't do that on his own.

He considers for a second. Then he walks as fast as he can without calling attention to himself. Last time he saw Carson, he was holed up in their room, where he spends most of his day on their Switch. The game console is supposed to be both of theirs, but they're only allowed to recharge the batteries once a day, and Carson always uses it up.

As Max walks to their place, he checks his watch. He used to have a knockoff smartwatch, but they can't charge those here, so it's a regular one with hands that take him a moment to figure out the time. Nearly five thirty, when Mom will get off work and come home. He has to move fast.

There are a few types of residences in Haven's Rock. Some of the staff live in lofts over businesses. A few have their own place, like Sheriff Eric and Detective Casey. The residents—and some of the staff—live in what Mom says reminds her of college dorms.

The people who come to Haven's Rock by themselves get a little bedroom of their own, and they share the living area and kitchen and bathrooms with everyone in their building. For the families, like Max's, there's a building with apartments. Theirs is really tiny, like everything else, but it has two bedrooms, a bathroom, and a living area with a kitchenette, a dining table, and a sofa.

He finds Carson exactly where he expects him. In their room, playing a game on the Switch.

"Carson?" he says.

His brother ignores him.

Max counts to three. "Carson?"

"Wait."

Max glances toward the door. "It's important."

"You're ten. Nothing's important when you're ten."

Max's teeth clench. "Well, this is. I think I see it again."

"See what?"

"The bear-man."

Carson slaps the Switch onto the bed. "For fuck's sake, not this again."

Max doesn't tell him not to say "fuck." Carson is always giving Max crap for doing things that he thinks are cool, but then he does the same.

"There's no Bigfoot in the forest, Max," he says.

"I never called it a Bigfoot. I don't know what it is. I'm not even sure that's what's out there right now, but it's close to town, and I want to take a look. I need you to come with me."

"No."

"Then I should tell someone. Deputy Will or Yolanda or—"

"No." Carson swings his legs over the side of the bed. "You are not telling anyone. You've embarrassed yourself enough."

Max unclenches his jaw and barely manages to get the words out. "I have not embarrassed myself. Even if what I saw was a bear—which I don't think it was—everyone needed to know it's out there. They appreciate the warning."

Carson rolls his dark eyes. "Because they told you that. Because Mom won't *stop* telling you that. There's no Bigfoot, and there's no bear. There's just a scared little kid seeing bogeymen because his daddy got shot. You want to talk to someone? Talk to your therapist, the bartender chick."

"Her name is Isabel."

"Whatever." Carson picks up the Switch and thumps onto his back. "You tell anyone else, and I'll say there wasn't a bear the first time either."

"What?"

Carson doesn't even glance over from his game. "The only person who saw it was Gunnar, and he just said that to be nice to the kid whose dad died. They're all just being nice to you because they feel sorry for you."

Max's fists clench. "It wasn't just Gunnar. Kendra saw something, and Lynn heard it running away—"

"Being nice to the poor little kid who was *traumatized.*" He sneers the last word, and that makes Max madder than anything. Tears fill his eyes.

"I'm not the one who saw Dad get shot," Max says. "You are, and you keep acting like it's no big deal—"

"Yeah, I'm the one who saw it. Because you were hiding in the closet."

The tears stream down, hot with anger. "Mom told us to stay in the closet, and you didn't listen, and you could have been shot, too, and you saw Dad die and you saw Mom get shot, and you had to be scared, but you act like—"

"Are you still here?" Carson waves a hand, gaze still on his game. "Go away, little boy. You're scared of Bigfoot? Find a closet to hide in."

★ ★ ★

Max hates his brother, and he doesn't care if Mom says he should never say that. Carson hates him, so why shouldn't he hate him back? Carson's a jerk. An asshole, just like Gunnar said.

Mom keeps telling him to be patient, to give Carson time, to understand that he's going through some stuff. But they're all "going through some stuff." The worst stuff. That's what Isabel says. This is the worst kind of stuff, and it's okay to admit it's the worst, and it's okay to admit you're not fine.

Why can't Carson say that? Admit he's not fine instead of making Max feel like a baby for not being fine himself. Mocking Max and acting like he has no right to be "not fine" because *he* was hiding in the closet.

He was in the closet because Mom said to stay there. The men had broken in, and Mom said to get in the closet. They did at first, but then Carson left, and he saw Dad get shot and then Mom get shot, and then the police showed up before the men could shoot Carson, and maybe, just maybe, Mom and Dad wouldn't have been shot if Carson hadn't snuck out and been caught.

Did Carson ever think of that? He snuck out, and the men caught him and then they started shooting. It might be Carson's fault, and still he goes around acting like it's no big deal, like he's fine.

Maybe Carson *is* fine. Maybe he's such an asshole that he doesn't care that Dad's dead and Mom is hurt. Maybe the only reason Carson cares is because it means they ended up here, and he hates it, and otherwise, if they were still back home, he really would be fine.

Max has headed into the forest without realizing it. He just needed to get away before anyone saw him crying, and he didn't want to be anywhere his mom might spot him, so he'd taken his secret path into the woods.

The path heads toward the medical clinic, so if anyone sees him they'll think he just needs to talk to Dr. April. It's the quiet edge of town, with storage buildings and stuff, and there's hardly ever anyone there.

He walks into the woods and he just keeps going. He thinks he hears Deputy Will's laugh, but they're too far away to see him, and he's not going to tell them about the bear-man. He's not even going to try to see whether it *is* the bear-man. It wasn't on this side of town. All Max wants is to walk for a while and be by himself. Mostly, he wants to be by himself.

He takes what Sheriff Dalton calls a game trail. It looks like a path made by people, but it's from animals using the same route over and over. He's following that and swiping at his tears and trying not to snivel when a twig cracks right behind him.

He spins—and a figure lunges from the forest and grabs him.

CHAPTER EIGHT

Casey

We're almost back to town when someone shouts, "Max!" Dalton glances at me. It's dark now—after leaving Lilith's cabin, we'd spent a few hours searching for our wild man before eating a quick dinner and heading back out. I check my watch. Past eight.

"Bedtime for the kiddos," I say. "Max must be off visiting."

Dalton grunts. We don't have a curfew in town. In Rockton, we'd asked people not to be out past midnight, but only really enforced it when there was a problem. Even there, anyone out that late was usually returning from someone else's bed. There's less of that in Haven's Rock, partly because there are fewer people, partly because there are fewer singles, and partly because, well, the housing is communal. Chances are that if you're tiptoeing back to your bed, you're not leaving the building.

We do ask for darkness after sunset. Of course you can have a light on, but your shutters and blinds must be closed. That minimizes the chance of the town being spotted at night. It also means that, by nightfall, people are already hunkering down. In Rockton, it'd be a mix of hunkering down at home and at the Roc. Again, fewer people means our new Roc is far less active.

All that combines to create a town that's usually as silent at eight thirty as it will be at two in the morning. But even before we reach the outskirts, voices and boot clomps make it sound like midday.

Anders must spot our flashlight beam. He comes jogging out to meet us.

"Max is missing," he says.

"Shit," I say. "I figured Dana was just calling him in for the night."

He shakes his head as he falls in beside us. "He's been gone since dinner. Dana came home from work, and someone saw Max with Yolanda, so she didn't worry about it right away. A few people were going to the Roc for after-work drinks, and they invited Dana. She told Carson they'd go to dinner at six thirty—just come and grab her at the Roc. He was playing his game and lost track of time. Dana was enjoying some time out and also lost track of time. She remembered just before seven. When she went to get the boys, Max hadn't come home."

Anders pauses for breath, and I should let him go on, but my brain is already compiling a timeline. "When did Yolanda last see him?"

"Five. Max wasn't hanging out with her after all. He was with Gunnar. Which is causing a bit of drama, but we'll stick a pin in that for now."

"Okay. So Max was with Gunnar until . . . ?"

"Five. Same time Yolanda last saw him. Kendra needed Gunnar. Yolanda fetched him. She told Max she'd bring him a cookie."

"One of Casey's cookies?" Dalton says.

Devon confessed that Yolanda has been commandeering some of "my" cookies. I don't care, but I've decided to let Yolanda think she's putting one over on me. Maybe allowing this minor power move will keep her from needing bigger ones.

"I think so," Anders says. "Anyway, she brought him back a cookie, only he wasn't there. No big deal. He'd never actually said he was staying. Gunnar got back just before five thirty, and there was still no sign of Max. They figured he'd gone home."

"Who saw him after that?"

"A few people said he was heading in the direction of the family residences, but Carson had been there the whole time and never saw him."

"Did anyone see Max go inside? Or just head that way?"

"Just head that way. That would have been about five twenty. Before Dana got off work."

"And after that?"

"No one has seen him since."

We're back in town and taking over the search. Once Dana realized Max never went home, she checked with Yolanda, who got Anders. It took about thirty minutes for them to confirm that no one had seen Max since about 5:20.

Anders has had April and Kenny asking door-to-door while he organized a search. By the time we arrive, everyone has been questioned and everyone is looking.

I make a few adjustments to the search. Dana is certain Max is still in town, that if we told everyone not to leave, he wouldn't. While he's a curious child, he does what he's told, even more so since his father's death, not wanting to upset his mother. Dana thinks he went poking around and fell asleep in some nook or cranny.

Do I believe that?

It's possible, I guess, and here's where most of us aren't any help. We don't have kids. All we can do is think back to our own childhoods and evaluate the likelihood of that scenario.

"That's not what happened," Anders whispers to me as we search a storage-building underfloor compartment that has already been searched twice.

I glance up at him. "You aren't buying it."

"I found lots of hiding places as a kid. You need to get away, and you find a spot. Max needs to get away more than most kids but . . ." He shrugs. "How deeply can the kid sleep? Would he even fall asleep? He's not five. He's ten, and he's a mature and responsible ten. I'm not saying it's *impossible* but . . ."

"So what are the options? One, he's hiding and asleep and doesn't hear us. Two, he's hiding and angry, so he isn't answering, but he doesn't strike me as that kind of child either."

"Yeah, he'd never freak out his mom on purpose. That's what I keep coming back to. He's a sensitive kid, and I mean that in the best way."

"Intuitive and empathetic."

Anders nods as he shines his light around the goods stored in the cold compartment. "He knows what his mom's going through, and he's not going to get pissy and hide. And who would he be pissy with? The last people he interacted with are Gunnar and Yolanda, and he was relaxed and smiling."

"Option three is that he was hiding somewhere and got hurt. But the worst he's going to do is fall and twist his ankle, and we've searched all the spots where he might fall."

"You think he could have gone into the woods?"

We head for the hatch and climb out before I answer. "I think

Dana's right that he wouldn't deliberately defy her. Again, it's about not worrying her. He also wouldn't deliberately ignore a sensible order to stay out of the forest."

"He's not his brother," Anders says.

"Carson's having a rough go of it, but yes, if he was missing, I'd be looking in the forest. He doesn't seem to like it much, but if we told him he can't go there, that'd be a reason to do it."

"He's being a little shit." Anders catches my look and sighs. "Fine. He's being a teenage boy who witnessed something traumatic and is bound and determined to prove it didn't bother him. But I didn't fail to notice your use of 'deliberate' earlier. Max wouldn't deliberately go in the forest. He might under the right circumstances. Like—"

The storage-room door flies open, and Dana lurches in, leaning heavily on her cane.

"All right," she says. "I gave him the benefit of the doubt. Now I'm done."

"Gave Max the benefit of the doubt?" I say.

"Gunnar. He did something to my son."

Earlier, Anders had said there'd been some drama about Max being with Gunnar. I hadn't had a chance to ask what he meant, though I had an idea. I'd seen the way Dana flinched when she found out about the hike, that Max had been lagging behind the hiking group with Gunnar. I'd waited to see whether she had a problem with that. If she did, I'd respect her wishes and speak to Gunnar. Otherwise, while Gunnar certainly has his shadows and secrets, I don't get any twitchy vibes when I see him interacting with either of the boys. I've noticed he takes an interest in Max, but it's been nothing concerning.

When Dana didn't complain about Max walking with Gunnar, I took that to mean that she'd gotten past any initial concerns. Now I realize she'd just set that aside temporarily. It bothered her that Max had been on the perch with Gunnar, but she didn't want to point a finger only to discover that Max was holed up somewhere.

"He's not here," she says. "That means someone took him, and it's obvious who that someone is."

I wave her fully into the storage building. Anders motions that he'll leave us alone. Then he slips out.

I settle onto a box. Dana stays standing. She's in her late thirties, Latinx, with spiky dark hair and a slight figure. She wears a brace on one leg, from a shot to the knee.

I could pretend her attackers fired while she was in motion and happened to catch her in the knee, but I know better. That was torture. Torturing her for something her attackers wanted? Or shooting her to torture her husband? It's not part of the bare-bones story I've been given, so it can't matter. It just means that she wears a brace and has chronic pain.

"I heard that Gunnar was with Max before he disappeared," I say.

"Yes." She fairly spits the word. "I have made my feelings about that very clear."

"To Gunnar?"

A flash of discomfort and her voice drops a few notches. "To Max."

"He'd been forbidden to be with Gunnar?"

More discomfort as she leans against a box, finally taking some weight off that injured leg. "No. But he knew how I felt. I didn't want to forbid it. I should have. My gut told me to, and I should have."

"What has Gunnar done to make you nervous?"

"I don't like him." Her anger surges. "There's something very wrong with that man."

"And that something suggests he shouldn't be around your sons."

"He's . . ." She glances toward the door, though there's no sound of anyone there. Then she lowers her voice. "I saw one of the women coming out of the building where Gunnar has his little perch. He was up there, and she snuck out like she didn't want to be seen. Then I heard Kendra teasing him about . . ." Her cheeks flush. "It left no illusions about what the woman had been doing in there with him, which is none of my business, except . . . What Kendra said . . . It made him seem . . . like he does that a lot."

He does. Yolanda's construction crew had been mostly women, and Gunnar had made it clear he was available for any-one feeling lonely. Straight-up sex, no strings attached. He'd had plenty of takers, which meant he must have kept up his end of the bargain, providing exactly what he advertised. Erica Jong's "zipless fuck"—pure pleasure seeking for both parties. I sure as hell won't judge him or them for that.

I wasn't aware that Gunnar was doing that again—there are only a handful of single women here. But if he is? Well, it might require a conversation, to be clear he understands that the dy-namics could be different. These aren't construction workers and tradespeople on a job; they're potentially vulnerable people seeking refuge.

I don't say any of that. I just say, "Ah."

"There's more," she says. "I once saw Lynn sneak in that door when he was up there."

Shit. Lynn is married, and while I get the sense there's ten-sion there, we cannot afford to have extramarital-affair drama in a place as small as Haven's Rock. I can hope it's an open marriage, and Grant is fine with Lynn hooking up, but I doubt that. Which means I definitely need to speak to Gunnar. I know he has no problem with married women, having casually propositioned me.

"So Gunnar seems to be . . ." I stop before giving any of my usual jokey euphemisms and say the loaded word I'd rather not use. But anything else will seem as if I'm making light of it. "Promiscuous."

"Yes." She exhales, and it was clear she'd been circling that. "It worries me."

Here I must tread extra carefully. I don't like where this is going, but I can't appear biased. I need to treat her concerns seriously. But I also need to say what has to be said.

"Promiscuity isn't a warning sign for sexual predators," I say. "I know the media can make it seem that way, especially if the predator is a woman. I'm aware that Gunnar encourages short-term relationships, but it's consensual, and none of his lovers have ever complained about his behavior. If there'd been even a hint of that, we'd have jumped on it. This town is too tiny to let the whisper network handle problems."

Her cheeks flush again, and I can tell, as careful as I'm being with my wording, that even this guarded talk of sex is making her uncomfortable.

"I'm guessing," I say slowly, "that if you're bringing this up, you think it's a danger sign with your sons. That if Gunnar is promiscuous and he's taken an interest in Max, that's a problem. But . . ."

"Hooking up with a lot of women doesn't mean he's a pedophile."

"Yes."

She crosses her arms. "I know that. I just . . . He makes me uncomfortable, and I don't like seeing him around Max, and

I should have said something, but honestly?" She meets my gaze. "I shouldn't have had to. Yolanda saw Max up in that loft with Gunnar and acted like it was no big deal. She doesn't have children. Neither do you. I hate to play that card, because I know people do that all the time. *You don't have kids so you don't understand.*"

"Except that it's true. We don't have children."

"And if you did, you'd be nervous about any stranger taking an interest in them. You can tell yourself you're being paranoid, and nine times out of ten, you are, and it sucks if you're depriving your kid of a healthy relationship with another adult, but you cannot take that chance. Gunnar was wrong to take Max up in that loft without my permission, and Yolanda should have known that."

"Except," I say gently, "as you pointed out, we don't have kids. We don't understand the nuances. I don't want to lay blame on anyone. Gunnar would have topped my list for questioning anyway, as the last person to be with Max. In light of your concerns, I'll go harder at him, and I'll do it right away."

"But you don't think he had anything to do with it."

"I do not know Gunnar well enough to say that."

"Will you search his loft?" she asks. "For evidence?"

"I've searched it for Max, but now I'll search it and his room for evidence. Right after I speak to him."

I head out to talk to Gunnar, but instead see Dalton striding my way, Storm having to nearly jog to keep up.

"Max went into the woods," Dalton says. "Storm found his entry point. I'm going to take her in and see where it goes."

I don't hesitate. Yes, I'd promised to talk to Gunnar right

away, but finding Max is a lot more important. As we cross town, I spot Gunnar with Kendra and call Gunnar over.

"I need to talk to you," I say.

"Figured that. At the town hall?"

"Yes. Meet me there. We need to check something first."

He looks from me to Storm. "A trail?"

I make a noncommittal noise.

"If it's beside the clinic, that's not new."

Dalton stops and pivots to face him.

Gunnar raises his hands and takes an exaggerated step back, as if Dalton had lunged at him. I only shake my head.

I could say the two men don't get along, but they'd need to have an actual conversation to know that. It's as if they've decided they won't get along and don't bother to interact. That's mostly Gunnar, but if someone doesn't want to deal with Dalton, he's happy to leave them be unless they give him a reason to deal with *them*.

"What do you mean that's not new?" I say.

"I'm not saying Max didn't go in there tonight. But if your pup picked up his scent, it could also be old. That's Max's secret sneaking-in point. On the left side of the clinic. It's a blind spot, where you can't see him unless you're in my perch."

Dalton rocks forward. "So you've noticed Max going into the forest alone, which we absolutely would not want him doing, and you didn't say anything."

"He's ten, and he's got you telling him all these forest secrets. Of course he's going in. I would at that age. Hell, I do now."

I give him a look that says that isn't helping.

"The point," Gunnar says, "is that he's a responsible kid. *Too* responsible, if you ask me. He's had a lot of shit in his life, and it's made him nervous about doing anything wrong. That's good for his parents, but not so good for him." He lifts his hands.

"Which is never anything I'd say to Max himself. I'm not going to encourage a ten-year-old kid to act out. I saw him go into the forest and I watched—not because I'm a perv but because I thought he deserved a little safe rebellion time. He goes in maybe fifty feet. Pokes around. Sometimes sits on a log and hangs out. If he went further, I'd have told someone."

"You still should have told someone," I say, before Dalton can. "But I appreciate that you were keeping an eye on him."

"Which you're saying very nicely so you don't make me feel like a perv until you need to question me about the possibility that I *am* a perv."

"Yep."

"I'm not going to take offense at that."

"Good, because you were the last person seen with a missing child, after taking him up to your perch. I'm not saying you meant anything untoward, but I'd be a really shitty cop if I didn't consider that."

"I know. I'll be waiting at the town hall for you." He strips off his shirt. "Take this."

"Uh . . ." I say.

Dalton sighs and shakes his head. Gunnar has just handed me his T-shirt, and he's not wearing a jacket or sweater, despite it being about five degrees above freezing. Those of us who've acclimated to the cooler weather often dress lighter than others. That's not Gunnar's excuse. Yolanda once described him as having a serious clothing allergy. He just likes to wear as little as possible to show off what he's got underneath.

"For scent," he says, handing me the shirt. "I haven't been near where Max goes into the forest, and I want your dog to confirm it."

"That's not actually how it works, but yes, I'll ask whether she smells your scent there."

"She won't. You do that, and I'll be at the town hall."

"With a shirt on?"

He waggles his brows. "That's up to you." He stops so fast it's almost comical, and his gaze goes to Dalton. "That was a joke. I wouldn't hit on your wife."

"Not in front of me, at least?" Dalton shakes his head. "I'm not worried."

"Put on a shirt, Gunnar," I say. "Before you freeze."

CHAPTER NINE

We check the spot where Storm found Max's trail. It's exactly where Gunnar said it would be, and as we walk along it, Dalton and Storm both confirm Max has been back here a few times. There are multiple trails of his in the area, along with footprints and clothing fibers on an old log, presumably the one he sits on.

Did he come back here tonight? It's impossible to tell. If Storm can distinguish between a two-hour-old trail and a ten-hour-old one, I don't know how to get her to convey that information to me. She can only find trails and confirm they're recent.

Dalton can do the same. There are three trails that go past the log. All three end about twenty feet later. We can't tell which is the most recent. They're all newish, according to Storm and Dalton, meaning less than a week old.

Dalton is going to circle town again, but we don't have much hope. Of all our current residents, Max is in the forest more than anyone. He joins every possible excursion, and

Dalton and I take him on some of our own. We'd hoped that would keep him from making his own treks, but we must admit Gunnar was right there. He's a ten-year-old with an interest in the forest. He's going to take our prohibition with a grain of salt and decide we *really* only mean he shouldn't go far on his own.

Back in town, I find Gunnar on the front steps of the town hall. I still struggle to call it that. In Rockton, it was the police station. Here, we're trying to move away from that. "Police station" implies that there are residents who require policing . . . when many of them have escaped that sort of person.

We also considered doing away with our titles: sheriff, detective, deputy. We decided against it in hopes that the titles suggest protection rather than enforcement. We're here to keep you safe rather than "police" you. Maybe it's all semantics. I don't know.

"I didn't hear any commotion," Gunnar says as I approach. "I'm guessing that means you didn't find Max."

I shake my head.

"Did you find a trail that could lead to him?" he asks.

Another shake.

"Damn," he mutters. He holds the door for me, and we go inside. "What do you think happened?"

Gunnar takes my silence to mean he's not getting more, and he doesn't push, just drops into a chair.

"Yes, I was the last person to be with Max, apparently," he says. "But I left him alone and went with Yolanda. She returned before I did, and he was already gone. At that time, I was still helping Kendra."

I open my mouth, but he pushes on, "Maybe I shouldn't have taken him up to the perch. I was aware of how it could look. I had him go up first and get out to where people could see him before I went up."

"If you knew it was a problem, why do it?"

"Because the kid needed someone he could vent to."

"Vent about what?"

Gunnar's brows shoot up. "He told you guys he saw a bear with human eyes, and you took his statement and then held a meeting telling everyone it was a bear. You didn't even warn him first."

I sink into my chair. I hadn't considered that.

"He was angry," Gunnar says. "Angry and embarrassed. I brought him up there in case he wanted to talk."

"Did he?"

"A bit. Mostly, I just let him sit." He shifts forward in his chair. "I know his mom doesn't like him hanging out with me, which is why I don't usually do it. I don't know how to convince her I'm not a perv. Maybe I can't. Maybe I should accept that and back off."

"So why don't you?"

"Because he needs something he's not getting, and I understand that."

"Okay."

I let the silence fall. Gunnar squirms and then holds himself still.

"Look," he says, "I've had enough therapy to last me a lifetime, and it was all bullshit. I'm not saying Isabel isn't helping Max. She seems better than anyone I ever had. And Mathias is one scary fucker, but I think Carson needs that. But as much as they can try to understand what the kid's going through, unless something like that happened to them, they can't."

"Okay."

Again I just let the word drop. Again he shifts in his seat before stopping himself.

"I'm going to say this very fast," he says, "and I don't ever want it mentioned again. I'm only saying it because it explains why a grown man wants to help a kid like Max. It's between us, right? Confidential."

"It's confidential unless you hurt Max. Then everything's fair game."

"I didn't, so I'm not worried. Here goes. My dad killed my mom. Took a shot at me, but I ran, and when I came back with the neighbor, he'd killed himself. Don't say you're sorry because that's just awkward. It's not some sob story I'm telling to make you feel bad for me. I don't talk about it. Ever. But there it is. Max's dad was murdered and his mom hurt, and I'm not going to push myself at him like some kind of trauma-buddy, but if he wants someone to just be there, in case he needs to talk, I can do that."

It's really hard to not say "I'm sorry" even if Gunnar has told me not to. He just confessed to something horrific in his life, throwing it out there in a way that tells me he really *doesn't* want to talk about it and would rather never have mentioned it.

"I understand," I say. "It's a tough situation because you have a valid reason, but he's still a minor, and if his mom doesn't want him around you . . ."

"Yeah, I know."

"Maybe if you talked to her—"

"She'd think I was full of shit. That I'm a perv with a fake sob story that gives me an excuse to be around little boys. If *you're* concerned my story's fake, I can give you details to look it up. But I'd rather not if I don't need to."

"Understood."

"I was extra careful with Max, and not because of his mom. I had stuff happen to me after my parents died. Nothing major. Just people crossing lines. Kids like Max and me, I think we put out some kind of signal that pervs pick up on and know they've got a live one, a boy who might fall for their games, as if what happened makes us desperate and needy. I was careful with Max so he'd know I wasn't like that, but also trying to teach him how to be ready for people who *are* like that."

"Okay."

"So where do we go now? Search my apartment and whatever? I'm not sure where I could have stashed the kid, but I know you'll need to check."

"We will," I say.

"You want me on house arrest or anything? Until he's found?"

"No, but I'd like you to buddy up with someone. You'll move in with Will temporarily."

"So no one can accuse me of taking off at night to feed my hostage?"

"Just cutting off all avenues of concern."

"Yeah, I know. And I'm probably not the person to offer, but I'd like to help. Whatever I can do. I have no idea what happened—I can't imagine Max would go into the woods far enough to get lost—but I'd like to help."

"Thank you."

I head out with Dalton, to tell him about Gunnar. Then we continue searching. For hours, in the dark, we search.

When we return to town, Yolanda strides out. "You need to take a break."

"We're fine," I say. "We just came back—"

"To get some sleep. Tell me those are your next words, because you two have been out in those woods all night. See that yellow thing in the sky? It's the sun."

"We're—"

"No, you're not fine." She stops before us, arms crossed. "You're setting a shitty example, and it stops now."

"Excuse me?" I say.

"You've been out all night. Do you think Will got any sleep? Kenny? Your sister? As long as you two are up and searching, they're up and searching, because anyone who goes to bed while a child is lost is an unfeeling monster. So it's up to you two to be the unfeeling monsters."

I glare at her. She has a point. I just don't like how she's making it, as usual. And, as usual, I also have to admit this is a language I listen to. Guilt. Say I need a rest for myself, and I'll keep going. Say that others need a rest and I have to lead by example, and if I ignore her, I am indeed an unfeeling monster.

"Tell Will you're taking a few hours off," she says. "Suggest others do the same. If he wants to stay up while you sleep, that's fine, as long as he takes the next rest shift. We're all zombies, and do you know what zombies can't do? Think."

"Depends on the depiction," Dalton says.

She glares at him. "Don't pull that. You know what I mean. You are the mindless walking dead right now. Everyone is. We aren't thinking—we're just relentlessly seeking our target, which in this case is a boy instead of brains."

"Has anyone found anything?"

"Do you think I'd be telling you to get some rest if we had a lead?" She shakes her head. "You're exhausted, Casey, and you're not thinking straight. Go rest. I'll tell the others."

★ ★ ★

I don't expect to fall asleep, but my body has other ideas. I climb into bed and curl up against Dalton, and I don't remember another thing until someone's pounding on our door. Then I flail awake to find Dalton already out of bed and striding for the door, sweatpants in hand, with Storm at his heels.

As I dress, Dalton opens the door. A voice sounds, alternating between a high pitch and a lower one.

Carson. I haven't heard him talk enough to realize his voice is breaking, but now the words are tumbling out and it's cracking all over the place.

It's Carson.

Max's brother.

In a panic, his words a jumbled mess.

Oh no.

I barrel out of the door and take the stairs so fast I almost trip.

"I did this," Carson is saying. "It's all my fault."

"Slow down and come in," Dalton says.

Carson shakes his head. He's still in the doorway, dressed in a T-shirt and jeans, barefoot despite the freezing-cold morning. His hair is wild, his eyes even wilder, dark rimmed and shadowed. He's breathing hard, as if he ran the whole way here.

"I did this," he says.

"You did what, Carson?" I ask.

"Max. I did this."

Dalton glances my way as cold dread seeps in.

"Come in," Dalton says, hand landing on the boy's shoulder. "Or we're all going to freeze before you can explain."

He guides Carson to the sofa, taking his time, giving Carson a chance to catch his breath.

Dalton settles Carson on the sofa and then murmurs to me that he'll make hot chocolate.

When he's gone, I say, "What did you do, Carson?" my voice as neutral as I can make it.

"Lied," he blurts. "I lied."

"About what?"

"Max. I was the last person to see him. I know why he went into the woods."

Do not judge. Do not put him on the defensive.

"Okay," I say. "Tell me what happened."

"He came to my room. Before Mom got home. After he left Gunnar's perch, I guess. He said he'd seen the bear guy in the forest."

I stiffen. "The bear guy . . ."

"Bigfoot. Whatever. I was . . ." He meets my gaze with eyes red-rimmed from crying. "Max wanted me to come with him to get a closer look. When I said no, he wanted to tell someone. He was doing the right thing. He always . . ."

His voice cracks and his eyes fill, but he angrily wipes away the tears. "He's always so *good*. He always does what he's told, and I hate it. Everyone likes him. Everyone thinks he's so cute and sweet, and I can't even say he's secretly a jerk because he's not and—"

Carson takes a deep breath. "That doesn't matter. I was the jerk. I told him to stop talking about whatever he thought he saw in the forest, that he was embarrassing himself. I even said I didn't think he saw anything and Gunnar was humoring him, which isn't true at all. I just . . . Sometimes, I start being mean to him, and I can't stop."

I think about April, how often growing up I'd felt like she was being mean to me. In her case, it'd been her brutal honesty, and she hadn't done it to hurt me. But I remember what her seeming cruelty felt like. I'd been devastated.

Carson misdirected his anger at Max, and it felt good because it was cathartic. It's just that, like April, he was too young to really see how much it hurt his younger sibling. I understand that, but I am the former little sister who cannot help but put herself in Max's shoes and feel the devastation of a sibling's harsh words.

"I understand," I say.

I also understand exactly what Max would have done next. What I would have done if it'd been April telling me to stop being a baby, stop making up stories. I'd have stormed out, determined to prove her wrong.

Determined to get a better look at that creature in the forest.

"I was really awful." Carson's voice drops to a whisper. "I said other things, too. Things I should never have said. Things I don't believe."

"And then what?"

"He left. I didn't think about where he might be going. I just wanted to play my game. Mom came in just after that and said she was having a drink before dinner. Max and I were supposed to meet her at the Roc at six thirty. I didn't set an alarm or anything. I knew Max would be in by six—that's the rule. So I went back to playing my game, and the next thing I know, Mom's there, saying we're late for dinner and asking where Max is."

"And you said?"

"That I didn't know. Which is true. I wasn't hiding anything. Not then. She didn't ask when I last saw him, and I figured it didn't matter. I said he wasn't at home, and she took off to find him."

"What did you do then?"

He shrugs. "I put away my Switch and got a sweater. Then I

was hungry—I hadn't noticed that because I was busy playing a game. I found some bars in the kitchen and ate half of one before I went out to help Mom look for Max. I was mad. I wanted dinner, and he was being a baby, running off and hiding because I hurt his feelings." He sneaks a glance at me. "That's what I was thinking."

"So you helped look for Max."

"I checked some spots he likes. Then I heard Mom yelling at Gunnar and Yolanda. Mom never yells like that, so I went running over. She was saying they were the last ones with Max. At first, I thought that was good—they'd seen him recently. Then I realized she meant they saw him *before* I did. They asked whether he could have gone home, and Mom said no, I was there, and I never saw him."

"Ah."

"She must have figured I'd have said if I saw him, but I honestly didn't mean to hide anything. She came home and asked where Max was, I said I didn't know and she took off. Then she was telling everyone I hadn't seen him, and I . . . I didn't want to make her look bad."

And make himself look bad. Risk his mother's anger when she found out he hadn't told her the full story. I get that, but I only say, "Okay."

"At first, I thought it wouldn't matter. I was mean to Max, and he took off and hid somewhere. Everyone was sure he was hiding, so what difference did it make *why* he'd hide? Then I started wondering whether he might have gone into the woods to look for his Bigfoot, but by then, you guys were back and Sheriff Eric and Storm were already searching the woods."

"What made you decide to come tell us now?"

"I . . . I had a dream and . . ." He tugs at his collar, as if it's suddenly too tight. "It was about something bad happening. With the Bigfoot."

He'd had a nightmare. Once he fell asleep, his subconscious poked at his conscience. That's why he came running over. He woke in a panic and ran to tell us the truth.

"Does your mom know?" I ask gently.

His gaze drops, and he whispers, "No."

"Okay. Let's talk about how we want to handle this."

Carson and I agree that I'll tell Dana what happened. That's not as much about saving Carson from the experience as making sure it's conveyed correctly, which I suppose is still about saving Carson from *an* experience—that of breaking down in a puddle of guilt and self-recrimination that will panic his mother even more.

I relay the situation to Dana succinctly. Max thought he saw the bear-man again. Carson figured he was imagining it. They argued. Max stormed out, and when he went missing, Carson presumed he was hiding because of the fight.

Dana is upset, of course. Carson should have come forward. This is vital information. But I make the case for it being less vital than it seems—we were already searching the forest. The only difference now is that we know *why* Max might have gone into the woods.

I leave Carson with his mother to work it out. Then it's time to call a small breakfast meeting because this really does put a different spin on the situation, more than Carson could have guessed.

Max went into the forest to get a better look at his bear-man—the creature that, at the time, we all presumed was a bear. That's bad enough. But after what the miners said, we're pretty damn sure it wasn't a bear at all. It was a person, and that is so much worse.

CHAPTER TEN

Another staff meeting. This time, remembering how Yolanda felt being excluded from the last, my initial plan is to have all the staff attend. Then I realize that would include Gunnar.

Do I believe he could be involved in Max's disappearance? No, yet he must remain a suspect, whatever my gut says. I don't want him at the meeting because I don't yet have a firm sense of how much I can trust him to keep his mouth shut. And if he's not there, then I need to comb through the invitee list more carefully. Otherwise, everyone will know he's been snubbed, which pins the label of prime suspect on his chest.

Dalton and I decide to limit the list to staff who'll be part of the search teams: Dalton and Anders, obviously, and also Kenny, Yolanda, Kendra, and Phil. Phil won't join the search, but as the de facto "mayor" he should be there. The doctor should be available whenever possible, so I exclude April. Mathias and Isabel would join the search if prodded, but we aren't at the prodding stage. As for Gunnar, he needs to stay in town for the time being.

I start by telling everyone about our encounter with the mining-operation leader.

"Does he have a name yet?" Kenny asks.

"Mr. Rogers," Anders says. "Or that's what I'm calling him. Because I really wish he *wasn't* our neighbor."

"Mr. Rogers it is," I say, and continue his story about the wild man of the forest.

"Damn," Kenny says. "So the kid really did see a person's face."

"Seems that way," I say.

"A serial killer on the run?" Yolanda says. "Hiding in the north?"

Kendra makes a noise. "I don't mean to be rude, but as someone who's lived up here for most of her life, I've never actually encountered anything like that off a movie screen. Dangerous people, sure. Wild-*looking* people, sure, but . . ."

"Not actual wild people," I say. "They're miners and trappers who appear a little rough after being in the forest for months on end."

She exhales, as if relieved. "Yes. And also, being blunt, sometimes they're just regular Indigenous hunters who aren't dressed like white folks. Wearing a bearskin would be extreme but . . ." She shrugs. "Maybe?"

"The miner reported that it was a white man, at least as far as he could tell. And while the Yukon wilderness isn't teeming with serial killers, there is something else."

Having Kendra and Yolanda there means I need to explain about the hostiles. I don't know how much Yolanda knows from Émilie, but I give the bare-bones version.

"You think a leftover hostile followed us here?" Kenny says.

"I wouldn't say *followed*, but it's a theory we can't rule out."

Kendra says, "And you think—whether it's one of these 'hostiles' or not—that whoever that miner saw is the person who took Max? That Max spotted him and went to investigate?"

"Someone has come forward to report that Max said he saw his bear-man again. This person didn't believe him, and so didn't go to check it with him. We think Max went to investigate on his own."

No one asks who "this person" is. Carson is the only one who really fits that bill—someone Max would entrust with that secret and who might not be quick to tell what happened.

"Max goes into the forest for a better look," Kenny says. "And this man in a bearskin grabs him."

"It's a strong possibility, which means we're shifting the full search focus to the forest and traveling further than we'd expect Max to wander on his own. Does anyone have any questions or concerns?"

No one answers.

"All right then," I say. "We're not ready to recruit residents, so it's just us. We're also not ready to tell them what was seen in the forest. Eric and I will leave the search to Will. We're taking Storm into the woods."

We spend the remaining daylight following every possible trail from town. The only one that goes deeper is the main hiking path. After a quick late dinner, we're far along on that path, with Storm following Max's scent, which could be new . . . or could be from the many times he's hiked it with us and others.

When we broke ground at Haven's Rock, there were only pathways worn by animals going to and from the lake. We'd asked Yolanda to cut a trail for her crew, so they could take guided hikes. Yolanda's idea of a hiking trail was a path about a kilometer into the forest. Then you turned around and went back. It didn't lead to a pretty overlook. It didn't lead to the lake. It didn't even meander along a scenic route. It was literally the simplest possible path in and out, the wilderness equivalent of using a treadmill for exercise.

One of our key tasks since then has been the creation of more trails. Right now, we've focused on practical ones. Trails to the lake. Trails to berry patches. Trails to good hunting and logging spots. We've been linking those up to form a longer system for hikes.

Eventually, we'll cut and groom them properly. For now, we've made one primary hiking route, which links with others before looping back to town. In other words, it's a closed system. We need to find the spot where Max's scent trail leaves it.

There isn't one.

"Do you think it's possible Max *didn't* leave town?" I say as we walk.

Dalton doesn't answer. Of course it's possible.

"How possible?" I say after a few more steps.

He still doesn't answer, which may mean he realizes I'm not talking to him as much as I'm talking at him. Verbalizing my thoughts, while giving him the opportunity to respond if he has something to add.

"We know he saw his bear-man," I say. "Going into the woods after him is the obvious theory, but it's not a definitive answer. Everyone says Max did as he was told. He nudged the boundaries—like slipping a little ways into the forest—but would he go after this guy?"

"Depends on how angry he was."

"Which we can't know, not being in his head. If Max never went into the forest, he had to be grabbed by someone *in* town."

"Yep." Dalton moves ahead and bends to examine a broken twig.

When I don't speak, he waves for me to follow him and says, "Keep talking."

"We've searched everywhere in Haven's Rock multiple times. So even if Max was *taken* by someone in town, he's no longer *in* town. But if the culprit is a resident, they can lead us to him. That likelihood that someone in Haven's Rock took him determines how much time I spend questioning versus searching."

"You can question. I can search."

"True."

"You'd just rather be out here. Which, for now, I'd agree with. Unless we have reason to believe someone in town took him, we keep looking. . . ."

He trails off and bends near crushed vegetation and what looks like a partial boot print a couple of feet from the trail. The print is too faint to leave more than a half-moon heel impression. I bend for a closer look, shining my flashlight on it. Then I take a measurement and a cell-phone photo before we carefully make our way onward in that direction.

I start steering Storm around the print. Then I stop and ask her to sniff it. When she does, she snorts, as if clearing her nose. I frown and motion again for her to sniff. She obeys, with obvious reluctance, and then gives a low whine, her ears cocking down as if she's done something wrong.

There *is* something wrong. But it's not her. It's the scent. I've seen this before, when we ask her to pick up a scent, and there's some reason why she can't, such as when it's too faint. But that snort and reluctance suggests more. There's something about the scent, as if it's overlain with another smell.

I lower my own nose, and all I smell is loamy earth. Then . . . rot?

"Eric?" I say. "Could you come here a second?"

He's disappeared into the trees. When he returns, I tell him the problem. Then I lead Storm away so he can sniff.

I walk into a clearing, and I'm standing there, in the moonlight, when a glimmer in the sky catches my attention. A faint ribbon of green.

"Aurora borealis," I whisper to Storm as I smile. "We're going to get a light show to lead the way."

If only we weren't in the forest searching for a lost child, which kind of puts a damper on the beauty of the northern lights.

I'm still looking up when movement in the trees makes me startle. I look toward it and . . .

What the hell is that? I step in that direction, only to see something move out of the corner of my eye.

"Eric?"

That's all I need to say for him to come barreling through, as if I'd screamed in terror. I point toward the first thing I saw . . . and then the other.

"What the hell?" he says.

He strides to the first object. It's hanging from a tree, and when he reaches up, a noise from me stops him. He lifts his flashlight instead.

The object dangles from a branch at eye level for Dalton. It hangs there, twisting in the breeze, which is how it caught my attention.

I move closer and squint up.

"Eagle feathers?" he says. "Yeah. Looks like eagle. The central feather does, at least."

It's a bald eagle feather hanging straight down with three smaller white-gray feathers affixed to it. Two of those smaller feathers are at the bottom, jutting out at forty-five-degree angles. One is tied across the middle. Together, they form a stick figure. Where the hands and feet would be are black splotches on the pale feathers.

"Is that . . . ?" Dalton moves his flashlight even closer, and the black splotches turn dark red.

Blood.

I turn to the second object. It's a replica of the first. As I turn, I see two more. Four stick figures hanging from the trees in this clearing.

"How far from town are we?" I ask.

"Maybe five hundred feet that way." He points.

Close enough for these to be made by someone in town? Yes. But also far enough that they might not be.

"Can you see what they're attached with?" I ask.

"Vines."

String or fishing twine would suggest they were made by someone with access to a town.

Dalton's flashlight beam moves over the ground. At first, I think he's looking for footprints. Then I realize what else he could be looking for.

We're in a clearing with a bloody stick figure at each compass point, while we're searching for a missing child. When my gaze finds a slight rise in the middle of the clearing, my stomach clenches, and I'm terrified of seeing a mound of disturbed earth. I hurry over to find what looks like a campfire.

I'm crouching beside it when Storm lets out a low growl that has me laying a hand on her head. Dalton's head swivels as he listens. Then his eyes narrow. His gaze lasers in to our left, and his hand goes to his gun. I do the same, taking mine out, although I don't yet hear anything.

Then it comes. The rustle of something brushing through

the undergrowth. It's the faintest sound, one I'd never have noticed without Dalton and Storm detecting it first. Dalton motions that he's going to move forward. I nod and keep one hand on Storm's head, telling her to stay with me.

I cover Dalton as he heads into the forest. When a twig cracks to my left, I go still.

Storm stays focused on the direction Dalton's going. There's another whisper of undergrowth, definitely to my left, and that's when Storm notices, her shaggy head turning that way.

Has whatever's out there changed position, now approaching from the left? Or are there two presences in the forest?

I take a slow step left while keeping enough of my attention on Dalton. When I can't see anything, I take another step and . . .

And my target is a porcupine, ambling along. Storm doesn't do more than growl. After one encounter with the large rodents, she stays clear.

I swing my attention right, toward Dalton. I'd been distracted just long enough for him to disappear in the trees. I quickstep in that direction and—

A crackle in the forest. Then:

"Goddamn it!" Dalton snarls. "Really?"

I hurry over to see him holding Louie by the back of his collar, as if he'd caught the man making a break for it.

"This seems familiar," I say as I walk over. "What are you doing out here this time?"

"Searching for the boy. Obviously."

"So yesterday, when you weren't included on the hunting team, you went out on your own and caught a week of shit duty for it. Today, when you're not included in the search party, you thought you'd do the same thing and expect a different outcome?"

"Nah," Dalton says. "He just didn't count on getting caught again."

Louie squares his shoulders. "I didn't care if I got caught. A child's life is at stake, and I'm not letting you two morons screw it up."

"Morons." Dalton chews the word over as Louie yanks from his grip, as if getting out of the way before Dalton throws him down again. Which means he doesn't understand my husband very well.

"Morons," Dalton repeats. "Explain."

Louie turns to face him. "Explain what?"

"Why we're morons. Because it seems I'm too dense to see it myself, being a moron and all. Tell us how you reached this conclusion."

"You have no idea what you're doing."

"Continue."

Louie falters, confused when Dalton doesn't defend himself. Oh, there *are* ways to get Dalton to react. Even to get him to react physically. But calling him stupid isn't going to do it. He'll just congratulate himself on pulling off a very useful persona.

"Continue with what?" Louie says finally.

"Elaborate on how I am doing this wrong. I'm always open to constructive criticism."

I bite my cheek at that. Sure, Dalton accepts useful critiques . . . from the select few people whose opinion he values enough to listen to. Something tells me Louie isn't part of that club, but the man straightens, his chin lifting as he prepares to elder-splain Dalton's job to him.

"You have no idea how to conduct a proper search," Louie says. "You need grids and search teams."

I turn to Dalton. "He's right. I think I've seen that on TV."

Louie nods. "You should listen to your wife. I don't know

what actual law-enforcement experience you have, son, but you're doing this all wrong. You need to form teams and grids and get search dogs." He shoots a pointed glance at Storm. "That's a lapdog."

My brows shoot up. "You're a brave man if you want her on your lap. Last time she hopped on mine, I nearly suffocated."

"You know what I mean. That's not a tracking breed. She's a pet. Now, if you'll let me take charge of this search—"

"Glad to," Dalton says. "I just need to know your qualifications."

A sly look creeps into Louie's eyes. "Oh, but that's the problem. I can't provide them. My past is confidential. Just trust that I know what I'm doing. I've been on multiple searches."

"In what capacity?"

"I can't say."

"Law enforcement? Ranger service? Search-and-rescue?"

"Can't say."

Dalton nods. "I understand. Just as you'll understand that we need to confirm your expertise with the person who conducted your background check. We won't ask for details. We'll just say that you've represented yourself as a professional in this area. If they can confirm your credentials, then we will welcome your input. If they can't—" He steps toward Louie. "—your stay in Haven's Rock will be terminated for interfering with a critical mission."

Louie smirks. "Don't embarrass yourself with idle threats, Sheriff. You don't have the authority to kick me out."

Dalton does an excellent job of not laughing at that. "Maybe not, but if you misrepresented—"

"I said I've been on searches. That's all."

"In a professional capacity that would give you the right to question my own expertise."

"I never said—" Louie begins.

"How many searches have you been on?"

"Two."

"I've been on dozens, and I'm damn well going to bet my recovery rate was higher and my personal involvement was greater. Now, if you want to challenge my authority, go ahead, but if you do, then I am checking your credentials, and if they don't reflect your claim of expertise—which we both know they won't—then you are going home."

"You're doing this wrong, and I have a right to my opinion."

"Yep, you do. And you have a right to wait in town and give me that opinion when I return. You do not have a right to be out here, fucking up my search."

"Fucking up your search?"

Dalton continues toward Louie, making him back up. "You damaged a potential scene. You interrupted our search of that scene. We now need to abandon the scene to escort you back to town, after you've been barreling through this forest, fucking up my fucking search grid, filling it with trails that do not belong to the child we are looking for. There is a boy out here—"

"We both know that's not true."

Dalton rocks back. "Excuse me?"

"The kid's dead, and you know it. It's been twenty-four hours. We're looking for a body."

"Someone watches *way* too much TV," I say. "Statistically, after forty-eight hours, the chance of finding a missing person alive drops, but that doesn't apply out here. A few months ago, we found someone who'd been missing for days. Once, we found someone who'd been missing for a year."

Dalton takes another step. "If you go back to town and even mention the possibility that Max is dead, I will put you on shit duty for the rest of your stay. If you mention it and his mother gets wind of it? Consider yourself gone."

"His mother is the one you should be investigating, not that moron Gunnar, who hangs out with the kid because he's the only person in town with the same IQ."

Someone really likes insulting other people's intelligence. Coming from a family where my own high IQ is considered merely adequate, I've met plenty of people like Louie. They're slightly more intelligent than average, and they cling to that as their sole mark of superiority because they need to be superior, in some way, any way.

That's not the important part of what he just said, though.

"You think Dana has something to do with her son's disappearance?" I say.

"Please don't tell me you buy their story. I don't know the details, but I've heard enough to glean the basics. Anyone with a shred of intelligence could. Apparently, they're just an innocent family targeted by some drug cartel. Which happens all the time." He rolls his eyes.

"Drug cartel?" Dalton says. "Who told you that?"

"Again, Sherlock, no one needs to tell me anything. I can figure it out. You need to dig deeper into her story."

"And *you* need to leave detective work to the detective," Dalton says. "You're spending the night under guard."

"What?"

"You just said you think Max is dead and you think his mom has something to do with it. You really expect we'll throw you back into the general population to run your mouth off? You're on house arrest."

"You can't do that."

"Check your contract. Section 12, clause B. You may be reasonably detained if you pose a threat to the safety or privacy of other residents. Come on."

"Eric?" I say.

He turns.

"I'd like to stay and check what we found," I say.

He hesitates.

"We're only a few hundred feet from town. And I have backup." I motion from my gun to Storm.

He nods. "Fine. I'll be quick."

"Bring someone with you, please. For *your* safety."

He grunts, grabs Louie's arm, and heads out.

CHAPTER ELEVEN

After they leave, Storm and I return to that clearing. With my flashlight, I examine the scenario from a short distance, getting a sense of what I'm seeing. Then I move closer.

The central piece looks like a firepit in miniature. The ring of stones is maybe a foot in diameter. In the middle, sticks are arranged in a spoke pattern. The sticks look charred, but the fire hasn't been lit. Beneath them, there's still dry vegetation, and on top of them is a ball of some sort of dried plant, as if put there for fire starter but never lit.

I take photos of the firepit. Then I carefully remove the dried ball of vegetation and put it into an evidence bag from my backpack. When I shine the light on the exposed sticks, I pause. They aren't sticks. They're small animal bones. More photographs. Remove the bones and bag them. There's nothing underneath.

I examine the bones through the bag. Hare? Most likely. I'm not sure about the plant matter, but it gave off a familiar smell, as if it has a use I'd recognize.

I take down one of the feather objects and bag it. The others,

I only photograph. Then I prowl around the clearing searching for more. I can't see anything. The ground is dry and hard, and that single heel print is the only one I detect.

I return to that print and keep looking around it for more. When I smell something, my brain vaguely registers an unpleasant scent. Then I remember what I'd smelled here. Something that bothered Storm. I sniff again. I'd thought it was rot, and there's a hint of that, but let's be honest, while Storm can be something of a princess, she's still a dog. The smell of a dead animal elicits two reactions: mild interest or "Ohh, perfume!" followed by rolling on it.

This scent was different. When I first smelled it, I'd thought little other than that it kept Storm from getting the scent. Now, having found what we did in the clearing, I realize that's probably the point: hide the scent of whoever created this tableau.

I'm still considering that when Dalton returns with Anders. I show our deputy the scene and explain to both what I found on the campfire, complete with photos.

"Wasn't there something like that with the hostiles?" Anders asks. "Weird shit marking their territory?"

"This doesn't seem like a territorial marker, but yes, there's a troubling resemblance."

"Also don't like Louie just happening to show up again," Dalton says. "I confiscated his boots to check against that heel mark."

"Thank you," I say. "Last night, he conducted his own bear hunt because he claimed to be an expert . . . and proved he wasn't. Tonight, he conducted his own missing-person search while, again, claiming expertise he doesn't possess."

"The man really does think we're morons, as he puts it."

"Ready to swallow any story he feeds us? Both of his reasons for being out here do seem like half-assed excuses. First, he's searching for Max. Then, he claims to think Max is dead, which doesn't explain his fervor to search after dark. Finally, he's aiming blame at Max's mom."

"Eric told me about that," Anders says. "Louie doesn't believe Dana and her husband were innocent victims. Love how he jumped on 'drug cartel.' Wouldn't have anything to do with Dana being Latinx, would it?"

"Right? Again, I'm not sure he even cares whether we take him seriously. He's blowing smoke in our eyes."

"Better than blowing it up our asses."

I shake my head, and we search the clearing until we're certain there's nothing left to find.

I wake up to a sight even lovelier than the northern lights. Dalton is in our bedroom doorway, dressed only in a pair of sweatpants. His hands are braced on the top of the open doorway, and he's stretching, which probably means his muscles are stiff, and I should feel a pang of sympathy, but I'm too busy admiring the view. He's stretching up on his toes, sweatpants riding down, muscles flexed.

"Mmm," I say. "Looking good, Sheriff. Any chance I can get breakfast to go and use my extra time more wisely?"

His mouth quirks in a slow smile. "I believe that could be arranged. I was just coming up to see whether you were stirring. If not, I wasn't going to wake you."

I waggle my brows. "I could pretend I was still sleeping if you want to try waking me."

"Any suggestions for how I could do that?"

"Oh, I have all the suggestions." I flip over to brace on my elbow, but at the sudden move my stomach lurches, and I gag.

"Casey?" He hurries forward.

My hand flies to my mouth. "Wow. Definitely not sexy."

He pushes to sit beside me and lowers me back to the bed. "You look green."

"Is that a thing?" I say, struggling for a smile.

"Never thought so, but hell, yeah." His hand goes to my forehead. "Let me get April."

"For a two-second bout of nausea caused by a lack of sleep?" I shake my head. "I'm just annoyed by the timing. I was looking forward to that wake-up, and now I've spoiled it."

I'm waiting for him to say it's not spoiled. That's what he'd normally do if something—often a lumbering canine—interrupted us. Resolve the issue as quickly and efficiently as possible and then continue. When he doesn't, my stomach tightens, which only makes it lurch again.

"You *really* don't look good," he says.

"I'm fine." It's a little brusque, and I apologize for that with a cheek kiss. "We'll skip the diversion, but only if you'll promise I get to wake up again to you stretching in the doorway, 'cause that was hot."

He chuckles under his breath and kisses my forehead. "If you think it's hot, you're going to see it until you'll be gagging to make me stop."

"Oh, that's not happening."

"Give it thirty years, when I'm looking a little worse for wear."

I lay my head on his leg. "I'll still think it's hot when you're ninety."

He bends to kiss my head again, and I turn to give him a proper kiss and . . .

He catches me as I sway.

"Casey?"

"I . . . It'll pass. It has to, right?" I manage a wan smile. "Can't get sick in the middle of a missing-child search. I'm sure it's just exhaustion."

We don't get much in the way of viruses here. That's one advantage to being in a closed environment, although it does mean that when a new resident carries in the flu or a cold, it seems to circulate endlessly.

I continue, "Maybe I'll just have toast and coffee for breakfast. Or even tea."

"Let me brew some tea." He starts to rise and then pauses. "You sure you'll be okay while I'm downstairs?"

"You're fifty feet away, Eric. At worst, I can moan for help."

He squeezes my arm and then rises. I lie there a minute, making faces at my own weakness. That's another thing about living virtually virus-free—any illness feels like a personal failing.

I hope it's not food poisoning. We're *so* careful, but in a new town, it's more likely to happen, as we bring our safety protocols up to speed. I start leafing through my menu from yesterday, only to realize it was mostly prepackaged bars, eaten on the run.

Exhaustion then.

I rise. There, not so bad. Get to my feet—

The smell of coffee wafts up, and my stomach lurches, and I nearly double over. I run to the bathroom and make it to the toilet just in time.

When I finish, I push to my feet and look in the mirror, which is a really bad idea. I'd like to think I'm not vain—my parents hammered in the idea that their daughters' pretty faces would only give others an excuse to dismiss our intelligence. But I still have an ego, and when I see myself in the mirror, I'm surprised Dalton didn't back away slowly and call for an exorcist.

Looking green is an understatement. I could play the Wicked

Witch of the East *after* the house fell on her. My skin is gray and splotchy, and my eyes are dark holes.

I look like shit.

I *feel* like shit.

What the hell is wrong . . .

I see a partly open cupboard door, and through it, my box of tampons. A box I haven't had to use.

Oh no.

You knew you were late.

Yes, but . . .

But I'd told myself it was no big deal because "being late" was the only symptom I had.

Not anymore.

I'm knocking on April's door. I managed to hold it together enough for Dalton not to realize how sick I am—apparently, I vomit quietly. I'd asked for my tea and toast to-go and said I wanted to pop by the clinic for an antinauseant. He'd offered to come with me, but I'd asked him to take Storm for her morning walk instead.

When April finally opens the back door, she says, "Why are you knocking? The front door is—"

Then she stops and pushes the door wide to usher me inside. "You're sick," she says, and there's a note of accusation in her voice, as if I've gotten ill just to annoy her. I know that accusation is because I didn't come sooner, and so I don't take offense the way I would have at one time.

My sister has some neurodivergence that puts her on the autism scale. It manifests in ways that aren't uncommon for people like her. They're also the sort of behavioral quirks that others expect from a brilliant and driven neurosurgeon. She's exacting and brutally honest and ruthlessly analytical and can seem cold and unfeeling. She's far from unfeeling—she feels very deeply and just doesn't express it in the usual ways. That makes it easy to misunderstand her. If you think someone's cold and uncaring, then you'll interpret their annoyance as a sign you've disturbed them rather than a sign of concern.

"I don't feel good," I say, feeling like her baby sister complaining of a tummy ache.

"I can see that." She plucks the tea thermos from my hand as I step in. "Nausea?"

I nod. "I'm probably just overtired."

"You do not have a weak stomach, Casey. In fact, you might have a stronger one than I do. I have seen you drive yourself without sleep for days. It doesn't make you nauseous."

"Maybe food poisoning."

"When was your last period?"

My eyes fill, and I stumble to the nearest chair and drop into it. Tears fall, and I rub them away as humiliation fills me. We don't cry in my family, and I definitely don't cry around April.

"Casey?" she says, and her voice is almost soft.

She moves forward and hesitates there, as if she feels an obligation to embrace me.

"I fucked up," I whisper.

"How?"

I manage a wan smile. Anyone else would assure me I haven't. April wants the details before she'll assess culpability.

I look up at her. My sister is five years older than me. We're often mistaken for half sisters, because—despite the fact that we share the same parents—she looks white and I do not. I've come to realize that bothers her more than it does me. She feels as if half of her heritage has been erased, letting her blend into the dominant population. I won't pretend I fully understand, but it is yet another wedge that drove us apart as children.

"When I missed a few days of my pill," I say.

She frowns. "Yes. I remember that. But it didn't seem to be at the right time of your cycle, which is why I told you not to worry about it. However, I'm not a gynecologist, so . . ."

I find that tiny smile again. "I shouldn't have listened to you?"

"There was nothing to listen to. It was already too late for a morning-after pill. If you are pregnant now, then you will have decisions to make."

Here's one thing I love about my sister. Her pragmatism. Whatever medical decisions I made about a pregnancy would be my choice, with zero judgment, because it really *is* a medical decision.

I shake my head. "I want that right and that choice, but it's not for me."

"Unless there is a medical reason to consider it, such as the fact that you may not be able to carry to term, and it would endanger your health."

I say nothing.

"Casey?" Her voice sharpens in that way I know indicates distress. "If your health was in danger—"

"We're jumping the gun. I haven't taken the test. That's why I'm here."

"I'm not sure how necessary it is. You missed a few days of your contraceptive. Now your period is late *and* you're nauseated upon waking. There is a reason it's called morning sickness."

"Can I just get the test, April?"

"You should have sought answers to your gynecological questions years ago, Casey. At the very least, you should have sought them once you became serious about Eric. You've been together for—"

"Can we not, please, April?"

"If the problem is that you cannot carry a fetus to term, then there were decisions to be made—"

"*April.*" I meet her gaze. "Whether I'm pregnant or not, I *will* get those answers, okay?"

The clinic front door bangs open. Then a loud rap sounds at the door into the exam room.

"I am with a patient," April says.

"Your sister." It's Kendra's voice. "I know. She's needed at the town hall."

"She is presently occupied—"

"It's important."

I stand. "I'd better go."

"It will take two minutes to test—"

"Whatever the results are, they won't help me bring Max home," I say, and hurry out the front to follow Kendra.

"Yolanda found it," Kendra says as we walk. "She sent me to grab you and Eric, but someone saw him heading out with Storm and you heading to the clinic."

I don't ask what was found. Maybe she's waiting for that obvious question, but whatever it is, I want to see it before I hear more. Get a clean first impression.

When I notice movement in the forest, I stutter-step to a halt. My brain screams, "Max!" Then I see Storm's bulky form and try not to be disappointed.

"Eric!" I call. "We're needed at the town hall."

He cuts through the thin barrier of trees and catches up just as we reach the building. Kendra murmurs that she'll head back to the search party, and we climb the steps.

Yolanda is alone in the town hall. She's seated at the desk, and if I inwardly grumble that it's *our* desk, then that's only proof of how upset I am after that conversation with April.

The fact that April's right only makes it worse. I should have gotten those gynecological answers. The only thing stopping me was my own fear. If I didn't get answers, I could keep hoping that initial diagnosis was wrong or my body had repaired whatever damage had been done, and whenever we wanted kids, we could have them.

Which is not what I need to be thinking about now.

Yolanda rises as we come in, and she steps from behind the desk. There's a bag in her hand. A clear plastic bag. Inside is a piece of paper.

"This was under the door," she says. "It wasn't there twenty minutes ago. I went out to grab my morning snack"—she waves to a coffee on the desk—"and it was here when I got back."

I read the note.

ask dana where her son is.

"For fuck's sake," Dalton growls. He turns to Anders. "Tell me that whoever was keeping Louie under house arrest screwed up."

"Because otherwise," I murmur, "we have an even bigger problem to deal with."

CHAPTER TWELVE

Kenny was the one assigned to Louie-watch. We have a house-arrest apartment set up for exactly this purpose. It's windowless, with a single door. That door leads into a small room where, if we deem it necessary, someone can stand guard.

Down south, Kenny was a high-school math teacher. In Rockton, he was the town carpenter and head of the militia, and he'll continue the former here for certain and the latter if we decide we need a militia, which I suspect we will. He's grown close to April, and if I'm hoping they'll grow closer still, well, that's taking a while.

Louie is inside. Kenny swears he didn't drift off. When he'd gotten sleepy, he'd worked on carpentry designs for a chest he wants to build for my organization-loving sister. That kept his mind active, which meant he stayed awake. There's also no sign that Louie left.

I still bring Louie to the town hall for questioning. Giving me something to focus on keeps me from dwelling on the fact that I don't feel good . . . and the likely reason for it.

I sit behind the desk. Louie glances around. He's clearly looking for Dalton, who left again, searching with Storm.

"It's just us." I lift my phone. "And a voice recorder."

"How come you guys get phones?"

I stare at him, as if waiting for the part of this question that makes sense. When his jaw only sets, I say, "Because we have uses for them. Like recording a witness's statement."

"I was told there's no cell signal here."

I turn the phone toward him, showing zero bars.

"Then why have them?" he asks.

"Because they have other uses." I look at him and repeat, "Like recording a witness's statement."

His expression says he isn't buying that, and then I understand. He thinks we're lying about the cell signal. Even if we did have it—which we absolutely do not—we couldn't allow residents to have phones. They're in hiding. That requires being off-grid, unable to contact anyone . . . or be traced by anyone.

"This was pushed under the door this morning." I lay the bag containing the note in front of him.

"Then it wasn't me," he says, making no move to read it. "I've been in solitary confinement."

"House arrest," I say. "Temporarily."

"Still wasn't me."

"Read it."

He does, and then his lips twitch in a satisfied smirk. "Well, well, seems I'm not the only person with a brain in this town. Someone else realizes Dana's story doesn't make sense."

"Or you told someone it doesn't."

"Nope." He shoves the bag back my way. "I don't communicate with this bunch of scared rabbits."

My jaw tenses, and I try to hide it. "So you haven't told anyone your suspicions?"

"I don't need to. Her story has more holes than Swiss cheese."

"What do you know of that story?"

"Just what I said last night. Her husband was killed by a drug cartel because he saw something he shouldn't have. They killed him and shot her . . . and then let her live." He leans forward. "The only reason people like that let you live is if you have something they want. If you saw something, they want you dead. The dead don't talk."

"And if I said Dana only escaped death because the police showed up?"

"Then I'd say you've been fed a pack of lies." He leans back now, hands folding over his belly. "You don't know why *I'm* in this town. That means you don't know her full story either. I can only imagine what nonsense they spun for you guys. The police showing up just in the nick of time? Doesn't happen outside of movies, and if you were a real cop, you'd know that. If the police get an urgent call, they finish their doughnut first."

He's playing Whac-A-Mole, slamming insults in every direction. If I'm not actually law enforcement, that dig about "real" cops will sting. If I am? Then there's the doughnut comment, which really, would probably work better on anyone who hasn't heard it a hundred times.

"Dana's husband stole from the cartel," he continues, "and she knows where the money is. That's why they let her live. Now she's given you a sob story and trotted out her two 'traumatized' kids to earn her way up here. But she's not getting out of it that easily. Someone has come for her, and they took the boy." He pauses for obvious drama. "Or she took him herself. Maybe even killed him."

My jaw clenches at the obvious delight he takes in saying this.

I'll never understand the psychology of people who find a perverse pleasure in shredding victim stories. I could ask Isabel to explain, but that presumes I *care* to understand the psychology.

Could Dana not be an innocent bystander? Yes. Could Max's disappearance be about this, rather than a wild man in the forest? Yes. But it's too much of a long shot for me to do more than file it away until I have evidence making it worthy of investigation.

"Tell me I'm wrong," he says.

When I don't answer, his eyes widen for a split second. Then he chortles. "Oh, you *do* see my point."

"Why do you think this is the solution to Max's disappearance?"

"It's obvious."

"Because you know something?"

"No, because it's obvious." He waves a hand. "It's also obvious that you need some help with this. Tell me what version of the story you were given, and I'll poke holes in it for you."

"I got the same story you did."

"Bullshit. You must know more. That's why you think I'm wrong. Did you hear it wasn't a cartel? It obviously is."

"Because she's Latinx?"

He rolls his eyes. "No, because that's how they operate. It's either that or organized crime."

"Drug cartels *are* organized crime."

"You know what I mean. Cartels versus triads versus Mafia . . . The story is that her husband saw something, right? Let's start with that."

"Let's start with this." I flip my phone to a photo of his boots from last night, turned on their side for me to photograph the sole. "Last night, we found a possible scene."

"Crime scene? You found the kid, didn't you. He's dead."

I meet his gaze. "You should see your eyes right now, Louie.

They're shining with excitement at the thought that a ten-year-old boy is dead."

He yanks back. "What? No. I'm just interested."

"In the murder of a child."

"You're twisting my words."

"Nope, I don't think I am. A crime scene implies a spot where we think a crime took place. This was a scene of interest, one indicating someone has been in the forest for illicit reasons. Beside it was a boot print matching yours." I lift a hand before he can go on. "Only three people in town wear a twelve, and there's a notch in yours." I point to the picture. "This makes the print unique."

I'm bullshitting. Not about the notch or the size. But all I have is that heel print, which seems to roughly match a size eleven or twelve. He doesn't know that, though, and I study his face as his arms cross.

"I was out there," he says. "You already know that."

"Then tell me what I found."

Genuine confusion. "What?"

"I found this print beside a very curious scene, and if you did not create that scene, then you saw it. So tell me what it is."

"It was dark."

"Not that dark."

"I was paying attention to where I was walking. Looking for evidence. If I didn't walk straight through your 'scene' then I didn't see it."

"You seem to like the idea that Max is dead."

"What?"

"I mean that you like it as a theory. You think it's plausible."

He relaxes. "As a theory, yes. I don't like the *idea* obviously. That kid can't help who his parents are. But you're not going to find him alive—"

"Which you know. Because you killed him."

"What?" He shoves his chair back. "I was trying to be helpful. I was saying you won't find him alive after he's been out there nearly two days. Even if he's only lost, he isn't an adult capable of looking after himself. But he isn't lost. We both know that. The only way that kid is alive is if someone is holding him captive to put pressure on his momma. If that's the case, then you need to investigate her because it means she has definitely received a ransom note."

I question Louie a little more, mostly so he doesn't think he gets to choose when the interview ends. After that, I make my way to the Roc. It's open as a coffee shop during the day, and when I walk in, the usually wonderful smell nearly sends me back out again, as my stomach twists.

"Casey?" Kendra hurries over from the back of the line. "You don't look so good. Want some company walking to the clinic?"

I manage a smile. "Nice try, but I'm too busy for that. I'm looking for Isabel."

"She's in the back, brewing." Kendra sniffs the air. "Pale ale, if I'm correct."

My stomach heaves even without me inhaling. The thought of beer—or coffee—has my tea threatening to come back up. My gut even churns when I catch a whiff of my beloved cookies.

"You really don't look good," Kendra says.

"Too many protein bars and not enough sleep. Make sure you don't fall into the same trap. I appreciate everything you've been doing with the search, but look after yourself."

"You, too," she calls after me.

I duck around to a locked door and knock. "It's Casey."

When Isabel opens it, she sees me and blanches. Then she lowers her voice and says, "You found Max," in a way that suggests we did not find him alive.

"No, no." I wave around my face. "This is just how I look today. Run-down and feeling run over. I need to talk to Dana, and I'd like you to join me. It's a tricky situation, and I value your professional opinion."

"Also, both Eric and Will are out searching, so I'm next in line."

"I wasn't going to say that."

"Let me finish up here first."

CHAPTER THIRTEEN

As we walk to Dana's building, I tell Isabel about Louie's accusations. She rolls her eyes and says, "Drug cartel. Obviously."

Isabel has light brown skin. Some mix of backgrounds, like my own. In her case, the combinations aren't obvious and, since she has never volunteered more, I don't know more.

"I know," I say. "Which means if it is a cartel, it's only going to make things worse. Louie is convinced that her husband did something. I'm not asking your opinion on that—because it would be tainted by information you gained in therapy with Max. It's none of my business whether they're purely innocent or they made a mistake. Émilie judged them worthy, so they're worthy. Whatever the parents did, the *kids* would always be worthy."

"My opinion, which you didn't ask for, is that it really was a case of witnessing something as innocent bystanders. Their only 'mistake' was refusing to keep quiet."

"Okay. But there is still the faintest possibility that Max's disappearance is connected to what happened to his parents. We know he saw his bear-man in the forest. We presume he went to investigate. That doesn't mean he *did* go . . . or that if he did, there wasn't someone else waiting to snatch him. Highly unlikely but . . ."

"Not impossible."

"If that's the case, then Max is being held as leverage over Dana, and she would have received a demand by now. So while it's a long shot, I feel obligated to address it. If this is the case, I need Dana to confess so I can help her."

"Which is where I come in."

"A bit. This isn't my first time doing something like this. I'm looking for any insights you can add, along with any advice. Oh, and I'd like you to be present at the interview to allay her concerns. I'm not questioning her story. I'm asking after anything that might help, but mostly I'm concerned about her wellbeing, which is why you're coming along."

"The *real* reason I'm coming along." She gives me a hard look. "As a prop, not an advisor."

"It's fifty-fifty."

Her eye roll disputes that percentage split. I explain my plan, and she doesn't see any issues. She does give me a little insight into Dana—from their sessions, but nothing that could be construed as breaking confidentiality. Technically, there is no client-patient confidentiality in Haven's Rock. If Mathias or Isabel or Kendra learns anything that raises concerns, they'll bring it to us. That's part of their job. This kind of isolation can cause psychological issues, and we need to be aware of any cracks immediately.

According to Isabel, Dana is struggling as much as one might expect. She puts on a brave face for her boys, but she's grieving for her husband. She's frustrated by her lingering injuries and how they impact her ability to do things with her boys, especially Max. Her son has discovered a love for the forest, and she needs to cajole Carson to join him on walks when she'd love to do so herself.

The pain meds are also a problem. Dana doesn't want them. She's afraid of addiction, leaving both April and Isabel playing nursemaid, urging Dana to take the meds.

"Is there any indication that she has a reason to fear addiction?" I ask carefully.

"Like from when her husband was part of a drug cartel and brought home oxy as an employee bonus?"

I sigh.

"I'm teasing you," she says, lowering her voice as we near the residence. "While I don't think that's the family's truth, there's always the possibility their truth isn't what they claim, which would be a problem if it came out."

"Giving Louie—and whoever sent the note—reason to say they told us so."

"Also the fact that it came from someone like Louie might affect your impartiality." When I glance over, she lifts her hands against my look. "Understandably affect it."

"The fact he's an asshole doesn't mean he's wrong. That's why I'm here." I motion at the family residence and lower my voice. "Was that your way of ducking the question about addiction?"

She shakes her head. "No. If that was an issue, I'd tell April so she understands the situation. I think there's been oxy addiction in Dana's circle of family and friends, but these days, that goes for pretty much anyone. I had an uncle who got hooked on it after surgery."

"And I had a detective partner whose wife got hooked. So, yes, nothing remarkable there."

We reach the family residence building. It's two stories, with three units top and bottom. Right now, we're letting couples stay in the empty ones, with Dana having the only family. All these units have exterior doors—there's a balcony along the second level. It's not much in the way of privacy, but conservation of space is too important to give families private homes . . . which would also have the singles complaining over their own dorm-style living.

I rap on Dana's door. When no one answers, I knock again. Still nothing.

"Are they out with the search teams?" Isabel asks.

I shake my head. "Dana joined for a while last night. We didn't feel right saying she couldn't. But she should be home sleeping now. She has the day off work, obviously. Carson's usually doing his schoolwork at this time, but again, no one expects that. I asked him to help Mathias today." That was mostly for Carson's sake, so Mathias would be there if he needed to talk about what he'd done to Max, ignoring his claim to have seen the bear-man.

I knock again. Still no answer.

I turn the knob. It's unlocked. That's common here, almost as if some leaving their doors open obligates others to do the same, to prove they have nothing to hide.

When the door opens, I stick my head in. "Dana? Carson?"

No answer. I glance at the tiny entrance, with a mat for shoes and boots. It's empty.

"She's out," I say to Isabel.

At this point, I should retreat and shut the door. I don't. I peer into the dark apartment, the blinds drawn.

I have the right to search any apartment at any time.

The *technical* right, granted by the contract residents signed.

The *ethical* right, though? To paw through their belongings without a solid reason to do so?

Louie is an asshole. He's jumping to ugly conclusions based on bigotry and a perverse glee in insisting Dana's story is a lie.

Isabel warned about dismissing his concerns on the basis that he's an asshole. If anything, I'm liable to overcompensate and investigate this lead because I'm concerned about bias.

When Louie first raised this possibility last night, Dalton and I dismissed it out of hand. And now I'm at Dana's door, contemplating a quick search of the premises, looking for evidence that Louie could be on to something.

Looking for evidence to support his claim?

Or to refute it? To dismiss him and move past a theory I really don't like?

I back up a step and bump into Isabel. She retreats out the door, and we say nothing as we walk toward the corner of the building and—

"Oh!"

It's Dana, coming around that corner with her cane.

Dana's moving so fast she barrels into us and then falls back, pulling her jacket tight. Her gaze drops as she fusses with the coat.

"Sorry about that," she says. "It's getting so cold out here, and I was in a hurry to get home."

She pulls the coat together and shivers dramatically. Then she goes still, and color flushes up her cheeks. "And here I am complaining about the weather when . . ." She swallows. "Dare I ask if you've found anything?"

I shake my head, and I keep studying her face, making no effort to hide my scrutiny. She pulls the coat tighter and hunches her shoulders. I let the silence drag for a moment before I say, "We were coming to talk to you."

"Oh?" She sounds flustered and glances around, as if we might be talking to someone else. "Of course. Yes. Sorry I wasn't home. Let's go inside."

Sorry I wasn't home.

No explanation given. Not even a false one.

We head inside. My plan had involved starting with concern for her well-being, and Isabel offering support. I don't do that now. Something is up, and I'm not softballing this.

Once we're inside, Dana invites us to sit. Isabel does. I stay standing.

"Can I get you a coffee?" she asks. "Tea? Water?"

"No need," I say, a little brusquely. Yes, part of me is deeply aware that I'm questioning a woman with a missing child, but the way she acted a moment ago tells me something is up. It also tells me I need to keep her off balance.

"You know that Max spotted his bear-man in the woods," I say. "We've been investigating that angle. We aren't completely convinced it's the answer here. We see no evidence that someone in the forest grabbed him."

"Then Gunnar," she says. "It's Gunnar."

"He is not a suspect at this time."

Up until now, she's been unsettled. With that, her eyes flash. "Not a suspect?"

I could tell her why. I don't. Instead, I say, "You believe Gunnar is the most likely suspect, yes? What do you think he's done with Max?"

Dana's eyes flash in outrage. "Excuse me?"

"Casey doesn't mean it like that," Isabel slides in. "She's clarifying why you think Gunnar would have taken Max."

"He's a grown man taking an interest in a little boy," she says. "Do you really need me to spell it out?"

"Actually, yes," I say. "Otherwise, I'm putting words in your mouth."

"I think he's a pedophile. I already suggested that, so it's not putting words in my mouth. I've said them, and I'd rather not keep saying them."

"What has Gunnar done to suggest that? Besides his mild interest in Max? And his promiscuity."

Isabel clears her throat. "Promiscuity does not suggest pedophilia. In fact, it's the opposite. Gunnar's active sex life suggests his needs are being met."

Thank you, Isabel.

"Yes," I say. "I said that earlier, too, which is why I'm putting the question to you again, Dana. You think Gunnar is a suspect. You think his interest in Max is suspicious. If we're going to consider him as a suspect, we need more than him taking a friendly interest in Max and being sexually promiscuous." I meet her eyes. "Can you think of any other reason why someone would take Max?"

She should bring up the possibility that someone followed her here. That someone took him to threaten her.

"What about this bear?" she says. "Or a man everyone mistook for a bear. Why are you dropping that?"

She hadn't questioned it before, when I first suggested that the investigation has pivoted. But she does now, when it's useful. When it'll divert my attention back to a bogeyman in the forest.

"We are still investigating all possibilities," I say. "Getting Max back is our priority."

"Then why are you here questioning me? My son is out there." She waves toward the window.

"Eric is searching. I'm here, investigating, in case there's a chance whoever took him is from town. Do you have any idea who—besides Gunnar—might do something like that?"

"No, because I don't know anyone here, Detective," she says.

"That's the point, which is also the problem. I don't know anyone's background. I only know they're in hiding. For all I know, we could have a town filled with pedophiles."

I lower my voice. "Do you really think we'd bring your sons here to that?"

Her gaze cuts away, but she says nothing.

"No one in Haven's Rock is running from crimes they committed. Mistakes they made, possibly." I let that sit for two seconds. "But everyone makes mistakes, and sometimes the price they're being asked to pay is too high. No one here is running from the law. No one here is a known pedophile. But as for how much you know about them?" I shrug. "Is it any different than down south?"

She glances at me.

I continue, "How well do you know your neighbors there? Your sons' teachers? Their friends' parents? Their coaches and instructors and everyone your sons come into contact with in their lives? When I say no one here has ever been accused of crimes associated with children, that's more than you can say for your neighbors at home."

She doesn't answer. Just keeps looking out the window.

"I investigated Gunnar," I say. "I am still keeping an eye on him, and he's been assigned a roommate until this is over. He is not allowed to leave town, even to join the search. If you have any reason to suspect anyone else, we will take the same steps. And if you know a reason why someone might take Max— even without being able to name a suspect—I need to know it."

She shakes her head and says nothing.

"All right then," I say. "I'll get back to work. We're doing everything we can to find him."

At that, something in her cracks, her shoulders shaking, her voice breaking as she says, "I know." She looks up. "I'm sorry if

I snapped. I'm just . . . I don't know what to do. We came here to be safe and . . ."

And now this.

She doesn't say it, but I still feel it.

I feel every bit of it.

CHAPTER FOURTEEN

Right after that, Dalton comes out of the forest for a late lunch, which is perfect timing. I can head back in with him, both to search and to talk.

He doesn't know what to make of Dana's behavior any more than I do. He can only agree that it's suspicious.

Is it possible she's received a demand already? That Max has been kidnapped to force her to undo whatever she and her husband did, even if it's only retracting the statement of innocent bystanders? If that's the case, what's the chance she'd keep it from us?

High. One of the first things kidnappers do is warn their target not to contact the police. Of course they don't want you contacting the police. Just like police don't want you lawyering up. In both cases, if you listen, that's in their best interests, not yours. But television and movies are filled with dramatic kidnappings where the target brings in the police and everything goes horribly wrong, because otherwise, it'd make a boring show.

Has Max's kidnapper told Dana not to involve us, or her son will suffer the consequences? Is that why she was out when

Isabel and I arrived, why she'd seemed harried and distracted? Why she'd been on the defensive?

Except, well, I *put* her on the defensive, didn't I? I *wanted* her defensive to see what happened, and her response wasn't what I would expect from a woman whose son had disappeared into the wilderness.

Are we making a mistake concentrating on the forest search?

We head by Lilith's cabin again. She's still not there, and Nero still *is* there, standing guard and not letting us get close. Then we check the spot for messages from "Mr. Rogers," but there's nothing.

"There *is* someone in the forest," I say. "Max's bear-man. Almost certainly the same guy Mr. Rogers's miner saw."

"Agreed," Dalton says.

"The question is whether he's involved in Max's disappearance."

"Yep."

"We know Max saw the bear-man. The obvious answer is that he went out to get a better look."

"Yep."

"But it's also not the *only* answer."

"Yep."

I scowl over as Dalton holds back a branch for me. "You aren't helping."

"You want someone to needlessly argue with you, ask the new Jen."

I glance at him.

"Yolanda," he says.

I roll my eyes. "Jen enjoyed making my job ten times harder than it had to be. Yolanda's worse. She's not *trying* to make my job harder. She just is. And while I know you're joking, I may actually run this past her, though I don't expect to get anything more than a lecture on how this proves our town is doomed to failure."

"If it's doomed to failure, why is she still here? Do we need to buy her a violin?"

I glance over. "A violin?"

"So she can fiddle while Rome burns? Not that there's any evidence Nero did that. He was still a shit emperor, though, one who made a lot of money from that burning. But in Yolanda's case, I don't see the need or desire for profit, nor any way our demise benefits her."

"Maybe she's just sticking around to say 'I told you so.'"

"Probably."

I slow as I peer into the forest, already dimming as the sun drops. "Did we make a mistake letting children into Haven's Rock?"

As the words leave my mouth, I realize the full import of them. If I am pregnant, if I could carry to term, would that be a mistake? We couldn't even keep Max safe. How would we dare raise a child here?

But Dalton had been raised in Rockton. It couldn't be called an idyllic childhood, given the circumstances, but in many ways, it *had* been idyllic. Despite all the problems, he still never wanted to leave Rockton. It was his home.

"If we did," he says slowly, "then the mistake was in being unprepared because our only template was my own experience. I grew up in this forest. Doesn't mean I wouldn't have made the mistake we think Max did—walking into the woods to get a better look at something. Hell, at least he tried to get his brother to go with him. I wouldn't have bothered."

I understand what he's saying, but I also hear what he's not saying. That our first young residents were, however unintentionally, guinea pigs.

In the end, everyone in Haven's Rock is a guinea pig. We're trying something new, and we'll adjust as we see how things work out. That's fine if it's something like realizing kids need more physical activity than we're offering. It's not fine if it means realizing we didn't protect them as well as we promised, if someone in town—or out of it—could grab them and—

I take deep breaths to calm my breathing. Don't think about that. Focus on finding Max.

On finding a needle in a haystack.

How many times had we searched for someone lost in the woods outside Rockton? Each time, I told myself that we were learning. Refining the process. Yet here we are, with our two best trackers, doing little more than tromping through the woods, hoping to pick up some sign of Max.

I need to remind myself that we've had plenty of successful searches. But it's like those Hollywood kidnapping cases where calling in the police ruins everything. It's the failures that stick in my head, the times when all our resources felt as useless as a magic people-finding wand bought off eBay.

These are the times when a little voice whispers that maybe Yolanda is right. Maybe we are dragging innocent people into our savior fantasies, and they are paying the price.

And then another voice, which sounds a whole lot more like my sister, snaps that I'm being ridiculous. If I have a boat, and I see a sinking ship, do I avoid picking up survivors for fear that one might fall into the ocean and drown? I'm not saying we're these people's only hope. But witness protection didn't save Dana's husband either.

Can we save her child?

Is it already too late?

And just then, as if in answer to my worries, Storm lets out a bark. A very particular, very happy bark. One that says she's smelled something we're looking for. Some*one* we're looking for.

"Show me," I say to her.

She takes off lumbering across an open area, and as we follow, I'm squinting into the dim light, hoping to see a small figure standing somewhere ahead of us. That's what I want. Max's figure—

"There!"

The word comes before I can stop myself. I'm not myself today, and when I spot his jacket, I can't help but cry out. It's only after I utter that word—and remind myself I could be running toward a kidnapper—that I put on the brakes.

"Storm!" I call. "Wait!"

She stops, and I catch up, and by then I have my gun out but lowered. I approach with my gun down, well aware that if I'm stepping into a hostage situation, I've already tipped off Max's captor.

I'm moving slowly, my gaze on that jacket. I can only see enough to know that it is Max's and it isn't lying on the ground.

Dalton grabs my arm. I'm turning to frown at him when I catch another angle. An angle that places the jacket higher than it should be.

It's in the air.

Hanging in the air.

My heart jams in my throat, but I force myself to keep moving at that slow and steady pace, to not think about why Max's jacket is suspended in the air, turning slightly in the breeze, as if its owner is hanging—

Not thinking about that.

One more step, and I clear the trees blocking my view, and when I do, I let out a simultaneous exhalation and a curse.

"Fuck," Dalton says behind me, growling the word.

It is not Max hanging from a tree. It's just his jacket, suspended by the shoulders.

I start to stride forward, but Dalton catches me and murmurs, "Trap."

Yep, I'm really not myself today. I motion that I'll cover him while he approaches. In this mental state, I can't be trusted to do it.

He steps into the clearing past the trees and lets out another profanity.

"Clear," he says. "Come on in."

As soon as I step in, I see what prompted the profanity. Max's jacket hangs at the northern compass point. At the other three are those same feather stick figures we'd found earlier. And in the middle of the clearing, another of those strange fires made of bones and unburned dried plants.

This time, I don't pause to examine the scene. I set Storm on it. At first, she's enthusiastic. She smelled her target—Max— and so he must be here. But it doesn't take long for that enthusiasm to evaporate. She circles the clearing three times before walking toward his hanging jacket and whining.

"He was never here," I say. "Someone just hung up his jacket. That's what she smelled."

"Whoever did it exited here," Dalton says, pointing to signs in the undergrowth.

I bring Storm over. She lowers her nose and then huffs, like she did before.

"Same thing as the other one," I call after Dalton, who's disappeared into the woods. "They're disguising their trail by covering it with a scent."

"Wouldn't have mattered much anyway," he says as he returns. "Trail goes straight to a stream. She'd have lost the scent there."

We spend more time searching for evidence, but there's

nothing except those signs of passage. We hope to find a foot-print in damper soil near the creek, but it's all rock.

When we return to the clearing, I walk to where Max's jacket hangs.

"Two clearings with these stick figures and ritualistic firepit. The jacket suggests both are connected to Max's disappearance."

"Seems so," Dalton says.

"Which means we really should be hunting for a wild man of the forest."

"Seems that way."

"*Seems,*" I say, and catch his eye as he nods. "Because this might be a clue . . . or it might be someone feeding us a clue."

"Yep."

"So are we looking at the work of an actual wild man of the forest, performing some strange ritual, having kidnapped Max for it?" I glance over. "Or are we looking at someone who kid-napped Max knowing he saw a bearlike person in the woods, and is doing this to divert attention?"

Dalton considers. Then he says, "We know the bear-man exists."

"Yes."

"We know he could be dangerous. We also are concerned that Lilith doesn't seem to be home."

"Yes."

"But if I were going to kidnap a kid, and I knew the kid reported seeing Bigfoot in the woods? Hell, yeah, I'd use that."

"Keep us chasing phantoms out here while they negotiate with Dana."

"Yep."

★ ★ ★

We're back in town. We don't call in the other searchers. We aren't certain enough about our theory for that. We act as if we just came back to grab dinner, which we'll eat at home before heading back out. Only we don't head back out.

Instead, we make a call.

With Rockton, we were expected to report everything to the council, and we did our best to avoid it. The council wasn't there to advise us. It wasn't there to make the hard choices for us. It wasn't even there to reprimand us when we misbehaved—though it did plenty of that. Mostly, it seemed to exist to tell us to stop. Whatever we were doing, stop.

Worried about the hostiles? Batten down the hatches and avoid them. Want to better understand what caused them? Stop. Just stop.

A resident goes missing? Sure, look for them, but not at the expense of letting town responsibilities slide because the missing person made their own choice to cross the town border. Insist on searching even when hope seems gone? Stop. Just stop.

A resident turns up dead? Suspicious circumstances? Are you sure they're suspicious? Maybe you're overthinking this. Insist on digging deeper? Stop. Just stop.

They had so much to hide, more than I think we ever fully understood. But living in Rockton had been a constant battle of wills, and our only saving grace was that the council was an absentee landlord. Sure, we were *supposed* to report to them, but what they didn't know never did hurt them—and telling them could hurt others.

Now we have no council. Émilie is more than willing to help but also understands that we're still licking our wounds, not ready to trust anyone, especially another voice on the end of a satellite phone. She has let us know that she's there for anything we need, but we aren't required to update her on *any* events in Haven's Rock.

Now, though, we make that call of our own volition. We still do it with trepidation, worried about setting a precedent, but Émilie has resources we lack, and we need to use them if they can help residents.

We call her from our living room. Dalton is sprawled on the sofa with a beer, with Storm below him, dozing by the fire. I'm in my favorite chair, with my note pad, pen, and tea, legs pulled up and crossed.

I tell Émilie everything that has happened, starting with Max seeing a man in the forest. When I'm finished, she's quiet.

"I know," I say. "Our first child residents, and we've already lost one."

"Not lost," she says. "Taken. I'm certain of that. Max is a clever and cautious child, and Eric has been teaching him about the forest. He's not going to wander off and get lost. If he had, Storm would have found his trail. He's been carried off and, presumably, he's being held somewhere."

Presumably? She means hopefully.

Émilie continues, "I think you're right that Max's captor has used this 'bear-man' as a smoke screen. Yes, there is someone out there. Yes, that's what Max and Gunnar saw. Whether or not it could be a hostile is impossible to say, and it hardly matters right now. There is someone out there, which is an absolute fact because it was independently confirmed by your neighbors. I hope this wild man isn't responsible for Lilith's apparent disappearance, but we have to set that aside. Max is our priority."

"You think someone used the bear-man sighting to grab him. Possibly even imitating the bear-man to lure Max out."

"No, that's what *you* think, and I'm confirming it's a valid theory. Which leads to your actual point for this call. Not to update me or to get my opinion but to see what I can add, as the one who knows all Dana's details."

I sigh. "You're the second person today who's called me out on my motives for talking to them. I need to up my game."

"No, you need to find your game. Anyone who knows you realizes exactly where they fall on your scale of advisors, Casey, and unless their name is Eric Dalton, you probably have an ulterior motive for consulting them."

"Well, I still do value your opinion."

I swear I hear the smile in her voice as she says, "I know you do. But in this case, my opinion matters mostly because it will help determine whether I feel comfortable sharing confidential information with you two, which I would not if I thought your theory was wrong."

"If you thought we were wrong, that would tell us we don't need those details."

"True." A rustle and a click, as if she's moving and getting out a laptop or tablet. "All right. First, while you didn't ask, Dana isn't running from a drug cartel. It's not even organized crime, per se. It's one very bad person with a very big grudge against her . . . and the resources to pursue her family until they get what they want, which is revenge."

"Okay."

"Keeping the details to a minimum, Dana and her husband witnessed a murder. They told the police what they saw. Then came the offer of a bribe."

"To retract their story."

"Yes. When that failed, the carrot turned to a stick, with threats, and soon what they'd presumed was a simple matter of testifying against a killer turned into something much more dangerous. They weren't accusing an average citizen. This man had money. A lot of money, and a lot of dangerous people in his contact list, ready to take some of his money to help him stay out of prison. Dana's family was put into witness protection. The man went to prison, which should have been the end of it, but his wife was determined to get him out and since his conviction hinged on eyewitness reports . . . ?"

"She thought getting Dana and her husband to retract their story could lead to at least a new trial."

"Yes, but by then, they'd disappeared into the witness-protection program. A year ago, the man Dana and her husband helped convict died—killed in prison—and his wife now wants something else."

"Revenge."

"She tracked them down and hired men to stage a home invasion and murder Dana and her husband. But the police arrived before Dana could be killed."

"And the police are certain this man's wife was behind it? That it *wasn't* a home invasion?"

"The two men weren't going to kill Dana and her husband without letting them know *why* they were dying. The home invasion was staging for the police. It failed because Dana survived. Carson also overheard enough to confirm why the men were there."

Dalton calls over, "So why wasn't the wife arrested for hiring whoever killed Dana's husband?"

"She's too careful. The men escaped, meaning no one can roll on her. The police are continuing to investigate, but she's covered her tracks well. The only way for Dana to get away was to truly get away."

"Come up here," I say. "Except she might not have gotten away. So the question is whether someone followed them and is waiting outside Haven's Rock . . . or followed them *into* Haven's Rock. The first possibility means someone tracked a plane and is in the woods. The second means someone is in here, having come under a false story."

"I can't see how someone would track the plane, but having someone slip in is even less likely. I'll comb through all the files, though, in case I've made a mistake."

"Thank you," I say. "I'd also like to know more about Louie."

A pause, one that stretches long enough for me to take a sip of my tea.

"Not as someone who followed Dana here," I say. "He was in Haven's Rock before her."

"Yes, and my person found him before the home invasion even occurred."

"Which means he didn't come here because of them. Nor did he slip that note under the town hall door. But he's up to something. None of his excuses for being in the woods make sense. It might be completely unrelated to Max. But while he didn't come here for Dana, that doesn't mean he isn't working with someone who did."

"Ah. Yes. That makes sense. All right. Let me pull up his file."

If Louie had any hunting experience, it wasn't in the file we received . . . or the broader one Émilie has. Likewise for any search-and-rescue experience. Does that mean he was lying? Not necessarily.

There are things we need to know and things we do not. Hunting and searching experience may come in handy, but it's not a criterion for choosing whom we let in.

Émilie doesn't tell us why Louie is here. What matters is whether his reason for coming raises any red flags in the current situation. It does not, apparently. He is a legitimate resident here for a legitimate reason, and while she'll dig deeper, this isn't the old Rockton, where anyone paying enough could get the council to accept their story at face value.

Émilie has someone who investigates the backstories and confirms details. All she can do now is double-check. Mostly what we need her to double-check is Louie's background beyond his reason for being here. Are we sure he's never been charged with or accused of a crime? Whatever he's doing in the forest, he's up to something, and his disdain for law enforcement raises red flags.

We also ask Émilie to double-check Gunnar's background for any hint of crimes against children. Obviously, he'd never have gotten on Yolanda's crew with a conviction, but we need to dig deeper. Even a whiff of concern would be enough.

Once we're done talking to Émilie, it's after midnight. I might long to get back out there, searching, but I'm no longer convinced that's the most expedient way to find Max. I want to talk to Louie again, and I want to talk to Dana again, and I want to find out who slipped that damn note under the town hall door.

All that, though, has to wait. It's late, and if we have the chance to get a decent night's sleep, we need to take it, whether we want to or not.

CHAPTER FIFTEEN

Max

It's the third night since Max was taken, and he's huddled under a scratchy blanket, shivering and trying very hard not to cry. Crying won't help. He knows that, but the tears are half fear and half frustration. He spent the first day trying to escape, but that didn't do any good. Whoever has him isn't giving him that chance. His legs had been tied except while they were walking, and in the beginning, he hadn't even been allowed to walk. He'd been wrapped in a stinking blanket and carried.

That had been so Storm couldn't track him. If he walked, she could follow his scent. Even if his captor carried him, she could pick up his scent in the air. That's why he'd been wrapped in a blanket, and that's why it stank.

His captor would carry him for a ways and then put him down to rest, and then carry him some more. Eventually, Max was allowed to walk, but his captor would still sometimes carry him, as if trying to mess up any trail he left. Max was too heavy to carry as far as his captor wanted. He'd realized that, and he'd thought maybe he could use it to his advantage—escape while his captor got tired—but the man never lowered his guard.

It *was* a man. Even though Max had been blindfolded from the start, it was obviously either a man or a very strong woman, and while his captor hadn't spoken, the grunts and noises sounded male.

Could his captor speak? When he removed Max's gag to let him eat or drink, Max had tried talking. He'd seen that in a movie once, where a kid had been taken, and he'd talked and talked and eventually his kidnapper got to know him and wouldn't hurt him. But when Max talked, his captor put the gag back on until Max was quiet again, and if he kept trying to talk every time the gag came off, then he didn't get to eat and drink. Eating and drinking seemed more important than talking. Keep his energy up.

Still, Max had begun to think that maybe his captor *couldn't* speak. That he'd been taken by the bear-man. While that seemed obvious, Max still wasn't sure. After he'd left Carson, he hadn't marched into the forest at the spot where he'd spotted the bear-man. He'd entered at his usual place, away from the bear-man, with no intention of getting close to it. Yet he'd still been grabbed.

At first, he'd figured his captor was sent by the people who'd killed his dad. They'd tracked them down to Haven's Rock and kidnapped him.

Max still thought that *might* be the answer, but the not-talking part had made him think it could be the bear-man after all.

It should have been easy to work that out. The figure he'd seen had bear fur and bear claws and bear ears. All Max had to do was touch his captor and see whether he felt fur. But he wasn't getting that chance. Once when he'd tried reaching out, the man tied his hands up again and fed him.

One thing that made Max think it *couldn't* be the bear-man was the hands. If his captor could tie and untie him, that seemed to mean he had human hands, and Max had seen bear claws on the figure in the forest. When he'd first been grabbed, he'd caught a glimpse of his attacker's wrist. He'd seen a bare underside of white skin with a streak of dirt.

What if the bear-man's hands were part bear and part human? Maybe human fingers with long claws. Could he still tie ropes?

These were the questions that had consumed Max, as if figuring out who had him—or *what* had him—would help him escape. Tonight, though, he can't summon any hopes or fantasies. Tonight there's just frustration, with a little bit of fear, but even that fear is knotted together with the frustration. He doesn't know who has him. He doesn't know why he's being held. The not knowing is getting worse, the fear of that eating into the frustration.

What does his captor want? If his captor can talk, he isn't explaining or asking for anything. He just watches Max. Even blindfolded, Max can *feel* him watching.

He remembers what Gunnar said about trusting that twist in his stomach. He feels it now. The sense that he faces a certain kind of danger here, that this man has a certain kind of interest in him, from the way he sits too close, the way he touches Max's shoulder or arm, a tentative touch before roughly checking his bonds.

It's not proof of anything. Carson would scoff. And yet . . .

After what seemed like endless walking, they'd ended up in some kind of space. A cave? Maybe. The sounds outside were muffled, but he's been in caves with Deputy Will and Detective Casey, and they had a smell and a chill, and this doesn't have either. He only knows that he's lying on hard ground with a scratchy blanket over him.

Once or twice, he's woken and thought he was alone, but then his captor returns. Other times, lying here with everything quiet, he'll think his captor is asleep. He'll hear him breathing, right beside Max, but if Max moves, that breathing catches and he knows his captor is not asleep. Just sitting there, watching him.

Max thinks it might be night, but he has no idea. Everything is dark behind the blindfold, and his meals aren't breakfast, lunch, and dinner food. They're just meals. Dried meat and what tastes like bread and then water.

When his captor squeezes Max's shoulder, Max jumps, but he's come to know what this means. Apparently, it's time to eat.

His captor grunts, which Max knows means he's supposed to hold his arms out straight so they can be untied.

Max does that. He doesn't fight. Not anymore. The first few times, he'd lashed out, only to get cuffed so hard he'd sworn he'd seen stars, like in that old saying. Bright lights had popped behind his blindfold. Was that from his eyes? Or his brain? He'd need to look that up when he got home.

Back in Haven's Rock, Max has a list of things he wants to look up once he has the internet again. This is something he'll add, and if a little voice tries to change "*when* he gets home" to "*if* he gets home," he isn't thinking about that.

He holds out his hands and lets his captor untie them. Then his captor starts tying his one hand to something else, like he always does when Max eats.

His captor is in the middle of doing that when he stops.

"Shh!"

Did his captor just shush him? It sounded like it, but Max hadn't said anything, so maybe that *shh* was just a noise?

Then Max catches another sound. A voice.

His head jerks up.

Someone's out there.

He opens his mouth to call out, but of course he can't. He *can* make noises against the gag, and he almost does, until some instinct warns him to shut up.

The voice outside is faint. So faint he can't tell whether it's a man or a woman. Even if Max screams against his gag, they'll never hear him, and all he'll do is make his captor mad. Better to stay still and act like he hasn't heard anything.

His captor quickly finishes tying the knot. Then, in a guttural voice, he says, "Stay."

Max looks up in the direction of the voice, trying to act confused. The only response is what sounds like footsteps on hard ground.

His captor is leaving.

Going to see what's out there.

Max holds his breath and strains to listen. Soon he catches the faint sounds that Sheriff Eric taught him to listen for in the forest. A footfall. The crack of a branch.

His captor is gone and heading in the direction where Max had heard a voice.

He's left Max with one hand untied.

Max yanks off the blindfold, and that's a mistake, because as soon as he can see his surroundings, he pauses to take them in. It's not dark. It's barely even twilight. He's in what looks like the ruins of an old shack, with a dirt floor and half a roof and—

And *move*! Is he going to sit here gawking at a place he needs to escape?

Max listens for any sound that might mean his captor is right outside. When nothing comes, he reaches for the rope tying his hand to a half-broken board. His fingers fly to the knot, and when he finds it loose, he almost stops, his brain screaming that it's a trap and he has to get his blindfold back on *now*.

But it's not a trap. His captor heard the voice outside and quickly finished tying Max's hand, distracted by the possibility of an intruder.

Max finds the loosest loop and tugs. When the end doesn't move, he tugs another and feels the give. He keeps pulling, as fast as he can, until the knot is undone and his hand is free.

He starts to pull off his gag next, and then realizes that's the *least* important thing. He can handle that once he's running, and in order to run, he needs his legs.

His feet are bound together, and it doesn't take long for him to realize they're tied a whole lot tighter than his hand had been. He makes himself stop frantically yanking at the knot and look around instead.

There's a piece of broken wood a few feet away. Maybe the edge is sharp enough to saw . . .

Or maybe he can use his knife . . . which is sitting right there.

He blinks, as if he must be seeing things. No, he's not. His knife has been left beside a couple of apples, as if his captor was using it to slice them. The blade is still open.

Max grabs the knife and starts sawing at the rope. For a second, he makes the mistake of sawing inward, and then has an image of the rope snapping and the blade cutting right into his ankle.

He gets the blade inside the rope, cutting out, and that makes it easier, pushing against the rope as he saws. The blade is sharp, and pride surges in him at that. He always keeps his knife sharp, like Sheriff Eric showed him, even when Carson said sharpening it was kinda creepy. Soon he's throwing the rope aside and pushing to his feet and—

Max falls. His ankles give way, as if the muscles have stopped working. Or as if they're asleep from the rope being so tight.

Max is rubbing his legs hard when a shout comes from deep in the forest.

A man is shouting. He can't tell what the man says. He doesn't even think it's a word. Just a shout. A cry of alarm.

Max bolts for the door. Then he pauses, runs back, and grabs two of the apples and some of the dried meat and shoves it into his pockets.

He won't need it. He's about to be rescued. He's sure of that. But . . . just in case, that little voice whispers. Just in case whoever's out there isn't from Haven's Rock.

With the food in his pockets and the knife in his hand, Max runs out the door. Then he stops short and looks around. He heard a shout, which would seem to mean that his captor is too far away to race back and catch him. But he can't say for sure that his captor was near whoever just shouted.

Max takes it slow, peering around the gloom. There's no sign of anyone. Just trees and more trees. No, that's not completely true. If he listens, he can hear water. A creek maybe. That would make sense. Whoever built that shack would have put it near water.

Max keeps moving until he's in the forest. Then he stops and listens. No other sounds have come since that single cry.

He squints in that direction and sees nothing.

Should he head that way?

If it's a rescuer, then yes.

But what if his rescuer is the one who cried out, the one who is in trouble?

The cry could have come from his captor, though. What if that first voice had been Sheriff Eric or Detective Casey and they'd taken down his captor?

Then he should hear his captor being interrogated—Sheriff Eric or Detective Casey asking where Max is. He hears nothing.

And then he does, and it's not a voice but the crack of a twig. Then a heavy footfall.

Someone is coming this way.

Max looks down at himself. He's dressed in jeans and a dark long-sleeved shirt, his captor having taken away his jacket on the first day. His face is the lightest part of him, so he pulls up his shirt collar as high as it will go, covering halfway up his nose, and he eases back more into the shadows.

A figure appears, but it's partly hidden behind a bush, and all he can see is someone walking near the old shack.

Sheriff Eric? The figure looks tall enough. Maybe even tall enough to be Deputy Will, but that's all Max can make out. A tall figure.

Max eases to one side, and he almost crunches dead leaves underfoot, but at the last second he realizes it and stops himself.

The figure disappears and Max goes still, holding his breath. Is it behind the shack? Inside it? Somewhere else? It steps out and—

And Max sees fur. Brown fur and long hanging claws.

He lets out a whimper. He doesn't even know he's doing it until he hears the sound.

The bear-man turns, and all Max sees is a glimpse of eyes and a blur of brown fur. Then Max turns and runs.

CHAPTER SIXTEEN

Casey

I wake up sick. Oh, there's a moment there where I first open my eyes and I feel just fine. Then I sit up and nearly puke over the side of the bed. Dalton's already downstairs, so I manage to creep into the bathroom to throw up as quietly as possible.

I need to speak to April. Take that pregnancy test to be sure and then deal with it.

And I need to talk to Dalton. Yes, I want to shove this aside and focus on the case. Whether I'm pregnant or not doesn't change the fact that Max is missing. But I need to tell Dalton before he figures it out for himself, and to do that, I must first take the test.

"Good morning," Dalton says as I come downstairs.

I wait for him to ask how I'm doing. I wait for that eagle-eyed stare that *sees* how I'm doing, however hard I'm trying to hide it.

"Good morning," I say cautiously.

He doesn't look up from where he's crouched, peering into

our underfloor icebox. "You up for a proper breakfast? Or toast and tea again?"

"Toast and tea, I think. Just for one more morning."

"That's what I figured. Tea's ready. Let me pop bread over the fire, and you'll have toast. I need to go out, but I should be back before you're done eating. Anything I can get you from the café?"

My stomach lurches at the thought of coffee. "No thanks."

"You rest, and we'll come up with a game plan when I return."

"Sounds good."

Dalton's gone, and I'm worried. Maybe that seemed like a normal couple conversation, but it was a little *too* normal, if that makes sense. Like a scripted early-morning chat between people who are definitely not us.

Dalton didn't ask how I was feeling, even after I opted for toast and tea. He didn't tell me what he had to do so early in the morning or ask whether I wanted to come along.

He's distracted. Something is on his mind, and he was too wrapped up in it to notice how rough I looked.

Did he think of a clue overnight? A lead he wanted to check before telling me? That's not like him and yet . . . Well, he is still the acknowledged junior partner in this detective duo, and it is possible that if he had a wild theory, he might look into it before telling me.

I'm reading too much into this. If he's gone, though, I have a chance to slip off to April's without telling him that I need—again—to speak to my sister about my stomach troubles.

I take a few bites of toast, so it'll look as if I made the effort.

Then I put my tea into a thermos and head out. Even the toast has my stomach churning, but I try to ignore it. The fresh air helps, and I gulp it in as I take the forest route to the clinic.

I go up to the back door. April doesn't like to lock it, and I've been asking her to. Now that we have someone in the forest, I definitely want that door kept locked, since it also leads to my sister's quarters over the clinic.

I ease open the door as I glance at my watch. Still too early for me to interrupt her with a patient. Good, because I'd definitely catch shit for that.

I have the door halfway open when I hear her voice and stop. Early-morning appointment?

Then I catch the second voice.

Dalton.

That's where he went.

Did he hurt himself this morning and didn't want to worry me with it? Whatever the answer, any medical appointment—whether it's with my husband or not—is private, and I start to beat a hasty retreat when a word stops me dead.

"—morning sickness," Dalton is saying. "I don't want to mention it to her. I know it's a loaded subject with her medical issues, but this is the second morning she's been sick. I think she's late with her period, but again, I don't want to ask. Can you bring it up? Get her to test before she has time to worry about it?"

"She's had plenty of time to worry. She came to me for a test yesterday."

My heart thuds, and I try to propel myself forward, to stop April before she says more, but I'm frozen in horror, guilt freezing my entire body.

"What?" Dalton says, and it's a genuine question, as if April can't be saying what she seems to be.

Again, I try to move. Again, it's as if some power holds me there, forcing me to bear full witness to Dalton's bewilderment.

Bear full witness to the consequences of my mistake.

"Casey came to me for a pregnancy test yesterday," April repeats. "She should have done so as soon as her period was late, but of course she didn't. Then she went running out of here with Kendra before she could take it."

"I don't think you should be telling me this, April," Dalton says, his voice low.

He's right, of course. She's breaching patient confidentiality. But in this moment, she isn't my doctor. She's my big sister convinced that I have, once again, proven myself incapable of managing my own affairs. The screwup who needs April to come to my rescue.

I should be furious. Maybe I will be later. But right now, getting angry with April feels like an excuse to absolve myself of guilt, and I deserve every drop of it.

"Casey needs to take the test," April says. "If it's positive—as I'm certain it is—she needs to get down south to a proper gynecologist, because we don't even know whether she can carry a baby to term."

Silence. Complete silence from Dalton. Tears well in my eyes, but I still cannot move.

"You're certain she's pregnant." His voice sounds hollow, and when I hear that, blood pounds in my ears.

"She missed a few days of her birth control when things were hectic. She confessed it to me, but she'd realized it too late to take a morning-after pill. So there was nothing to be done."

"You knew she could be pregnant—"

"Missing a few days only reduces effectiveness, and she didn't seem to be at the time of her cycle to conceive, if she was able to conceive at all. Which she should have known. She should have seen a gynecologist years ago, and if she wouldn't, then you should have insisted. It was irresponsible of you—"

That's what releases me. The moment blame shifts Dalton's way, I'm through the door, saying, "No."

April blinks at me. "You aren't pregnant? Did you start your—?"

"That's not what I'm saying." My voice is nearly a growl. "I mean 'no' to what *you* were saying."

At first, I think I'll have to explain it. I don't. Whatever my sister's idiosyncrasies, she's no different than anyone else in sometimes saying things she doesn't mean, and she flushes.

"I'm worried," she says. "I'm sorry, Eric. I didn't mean to blame anyone."

"Can you leave us alone, please, April?" I say.

"You really need to take that—"

"Leave us alone, please, April."

My tone tells her not to argue, and for once, she backs down. She murmurs something and leaves.

Dalton is standing right next to the wall, as if he'd been casually leaning against it while asking for the test, and then he'd straightened in his shock and confusion.

"I'm sorry," I say. And I burst into tears.

I feel his arms go around me as I blindly wipe away the tears, angry with myself for the outburst that keeps me from saying what I need to say.

I step away from him, swiping at my tears, but they just keep coming, and when I catch a glimpse of his face through the wash of them, his panic is palpable, as if I'm bleeding uncontrollably.

"I'm so sorry," I say, though I'm not sure how clear my words are. "I—I didn't want to tell you about the missed pills. It was already too late, and I just wanted to forget it and do better, and now I might be pregnant, and I know you're not ready, and if I'm pregnant, it's my fault."

Before I can protest, his arms are around me again, and this time, I don't have the will to protest. I just sink into him as he moves us to a chair and sits with me on his lap.

"Not sure how it's your fault, Butler," he says. "Pretty sure it takes two to make a baby."

I know he's trying to make light, but I start blubbering uncontrollably.

His lips go to my ear. "You said you know I'm not ready. Did I say that recently?"

"I heard you. When April said she thinks I'm pregnant. I heard your tone."

A moment's pause. Then his arms tighten around me. "Did I sound like she'd just punched me in the gut?"

I nod against his chest.

"Well," he drawls, "that could be because she said she thinks you're pregnant and reminded me that we aren't sure you can carry a baby. I sounded like that because not being able to carry a baby to term might mean a miscarriage. Or it might mean you'd be in danger, and that was an answer—as April said—that I should have gotten before now."

"It wasn't your responsibility."

"Yeah, it was, Casey." He pulls back a bit to look down at me. "It was like me dealing with my past. I didn't want to. It hurt, and I wasn't sure I wanted answers. You gently pushed me to get them, and I needed that, but not as much as you needed *these* answers. If there's a chance that having a baby could be dangerous to you, then we should have been discussing long-term solutions, not taking temporary birth control."

"I might not be pregnant," I say quietly. "If I'm not then

we'll double up on protection or whatever we need to do until I can get answers."

He says nothing.

"You think April's right," I say. "Between the missed pills and the late period and the morning nausea and the bursting into uncontrollable tears . . . there's not much chance that test is coming back negative."

"Take it," he says. "Let's get our answer."

Ten minutes later, I'm sitting in our living room, holding the test strip with its double lines. Dalton is across from me, scratching his beard stubble, his gaze down, and I want to cry again. Not for those double lines, but for the look on his face, the way he can't even meet my eyes.

"Eric?" I say. "This doesn't mean anything."

He nods, still not looking up.

"If it's not what you want, then it doesn't have to happen. Regardless of whether it *can* happen. If we aren't ready, then . . . this can all go away."

He drops his head and runs his hands through his hair.

"Okay then," I say softly, ignoring the clenching in my chest. "As soon as we find Max, I'll go south. Afterward, I'll see a gynecologist and get answers for the future, and we'll make decisions."

He raises his gaze just enough to meet mine, his head still down, hands laced around the back of his head like he's about to get sick himself.

"Is that what you want?" he asks, his voice barely audible.

I force my expression to stay neutral. "I made a mistake. I missed the pills. We didn't decide we wanted to try for a baby, and therefore, the ball is in your court. Whatever you want is fine with me."

He runs his hands through his hair again and groans. "Can you not do that, Casey? Not now. Please."

I'm taken aback. "Do what? I'm trying to be fair."

"Fuck fair. This is not the time to be rational and tell me that you'll do whatever I want as if it doesn't make a difference to you. What do *you* want?"

I tense. It's an old argument, one we haven't had in a while. Maybe it's my upbringing—emotionally distant and demanding parents and a sister with autism. Maybe it's because I shot a man and spent over ten years of my life waiting to be punished for it. I didn't come to Rockton because I wanted to. I didn't *want* anything. I didn't allow myself to want anything. Dalton has spent years propelling me into a place where I can want things and admit to it.

"This isn't the same," I say.

"Maybe not, but we're talking about your body and your health. Even if it's a normal pregnancy, it's still a risk, and you're still the one puking in the morning while I'm enjoying my breakfast."

"That's only the first nine months. After that, you'd be the one cleaning up the puke while I have my breakfast, because I am a lousy nurse. Just ask my sister."

His lips twitch, just a little. Then he comes to where I'm sitting, picks me up, and carries me to the couch so he can sit beside me, my hands in his.

"All right," he says. "I know you're afraid to say anything one way or the other, for fear that I'll feel pressured to agree. When we took our vows, we made it very clear that we are two separate people joined in partnership. That means I don't need to share your opinion. We can both give ours and work out the differences."

"Then why won't you go first?"

He mock-glares at me.

I lean against his shoulder. "Neither of us wants to go first for the same reason we struggled with the baby question three years ago. What if I say I'm ready and you're not. Or vice versa. This isn't like disagreeing over whether to let Storm on the bed. It's huge."

"Agreed, but again, this is your body. Your health. Therefore, your opinion takes priority."

"I don't want my opinion to take—"

He puts his hand to my mouth. Now I'm glaring at him.

"Yes, I'm being rude," he says. "I don't care. I *am* rude. Ask anyone. Tell me your preference, Casey." He meets my gaze. "Please."

My eyes fill, and I swipe at them. "Great. This again."

"Crying isn't weakness."

"No, apparently, it's hormones." I take a deep breath and try to look at him, but I can't, as my voice drops to a whisper. "I want to keep it. If I can, I want to keep it."

"And if you can't? If a doctor says you are at risk—any significant risk to your health . . ." He takes my chin in his hand and turns my face to his. "This is the part I'm struggling with, Casey. This is the part where I need to be perfectly clear and perfectly selfish. Before I can answer the question of whether I want this, I need to know what happens if there's a risk. I need you to say you'll put yourself first. That for once in your damned life, you'll put yourself first."

I nod.

"Can't hear you."

I roll my eyes. "Yes, okay? If there is a more than average risk to me, I will put myself first."

"Good." He shifts and meets my gaze. "This might not be what we planned, but I *am* ready. I *do* want it."

It takes a moment for me to assimilate that. "So we both want to continue the pregnancy, then? If that's medically sound?"

"Yes."

I burst into fresh tears, and he gathers me in his arms and holds me while I cry.

CHAPTER SEVENTEEN

April wants me to come in for an immediate examination. She isn't a gynecologist or even a general practitioner, but she's had to become the latter, and she's dedicated the past three years to learning about the role she'd been thrust into. She knows how to conduct the preliminary examinations and oversee a pregnancy, and she wants to do that exam right away. But we have a little boy to find. Until I need to take a break, I'm on the job every waking hour.

Back to the case then.

Last night I wanted to go in hard again on Dana and Louie. And now? Now I'm not sure that's the right move. I don't have anything to go in *with*.

Knowing Dana's story makes me confident that Louie is wrong. She's no less of a victim than she seems. She did witness a murder. Émilie's investigator confirmed that by matching up the details with a case, which led to Dana's previous identity, which allowed the investigator to verify her background.

We don't need to know her name or details on her background. We just needed confirmation that Dana and her husband didn't have any criminal connections to suggest they weren't innocent bystanders. There was also an actual home invasion, during which her husband was killed. Police reports confirmed all that for Émilie's investigator. Dana and her sons are here for exactly the reason they seemed to be.

So why was Louie convinced otherwise?

Maybe because he wanted *us* to be convinced otherwise. He presumed we couldn't follow up. The "not following up" misconception seems legitimate given the way he blustered about his own past, even when we threatened to check.

He's mistaken us for mere employees, as we were in Rockton. Sure, we could go to our "boss" and demand answers, but were we entitled to those answers? No. He'd been promised privacy, and he doesn't know that *we* are the people promising it. That's the way we've set up Haven's Rock. No one knows we own it, and if we seem more like mere employees, that's to our advantage.

Louie claimed hunting and search-party expertise, but when we pushed, he dialed that back to what seemed like a few hunting trips and participation in a couple of search parties. Covering his ass, in case we really could check?

I am ninety percent sure he lied about why he was in the forest. He was out there doing something and—

"Us," I say aloud.

Dalton and I are in the forest with Storm, ostensibly searching for Max, but mostly giving me fresh air so my stomach can settle . . . and giving us quiet time to process our news while doing something productive. We're holding hands, not talking, with me mentally working through the case while Dalton checks for fresh signs that anyone has been out here.

"Us . . . ?" Dalton says. "I'm guessing there's more to that exclamation, unless you're just randomly proclaiming our love to the world." He pauses. "Or you're shouting the title of that horror movie we saw, which I'm really hoping isn't the answer, because I don't even *want* to know how it relates to Max going missing."

I shake my head. "I was thinking about Louie. Why he was in the forest. What he was up to." I look at Dalton. "Us."

"This is payback, isn't it? You're sick because of something—one could argue—that I did, and so you're repaying me with cryptic clues."

I bump my head against his shoulder as we walk. "I'll give you a hint. What was Louie doing in the forest? The answer probably isn't that he just happened to bump into us twice."

Dalton curses. "Of course. There's a whole fucking forest out here."

"He was spying on us. Hopefully not the whole time we were out there, which would be really embarrassing if it took us that long to notice him."

Dalton shakes his head. "Storm would have realized it even if we didn't. My guess is that he was keeping his distance until he needed to get closer to hear us."

"So he was spying on us. . . . To make sure we were actually searching for the bear and then for Max?"

"Well, if someone kidnapped Max by pretending to be his bear-man, that kidnapper knew more about the situation than we'd told the residents."

I nod. "Which Louie could have overheard us talking about. We'd been doing that when Storm smelled the black bear."

"And then once Max goes missing, whoever has him stashed might want to be certain we don't get too close."

"And divert us if we do?"

Dalton shrugs. "Louie did make enough noise for us to hear him. And it did keep us from going further."

"So we should head back and search that area."

"Or I should, while you chat with Louie. See if you can get him sweating. Take . . ." He tilts his head. "Take Yolanda. I get the feeling he'd rather talk to a man. Or a woman he can patronize."

"Not many of those in Haven's Rock. Yes, I think Yolanda will do nicely here."

We circle just close enough to town for Dalton to be confident letting me continue on my own, and if I feel a bit like a child whose parent lets them "walk the rest of the way" once they can see the school . . . well, I don't say anything. He's always struggled against an overprotective streak, and I suspect my "condition" is going to make that a losing battle. I'll allow it up to the point where he insists on carrying my gun for me, so I don't lift anything heavy.

I'm at the edge of town when footfalls have me reaching for that gun. I don't grab it. I just let my hand fall in that direction. Then I see it's Gunnar, and I don't exactly relax, but I do let my jacket close over my weapon.

"Hey, you wanted me to keep an eye on Dana?" he says.

We'd asked Anders to assign someone to that role, and I'm surprised he picked Gunnar but . . . maybe not so surprised. Gunnar's perch makes him our best town spy, especially since everyone expects to see him there anyway. If Anders trusted him on this, then I trust Anders.

"Something's up?" I say.

"I'm not sure. She was at home until after Carson left. He's with Mathias again today. She stayed in for about ten minutes after that and then snuck out."

"Snuck?"

"Yeah. I saw the curtains move, like she was peeking to see who was around. Then she came out slowly, looking around, and ducked behind the building. She seemed to be heading for one of the storage sheds. I couldn't see her over there, so I climbed down. I thought I had eyes on her. I didn't. She wasn't at the shed or anywhere in sight. I think she went into the forest."

"Goddamn it."

"Yeah, I was going to tell Will or Kendra or Yolanda, but then I saw you heading back."

I pick up my pace. "Which storage shed?"

He's telling me just as I spot my sister cutting along the edge of town.

"Go back to your perch," I say. "I'll handle this."

I pick up speed and call my sister's name, but she's moving fast. She disappears from sight behind one of the residences. I follow, but by the time I get there, she's gone.

I curse under my breath and look around. I should take someone with me to go search for Dana, but all I see are residents.

I peer toward the forest. I won't go far. I'd literally just been mentally joking about Dalton getting overprotective, but he really will be. I know him well enough to judge that, and I've already seen how worried he is about my pregnancy. He's going to be on edge, and I need to respect that.

Even under normal circumstances, I'd think twice about venturing into the forest alone while we might have a mentally ill person out there, in the form of our "wild man."

I'll get a look around the storage shed. See whether I find

any proof that Dana went into the forest, and if so, then I'll get backup.

I look around again, still seeing only residents, and few of those. It's past nine, and most people are at their jobs. I consider taking out my gun, but there are too many people around for that. I settle for opening my jacket as I circle around the building.

The storage sheds are on the edge of town. This one backs right onto the forest, with the lake just beyond a thick stand of trees. I might not be Dalton, but I should be able to see signs of anyone walking through that treed barrier.

I move along the back of the building, my gaze fixed on the undergrowth. I'm looking for broken twigs, footprints, crushed plants, anything to tell me that—

My gaze swings to the wooden wall. The shed is raised off the ground, like most of our buildings. Permafrost means that cold that will seep through a floor as well as unsettle it. This building, though, has a skirt, like many others, providing cold storage. Hatches on all sides allow easy access. The hatch door for this one is ajar.

I bend at the hatch. We don't lock this one—it's not food storage, and nothing else is going to tempt residents to sneak around back and pilfer. Still, it has a bearproof latch, which means it didn't just pop open.

Did someone leave it open? I can't even remember what we're storing in here. Nothing, I think. We've maximized our storage potential to allow for growth, but a lot of that is unused, and I'm pretty sure we don't have anything in here. Which means no one came to fetch goods and forgot to fasten the latch.

I open the hatch. Inside, it's pitch-dark. I pull out my flashlight and before I can push it past the opening, I spot a folded piece of paper, a few feet inside.

A stone weighs down the paper, meaning it hasn't somehow blown in or fallen out of a pocket. Flashlight in hand, I creep into the crawlspace. When I realize I can't reach the paper while holding open the hatch, I stretch awkwardly to keep one foot braced against the hatch door while I reach as far as I can, my fingers grazing the paper—

At a sound beside me, I roll fast, the hatch swinging shut as a figure lunges. It hits me in the side, and I punch hard. A sharp intake of breath. My flashlight is on the ground, beam pointing away, and all I can see is a dark shape.

I rise onto my knees, head still ducked to clear the floor above. The figure comes at me again, and I strike, but sharp pain slices through my hand. I let out a hiss, and the figure kicks. I feel that kick in my side, dangerously close to my midriff, and something inside me panics, one hand flying to instinctively shield my abdomen even as an inner voice screams that it's too soon to worry about that.

I roll, and another kick lands, this one on my back. My hand is hot and slick with blood, and I'm about to scramble up when a knife pokes into the back of my neck.

"Don't move."

The voice is a hoarse whisper, but I still recognize it.

"Dana?" I say.

"I should have guessed it was you," she says. "I didn't want to, even after yesterday, when I found you in my apartment."

"I have no idea—"

"You were in my apartment, poking around. You even hinted that I knew more than I was saying."

"I did not poke around. Ask Isabel."

"Your *friend* Isabel? That's your witness?"

I take a deep breath. "Dana. I do not know what you are

talking about. You're the one who came back to your apartment acting oddly. That's why I pushed."

"You dismissed my fears about Gunnar. You didn't want me thinking that it was him because then I'd ignore the note."

I go still and resist the urge to look back at her. The knife point still pokes into my neck, shaking slightly, and I'm not moving and giving her any excuse to react.

"You got a note," I say.

"Stop," she hisses. "You have my son, and if you doubt what I will do to get him back . . ."

She doesn't finish the threat. I'm not sure she can. From the way that knife is shaking, I know my gravest danger here is making her react on impulse.

"I've been in the forest with Eric all morning," I say. "I was coming back when someone said they saw you head this way. You were under observation because your behavior yesterday suggested something was wrong, and I was concerned that Max's kidnapper had reached out and told you not to involve us. The person watching thought you went into the forest. I was heading there when I noticed the hatch undone. I opened it and spotted the note."

She doesn't answer. I'm making sense. Good.

I continue, "There was also a note shoved under the town hall door yesterday morning. That's why I'd gone to talk to you. It said to ask you where your son is."

"Me?" Her voice rises as that knife point digs in. I've lost points on credibility.

"I didn't believe it," I say. "But I had to take it seriously. Both the contents of the note and the possibility that whoever sent it knows where Max is. I have the note. Multiple people have seen it. I'm guessing you received one, too."

She doesn't answer.

I continue, "I'm also guessing that you received a message—now or then—telling you to leave something here. A reply maybe? Then you lay in wait to see who came to get it."

"Which was you."

I exhale. "Dana, if I were the kidnapper, would I really crawl in here without looking around first? Without making sure you were someplace else so it was safe to come? Would I do it in broad daylight? I'm a cop. I'd know better."

Silence.

I continue, "I've been investigating the possibility that Max was kidnapped to get to you. I'm not sure how that would happen—whether we have a leak somewhere—but I'm definitely not saying it *couldn't* happen and focusing all our efforts on a wild man in the forest. You have information that can help me, and I'm going to need it."

"How do I know you didn't take him?"

"You tell me. What proof do you need? I'm not even sure any I could give would be good enough. I was in the forest hunting for a bear when Max disappeared, but the only one who can prove that is my husband."

"That doesn't help."

"I'm cutting through the crap, Dana. You can demand proof, and I can offer proof, but in the end, you'll only see ways I could still have done it. The point is this: What would I do with Max? What would be my motivation? Unless we built an entire town to lure you in, I don't see how I could be involved with the people who're persecuting you."

"We were supposed to be safe here."

My shoulders slump. "I know," I say softly. That's all I say. It's all I can say.

"Can we go to the town hall?" I say. "I have the note there, and you can bring yours, along with anyone you might trust."

"I don't trust anyone here. Not anymore."

"Understood. But you're going to need to at least trust that I seem to be trying to get Max back."

"Fine." She withdraws the knife blade. "Let's go."

CHAPTER EIGHTEEN

I don't go straight to the town hall. I track down Anders first and ask him to stand guard behind that shed and let me know whether anyone goes poking around it, though I suspect we've lost our chance to catch whoever was expecting that note. Of course, Anders notices my bloody hand, but I insist I'll look after it, which I do with the first-aid kit at the town hall.

Dana meets me at the town hall. Yesterday, she looked frazzled and spooked. Today, she's furious, and I cannot say I blame her. It's one thing to think someone from the forest snatched her wandering son. It's another to think we failed and the person who murdered her husband is now responsible for grabbing Max.

She marches over, barely using her cane, and slaps two notes down on my desk.

The first reads:

Western storage shed. Go around back. Open the hatch.
Look inside.

The second:

It's time for your confession, Dana. That's how you'll get your son back. Tell the truth and sign it. Not your fake name either. It's time to stop living a lie. Write it out and put it where you found this note, and I'll decide whether it's good enough.

I read through both notes a couple of times. As I'm rereading, she says, "The first was put in my boot. I found it yesterday morning, when I was going to get a coffee. I ran to the storage shed. I thought Max was there. Instead, I found the second note. That's when I came back, and you were in my apartment."

"Because I came to speak to you," I say. "I was there less than thirty seconds, and while you don't trust Isabel, multiple people saw us. Someone will be able to confirm that I did not have time to do anything in your apartment, and when you saw me, I was clearly leaving."

I pick up the first note with tweezers. "This was in your boot. Inside the house?"

She nods. "Our door wasn't locked. I presume they put it there so I'd be the one to find it, not Carson."

"When did you last wear them?"

"The day Max disappeared. I was helping Kenny in his carpentry shop, and the boots are steel-toed. I didn't wear them again until I was going to grab coffee, and even then, it was only because I couldn't find my sneakers. The night before I wasn't in a state to put them anyplace I'd remember them."

So it'd been pure happenstance that she even found the note, given that it wasn't wet or cold enough to need boots. Whoever put the note there thought they were being clever, but it could easily have gone undiscovered for days.

Why two notes? One only led her to the other.

To establish a place to exchange messages, and to be sure she found it. Maybe also to avoid putting too much into that initial note. Still, like sticking the first one in her boot, it's someone *trying* to be clever, but really only making their plan more convoluted.

"I'll need your boots," I say.

"For what?"

"Fingerprints. Everyone provides them on entry."

"You can actually check that?"

"Yes, because I'm *actually* a detective. Is that why you didn't bring this to us?" I wave the note in the tweezers. "You didn't think we could help? You don't seem to have been warned to leave us out of it."

"I trusted law enforcement before," she says. "It got my husband killed. I didn't need to be told to leave you out of it."

"Understood. But now that I'm in it, what else can you tell me? This note says to stop lying. I don't need details, but do you know what this means?"

"No." She meets my gaze. "I honestly do not, Detective. I've been telling the truth since the day we saw that man get shot. My husband and I did nothing *but* tell the truth and look where it got us. Years on the run, him dead, and now our son taken. We did tell the truth. *That* was the problem."

"Do the people chasing you think you lied?"

She shakes her head. "No. They wanted us to lie. Now . . . Well, now lying wouldn't do any good, so they want us dead." Her voice drops with bitterness. "They got half of that."

The man they put in jail is dead. Dana can't undo the damage by retracting her statement, so it's all about revenge.

Revenge would be murdering Max.

Revenge would not be taking him captive and demanding that Dana "tell the truth."

An inkling of an idea creeps in.

I read the notes again.

"Has anyone in town seemed particularly interested in your story?" I say.

She slumps, now more defeated than angry. "Everyone's interested in it. I made a mistake with that. I thought we should stick to the basic truth when we came here, for the boys' sake. So that people understood what they'd been through."

"That their father was killed for testifying against a criminal."

She nods. "I should have just said their father was murdered and I was shot. That would have been enough. But I didn't want them needing to lie. The version I let everyone know is the version the boys know. I thought that was the right thing to do."

"People were still overly interested. Curious."

"Some were. No one pressed for details, if that's what you mean. We all get the talk about that—everyone here has the right to privacy. It was just more uncomfortable than I imagined, with everyone knowing what happened. I got the feeling . . ." She glances away. "I got the feeling I'd said too much. That it made some people wonder whether we'd done something."

"Whether you were as innocent as you seemed."

Her eyes flash. "We were. We *are*."

"I know that. But you suggested that people questioned your innocence. I'm asking for names."

She shakes her head. "No one said anything to our faces. It was just a sense. Maybe I'm being paranoid. I just felt like, if I'd only said that my husband was murdered, it'd have been more clear-cut but . . ."

A twist of a humorless smile. "I'm kidding myself, aren't I? They take one look at us and they think they know the answer. Crime. Probably drugs." Another twist. "Someone did say something like that to me. Started talking about drug cartels and how violent they are and how even whole families could get caught up in it, as if I knew all about that."

"Who?"

I expect her to say "Louie."

She doesn't. And with that, I have a new lead.

I find Gunnar at his perch. I climb up, and he's there looking out, watching.

"Tell me about Lynn," I say when he turns.

"Who?"

I give him a hard look.

"Oh, right. The chick married to Grant. Don't know her. Why?"

"You sure you want to stick with that story?"

He frowns, and it seems genuine.

"She was seen coming up here," I say.

"Ah." He glances toward the town and then back to me. "Look, that's a little awkward, and if someone saw . . ." He exhales and swears under his breath.

"I don't care what happens between consenting adults, Gunnar. I just want to ask you some questions about her, and as a staff member, you're expected to give me that. In confidence. It helps me get a handle on someone before I go asking other residents."

"I don't know anything about Lynn. Yes, she came to my perch, but I sent her away. I don't have a problem with married women, but it was clear she wanted to cause trouble, and I wasn't getting in the middle of that."

"Trouble?"

"She's unhappy with her husband and looking to stick it to him by screwing around with me. I said no as gently as I could."

I can tell by his expression that there's more to it, something he'd been about to add and then changed his mind.

"And then?" I say.

He exhales. "I don't want trouble."

"Anything you say is in confidence."

"Yeah, but if you confront her on this, she'll know I told you. Lynn . . . she sent me letters. Like sexting, only in actual letters, since we don't have cell phones. I asked her to cut that shit out. She did. That was weeks ago. It's handled, and I didn't want to make a big deal of it, but since you asked."

"Do you have those letters?"

"Uh, no. I mean, if they were good, I'd have kept them. But they were pretty awful."

I struggle to keep a straight face. "They were handwritten?"

"No other way to do it here."

"If I show you samples of handwriting, can you make an ID?"

"Like a handwriting lineup? Sure."

Gunnar has made his ID. He recognizes the handwriting on one of the three notes.

The note that had been shoved under the town hall door.

That one is done in cursive. The other two are printed. Is it one person trying to disguise the fact that they wrote all three? I don't know. But I do know who seems to have written that one note.

I find Lynn at work in the restaurant, doing prep for dinner, and I bring her to the station.

"You wrote this," I say, slapping it down in front of her.

She barely bothers to deny it. After all, she didn't bother to disguise her handwriting, did she?

"You need to talk to Dana," she says, after admitting to it. "She knows more than she's saying."

"Which you know because . . ."

"It's obvious, isn't it?" She gives me a look that borders on sympathy and lowers her voice. "Look, I understand this isn't what you signed up for. Like me chopping vegetables. I haven't done that since I was fifteen with my first job. Going back to it now is . . ." She shrugs. "Kind of humiliating, you know? But I get it. Someone has to do it. Like your case."

"My case?"

"You're obviously not a cop. You're too smart for that. Look at your sister. She's a doctor. That makes sense. You people are really good at math and science."

I don't ask what she means. I don't need to.

She continues, "I don't know what you did down south. Some kind of scientist or engineer? Maybe computers? But now you've come here and Eric's a cop, and the town needed cops. So you have to play detective."

Sometimes, if I can't explain without sounding defensive, I just don't. Do I really care whether this woman thinks I'm playing detective? Nope. If she kidnapped Max, she'll find out how much I'm "playing."

When I only look at her, she has the grace to squirm. Then she comes back with, "You're doing a good job, though."

"Uh-huh."

"You just . . . well, I'm going to guess you lived a pretty

sheltered life. You people usually do. Really close families and communities. Not a lot of crime."

I bite my tongue. Hard.

She continues, "You accepted Dana's story because you're a good person from a good background. To everyone else, it's obvious she's lying."

"Enlighten me."

She blinks. "What?"

I take a seat behind the desk. "We're going in circles here, Lynn. I asked how you know Dana's lying, and you said it was obvious and then made a whole lot of judgment calls about me, based on . . ." I circle my face.

She flushes. "I was just saying—"

"A whole lotta judgment calls, all of them wrong, which has to make me wonder whether you've done the same with Dana. Took one look at her and decided she was complicit in her own situation."

She sputters and squawks, but in the end, it seems she's made the exact same presumption as Louie. Is it racial prejudice? Maybe, but mostly I threw that out to knock her off balance. If Dana had been white, Lynn might have decided Dana and her husband were mixed up in meth or white-collar crime, depending on her assessment of their social standing.

The truth, I think, is that Dana is right. We underestimated the human capacity for blame. In the real world, I wouldn't have made that mistake. I've seen how the most innocent of victims are treated, with someone always questioning what they "did" to deserve it. They carried an expensive purse and got robbed. Walked home at night and got assaulted. Cut off someone in traffic and got shot. No crime is so horrific that someone won't blame the victim. That person made a mistake that they'd never make and therefore they are safe.

My mistake was in hoping that people who'd been victims themselves would be more understanding. In Rockton, no one openly shared their stories. They might tell a few people they became close to, for support and commiseration, but you arrived knowing that you weren't supposed to share, and most gratefully accepted that.

Yet while we've been busy setting up our town, suspicion has been festering. Lynn insists she came up with it on her own and told no one. She didn't think it was relevant until Max disappeared and then, like Louie, she decided it was very relevant. That's why she put the note under the door. For the fake cops who were too clueless to see the obvious.

How many other residents are questioning Dana's story? Any staff? Are there others out there who'd decided it was none of their business, but are now eyeing Dana, whispering among themselves that she knows more than she's letting on?

Did Lynn have anything to do with Max's disappearance? I don't think so. There'd be no point in tipping us off if she did. For now, I'll be assigning someone to watch her, and I'll quickly search the apartment she shares with her husband. My real concern, though, is finding the person who sent the other notes—the person claiming to have Max.

As I search Lynn and Grant's apartment, I think about the other two notes. I haven't dismissed the possibility that Lynn wrote them. Or that Grant did, the two of them working together. But the more I consider the trio of notes, the more Lynn's seems to work at cross-purposes with the other two.

Lynn's note turned attention on Dana. It urged us to look at her more closely. The other two notes are for Dana herself, and they function to open a direct line of communication. Presumably something would follow, and presumably it would be a demand for payment, in return for her son.

If Lynn was behind the other two notes, she sure as hell wouldn't want us taking a closer look at Dana. That would defeat the purpose.

Or would it?

Could tipping us off be a way of applying pressure to Dana? I'm not sure, but that twinges another thought.

There's something very odd about that final note, isn't there? About what it asked Dana to do.

Tell the truth and sign it. Not your fake name either.

Now look at the timeline. We know whoever left the note in the boot did it between Max's disappearance and the next morning. What about the follow-up note? She'd retrieved it the next day, but it would have needed to be in place as soon as the first note was left.

The timing works. It all works.

CHAPTER NINETEEN

I've been outside the storage shed for an hour now. Dalton is back, having found no sign of Max, and he's joined me after leaving Storm with Kenny. I've explained everything, and he agrees with my logic. Now we're waiting.

Our target finally slips through the forest. We're far enough away to hear them coming and hunker down. They stay just inside the trees and then make straight for the hatch. We let them go in. We let them come back out again and leave. Then we ease toward the hatch, and I stand watch while Dalton goes inside, because I've had quite enough of crawling in the cold dirt for one day.

Dalton comes out. "Nothing."

"That's what I figured. He has what he wanted. No need to make any more demands."

"Bring him in."

In a proper crime drama, our suspect would be a surprise to everyone. He'd be that person glimpsed at the beginning of the show, maybe given a line or two, quickly dismissed . . . until all the pieces fall in place and he is revealed as the killer.

It can work like that in real life. But more commonly it's like it is today, where the person in our interrogation chair is exactly who we expected to be there.

Louie sits in front of the desk. I'm behind it. Dalton leans against the fireplace mantel with his arms crossed. He's just far enough out of Louie's line of vision to make our suspect nervous.

"Whatever you think I did," Louie begins, "I couldn't have done it because I've been in custody for two days."

"House arrest," I say. "Which ended an hour ago, where-upon you were seen crawling under a storage building."

He shrugs. "I was thirsty, okay? I wanted a beer, and someone said the bartender hides the beer there. They lied. It's empty."

"Not completely empty." I take out the note I found in his pocket. "You took this."

He shrugs. "I was curious. Weird to find a note under there."

"Speaking of notes . . ." I lay the two other ones in front of him. "Look familiar?"

He doesn't even glance at them. "Nope."

"Huh. That's strange, because while you were sitting here, I conducted another search of your room, specifically looking for this paper and a pen. I found them."

He rolls his eyes. "It's standard-issue paper and a standard-issue pen."

"Maybe, but have you ever seen that trick where you write a note and the impression goes through onto the next page? No, I don't suppose you have . . . or you wouldn't have made that mistake."

I'm bluffing. Yes, I'd found the pad of paper, but all I could pick up were a few scratched impressions. Still, that was enough to tell me he'd written a note on the pad, and his blanch tells me it was *that* note.

He shakes it off. "I was in custody, remember?"

"Both notes would have been planted before that. You kidnapped Max and then reached out to Dana with your demand."

"What? There's no demand . . ." He trails off on realizing he's saying too much, but then, with a roll of his shoulders, he seems to decide there's no point denying it. "There's no demand, and I never said I had her kid."

I push forward the second note. "Read the first line."

His mouth sets. "It was a bluff, okay? I might have *suggested* I had him, but what I really meant was that you guys won't be able to find him until she tells the truth. You need all the information. I told *you* there was more to her story. Why would I get involved if I'd taken the kid?"

"Begging for scraps."

His face screws up. "What?"

"You were sniffing around for scraps. Trying to find out what we knew about her case. You claim it's a cartel and we say 'Ha! You're wrong. It's the Mafia' or some such thing. That's also why you were following us."

"Following you where?"

"In the forest. First after Max saw a bear, and then after he went missing. You were trying to overhear what we knew. Was the bear something you could use? What exactly did Max see? We said enough for you to impersonate a bear-man and lure Max out—"

"What? No. I was out there looking for the bear."

"With a knife?"

He chews that over while glowering as if I'm the bad guy for poking holes in his story.

"Fine." He spits the word. "I wanted to know what the boy

saw. I heard something about it being some kind of Bigfoot, and you were all pretending it was just a bear. I followed for more information. And I was right. You lied." Satisfaction surges so strong you'd think he'd uncovered us as Max's kidnappers.

"We believed Max saw a bear," I say. "If you overheard us talking, you heard that, too. Either way, our conversation gave you an idea of how to lure Max out. You kidnapped him and planted those notes. Then you followed us on our search for Max, hoping for more useful information, such as what we suspected and whether we were on to you."

"No!" He pushes his chair back and rises. "I didn't take the kid. I was investigating, just like you. Helping."

"By spying on us? That doesn't sound like helping. It sounds like investigating our investigation."

"I was concerned you weren't doing a good enough job. You weren't looking at Dana as a suspect, but now you've seen what she wrote. I was right, wasn't I?"

I take out the note we removed from his pocket. I spread it on the desk between us, flattening it with my hand, letting the silence stretch.

"You have read it, right?" he says.

"I have."

"And you see that I'm right. She confessed to everything."

"Confessed and signed her real name, just like you asked. Which means you owe her something." I look at him. "Her son."

"What? No. Are you listening? I don't have him."

"Then what's this?" I shake the note. "What is the point of making her confess?"

He goes still. That's what snagged my attention—the oddness of that "demand." A confession, complete with her real name.

"It was for you," he says finally. "Helping the investigation. So you'd know she's a real suspect and investigate."

"A real suspect for what?" I lift the note. "This confession says that she stole money from a cartel and that's why they're after her. What does that have to do with Max? She kidnapped her own son? For what?"

That pause again, the wheels turning fast. Then he blurts, "The cartel tracked her here. That's what I mean. They obviously tracked her, and they're holding him captive until she gives back the money."

"How? By wiring it from her phone?"

"No . . ." *Think fast, Louie. Think fast.* "By promising to wire it once she's out of here."

I stare at him. I don't need to say a word before he realizes how preposterous that is and starts spouting alternate theories.

I lean forward. "We have a problem, Louie. Nothing upsets people more than a missing child. Now we've held you under house arrest and questioned you and searched your room multiple times. That's going to make people suspicious, and they're going to turn that suspicion on you." I pause. "I'm sorry to say this, but I don't think you can stay in Haven's Rock."

His face lights up. Then he tries to cover it, muttering, "That's not fair, but whatever."

"I'll need to keep investigating you."

He nods, his gaze averted as he tries to hide the shine in his eyes.

"You'll need to stay in a secure facility until this investigation is complete."

That light starts to dim, his eyes narrowing. "Secure facility?"

"Comfortable. It's not prison. And you . . ." I draw this part out as I watch his expression. ". . . might have access to the internet and such."

"Might?"

I shrug. "I can arrange it, if you cooperate."

Now I have his full attention.

"Oh," I say, "I should probably mention that I wrote the letter."

He freezes. "What?"

I poke the letter. "I made this up, including Dana's so-called real name. You wanted a confession, so I wrote one for you."

Louie rises slowly, plants his hands on the desk, and leans toward me. Across the room, Dalton rocks forward but stays where he is.

"You made this shit up?" Louie says.

"Yep." I look him in the eye. "Why did you want her name and story, Louie? Skip the bullshit about giving it to us. We can get it, along with the investigator's report that confirms it. We don't need this confession. So why did *you* need it?"

He blusters about how he was only trying to help.

"Sit down, Louie," I say.

"I don't have the kid. I never did. I—"

"Sit."

It takes Dalton moving forward before Louie obeys.

"I didn't do anything," Louie says. "I was only trying to—"

"Stop talking and listen. You are our number-one suspect, and if you don't shut the fuck up and listen, then I'm going to open that door and let you walk out with everyone knowing we think you took Max."

Genuine panic lights his eyes, his bluster evaporating. "But I didn't. I—"

"Are you listening to me? Or do you want me to send you on your way?"

He stops talking.

I take the note. "I wrote exactly what you expected to read, and it still wouldn't have helped Max, so stop telling me that was your plan. See this?" I point to part of the note. "You specifically demanded her real name, because that's what you need to track down her story in the outside world."

It takes him a moment to screw up his face in exaggerated confusion. "Why would I want to track her down?"

"Not Dana. Her story. What she saw. Who's after her. Because that's the golden egg."

He tries to find words but only makes choked noises.

I push the note toward him. "Get her name. Get her story. Then, once you're back home, find whoever is targeting her and offer to sell whatever information you have."

He stares, and then gives a belated "What?"

"You might not have kidnapped Max, but you did something nearly as heinous. You took advantage of a child's disappearance. You pretended to want to help, but all you wanted was useful information. You got what you could from us, but what you really needed had to come from Dana herself. So you pretended to have Max to extort information you could sell to someone who wants her dead. You were willing to trade her life—and the lives of her children—for a bit of cash."

His mouth works, but he can't seem to find words.

"Oh, sorry," I say. "A *lot* of cash. You wouldn't do it for a few grand. It's only the big money that's worth sacrificing lives for, isn't it? You were willing to see innocent people murdered—"

"She's not innocent. She can't be."

I stare at him until sweat trickles down his face.

"So that would have made it okay," I say. "If Dana has done something, it would be okay to sell information that could have led to the death of her and her two children."

"They wouldn't hurt the children."

I stand and turn to Dalton. "I'm done here. If I keep talking to this piece of shit, someone's going to be cleaning up a mess."

"You aren't allowed to hurt me," Louie bleats.

"I meant that I'd throw up," I say. "But now that you mention it, that might work even better. I'll let Eric look after that, though. I can't stomach you for another second."

CHAPTER TWENTY

Dalton doesn't do anything more than lock Louie up. But if Louie spends his time in that cell expecting someone to beat the shit out of him, I don't have a problem with that.

I can't abandon the possibility that Louie—or even Lynn and Grant—kidnapped Max, but I don't see a motive. It's not as if they can demand ransom from Dana when she doesn't have access to a bank. Lynn was just sticking her nose into my investigation because clearly I was too inept to see the obvious—that Dana wasn't an innocent victim. As for Louie, he'd done something far worse. He looked at a boy's disappearance and saw an opportunity for profit.

Once again, I am reminded of an ugly and uncomfortable fact. That the people who caused trouble in Rockton weren't always the criminals the council snuck in. They were often ordinary people like Louie, who'd come here for a legitimate reason.

I could say that Louie must have lied and wasn't a real victim, but that's like him seeing Dana's case and deciding *she's* not a real victim. Horrible things can happen to innocent people like Dana. And innocent people like Louie can do horrible things.

Now we need to deal with Louie, and I absolutely do not have the time or the inclination for that while Max is still missing. So I bring Isabel and Phil up to speed, and we leave his fate in their hands while we go back to searching.

So much progress, and none of it got us an inch closer to finding Max.

Now that we're back in the forest, I'm laser focused, no longer feeling the tug of doubt wondering whether someone in town kidnapped him. Having set aside the "resident as kidnapper" theory, I'm confident roaming farther from town. Either someone is holding Max captive out there or they've taken him south, and if it's the latter, we should find a spot where the plane landed, because that's the only reasonable way to get him out of these woods.

We focus our search on the section we've been avoiding—the land that marks the territorial border between our town and the mining camp. We're supposed to warn them first, and there'd been plenty of land to cover before we got to that.

We don't know exactly where their settlement is, but we have a good idea from the distant noise. So we're staying far enough from their camp that we won't get shot as trespassers, while searching what is indubitably their self-claimed territory.

Louie mocked us earlier for not following a grid pattern, as if we were randomly tramping over the land. He's right that we aren't utilizing the standard grid, but that only works when you have either very little land to cover or a whole lot of people to do it.

What we do instead is a loose version, where we have divided the land into sections. We comb through those sections as best we can. We're following every possible trail, whether left by human or animal, because wherever Max is being held, they had to use or cut a trail to get there. We're on a very old one, overgrown but demarcating a clear passageway, and we're trekking along it when Storm goes still. Her nose lifts, and she lets out a whine and looks from me to the bag at my waist, the one carrying Max's scent.

"She smells him," Dalton says, and his voice is almost rigidly neutral. The last time Storm smelled Max, she'd taken off in the joy of finding her target, only to discover his empty jacket. Now she's wary, and so is Dalton, because that last experience might not be the only reason for Storm to be uncertain. She'd act the same way if she smelled him . . . and his scent said we might not find him alive.

I pat her broad head and lower myself to her level. "Thank you. It's okay. Whatever it is, it's okay. Now show us."

I give the command again, and she's off at a trot. She goes about twenty meters before veering off on a path I would have missed, being even more overgrown.

"Someone's been this way," Dalton says. "They cut through."

I don't see what he does, but I take his word for it. Storm continues down that path until she slows up ahead and Dalton grunts, and it takes me a moment to see why.

A cabin. There's a cabin ahead.

I crouch and quietly call Storm back so we don't alert anyone inside. Then I take her off the path and ask her to wait while Dalton and I get a closer look. She lies down with a grunt, her head resting on her paws, resigned.

I let Dalton pick a path forward through the trees as I follow right behind. He circles wide until we have a better view of our target.

I said it was a cabin, but "shack" would be a better descriptor.

An old and abandoned shack, with part of the roof missing, the rest sagging. It'd be just barely big enough for two people to stretch out sleeping bags.

We have come across the ruins of other shacks out here, and those were among the first places we checked. But with this one being on the wrong side of our boundary, we've never seen it.

We approach now with guns out. After a few steps, I tap Dalton's arm to get his attention and point at a spot where boards have rotted and one has half fallen, leaving a place where we can look inside.

There aren't any windows in the shack, which is to our advantage. As long as we don't make noise, our approach won't be noticed. We continue until we're pressed against that back wall. Then I bend to look through the opening left by the falling board.

I peek through and inwardly curse. It's early evening, not yet dark, but the lack of windows means it's black inside. I can make out a bit of light from the broken roof, and when I inch forward, more light comes from an open doorway on the far side.

I blink hard to let my eyes adjust. Then I look again.

There's a table and a chair. No sign of anyone on the chair. My gaze moves to blankets on the floor. Empty and discarded blankets.

I rise and whisper in Dalton's ear. "I can't spot anyone inside, but I can't see the whole interior either. You try."

He does and comes back up saying the same. It's quiet and still inside, and if someone's in that small space, they're out of our line of sight.

We back off then, and I tell Dalton that it looks as if the door might be missing. He agrees. That means no sneaking up around the front and yanking open the door to surprise any inhabitants. There's also the possibility of more missing boards that could act as unexpected windows and give us away as we pass.

I motion up.

"Don't tell me you're thinking of going on the roof," he says.

"They won't expect it."

"Yeah, especially when you crash through the rotted boards and land at their feet."

"I'll be careful."

He grumbles, but I can tell he's going to agree. Then his gaze drops to my midriff.

"No," I say. "It's a collection of cells well protected by muscle and fat. I'm nowhere near the stage of needing to worry about that."

When he finally relents, I could celebrate my victory as a sign of victories to come, but I get the feeling he's only decided to hold out for bigger fights.

We return to the shack, and he boosts me up. The building is low, with a roof barely seven feet off the ground. I easily find a safe spot and crawl up. As soon as I'm there, I can see down into half of the shack. Unfortunately, it's not the half anyone has been inhabiting, given that open roof. The blankets and furniture have been shoved into the section beneath me.

I take it slow. When a board creaks, I go still. Everything stays quiet. I switch direction to avoid that board and I continue until I'm near a smaller hole in the roof. Through it I can see the table. It's empty. Another few inches and—

The boards groan. I freeze. Then I listen. Nothing.

I reposition myself and peer down. I can see the blankets and part of the floor. No one is there. I mentally map the small space. Unless someone's plastered against the wall, it's empty. But that still means I have to make sure no one is plastered against the wall.

I creep to my left and look. There, I can see the one section of wall that had been hidden.

I retreat to the edge and let Dalton help me down.

"Empty," I tell him.

We still don't run around the front and through the door. We take it slow, and then Dalton swings around while I cover him. Within seconds, we're inside an empty shack.

I whistle for Storm. I don't want her out there any longer than necessary, but I also need her nose. She comes at a lope and lumbers in, and I can almost see her slump when she doesn't spot Max. She goes straight to the pile of blankets and noses them.

"He was here," I say.

Dalton looks around. "Decent spot. Well hidden. Partially sheltered."

"So why leave? That's what you're thinking."

"I am."

I look around from where I stand. There's not much to see. There are those blankets, old and moth-eaten. A handmade table and chair that I suspect were already here. Trash is piled in one corner, but when I dig through it, there's nothing less than a decade old.

"They cleared out," I say. "But why?" I stand and look around. "We'd have heard them leaving, and everything's gone—not so much as a wrapper or sock left behind when they fled with Max. Gone for a while, then. A planned departure."

I pace around the tiny building. "Temporary lodgings on the way to somewhere else? Or while waiting for a plane?"

Dalton doesn't answer, which means he has nothing to add. My reasoning is sound.

"Let's hope there's a trail for Max," I say. "Considering we know he was definitely here, that should be helpful. Storm? Come—"

An unearthly yowl splits the air.

CHAPTER TWENTY-ONE

We run outside. The sound comes again, sending shivers through me. The undulating "ahhh" sounds like a cross between a spook-house ghost and a pain-racked human.

"Lynx," Dalton says.

I knew that. Or I would have after my initial creep-out passed. It's two lynx in a territorial dispute, and knowing that almost makes it creepier, because it really does sound human.

"Go see what they're fighting over?" Dalton says.

"We'd better."

The sound comes from a couple of hundred feet away. We'd veered off the old path onto this fork, and the lynx seem to be farther down the main one. We have our guns out, and Storm sticks close. She's not overly concerned about the lynx. They can be as tall as her, but they're a third of her weight, and on the rare occasions we spot one of these ghosts of the forest, they melt away as soon as they smell her.

The sound gets increasingly loud, until I'm wincing. They're so wrapped up in their argument that they don't hear us, and soon we can see two leggy felines with short tails and tufted ears. They're staring at each other, making no move to attack, just arguing with those eerie yowls.

"Hey!" Dalton shouts, and they turn, like people who've been caught arguing in public, startled and annoyed at the same time.

Storm growls. They look at her. They look at us. Dalton takes another step forward, and then they are gone, as soundless as wraiths.

"Okay," I say. "Now let's see what you two were fighting over."

"Probably territory," Dalton says. "I don't see anything else here."

I keep walking, gun still out. He's right. The path stretches past where the lynx had been arguing, and there's nothing there.

Then Storm whines. It is the politest little whine, as if she hates to interrupt and point out that we've missed something but . . .

I look around. She glances to the left, and I follow the direction of her gaze to see what looks like an empty spot in the undergrowth. The brush has been flattened by something. From here, I can't see what, but when I take a step, Dalton says, "Hold up."

He crouches by the side of the path, his hand to the ground. At his fingertips is the clear outline of a boot heel. Beyond that, crushed vegetation leads toward that small cleared space about ten feet away.

We start in that direction, one step at a time.

The smell hits first. It wafts over, faint enough that I have to hesitate, not sure I caught it. We're upwind of that cleared spot, but after another few steps, Dalton's putting his hand to his nose, and my still-unsettled stomach flips.

The first thing I see is a hand. It's outstretched, with the fingers poking through the undergrowth, and at the sight of that, I relax a little. Yes, that's a terrible reaction to have when the smell of putrefaction tells me I'm dealing with a dead body, but seeing the size of that hand, I know it's not Max.

I take another step, and the figure becomes clear. It's a large man lying facedown in the undergrowth. His back looks wet until I shine my flashlight to see it's dried blood, the rear of his jacket a patchwork of stab wounds.

"Shit," Dalton says as he steps through.

My light passes over the man's body. It's not just his back. He's covered in blood, his clothing nearly in ribbons. There are some signs of predation from small scavengers, but the preciseness of those holes speaks to knife work.

Someone stabbed this man to death and then kept stabbing long after he stopped moving.

My mind slips, almost traitorously, to the small penknife Dalton gave the boys. But whatever blade killed this man is larger, and no matter how panicked Max might have been, he wouldn't have stabbed his captor this many times.

I'm also not sure this *was* his captor.

The man is dressed in work clothes—heavy canvas trousers with a myriad of small pockets, plus what looks like a flannel shirt showing through his torn windbreaker. He's wearing the sort of boots I'd expect from someone in construction. All of it shows signs of wear, but it's new and sturdy, and not what our man of the woods would have been wearing under his bearskin. There is also no sign *of* a bearskin. Not here and not in the shack.

I dig my phone out of my backpack and hit Record.

"The deceased is a white male. Indeterminate age, as he is lying facedown and I'm not ready to turn him over yet. Height approximately . . ." I look from the dead man to Dalton, who stands silently with Storm, letting me work. "Six foot one, possibly six two. Heavyset, perhaps two twenty-five. He's lying on his stomach with one hand outstretched. We're approximately ten feet off the main path. I didn't see blood spatter or drops that would indicate he was injured on that path, but we'll take a closer look."

Dalton motions to ask whether I'd like him to do that, and I nod. Once he's gone, I hit Record again.

"There are signs of predation, though not as much as I'd expect, given the amount of blood. That could be the location, which is heavily wooded."

I reach down and move the man's outstretched arm. "The body is mostly in rigor. Early putrefaction means it's coming out of rigor, not going in. That suggests death took place last night. Multiple stab wounds to the back, legs, and arms suggest a frenzied attack. I'll get a closer look once I remove clothing." I pause. "I'm going to conduct a full on-site examination, as I suspect I will not be taking this body back to town for autopsy."

I pause again. I have a theory about this man, and I want to pursue it, but I need to proceed in an orderly fashion here. Whether I'm right or wrong, that theory won't impact the process.

Dalton returns as I'm rising to my feet. "No sign of blood out there. No sign that the body was dragged either. There's just the one partial boot print. Looks like a possible match to what he's wearing but . . ." He shrugs. "It's also a match for mine. Not enough definition to be sure."

I nod. "I'll need to do a full examination, but that will risk messing up my scene. So the scene comes first."

"I definitely see blood here."

He's right. With the gloom of early evening, I hadn't noticed it, but a sweep of his flashlight shows blood spatter on leaves and trees. Less than one might expect, given the degree of damage, which means a lack of arterial spray. The man is stabbed. He goes down quickly and continues to be stabbed. There's blood everywhere around him, supporting that story.

"Stabbed in the back?" Dalton says.

"Seems likely, but I won't know that until we turn him over and see his chest."

Before the sun sets further, I record observations of the scene. We find a few footprints, but they're all smudged, as if captured in motion. I still take pictures of them, in addition to the boot print and the scene in general. Then I snap more photos of the body under the glow of Dalton's flashlight.

I record additional observations before putting away my phone. "I'm going to check his rear pockets before turning him over."

There are a lot of pockets to check. Most of them are empty. I do find a chocolate-bar wrapper, which I set aside. Then a half-finished pack of chewing gum, some kind of multi-tool, and a small pocketknife. The last one has Dalton snorting.

"Would have done him more good if it wasn't in a buttoned-up pocket halfway down his leg."

"Agreed." I hunker down and then shine my light at the pocket that had held the knife. "There isn't even a smear of blood on the pocket. Either he forgot he had the knife or the attack happened so fast he never even had time to fumble for it. Same as the multi-tool. That was closer to hand, but again, there's no sign he went for it."

I look at the other items. "Gum and a Hershey bar. Even more evidence we aren't looking at our wild man of the woods."

"American chocolate bar, too."

I shrug. "Hershey is American, but it's available here . . . Oh." I smile over at him. "Good eye."

"No French on the packaging. That means it's American. The gum, too. You want me to flip him over now?"

"Please."

I turn on my recorder and make notes of what we found in the pockets and the condition of the ones containing potential weapons. Then I continue, "Victim is now on his back. He appears to be in his mid-thirties. A short beard. Short medium-brown hair. No distinguishing marks immediately apparent." I open one eyelid. "Brown eyes. No signs of trauma to his face."

My gaze continues down the body. "No obvious trauma to the front of his body at all."

I'd noted a lack of defensive wounds on the one hand I could see earlier. The second hand had been under his body. Now I examine it. "There are no defensive wounds on his left hand either. I don't see anything to indicate a struggle. It is as if he was surprised by his attacker, who approached from the back, and he was incapacitated before he could fight. That would seem inconsistent with the number of wounds."

I hesitate and think it through. "One possibility is that, while the victim did not fight back, he did attempt to flee, and so his killer continued to stab him until he went down, and then kept stabbing in a panicked state. Or, as mentioned earlier, the number of wounds could suggest a frenzied attack."

I turn off the recording and look at Dalton. "Thoughts?"

"I'm leaning toward frenzy. If this guy did try to escape, he didn't get far. The blood on the ground doesn't go beyond this very small clearing."

"So he was incapacitated quickly, and his killer just kept stabbing."

We know Max saw what seems to be a wild man out here,

who was also witnessed by a miner. We also know that wild man may have lured Max into the forest and kidnapped him, and nothing in the ruined shack contradicts that theory. Therefore, if this man was murdered by our bearskin-wearing wild man, signs of frenzied attack would only cast our preconceptions into stone, and we need to be careful about that.

There is a wild man out here, one who may be both unstable and dangerous, and he has kidnapped Max, possibly taken Lilith, and now horribly murdered this man.

That must remain a theory until evidence further supports it.

"I think this is one of the miners," I say. "The clothing would support that."

"It does."

"So would the imported candy. We don't know where the mining company originated, but it could be American and if so, it could be shipping supplies over the Alaskan border."

Dalton nods. "With the clothing and the multi-tool and the fact we're on their side of the boundary line, my first thought was that he's one of them. Then I wondered, if a miner went missing, wouldn't they tell us? Ask for our help?"

I consider that. "They did ask for it with the bear-man, but I don't think they'd be quite that fast to ask for our help with a missing employee. Not with how cagey they've been. And if this is their man, I doubt they'll let us take him to Haven's Rock for an autopsy. We can offer but . . ."

Dalton goes quiet enough for me to know he's thinking something. Then he says, "Yeah, I don't think they'd let us take him, and I'm not sure we should offer . . . or tell them we found him."

I frown at him.

He continues, "If we don't think we can get the body for an autopsy, then maybe we don't want them knowing we've found him and have potentially done a little crime-scene investigating."

"I want to do as much as I can here," I say. "Nothing invasive, but a thorough external exam. First, though, I want to get back to that cabin and see whether we pick up a trail while it's fresh."

"Agreed."

Storm finds Max's trail. She does not find Max.

She managed to follow his trail for long enough that I really did get my hopes up. He left the shack and went deeper into the mining company's territory. At several points, when the forest thickened, Dalton could find signs of what seemed like running, where the undergrowth was trampled and torn.

Does that indicate Max and his captor on the run after his captor killed a miner who'd stumbled too close to the shack? At one point, I'd even dared hope that Max had escaped. We found two of his footprints, clear in a muddy patch. But then farther down, we found his print plus a larger one. Both of them running, then, his captor agitated enough that they didn't carry Max or make any attempt to hide their trail . . .

Until they did.

Until Max's captor obviously calmed down enough in that mad flight to realize they were laying a clear trail and took to a stream instead. It's the classic way to lose a dog, and it works. We find where they went in, and we cannot find where they came out.

We mark the spot to keep searching in the morning. Then we return to the dead man to continue my examination.

★ ★ ★

I've conducted my exam, and now I'm back to recording.

"Victim has sustained thirty-three wounds," I say. Then I list the locations. All are on his back side, over half on his back itself.

"Victim is in good physical condition, heavyset but also muscular. Further examination of his hands reveals calluses that seem relatively recent. Distinguishing features are two tattoos and several scars. One tattoo is Celtic knotwork encircling his right biceps. The other is a Celtic cross on the underside of his left forearm. There is one surgical scar on his right calf and a possible surgical scar on his chest, plus a scar indicating a past injury on his right knee. Photos of all have been taken. There is also . . ."

I shine the flashlight on his shoulder blade, where what looks like a recent small scar has been healing, almost hidden by one of the knife wounds. I describe that. It's an interesting place to get a scar, particularly one that looks almost surgical in its precision. Had he cut himself there? How? The stab wound mangles most of the already small scar tissue, and I might have missed it if my flashlight beam hadn't caught the skin in just the right way for me to see the raised mark.

I note all that for the recording. Then I continue, "Returning to the stab wounds, the pattern suggests attack from behind. One penetrated between his ribs and likely was the cause of death. The blade went in at what seems like exactly the right angle, suggesting intent rather than accident. Other wounds appear more random, with varying degrees of penetration, many seeming more slashes than stabs."

I ease back and shut off the recorder before I glance at Dalton. "Anything to add?"

He shakes his head. I've taken photographs of all injuries for my sister, which is the most I can do, as much as she'll complain that it's no substitute for a proper autopsy. She'll also complain about the tentative conclusions I've drawn in my verbal report. But we're not down south, where I'd need to be more careful and more formal. No defense lawyer or judge will ever hear those recordings. They're just for us.

Once that's done, we reclothe the body and return it to where it lay, positioning it as we found it. Then we take another half hour making sure we haven't left any trace. If we're going to pretend we never found this body, we need to do a thorough job of erasing ourselves. We've been wearing gloves, keeping Storm out of shedding distance, and watching where we set our feet, but now we comb through and remove every sign that we were here.

By the time we're done, it's fully dark, and a glance at my watch says it's been that way for a couple of hours.

"Do we need to get back?" I say. "I hate leaving when we've found Max's trail, even if we lost him. He's been out here, recently, and going back to town feels . . ."

"Like abandoning him? We've got enough to stay out overnight."

"Good. Thank you."

We retreat to the other side of the boundary line, where we deem it'll be safe to spend the night. We don't have sleeping bags, but we did bring a lightweight thermal blanket. We curl up on a sheltered bed of moss, me on my side, with Dalton behind me, his arms around me, the heat of his body enough to ward off the chill. Storm settles in front of me, sharing her body heat, which reflects off the blanket over all three of us.

We did not find Max. But we found evidence of him. Those small footprints told a story, and that story says that, at some time in the last twenty-four hours, Max was alive and well enough to run. Now we just need to find him.

CHAPTER TWENTY-TWO

Max

Max is still walking, still hoping to spot some sign of Haven's Rock. After he escaped, he ran all night. The bear-man had chased him for what felt like miles, no matter what he did—running through thick undergrowth or sneaking across open land and hiding.

Max finally lost him using a trick he'd seen in a movie, where a man had been running from tracking dogs. Max had taken off his shoes and socks and waded in a stream. He figured the bear-man must be able to track his scent, in order to follow him so well. Carson would roll his eyes at that. It was a man, not a bear. But Max knew what he'd seen, and he knew that he didn't lose his captor until he went into that stream.

The water had been so cold that Max couldn't feel his feet, but he'd walked through it as far as he could. Then he'd crouched on a rock in the middle and warmed his toes so he wouldn't get frostbite. Once they were okay, he went back into the water and kept walking until he came to a place where it cut through rock. There, he put his shoes back on, climbed up the rocks, and crawled across them. Then he hopped down to ground level and kept running.

The trick worked. He hadn't seen or heard the bear-man since he went into the stream. He still didn't stop until the sun rose. Then he was too tired to go on. He crawled under a fallen tree, hoping it hid him, and he fell asleep.

When he woke, he'd decided he was safe from his captor. Which meant he was halfway to his goal. He had escaped . . . now he needed to get back to Haven's Rock.

He thought he knew how to do that. Otherwise, he wouldn't have been able to sleep.

Sheriff Eric had insisted both Max and Carson take note of the landmarks in the area, so if they were ever lost, they could get back. He'd also given them compasses and shown them how to use them.

Max knew that the mountains were his best landmark. He needed to find the right one. Easy enough. He'd studied the profile of that mountain so he could recognize it from anywhere.

Sheriff Eric had warned that if they got too far from Haven's Rock the mountain wouldn't look the same. They had to see it from the correct angle and distance to make out the profile. When Max woke up and looked for the mountain, he realized he hadn't paid enough attention to that part of Sheriff Eric's warning.

Max could see mountains. One was right in front of him—he was even partway up it. But he couldn't tell if this was the right mountain, and if it wasn't, then he couldn't tell whether the right one was the one to his left or his right. He also didn't have his compass.

He thought it was still morning, which would mean that the

sun should be in the east. Except . . . hadn't Sheriff Eric said it was a little different here, especially as the seasons changed? That would make the sun more in the north, right? Or would it be south?

And *had* he woken in the morning? Or was it already afternoon? That made the difference between heading east or west. Also, how did that even matter when he wasn't sure whether he was east or west—or north or south—of Haven's Rock?

He'd known he had to get away from the mountain so he could see it properly. That had seemed so easy. It wasn't easy. He'd soon discovered that he had woken in the afternoon. *Late* afternoon. And he was still walking when it got dark.

It got dark and then darker, and then even darker, until he couldn't see the mountains. He was lost and tired and hungry. He'd eaten the apples, and now he had nothing left, and all he wanted to do was lie down and sleep.

No, all he wanted to do was reach Haven's Rock. To keep walking until he saw the light of it in the distance.

Except there wouldn't be any light, would there? They were supposed to keep the blinds shut after dark.

But he might still see a flashlight or the faint glow of the town. He's thinking that and stumbling along, and when he does see light, he's sure it must be a mirage. He'd heard about those. People lost in the desert spotting water, only to discover it's an illusion.

Could that happen in the forest? Wanting to see light so badly that you imagine it?

Max keeps walking toward that soft glow through the trees. Even as he draws close, he can't see where the glow comes from. A floating light in the darkness.

A flashlight? A lantern?

He nearly crashes right into the cabin. In front of him rises what looks like a wall, but even when he squints, he doesn't seem to be looking at a building. More like a hobbit hole. An odd little house that blends right into the forest.

Something catches his eye near the ground, and he looks down to see a painted fox peering from behind a real bush. Any other time, it would have made him smile, but out here, it's just too strange. Strange is men who look part bear. Strange is dangerous.

He's stepping back when he hears a growl, and for a second, he thinks it comes from the painted fox, which would mean he hasn't woken up yet, and he's dreaming.

The growl comes again. He follows it up and then gasps as he stumbles back.

It is not the painted fox.

It's a wolf. A real wolf.

The beast stands less than ten feet away, its golden eyes fixed on him.

Max is imagining things. He must be. Even if he is awake, this has to be a husky. People use huskies instead of wolves in movies all the time. Except Max has always been able to tell the difference, and if he saw this canine in a movie, he'd know it was an actual wolf. Its head comes up to his chest, but most of its height is legs. Long legs and a powerful body, with gray and white fur rippling in the breeze.

He is looking at a wolf.

He knows how he should react. Caution but not fear. Even before he met Sheriff Eric, he'd done a school project on wolves, and he knew that attacks on humans were much, *much* rarer than bear attacks or mountain lion attacks or even moose attacks. A single wolf is only going to go after him if it's starving, and this one clearly isn't. Nor is it making any move to attack. It just stands there, head slightly down, growling softly as it watches him, as if trying to figure out whether *he's* a threat.

"Hey," he says, and he extends his hand, because that's what he does with dogs.

The wolf's head snaps up, as if he's thrusting out a knife. Max pulls his hand back.

"Hey," he tries again, and the wolf's ears swivel.

Now what?

Back away. That's what Sheriff Eric would say. Back up slowly, keeping your gaze just below its eyes, not submissive or aggressive.

He takes a step back . . . and the wolf steps forward. Max's heart leaps into his throat. He tells himself to be calm. The wolf is just curious.

Another slow step back.

The wolf matches him.

Max swallows. Yes, it's curious, but it can also be curious about things like "Would that two-legged creature taste good?" and "Would it be easy to kill?"

He reaches into his pocket, fingers closing around his knife. He's pulling it out when a noise sounds in the strange little cabin, and the wolf lunges at Max, snarling. Max leaps back and stumbles, and for a second, he imagines the wolf leaping on him. He twists, managing to avoid a fall, and starts to run.

He makes so much noise running that it takes a moment to realize that's the *only* noise he hears. He slows and glances back.

There's no sign of the wolf. It didn't come after him.

He's considering what to do next when he hears a voice.

A woman's voice.

When he strains, he picks up words. "—out here, Nero? Whatever you scared off, it made a hell of a racket. I don't suppose you'll tell me what it was?" A pause. "No? Come on inside then. I picked up some treats in town."

Silence falls as he continues to strain, hoping for more.

That was a woman. He was sure of it. A woman who seemed to be talking to the wolf, promising it . . . treats? Really?

Was it a husky?

No, he was certain it'd been a wolf.

Max flexes his hand around the knife. The strange little cabin belongs to a woman. She seemed normal enough. Well, except for talking to a wolf, but if he had a wolf, he'd talk to it, too. As for having a wolf at all, that was weird, but also kind of cool.

Should he go back there? She seemed to take the wolf inside with her, so it won't be outside anymore. He knows just because she's a woman didn't mean it's safe, but it feels safer than walking up to a cabin with a man inside.

A woman living in the forest with a wolf? a little voice whispers. *She might as well have a house made of candy. She's a witch, obviously.*

He scoffs at the voice. That's baby Max talking. Scared Max. He needs to be grown-up Max. Practical Max. He's lost in the forest, after being held captive by a man who's part bear. He needs to get back to Haven's Rock. If he has the chance to get help, he should take it.

He licks his lips and swallows.

Should he wait until morning before he knocks on her door? He'd be safe sleeping out here.

Unless she lets the wolf outside again, and it finds him.

He should knock now. It's not completely dark yet.

He takes one step, and brush crackles behind him. He's whirling when a hand slaps over his mouth and another grabs him by the neck.

The hand on his mouth is human. He can feel that . . . yet when he fights, claws flash in a weird floppy way, and he realizes what he's seeing. A big bear paw, only it's just the fur and claws, like on a bearskin rug.

Not a person who is part bear.

A person *dressed* like a bear.

Figuring that out takes a moment, a moment where he's thinking when he should be fighting. The man withdraws his hand from Max's mouth, but before Max can scream or even speak, that hand joins the other, and both of the man's hands are around Max's neck, squeezing so tight that all Max can do is gurgle.

They keep squeezing until Max can't breathe.

He can't breathe.

The man is choking him.

Choking him.

A voice at his ear, rough and low.

"Sorry, kid. I hate to do this, but you're too big a risk to—"

Max doesn't catch the rest, because that's the moment when his brain screams, *Knife! You have a knife!*

Max pulls his arm up and, with everything he's got, he stabs backward.

The man shrieks and lets go. Max still has his hand on the knife, and when he lunges forward, the blade pops out of the man's leg, nearly sending Max flying. He's twisted enough to see a bearskin and a very human arm slapping down onto the man's leg, where blood gushes from his thigh.

The man tries to lunge, but Max is already running.

CHAPTER TWENTY-THREE

Casey

We wake the next morning still curled together. It's barely dawn, and I'd love to get a little more rest, but my bladder isn't going to allow that. I've barely started pushing up when my stomach heaves, and there's a moment where I'm confused.

Why do I feel sick? What did I eat last night?

Then I remember. Before I can resume moving, Dalton stirs and mumbles something I don't catch. I glance over to see his eyes half open and feel his hand squeezing the front of my thigh.

"How you feeling?" he says.

I make a noise in response.

"Anything I can do?" he asks.

I shake my head and push up. "I'll talk to April when I get back, but I'm guessing the only real course of action is to take it easy on morning foods. No coffee for me."

"Good thing I brought tea then. And crackers."

I lean over to kiss his cheek. "I love you."

I manage to get into the bushes and resolve the bladder issue without puking, which seems like a win. I'm moving slowly and taking deep breaths of sharp morning air.

Storm pads along after me, keeping a watchful eye. I make sure I'm not going to vomit and then I return to the camp, where Dalton is already starting a fire.

I sit down cross-legged near it and take a few moments of quiet pleasure watching him work. He'd prepped the campfire last night, and now only needs to light it. He'd filled our canteens last night, too, and while our backpacks don't hold a kettle, he gets the water boiling in our metal cups instead.

"Can we talk about something?" he says. "Tell me no if you're not up to it."

"I think I am. It's eating and moving that sets it off."

He hunkers down to adjust the cups over the flame. Then he says, "I'm not certain how to . . ." He scratches his cheek. "This isn't what I imagined, and I'm having a bit of trouble."

"What you expected . . . ?"

"Having a baby."

I swallow and try to sound upbeat. "It's a surprise. I know. And whatever you said yesterday, you have the right to change your mind, now that you've thought about it."

"Stop." He meets my eyes. "Please, Casey. Stop."

My hands clench on my lap.

He lowers himself onto the log with me, takes my hand, and draws my attention to him. "Please stop interpreting everything I say about this as a complaint. If there is a problem, *that's* it. I don't know what to say because I'm afraid it'll make things worse."

"Worse than they already are, you mean." I hear myself and close my eyes. "I'm sorry. *That's* what you mean. I need to stop doing that."

He presses his lips to mine in a kiss that has me opening my eyes.

"I said this isn't how I imagined it," he says. "Because I imagined it—however it came about—as nothing but joy. Being excited. Picking out names. Making plans. Which does *not* mean I'm complaining because this is different. I'm just trying to figure out how to approach it, if we don't have answers yet on whether you can carry to term. Is it okay to be excited? To talk about it? Or is that going to make things worse, if we don't get the answers we want? I honestly don't know, and . . ." He shrugs. "I'm in a weird kind of limbo, and I need some direction. Can we act like this is real, like there's a baby coming? Or should we ignore it until we get answers?"

He's articulating something I've been feeling since I got the news. I have moments where my mind starts throwing open doors to a new future, wanting to plan and dream. Then it slams those doors fast because this isn't a guarantee. Except . . . is it *ever* a guarantee?

That thought hits me, and I take a moment to process it before I say, "I think, if we wait to be sure it's going to happen, we'll be waiting until we're holding a baby in our arms. It's the same for anyone. I read somewhere that one in four pregnancies ends in miscarriage. The gynecologist could say everything's fine, and I could still miscarry. I could be on permanent bed rest and still miscarry. Nature decides that, not us. Or something could go wrong, and *we'd* need to make that decision."

"We might need to make it anyway, if your health is in danger."

"Will that be harder if we have names picked out, and we've started planning where to put a nursery? Absolutely. But I made you a promise. If there's a significant danger to my health, then this doesn't happen, and no amount of broken dreams changes that. Whether we dream together or separately, we'll still dream.

We can't help it. And if things go wrong, then we'll grieve for what can't be. But that's . . ." I look at him. "That's the chance we take with everything, isn't it? It's the chance we took when we got together. It's the chance we took when we built this town. We start to craft a dream for the future, knowing if something goes wrong, it'll hurt so damn much, but . . ."

I shrug. "What's the alternative? To not dream? If our relationship didn't work out, would I have regretted meeting you? Never. If Haven's Rock fails, will I regret building it? Never. We don't get to decide whether this"—I put my hands to my stomach—"is real. It *is* real, whether it lasts or not. So I say we let it be real for as long as it lasts."

I look up at him. "Is that okay?"

He catches me up in a tight squeeze. Then he lowers his lips to my ear and whispers, ever-so-gently, "I like the name Eric. Boy or girl."

I laugh. "Eric or Erica?"

"Nope, Eric either way. Eric Junior."

I laugh, pulling away and swatting him. "Make my tea, Eric Senior. We have work to do."

We're heading to pick up Max's trail again when we catch the sound of people in the forest. The noise comes from a few hundred feet away, likely over the border to the mining company's territory.

It's at least two sets of footfalls. They seem too heavy for one set to be Max's, but we still stop to listen.

Someone bellows "Sandy!" and we both look at each other.

"Nah," Dalton says. "I appreciate them helping us with baby names, but Sandy doesn't do it for me."

I roll my eyes. "Wanna bet Sandy is the name of the dead guy we found last night?"

"Nope. Because that is a bet I'd lose."

"Time to get ourselves in on this missing-miner investigation?" I say.

In answer, Dalton shouts, "Hello!" He waits a moment and then repeats it, adding, "It's your neighbors. We were just coming to leave a message for your boss."

It takes a few minutes to get a response, and I can imagine the men conferring. Then one shouts back to meet at the message spot. That's close enough that it worked for Dalton's excuse, and we head there.

We arrive first. Soon after, two men appear on the path. They're part of the mining company's security team. I don't know how many there are. That would require being able to tell them apart. These are two guys in their late twenties, both white with brown hair clipped short, both dressed in khakis and carrying rifles, which they have trained on us.

"You see us holding guns on you?" Dalton calls. "Lower them."

The men glance at each other.

Dalton continues, "Out here, approaching with your weapon drawn is acceptable caution. But once you see that the other party isn't armed, you lower yours. Or else you're telling us it's okay to take out our weapons. That what you want?"

"There is a hostile individual in the forest," one of them says. "We've been told to be armed and ready at all times."

"Fine."

Dalton reaches for his gun. I train mine on the closer guy's forehead.

"Head shot?" Dalton says. "Now you're just showing off." He aims his gun at the other man's chest. "I'm not as good.

I'll have to go for biggest body mass. Okay, we're all set. Let's talk."

The men exchange another look. Then one lowers his rifle muzzle. When the other does the same, we drop our handguns to our sides.

"Whew," Dalton says. "That was gearing up to be a very awkward conversation. And we hadn't even gotten the dog involved yet."

As if on cue, Storm growls.

"Stand down, pup," Dalton says. "We have reached an understanding. Now, we heard you boys shouting out there. You seem to be looking for someone."

When they glance at each other, Dalton sighs and turns to me, waving toward them. "See? This is the problem when no one is in charge. You just keep gaping at each other, waiting for the other person to make a decision."

"Nah," I say. "That's just them. With us, if no one's in charge, we're *both* making decisions. That's why I'm the boss."

Dalton snorts and shakes his head. Then he turns back to the two. "I don't actually care whether you have a man missing. I thought you might want our help—and our dog's nose— but that's your own business. We were coming to say that we have a boy missing. We think he just wandered off—you know kids—but with that yahoo in a bearskin wandering around, we are concerned. We need to speak to Mr. Rogers and obtain permission to search on your side of the boundary. If you are also missing someone, we would grant the same permission. But that means we're both missing someone, which is a little concerning."

"Mr. Rogers?" one says.

"Our friendly neighbor. He hasn't given a name so we assigned him one."

The one man's lips twitch. The other says, "We're supposed to post something at the message spot if we don't find our man today, but since you're here, I guess there's no sense denying it."

"Good call. So you *are* missing someone?"

"Affirmative."

Now I'm struggling not to exchange a look—or an eye roll—with Dalton. I've decided to stand back and let him handle this, and I continue to do so.

"What can you tell us?" Dalton says.

"He's an employee. One of the miners. He went for a walk the night before last and never came back."

"You let your employees wander around the forest?" Dalton says.

One of the men shrugs. "They know the risks."

"Even when you've already encountered a threat in these woods?"

"How he went missing isn't important," the other man says. "He left of his own volition. We're certain of that. He told his roommates that he was going out for a walk, and he never returned. They didn't realize it until morning. We've been searching for him since then."

"Can you give us any details?" Dalton asks. "Physical description? Clothing?"

"He's the only one of our men missing, so if you find one, that's him."

Dalton chews on that, and now I do cut in, before he gets annoyed.

"What about weapons?" I say. "What can we expect? We don't want to track him down only to find ourselves at the end of a gun."

"Our employees are not permitted guns of any variety. They are issued a pocketknife and a multi-tool."

Well, that confirms who we found.

"All right," Dalton says. "Do we have your permission to look for our missing boy on your side of the boundary? And we can look for your man at the same time?"

"We can't authorize that."

"Unacceptable."

The man blinks, as if thinking he's misheard Dalton.

Dalton crosses his arms. "Yeah, I asked for permission, but it was a formality. We have a missing boy. We will be searching for him over here. Now, in the interests of privacy, you can tell us where we're allowed to begin searching—north or south— and we will restrict ourselves to that section until we've had a chance to speak to your boss. We should also get a scent marker from your missing man—a piece of used clothing for our dog. While we wait for that, though, we're going to start searching. If one of you two wants to remain with us, that's fine."

Dalton's tone might be belligerent, but his suggestion is reasonable. The men decide that one of them will indeed stay with us and the other will return to fetch their boss and a scent marker.

Once one has left, the other wordlessly leads us north.

"Guess this is the direction we're going," Dalton says.

"Seems like it," I murmur, and we follow.

The direction we're allowed to search is the direction we want to search—the general area where we found the man who is presumably "Sandy." We don't get our guard's name, even when we ask. We don't get anything. He leads us north and then moves behind us, and if we feel a bit like we're being marched off at gunpoint, well, at least there's no actual gun pointed at our backs. They got the memo on that one.

"Have you found anything while you've been out here?" Dalton asks.

"Negative."

"What areas have you searched?"

No response.

"I'm presuming if you're leading us this way, you haven't looked here yet?"

"Affirmative."

"You actually former military?" Dalton says. "I'm asking, because I've got a buddy who served, and he doesn't talk like that. Seems like an affectation, if you ask me."

Silence, and I have a strong feeling the guy is trying to figure out what "affectation" means and whether it's an insult. Dalton's casual tone suggests it's not, so he decides not to answer.

Dalton stops and looks up and down the path. "You know your guy didn't come this way, right?"

Silence.

"Do you see what I do?"

Nothing.

Dalton sighs and glances at me. "How about you?"

"The path back here is open, meaning someone could have passed this way. But up ahead, it's overgrown. Anyone passing through would have left a trail we'd see."

"Gold star." He turns to the security guy, whom I'll now call Joe, for G.I. Joe. "You're better acquainted with this part of the forest. Is there a path in this region your guy would be more likely to take? One that's less overgrown?"

Joe points.

"Lead on," Dalton says.

Joe takes us back the way he and his partner had come. He's heading west when Dalton slows and squints off to the side. "What about that one?"

Joe looks at the trail to our right and shrugs. Doesn't say anything, just shrugs, but he stops walking, which we presume means he's fine following that one . . . which happens to head in the direction of the body.

We continue down that trail. Dalton plays it up more than I would have—starting down a "wrong" trail only to declare it unlikely and circle back. He really doesn't want them to know we'd already found the body. He doesn't even want them later wondering whether we'd stumbled on it a little too easily. I'm not sure that much subterfuge is required, but I'll trust him. He pulls off the performance better than I would have, and he's so good at it that Joe relaxes and even starts offering suggestions.

What's that over there? A footprint?

Hoofprint, probably moose, see the hoof points?

Is that another trail?

Game trail, from animals, but we should make a note of it for later, in case your guy went that way.

When we near the spot, it's Joe who suggests splitting off onto the proper fork, saying, "That one looks good."

We get about fifty feet along it when Storm sniffs the air. Dalton makes a show of that, too.

"What is it, girl?" he says. "Do you smell something?"

I put my hand over my nose and mouth. "You don't?"

I can't smell a thing—the breeze comes from the wrong direction—but Joe snaps to attention and inhales deeply.

"Smell what?" he says.

"Some predator's eyes were bigger than its stomach," Dalton says. "It cached its leftovers nearby."

"You think it could be Sa—our guy?"

"What?" Dalton frowns over at him. "Oh. Nah. Didn't mean to spook you. It's just some dead critter bits. Maybe a moose haunch." He peers into the forest as we walk. "Should probably check it out, though."

"You can do the honors," I say. "I've stumbled over enough carcasses out here." I look at Joe. "The last one was a dead caribou that started moving. Turned out to have a weasel inside of it."

"Stay here with the pup," Dalton says. Then to Joe: "Is your stomach up to this?"

Joe straightens. "Yes, sir."

The two men head for the spot where we know Sandy lies dead. I count to five. Right on cue, Dalton says, "*Fuck.*"

"Holy shit," Joe says. "What the hell happened to him?"

"Guys?" I make my own show of frantically fighting through the undergrowth to get to them. "What's wrong? What did you—?"

I clap my hand to my mouth as I see the body. "Oh!"

"That your guy?" Dalton says. "Might be hard to identify, with him being facedown."

"No, it's our guy," Joe says.

"Well, then, I'm sorry to say we found him."

CHAPTER TWENTY-FOUR

We leave Sandy's body where it lies and go back to meet up with Mr. Rogers. We arrive at the meeting spot to find he's already there with the other security guy and a third one, a young Black man I believe I've seen before.

When we arrive, Joe takes Mr. Rogers aside to tell him what we found. Then Rogers returns and tells both of the other security guys to stay right there, awaiting further instructions.

Rogers looks from me to Dalton, and says, "Well, you two might as well come along."

We do that. There's no conversation on the way. Joe must have mentioned that we have a child missing, and yet Rogers says nothing about that. Not his concern. And now that we've found his missing man, I have to wonder whether we've made the wrong play here.

We wanted to lead him to the dead man so we could get answers, and also so we didn't need to worry about avoiding that area in our own search—which we aren't going to do when Sandy's murder is almost certainly connected to Max's disappearance.

But by finding Sandy, we've incinerated our excuse for searching off our own territory. We can't say we're also looking for their man. Therefore, if they grant us permission to hunt for Max there, it's a favor, and these are not people I want to owe a favor.

I won't worry about that now. Whether Rogers allows it or not, we'll search where we need to search. The only question is whether we ask permission.

Finally we reach the spot. We let Joe and Rogers go in first. There's no curse of shock or disgust or grief. No sound at all.

We follow and stay on the periphery, keeping Storm with us.

Rogers turns to us. "I will admit that I know nothing about life in a place like this. Can I presume I'm looking at signs of an animal attack? Something with claws? A bear or big cat?"

"May I come closer?" I ask.

He nods, and I leave Storm with Dalton as I approach. I bend beside the body and examine the wounds.

"They're clean cuts," I say. "That's not consistent with an animal attack." I glance at Dalton.

"Yeah, I don't even need to come closer," Dalton says. "No animal did that. Something's been eating him"—there are more signs of that today—"but those other wounds don't make any sense for a predator. They're going for your throat or your belly. Not carving up your back."

"Looks like a blade," I say.

"Hunting knife maybe?" Dalton says.

I shake my head. "Too small for that."

"What about his own knife?" Dalton looks at Rogers. "We were told he had a pocketknife."

"Possibly?" I say. "The wounds seem a little large for a pocketknife. The weapon isn't large, but it's not small either."

"The guy who attacked him had a knife," Joe offers. "That's what he said."

I hesitate, parsing that. Clearly whoever attacked Sandy here had a knife. But that can't be what Joe means.

"Wait," Dalton says. "This is the guy who saw the fellow in the bearskin?"

Rogers turns a very cold look on Joe, one that promises disciplinary action for that slip. Then Rogers hesitates. I catch the look he sneaks our way, assessing and deciding, and I pretend not to see it, solemnly intent on the wounds of the dead man before us.

"Yes," Rogers says finally. "This is the employee who had a run-in with our local shaman. That isn't a coincidence. After his encounter, we asked our men to stay inside the settlement limits unless going out to work. However, we did not enforce it. They are adults capable of making their own decisions, and I believe in allowing people to do that. Free will and self-determination."

I say nothing. I also believe in free will and self-determination, while placing public safety above that. If this man—Sandy—chose to enter the forest after seeing what was out there, that's his choice, right? If a resident of Haven's Rock chooses to go into the forest after being warned, that's their choice, right?

Seems logical. But how many times has someone broken our rules only to find themselves in danger and, on being rescued, blamed us for not being clear enough? And if we *couldn't* have been clearer? Then why the hell were we—the experts—trusting newcomers to judge their own safety in the wilderness?

We must also acknowledge that someone breaking our rules isn't only endangering themselves. People—including us—have been hurt finding them. They also run the risk of stirring up trouble—with predators or humans—that can follow them back to town.

Giving Rogers the benefit of the doubt, he's treating his employees like adults and doesn't have the experience to know that Sandy could have riled up someone in the forest who will now be a danger to everyone.

So I don't react to his little speech. I just wait for him to go on. When he doesn't, I say, in a neutral tone, "You'd advised the workers not to go out, given the circumstances, and this employee—the one who originally saw the bearskin-wearing man—didn't listen."

"He wanted another sighting," Joe says.

I frown. "Another sighting? Of a bearskin-wearing man with a knife?"

Rogers looks at Joe. "Explain."

Joe turns to me. "Sa—this employee—was being teased by some of the others. He took it as harassment, although when he made an official report, we decided it was just teasing. His coworkers didn't believe what he'd seen and joked about him wanting time off for 'trauma.' He was determined to prove them wrong. He'd been out a few times, including that night."

"When he didn't return."

"Yes, ma'am."

"What was he hoping to do? Take on the man himself?"

"I don't think so. Someone says he mentioned finding the guy's 'lair.' That's what he called it. The mountain man's lair. He wanted to find it and then lead us to it, so we could deal with the guy."

"Which would prove your employee had seen what he claimed to have seen."

"Yes, ma'am." He looks down at Sandy's body. "I guess he found the guy after all."

"We don't know that for sure."

Joe looks at me, brow furrowing. "Don't we? He went looking for some crazy forest man who'd already attacked him with a knife. Now he's been stabbed dozens of times with a knife, in the forest."

Rogers lifts his hands. "Our neighbor is being cautious, in the event this isn't what it seems. Now my employee here says you have a young man who went missing . . ."

Young man? I think back and realize when we said "boy" or "kid," Joe must have presumed "teenager." Do I correct Rogers? No, this is better. I should have been more careful not to say anything to suggest our town has children.

"He's our top priority, obviously," I say. "Even above finding this man's killer."

"Understood. You have my full cooperation with whatever you need. And, yes, hunting for your young man is *also* hunting for my employee's killer, so it is not entirely an altruistic offer. But it is genuine." He meets my gaze. "I know we have taken an adversarial position, but I think you also realize that is to protect my employer's mineral interests. I'm here to run our camp *and* to protect the find."

"Understood," I say.

"Good. Then you'll also understand that 'full cooperation' will still have some restrictions."

Dalton says, "Got a different definition of 'full,' huh?"

Rogers ignores him. "Your skills for searching out here surpass my men's, which is why I'd asked you to look for this mountain man."

He pauses, just long enough for us to know that he considers his man's death at least partly our fault. I could point out that Sandy died on his territory. I don't bother. This *isn't* our fault. Rogers might say we're more skilled in this, but he still pawned the search off on us, without offering any help.

When I don't respond, he looks slightly disappointed. Then he continues, "But you will now have the complete use of all my men who would otherwise be assigned to watch over our miners. Our operations will cease while you find this killer."

"And the restriction you mentioned?" I say.

"Territorial, of course. My employers will not allow me to grant you full access to our settlement or employees. I can speak to them, given the tragedy that has occurred, but I can say, with some certainty, that they will not be moved. Their interests come first."

That sounds familiar. It might even rouse a pinprick of sympathy for Rogers. He's not the guy in charge. He's just the mouthpiece. Like Phil was before being exiled to Rockton.

If that's the case, I suspect Rogers will soon understand the full weight of his situation. It's the same one we had in Rockton, where we were on the ground dealing with threats while policy and procedure was dictated by people sitting in their comfy homes down south.

It's easy to put profit first when you don't need to see the dead body of your employee lying at your feet, stabbed thirty-three times and left for the scavengers to feast on.

"All right," I say. "So lay it out for me. Where can't we search."

"We'll set up a perimeter, which we will search ourselves, though I can't imagine this man would be lurking a few hundred feet from our camp."

"And the body?" I say, nodding at it. "I presume you have a doctor who will perform an autopsy?"

"He'll be shipped out for that."

Which means he's not telling us whether they have medical care. Just as we weren't keen to tell him that we do. It's one of the few things that could upset this delicate standoff. If they don't have a doctor and we do, it'll be a reason for them to come knocking on our door.

"Good," I say. "Then I leave that to you. Our priority is getting our missing boy back."

"I hope this didn't happen to him, too," Joe says, staring at Sandy's body. He catches everyone's looks and flushes, just a little. "Sorry. Didn't mean to bring that up."

"But it's obviously a concern, which heightens the urgency," Rogers says. "Now, let us discuss how this will work."

We let Rogers tell us how this will work. Then we tell him how it's actually going to work.

We'll accept his offer of extra men, and we'll assign them areas to search. They will stay on their side of the boundary. Our searchers will stay on our side . . . except for us. Dalton and I are free to go anywhere the trail takes us. Also, Rogers's men must stay where we put them—in their assigned search grid. We're not taking the chance that one of them will mistake us for their wild man.

On that note, we want only his steadiest men out there. Absolutely no one who will get spooked and fire at our missing resident. Everyone who is searching must be willing to do it with their weapons holstered.

We then tell Rogers where we want his men searching . . . which is not here. We don't want them finding that cabin or evidence of Max. We would allow it if we thought it could help, but the only thing they have to offer is extra eyes and feet. We'll take that. We just don't want them actually working alongside us. It would restrict what we can do and say and leave us open to slips, like the ones Joe has made.

We tell Rogers that we're going to let Storm track from the murder scene, in hopes of tracking the killer. For that reason, we need them to remove their deceased employee as quickly as possible and stay out of this area, to avoid leaving more scent trails.

Rogers leaves after that, and we do what we didn't have time to do last night—see whether Storm can pick up the killer's trail. She can't. Oh, she tries, but it isn't long before she gets hopelessly confused, when the trails seem to all head back to Sandy's body, as if the killer had paced around there, figuring out what to do next. The fact that animals have also been feeding complicates the scents, as does the nearly overpowering stink of decomposition.

When that fails, we take Storm to the ruined shack again. She picks up the trail easily, just as she did last night. She follows it . . . and she loses it at the creek. We spend more time trying to figure out where Max and his captor might have exited the creek but, again, we can't.

We need to get back to Haven's Rock. Anders knows not to worry if we're gone overnight, but there's a limit to how long before residents get nervous. Right now, we can't give them any more reason to be on edge.

I hate to leave Max's trail. I even try to come up with excuses for staying longer. I know we've reached the end of what we can do, but I absolutely dread going back to Dana and telling her we found Max's trail and walked away.

Fear of telling Dana makes a good excuse, but the truth is that *I* don't want to leave. We finally have tangible evidence that Max is alive, and it feels as if walking away is giving up.

That's not me being too hard on myself. I think of what I'd

feel if someone else came back to town, said they found Max's trail and left. Oh, I'd tell them they did the right thing, but deep down there'd be whispers.

Did they give up too easily?

What if they kept trying a little longer?

What if they tried a little harder?

It's as if we spotted him in the distance, spent a few minutes trying to find him again, and then gave up. Dalton feels the same. That's why I can't argue. Because if one of us wants to keep going, the other will agree, unwilling to accept the guilt of being the one who quit. This burden must be shared.

"We'll bring others and search," Dalton says as we walk. "Not rely on Storm's nose, but just search."

"Should we have let Mr. Rogers's men help us? If we need more eyes on the ground . . ."

"Not yet. Yeah, I know he's just doing his job, and breaking our balls is part of it. Hell, I'm doing the same thing. I didn't tell him we have someone who can perform an autopsy. I sure as hell won't let him near town searching for whoever killed his miner. If being an asshole protects Haven's Rock, then I will be an asshole. I have lots of experience. So I don't blame him for treating us like employees, but I don't have to like it either. Mostly, in this case, I don't trust his men. They're gun-happy. We might say they need to keep their weapons holstered, but I don't trust they will."

"Good point. Yes, their help comes with a risk." I glance at him. "How many security guys do you think they have? I'm having trouble telling them apart."

"Having trouble distinguishing between white guys with crew cuts?" He runs a hand through his own short hair.

"Fit white guys with crew cuts and steely gazes. It's a type." I squint at him. "Wait. Remind me who you are again?"

He knows I'm joking. Well, half joking. I could never mistake Dalton for one of Rogers's guys. Everything about them screams "Just following orders, ma'am," and that is *not* my husband.

"Yeah, I can't tell them apart either," he says. "There seems to be one Black guy, and one Latinx. Otherwise?" He shrugs. "I know there are at least two white guys, and only because we've seen them together. I've seen an older white guy, too. Those two were both younger than us. No women, though."

I nod. "Rogers said there aren't any women, which would include the guards presumably."

"So at least five security guards. Unless they're flown in on rotations. In which case, it could be as few as three in camp at a time—we've seen three today."

"Three would be reasonable. Even at our reduced size in Haven's Rock right now, we have you, me, and Will, plus Kenny part-time."

He glances over as we walk. "You're concerned."

"Hmm?"

"That wasn't an idle question. At first, I thought you were wondering how many men they could spare to help. That's not it. You're wondering whether the number of full-time security guards is a cause for concern."

"Is it cause for concern? That is the question."

He nods. "Yep. That is the question."

CHAPTER TWENTY-FIVE

By the time we make it to Haven's Rock, I'm ready to drop. Down south, I considered myself in good shape. I needed to be. If I'm chasing down a suspect, he'd take one look at a small female cop and decide fighting was his best option. That's actually to my advantage, given that my bad leg means he really *could* outrun me.

So I kept up my aikido skills and my strength conditioning, along with some cardio, even if it's my least favorite section of the gym. But then I came here and realized what I was missing. Endurance. The ability to effortlessly hike for half a day to get from point A to point B, in the same way I'd drive across the city as a detective. Oh, we have an ATV and my dirt bike, but I need to be able to walk for hours, including up mountainsides, while carrying a backpack loaded with gear.

Normally, I can do exactly that. But the morning sickness has me running on low fuel all day. I'm going to give the medical profession the benefit of the doubt here and presume they called it morning sickness because it's worst in the morning. The name, however, implies that once the clock strikes noon,

I'll feel fine. I don't feel fine. I just feel well enough to get a little bit of food down and keep it there.

Part of me is panicking at that. I'm eating for two! What if I'm starving my baby? Yeah, my "baby" could subsist on a bite of food right now. Me, on the other hand? I am not taking in enough nutrition to spend all day walking.

"Go inside," Dalton says when we reach our house. "I'll handle the updates."

"No, I can—"

"You don't trust me to update everyone?"

I scowl at him.

"Yeah, low blow," he says. "Go inside. Rest with Storm, who also needs it. Tell me what you want to eat—anything you think you can keep down—and I'll have someone bring it by for you."

"I'm fi—"

"And don't say you're fine, Butler. You're barely upright. I know you just don't want to be a burden. You want to soldier through and do your job. But here's the thing . . ." He glances my way. "When you insist on downplaying a health problem, you don't make things easier on others. We either need to trick you into accepting help or muddle through with you working at half capacity. That doesn't help you or us. And yeah, that's another low blow. But also? Truth."

He's right, of course. Better to rest and eat and come back at full capacity—or as near to it as I can manage.

I don't say that, because I'm tired and feeling like shit so, yep, I'm going to be a little pissy. I'll make it up to him later. For now, I grumpily wave for him to go and stalk toward the house.

"Love you!" he calls after me.

"Whatever," I call back, though I turn so he can see I'm smiling.

"You gonna give me a food order? Or do I have to tell them

to make a little of everything and deliver it plate by plate, like a royal banquet?"

That actually sounds tempting, but I shake my head. "If they have any plain cookies or muffins, I'll take those, plus some veggies. And if Isabel has lemonade, that'd be good."

"Done. I'll be back in an hour."

He picks up his pace as he heads to town, and I try not to grumble about that, too. *Someone* isn't feeling any worse for wear after a full day of hiking. Because someone's health hasn't suddenly been taken hostage, despite the fact that he contributed fifty percent of the DNA to the hostage taker.

Grumble, grumble. At least it's a relatively good-natured grumbling. I'm home, and as much as I didn't want to be here while Max is still missing, I can't suppress a shudder of relief on opening that door.

With yesterday morning's turmoil, we hadn't tidied up before we left, and my gaze goes straight to the coffee mugs on the hearth and the plate of half-eaten toast by the sofa. If I start tidying, though, I won't stop, and then I'll pull out my notebook and phone and start reviewing my notes from the examination of Sandy's body and . . .

Nope. My college dorm had looked ten times worse than this, mostly because I'd been rebelling against my parents' and April's obsessive tidiness even if the mess had driven me wild. Yes, for a supposedly rational person, I am apparently prone to acts of self-sabotage in the name of spite. Particularly pointless when my family had never visited my dorm to see the mess.

I collapse onto the sofa. With an equal groan of equal relief, Storm thumps onto her doggie bed. We both stare into nothing for five minutes. Then Storm is snoring . . . and I am still staring, my brain whispering that there would be nothing wrong with listening to my recorded notes from the crime scene.

Think of it as a bedtime story.

About a guy who was stabbed thirty-three times.

I'll want to talk to April about the wound pattern, but mostly what I need to do is my own crime-scene tech work. Revisit my notes on the weapon Sandy saw and compare it more precisely to the wounds I found.

Was Miner Sandy attacked by the bear-man? That is indeed the most likely explanation. Sandy had—in his witness report from earlier—described the knife the bear-man brandished, which seems to match the size of the wounds. I can picture the bear-man holding Max hostage in that shack when Sandy came rambling through the forest.

Did Sandy hear voices? They carry so far in the woods that I suspect that was the precipitating event. The bear-man leaves Max, presumably bound. He sneaks up on Sandy, who hears something in the woods and moves off the path, where he's attacked from the rear. The bear-man takes him down and then goes wild, stabbing until he's absolutely certain the threat is eliminated.

After that, the bear-man realized he needed to move Max. With Sandy dead, he had time to do a thorough job of clearing the shack, leaving only moth-eaten blankets. However, being agitated, he didn't think to hide his trail until they reached the creek.

Why would the bear-man take Max in the first place? I'm hoping that, in the man's deluded mind, he's looking for a son. Companionship in the wilderness plus a child to teach and raise in his ways. That drive is strong. I've seen it in otherwise rational people. Hell, I saw a version of it in my own parents. April and I were their legacy. We were supposed to follow in their footsteps and continue their work in the world. When I did not, I had failed them.

The drive for men to have sons is even more culturally ingrained. Is it possible that our bear-man spotted Max and envisioned a son? At ten, Max is the perfect age for that. He's independent enough to take care of himself and start learning the basics of wilderness survival, while not old enough—or big enough—to be a serious threat. It's roughly the same age Dalton had been when he was taken from the forest in a reverse of this scenario, Dalton being snatched from settlers and brought into a town as the son for a grieving couple.

If that's the answer, then Max is relatively safe for the time being. He's smart enough to see what's happening and do whatever it takes to relax his captor's guard. It also gives us time to find him. He will be traumatized, but not to the extent he would be if this is the scenario I fear most, the one where he has been taken by a sexual predator.

I'm trying not to think of that.

I should read through Sandy's interview notes from Mr. Rogers again, in light of his death.

I push to my feet . . . and there's a sound on the back porch.

I go still. Our cabin faces the town, leaving our back deck with nothing but a forest view. That means no one coming to our house is going to knock on the back door.

I listen, but everything has gone silent.

Did I really hear something?

I glance at Storm, who is so deeply asleep that I suspect we could be invaded by a family of grizzlies and she'd never notice.

Did we leave food on the porch? We're extremely careful about that. Food attracts pests, and around here, those pests can be a whole lot bigger than mice.

I pick up my gun from the table and head toward the kitchen. I suspect I was hearing things, but I'll still check it out. I round the corner just in time to spot a gray tail out the window.

A wolf?

That has me stopping short. I'm not generally worried about wolves, but if the shy predators start coming onto our porch and peering in, that would be a concern. The tail has disappeared, and I'm easing around the corner when Storm brushes my side, making me jump. I reach to give her a pat, but she just walks past me to the back door and looks over her shoulder expectantly.

When I don't move, she nudges the door handle.

Open this, please. I wish to go outside.

Okay. As much as Storm respects wolves, she's not going to be quite so blasé about one on her territory . . . unless it's a very specific instance of the species.

"Nero?" I say to Storm.

From outside comes an answering woof.

My gaze swings toward the window. Wolves don't woof. That sound came from a human.

I peek out. A face appears so suddenly that I know I'm supposed to jump back in terror. Instead, I only shake my head, as relief courses through me.

I yank open the door. "Lilith."

"That was underwhelming," she says. "At the very least, you should have pulled your gun on me for popping up like that."

"More like pulled my gun on you for skulking around like that."

"Skulking? I was patiently awaiting your return."

As I've said, Lilith looks very normal, if one ignores her beautifully handcrafted buckskins. She doesn't go so far as to craft her own boots—those are expensive hiking boots, a pair I haven't seen before. She's white, maybe in her late thirties, dark blond hair perfectly brushed to a sheen, and she wears stylish glasses.

Lilith might not look like a wolf-taming witch, but I'm still not convinced she isn't one. Part witch, at least, and part nature photographer, a very successful one, given her taste in expensive accessories.

"We went by your cabin twice," I say. "Only Nero was home. We left a note. We were concerned."

"I didn't see the note. Sorry to worry you. I suppose, now that I have acquaintances in this vast forest, I shall need to start posting messages when I leave. I'm gone for a few days every other month. Even a reclusive eccentric needs to answer her email every now and then. That's when I get my supplies, as well. I don't take Nero. I would love to, but people ask questions and occasionally call the authorities who, despite my charm, do not always accept my story that he's mostly husky."

"So Nero was guarding your cabin. That's a relief, considering we have a bearskin-wearing potential psychopath on the loose."

"A what?"

"Come in?" I say, motioning. When she hesitates, I say, "I can come out, but I'm supposed to be resting. We've been out for two days straight, and I'm not feeling well."

She hesitates again. "Is it contagious?"

"Definitely not. Will you come in? It's just me. Well, and Storm."

"Oh, I'm not concerned that you'll lock me inside and turn me into unpaid domestic labor. You'd see the error of your ways after a meal or two. I just don't like leaving Nero where he could spook a passerby." She turns. "Nero? Will you come in?"

He looks from her to the door as she gestures at it. Storm looks out around me, and I swear Nero nods before he heads inside.

"Good," she says. "Because if he doesn't want to go somewhere, he's not going. I suspect you have the same problem with that fur mountain."

"I do."

I usher them both in. "Can I get you something?"

"I'll take a beer if you have it, and I'll pretend that's just to save you from making a hot drink when you're unwell."

"Good excuse." I fetch a beer from the underfloor icebox and take a box of cookies from the counter. I hand her both.

"I do like your hospitality," she says. "And I'm also going to pretend I thought you meant for me to take the whole box, and since you're such a polite human, you'll hate to correct me."

"Fair enough."

We head into the living room and settle in.

"Now, back to the bearskin-wearing psychopath?" she prompts.

"That's why we were at your cabin. One of our residents spotted what he thought looked like a part-bear and part-human creature. We presumed it was a bear and went looking, concerned that it would approach a hiking party. Then Mr. Rogers—"

"Who?" she cuts in.

"Our not-so-friendly mutual neighbor."

"The miners I am studiously avoiding."

"Yes. One of their men seems to have seen the same creature. Except he got a close-up view and reported it was a wild-looking mountain man wearing a bearskin."

"Okay . . ."

"We were letting you know. Of course, on seeing you weren't there, we did get a little concerned."

Her lips twitch. "Thought I might have been snatched away as a mountain bride?"

"Somehow, I think anyone who did that would realize the error of his ways even *before* you cooked him a meal. But we had to consider the possibility you'd been hurt."

"I hope you didn't spend too much time looking for me." She catches my expression. "Or should I hope you spent at least *some* time looking for me?"

"We were searching for someone else, so you were just kinda lumped in with that."

"*Lumped in.* You do know how to make a girl feel all warm and fuzzy. So you do have someone missing then? That's what I'm here about."

My heart jumps. "You saw someone?"

"No, but I think Nero did. He was outside last night, and I heard him growl. I went out just as something—presumably an animal—ran off. I didn't think anything more of it until this morning, when I found signs of a person in the woods. Has another woman of yours gone missing? You do seem to lose a lot of them."

My heart speeds up. "A woman?"

"That's my guess. I found a couple of partial footprints, and they were small."

"Small enough to belong to a ten-year-old boy?"

"Boy?" Her head jerks up, eyes widening. "Oh, hell."

CHAPTER TWENTY-SIX

Lilith is full of apologies after that, losing her usual cool. Yes, she'd headed straight to Haven's Rock on seeing the footprints, but if she'd known it was a child, she'd have moved faster and she wouldn't have just waited outside our house for someone to show up.

She describes the partial prints with an artist's eye for detail, and they are undoubtedly Max's.

He was alive last night. I need to take comfort in that. He'd been alive, and he seems to have stumbled on Lilith's cabin before Nero frightened him off.

I can wish it'd gone another way. Wish Nero had been inside. Wish Lilith had seen Max and called him back. Wish Max had realized the wolf wasn't a threat and stayed until Lilith came out.

That's not what happened.

What did happen? That's what I'm working through even as I'm running into town for Dalton. Had the bear-man been leading Max through the forest when they both stumbled on the cabin?

That seems the obvious answer, and yet . . .

And yet there is another possibility my mind keeps pulling back, a little too eager to seize it.

What if Max escaped?

What if we'd misread the trail? We know Max was on foot when he fled the shack. We found his prints and his captor's. We presumed his captor killed Sandy, grabbed Max, and ran with no time to think about the trail they left.

What if it wasn't Max's captor running with him, choosing the creek to obscure their trail?

What if it was Max running with his captor in pursuit? Max wading into the water because he knew that was a way to hide his trail?

The bear-man hears Sandy. He hurries out before Sandy finds Max. But in his haste, he doesn't secure Max. While the bear-man is killing Sandy, Max escapes.

Max loses the bear-man with his creek trick. Then he stumbles on Lilith's cabin. But before she can come out, Nero spooks him and he runs.

If Max is alone out there, he is obviously still in trouble. We need to get to him before his captor does.

We're leaving Haven's Rock again, this time with Anders joining us. He's met Lilith, and normally they'd be lagging behind, talking, but no one is in the mood for socializing. We want to get to Lilith's cabin as fast as we can. We consider taking the motorized vehicles, but the noise could tip off Max's captor. Even if he no longer has Max, we don't want to tell him where we're looking.

Once we reach the cabin, Dalton orders everyone to stand

back. It's a testament to how rattled Lilith is that she doesn't argue, given it's *her* home. We understand he wants a scene that's as clean as it can be. Even Storm must stay with me while Dalton takes the first shot at deciphering the trail.

We watch as he examines the spot where Lilith heard someone running into the forest. Then we all wait while he works. I'm the least patient, pushing down the proprietary sense that this is my scene. It's not, of course. No crime was committed here, and Dalton's right that it must remain as pristine as possible while he tracks. Yet when he shouts for me, I'm off like a shot.

I circle wide around the area and find him in the forest. He lifts a hand for me to approach with caution. When I do, I see him pointing at something that has my heart sinking.

Broad leaves near the ground are splattered with dried splotches that reflect red in the sunlight.

I bend and scrape one with my fingernail. What flakes off is definitely the color of blood.

Did Max hurt himself, running to escape what he thought was a wild wolf?

Before I can consider that, Dalton points to a mess of footprints. Signs of a scuffle.

These are the first clear prints we've found. The rest have all been partial impressions—the curve of a toe or a heel that left us approximating size with no idea of the tread. These are clear enough for me to piece together entire footprints.

Two people were involved in the scuffle. One is Max. We can tell that not only by the size, but by what we can see of the tread. The other is a heavy boot slightly larger than Dalton's, with a tread that doesn't match our standard town footwear.

If Max had escaped, his captor caught up and grabbed him here. There's a flurry of wild marks in the dirt, as if the captor hoisted Max up while the boy fought, his boots scuffing the ground.

And then?

And then there was blood.

I can make out where Max's captor would have been standing when he held Max, and the blood radiates out from that spot, on the right-hand side.

"Here," Dalton says.

His voice startles me, and irritation flashes. I'd been deep in my thoughts, reconstructing the drama, and he's pulled me out of that. Then I see what he's gesturing toward—more marks in the dirt.

I gingerly walk around the marks and then crouch again. It's shaded here, and I need my flashlight to illuminate the spot. When I do, I spot clumps of dried mud. I pick up one and rub it between my thumb and forefinger. The tips come back red.

Blood flowed here. Flowed heavily into the dirt. My heart picks up speed. Max, injured and thrown to the ground, with marks in the dirt when he'd sat, bleeding. Part of a boot print and—

I stop and move my light over. There, in the dirt, is a partial handprint.

It is not a child-sized handprint.

"Can I get your light?" I say.

Dalton nods and wordlessly shines his flashlight along with mine. The pieces of the scene come together.

Someone falling, the force of that fall leaving a handprint in the ground. A man-sized handprint.

Max's captor falling, catching himself on that hand and then lowering himself to the ground.

And bleeding.

Max's captor was injured, and fell and bled here while tending to the wound.

I shine my light around and catch a footprint just beyond the area. Max's captor is back on his feet. One full print, and one toe print, and then a less clear repeat of the pattern.

Max's captor's leg is injured. He's limping on one full foot and one boot toe, while Max is running.

"It looks like . . ." I swallow, almost afraid to finish that sentence. "It looks like Max got away."

"Yeah."

I exhale in relief. Dalton agrees. Good.

Dalton continues, "I found three prints of Max's coming this way, including the one Lilith saw. No others. Scuffle over there, as if he was grabbed. But he has his knife. He stabs the guy, who goes down while Max runs."

"Remind me why you have a detective again?"

He walks over and kisses the top of my head. "Because she's super hot, and it is in my best interests to pretend I need her expertise. Yeah, I found the blood and the scuffle, but until you found that handprint, I thought Max was the one hurt. I didn't catch the significance of that pattern"—he points at the prints where the bear-man gave chase—"until I realized Max's captor is the one who was hurt. Stabbed in the leg. Limping. Good."

"The attacker gave chase but couldn't move very fast. Max could outrun him." I take a deep breath. "I hope he outran him."

We don't say why I hope that. We both know. The obvious answer is that if Max outran his captor, Max is still free. But the underlying one is a bigger concern. Max hurt him. If his captor catches up, he will retaliate.

I squint up at Dalton, the sun in my eyes. "Can you do me a favor?"

"Take Storm and follow Max's trail while you gather what you need from the scene?"

"Yes, but also take Will. I'll stay with Lilith."

He shakes his head. "Will stays with you. I have Storm. When you're done, Will can whistle and we'll meet up."

Anders and I process the scene as thoroughly as we can while I tell myself that Dalton and Storm have the tracking under control, and if they do encounter Max's captor, he will be no match for a .357 Magnum and a Newfoundland. That is true, and so I must get this done because when I look up, the sky whispers "rain."

What really messes with my focus, though, isn't Dalton's safety. I know he's fine. It's not even that I desperately want to be out there, searching for Max. It's that I want to be searching for Max . . . and I don't know if there's any point to what I'm doing instead.

I can tell myself that Max's pursuer might not be the bear-man, but it doesn't take long before I find the brown grizzly hairs that say otherwise. This scene isn't going to tell me who the bear-man is, and ultimately what matters is what he has done, and I cannot take this evidence to trial for that.

Yet we do have a murder—Sandy's—and this is the presumed killer. While I don't think Mr. Rogers is going to insist on a trial either, I need to compile the evidence. It is not my place to decide whether it's useful.

Lilith returns to her house with Nero while Anders and I process the scene. We take photos and measurements and even samples, bagging bearskin hairs and blood-speckled leaves and bloodied clumps of dirt. Only once I have everything does Anders whistle for Dalton.

I don't expect a response. It's been nearly an hour since Dalton left. Normally, we'd use flares or even the sat phones, but Dalton has one sat phone and the other is in town with Phil.

If Dalton doesn't answer, we must stay where we are. We don't have Storm. We cannot go tramping into the forest in the vain hope of locating Dalton and, more likely, giving him two more lost people to find.

It's Anders's second whistle that gets answered with a sharp birdcall we both recognize as Dalton's. He'd followed the trail east, but the whistle is from the northwest, meaning Max circled that way.

We set out in that direction, periodically exchanging calls in a game of forest Marco Polo. Dalton won't have stopped to wait. It's up to us to catch up.

He continues heading west. We can't tell how far ahead he is. We're sticking to trails where we can, but they're so overgrown that we wander off them without even noticing. I'm about to question the wisdom of this plan when we hit an actual trail, one clear enough that I glance over at Anders.

"We've crossed into Mr. Rogers' neighborhood." I point at saplings cut low to the ground, where they've cleared a path.

"Is that a problem?" he asks.

"As long as we don't head south, we have permission to be here. And even if we need to go south, I'm not stopping to ask permission. Also, whatever I might think of our neighbors, if Max stumbles over their camp, I trust they'll give him back."

"Yeah. They're corporate assholes whose concern is someone stealing their claim. That's not an issue with a ten-year-old kid."

I walk a few more steps, thinking before I say, "I *am* bothered about how much security they have."

"How much *do* they have?"

"I don't know. They're mostly military types, and I'm not sure whether I'm seeing the same few over and over . . . or not. We know they have at least three at a time, and that makes sense, right? Given the nature of their operation?"

"Like everyone says, miners are a paranoid bunch. If I were in charge, I'd want each work detail to have at least one guard. Two or three for that, then, plus two back at camp, one on duty and one off duty, resting for the late shift."

Anders oversaw our militia in Rockton, and he'll do the same here, with Kenny taking charge in the field. Anders knows scheduling, and which situations need which amount of security.

"So five or even six total would be reasonable," I say. "Even if they only have a couple dozen miners."

He waves at the forest. "Their biggest concern would be keeping the workers safe from men, bears, and men dressed like bears. Now, they could put miners on guard duty, like us letting residents join the militia, but if they can afford full-time security personnel?" He shrugs. "I'd take it."

Good. That's what I wanted to hear—that the security-team size and level of expertise weren't suspicious. We know Rogers is an asshole, but it's best for everyone if he's just a very ordinary sort of asshole. The face of a corporation with deep pockets and valuable mining interests they want to protect.

Those in charge of other settlements around Rockton were paranoid and sometimes dangerous, but we could work with them. That's what we need. High fences yes, but behind them, nothing more sinister than a corporation that'll gut you if you steal their assets. Which is fine with us, having no intention of stealing anything.

I'm opening my mouth to say more when a yowl cuts me short. We both freeze, hands going to our guns.

My first thought is *animal*. Like the two lynx we heard yesterday, fighting for the right to scavenge Sandy's body. Yet there's a sharp note in this cry, part outrage and part pain, that is very human.

"Eric!" I call out, proving I am not myself. I'm pushing too hard, corralling all my meager energy into focusing on critical tasks like analyzing a crime scene, and when I hear a cry, my exhausted brain leaps to the conclusion I fear most—that Dalton is at risk out there alone—rather than actually processing what I'm hearing.

Even before Anders turns a quizzical look on me, I know that wasn't Dalton. It sounded nothing like him, beyond being the cry of a human male.

"It isn't Eric," I say. "I know. I'm just . . . tired."

"Eric said you haven't been feeling well."

I only nod. When it comes time to tell someone, Anders will be at the top of that list, but we just heard someone call out in pain—this is not the time to tell him I'm pregnant.

"That was an adult, right?" I say as we move in that direction, continuing along the path faster now, guns out.

"Definitely adult."

"Good. Let's hope it means Eric found the bastard who took Max."

CHAPTER TWENTY-SEVEN

We're moving at a slow jog. The cry seemed to come from down this path. It also sounded a whole lot closer than we'd last heard Dalton's birdcall.

We don't need to go far before we catch the sound of ragged breathing. It's just up around a curve in the path. We slow even more, treading lightly, and I motion Anders into the lead. He doesn't question. I'm acknowledging that I'm not at my best. I need someone more mentally alert in front.

I follow right behind Anders. As he steps around that corner, a blur of movement has him yelling, "Stop right there!"

It's Joe—the young security guard. He's on his feet, gun trained on Anders, his eyes wild. He blinks hard.

Joe sees me and the gun drops, his shoulders slumping as he exhales. "It's you."

Anders lowers his weapon but doesn't holster it. I do the same.

I move in front of Anders. "We heard a shout."

Joe nods as he claps a hand to the back of his thigh. "Bastard got the jump on me."

He turns, and where his hand had been, blood seeps through his trousers. "I didn't even have my damn gun out. I'd stopped to . . ." He waves to where a canteen lies on the path, water spilling from it.

"You stopped for a drink and someone attacked from behind."

"Not someone. That damned shaman guy. The one who killed Sa—" He stops himself and then says, "Fuck it. Sandy. You already heard me say his name. I don't know why the boss doesn't want you to know it. Paranoid bastard."

"The guy in a bearskin attacked you? You got a look at him?"

"Enough to see the damned bearskin. Oh, yeah. He caught me by surprise, but I spun around before he could do what he did to Sandy. He still got this one slash in." He presses his hand to the back of his thigh and gives an angry wince. "I lunged at him, but I stumbled and he ran off."

"Better let me take a look at that wound," I say.

I holster my gun then and walk over. Anders hasn't said a word. He just stands there, gun out, menacing in a way that anyone who knows him would see right through. Joe doesn't know him. All he sees is a big guy who looks like he'll break him in half if he makes a threatening move.

"What were you doing out here?" I ask.

"I got first shift on search duty. This is my section."

"Where's your partner?"

"What partner?" Joe mutters. "Did I mention my boss is an asshole? We're just widgets to him. Us *and* the miners. Sandy's dead, and there's a psycho in the forest, and all he cares about is that someone might discover where the miners are working. He even thought this shaman guy could be a spy. You believe that?" Joe snorts. "A spy who dresses up in a bearskin and plays mountain man. For all I know, he might still think that. He's got half of us out here searching without backup."

I don't say anything. Joe's hurt and angry, and I'm happy to let him talk, but I'm not saying anything he might recognize as encouragement to sound off . . . and realize he's saying more than he should.

Anders speaks for the first time since ordering Joe to stand down. "You should have backup. Your boss obviously doesn't have any military *or* law-enforcement experience."

"Right? Corporate assholes. They don't know what a risk is, 'cause the only time they take them is on the stock market. Taking risks is what we're for. Cannon fodder."

Anders nods. Like me, he's not pushing. Nudging maybe, more than I would, but it works better coming from a guy who looks like he's played a human shield for others, whether on the street or the battlefield.

"I'm going to take a look at your wound," I say. "I might need to ask you to take off your trousers."

"Shit. If anyone comes around the corner and literally finds me with my pants down, I'm out of a job, even if there's an explanation." His shoulders slump. "Not that it matters much. I'm probably out of a job when I admit I let the guy get away."

"Hold off. Let me see if I can look." I pull apart the tear in his tan trousers. The cut inside is maybe three inches long. "It's going to need stitches. But even if I had a med kit, I don't have the skills."

That's a double lie. The truth is that Joe isn't about to bleed out, and Dalton is somewhere up ahead, tracking a killer. I don't have time to pull out my med kit and stitch Joe's wound.

"All I've got is a bandage roll," Anders says. "And I barely know how to use it."

Such liars. Both of us.

"Give me a roll," I say. "I'll get this wrapped up, and he can head back to camp."

"Uh . . ." Joe says.

I glance at him as Anders hands me the roll.

"I can't do that," Joe says. "If we encounter anyone in the forest, we've been told we cannot head straight to camp after leaving them or we risk leading them back. But my leg's not too bad. I can help you search. That way, I'm not abandoning my job."

I glance at Anders, whose shrug says it doesn't matter to him. An extra gun wouldn't be a bad idea, especially if it gives us a bit of time with a security-team guy who's pissed off at his boss and might tell us even more.

Once Joe's leg is bound, we set out. The first thing he says, with a sidelong glance at Anders, is "So, you're new . . ."

Anders only smiles, showing perfect white teeth. "Haven't seen me before?"

"No, just, um, her and, um, the guy." He glances at me. "I don't mean to be rude. I don't know names."

"Which seems to be how your boss likes it," I say.

"Yeah," Joe says.

"So you guys . . ." Another look at Anders. "You have your own security force."

"Kind of," Anders says. "It's a little more . . . irregular than yours."

Joe snorts. "More *irregular*? Or more *regular*? I don't see why we can't dress like you guys. We're not mall cops. What's with the uniforms? No one's going to see us except the employees, who already know what we are."

Anders shrugs. "Everyone has a different way of doing things."

"No shit, huh? I keep hoping if we're here long enough, things might relax a bit, starting with the dress code." He peers out into the forest. "Does your partner have the dog? That's another thing I envy you guys. I had to leave mine at home. I mentioned it to the boss after seeing yours, like maybe dogs would be a good idea. He said they're considering getting some German shepherds. That is *not* what I had in mind."

"Yeah," Anders says. "A big dog is good if you encounter wildlife, but mostly out here, you want something that can help you find anyone who gets lost."

"I'll tell him that."

Dalton bird-calls again, closer now, and Anders replies, and Dalton almost immediately repeats his call.

"He's found something," I say. "He must be getting close. Time to pick up the pace."

Joe falls in step beside us. "You found your little boy?"

"Not yet," I say. "But we have a trail."

He grins. "Good. Get the kid back and take that bastard down." He lifts his gun.

"Whoa," Anders says, waving for him to lower it. "I appreciate your enthusiasm, but we're not 'taking down' anyone. You wave that around, and you're staying here."

"Sorry. You're right." He lowers the gun. "I just . . . I liked Sandy. A lot of the guys gave him a hard time, but he was nice, you know?"

I nod, but I'm only half paying attention. Dalton has signaled again, and I know that means for us to get our asses over to where he is.

We break into a jog.

"I'm supposed to bring the guy in if I find him," Joe says as we run. "By any means necessary. I won't shoot him, but my orders are to bring him in and— Fuck!"

A thump and a hiss of pain. I spin, hand going to my gun, half expecting to see the bear-man attacking. Instead, Joe is on one knee clutching his thigh where it's bandaged.

"Tripped," he says as he pants. "My damn leg. Just give me—"

He starts to push up and lets out another hiss of pain. Anders extends a hand, but Joe says, "I've got this."

He doesn't have it. His leg is hurt too badly to run, and we can't wait for him. I glance at Anders.

"I can stay with him," Anders says.

"No, I'm fine." Joe grits his teeth, sweat breaking out on his hairline. "We need to get this guy. I can help—"

He takes one step, and his leg folds, and he falls with another yowl. "God*damn* it."

"We'll come back," I say quickly. I glance at Anders. "Help me get him against that tree."

We move Joe so he's sitting with a tree at his back, protecting it.

"Stay there," I say. "We'll come back."

Dalton bird-called twice more while we dealt with Joe. We should have told the young man to stay where he'd been attacked.

Maybe I should have taken Anders up on his offer to stay behind. But once we're out of earshot, Anders says, "That was the right move. He'll be fine."

I still don't like it. Neither does Anders. Joe is little more than a kid, and we've abandoned him in the forest with a leg he can't walk on. He's bleeding, and he could attract predators, and the predator we're most worried about has already attacked him. Worse, we let him believe we're chasing his attacker, which would mean the guy couldn't hurt him again.

I should have said something. That was an oversight—blame my exhausted brain.

We'll return to Joe as soon as we can. He's armed, and I'm sure he has some kind of paramilitary experience. He already scared the bear-man off once.

He'll be fine.

I hope he'll be fine.

But in the end—sorry, kid—this isn't about Joe-whose-real-name-we-don't-even-know. It isn't about a young man hired as security for a gold mine, a young man whose boss didn't even care enough to give his men backup. It's about our resident, the youngest one we've ever had, and if we are truly on Max's trail, we aren't diverting for anything or anyone.

Joe will need to look out for himself.

CHAPTER TWENTY-EIGHT

Max

Max had slept most of the day. He knew that was wrong. Animals came out to hunt at dusk and dawn, and he should be walking while the sun was high and then finding a place to hide until it returned. That was what his dad would have called "ideal circumstances." There are ideal circumstances, and then there are the ones you get stuck with.

Dad used that phrase a lot. Under ideal circumstances, they'd do x. But their lives hadn't been ideal circumstances for a very long time. The phrase had been, Max realizes now, a way for his dad to apologize for the life they led.

Under ideal circumstances, we'd have no problem with you spending the night at a friend's, kiddo, but . . .

Under ideal circumstances, you could sign up for that summer camp, but . . .

Under ideal circumstances, his father would be alive, and Max wouldn't give a damn about spending the night at a friend's or going to summer camp. But that isn't how things work.

Ideal doesn't happen when you're living in witness protection, and it doesn't happen when you're fleeing a kidnapper in the forest. Last night, after stabbing the bear-man, Max couldn't just run for ten minutes and find a place to sleep. He'd had to keep running until he was sure he was safe, and by then it was daylight. Like yesterday, he'd only planned to close his eyes, but once they were shut, they stayed shut.

When he finally woke, it was with a start. He'd heard something.

Footsteps? The low growl of the bear-man's voice? No. While he couldn't remember what he'd heard, the feeling it left was one of excitement, his heart tripping.

He'd fallen asleep in the crook of a tree. It'd been more comfortable than you'd think. Or it had been when he first got in, but maybe that was just because he was too tired to care. He figured the bear-man wouldn't look for him in trees, so that's where he went. Now, when he tries to move, everything hurts.

Max carefully stands on the limb, stretching his aching legs. His stomach growls, but he's not too thirsty. He's been drinking from streams when he can. Probably not enough, but it'll keep him from dying of thirst, which he knows is a bigger concern than starving.

It's still daylight. Strong daylight, meaning it's probably mid-afternoon. Good. That gives him hours to walk before dark.

He'd still been awake when the sun started coming up, and it'd been on his left. He'd even made a mark on the tree, so he wouldn't forget it. He has a feeling Haven's Rock is—

The sound comes again, and his head shoots up, some part of him recognizing it as the sound that had woken him.

A birdcall.

A birdcall he knows. Not the *kind* of bird, but that it's the call Sheriff Eric uses as a signal. He's been teaching it to Max, who really wasn't very good at birdcalls. Max starts to try calling back, his heart hammering with excitement.

Then he stops.

His birdcall won't sound like a real birdcall. What if that isn't Sheriff Eric? What if it's just a bird and Max makes the call back and the bear-man hears and knows it's him?

Just do it, a little voice whispers. *Take a chance.*

Max survived two days in captivity and two more on his own, and he hadn't done it by taking chances. He needs to be sure that's Sheriff Eric, and he needs to head in that direction, not stand in a tree making weird noises that might alert his captor.

He takes another look around. Then, just as he's about to slide down the trunk, the birdcall comes again, and this time, another sound follows. A whistle.

Max grins. He knows that whistle. As much as he respects Sheriff Eric's birdcall, he'd rather learn how to whistle like Deputy Will, who can be heard so far away it's like using one of those silver coach whistles.

Max isn't imagining things. Sheriff Eric and Deputy Will are out here looking for him.

In Max's excitement, he forgets he's six feet up a tree, and he jumps down as if he's standing on a chair. He realizes the mistake when it's too late to do anything. He hits the ground, and his ankle twists, and he crouches there, squeezing his eyes shut against the pain.

Not broken. That's what counts. His ankle isn't broken, and he can walk.

He looks around.

Sheriff Eric's birdcall came from the left. Deputy Will's answering whistle was more south and seemed closer. He should head for Deputy Will.

As soon as he starts walking, he knows his ankle is more than just twisted. Not broken, but definitely sprained.

Is sprained different than twisted? All he knows is that each time he puts his foot down, it screams. He tries to inwardly scream back, like his dad's drill sergeant voice, except Dad had been goofing around.

On your feet, boys. It is time for breakfast. Atten-tion!

On your feet, Max. It is time to get yourself rescued.

He might have laughed a little at that. Get himself rescued. That's exactly what he needs to do. Get to a place where he can be rescued, and to get there, he requires the cooperation of his ankle. No whining. No "But it hurts!" Just move.

Except inwardly yelling at himself does no good at all. His ankle still hurts. It hurts so much that each step is excruciating pain.

Excruciating?

Max swears he hears Carson's mocking voice.

You don't know excruciating. That's when you see your husband die and you get shot and the pain never goes away. It hurts Mom to walk every day, and you're whining because you twisted your ankle? Help is a few hundred feet away, and you're going to collapse and say you can't do it? Figures.

Max grits his teeth and keeps going, but it doesn't fix anything. He hurts and he's tired and he's hungry, so hungry that as soon as he thinks about it, his stomach feels like it's ripping itself apart from the inside.

Then don't think about it. Duh.

Maybe Carson could, but Max can't just not think about it and make it go away. Not the pain in his foot or in his stomach. He's so tired and sore and—

Are those tears? Are you crying? Such a baby.

Max swipes a hand over his eyes and snuffles, and he decides he doesn't care what Carson would do. He's not Carson. He also doesn't care what Carson would think of him. Carson doesn't matter. Not now.

In the end, the voice he pulls up isn't his brother's mockery or his dad's jokey drill sergeant. It's his mom.

Max? I know this is hard, and you just want to give up, but you're so close. Just a little further, okay? You can do this. You just need to get a little—

His ankle twists, and he falls with a yelp. He starts to clap a hand over his mouth.

Be quiet.

Or should he?

If Sheriff Eric and Deputy Will are close enough for him to hear them, why is he forcing himself to walk on a twisted ankle? Why not just shout for them?

Because he doesn't want the ending where the grown-ups come running at a little boy's cries and save him. He wants the one where he saves himself. If he can't stumble into town on his own, then he wants to find his rescuers on his own.

Maybe it's time to let that go. Time to say it doesn't matter how this ends. It matters how he survived. *That* he survived.

The birdcall and the whistle come again. The whistle is so close and—

Someone is crashing through the undergrowth. At least one person, maybe two, coming fast.

Not coming in his direction, though. They're heading toward Sheriff Eric. Which means, in a few moments, they'll be heading *away* from him.

Don't care about how this ends. Care about how it went.

He is still alive, and now he's going to get his rescue, even if it means they find him on the ground with tears in his eyes.

Max draws in a deep breath—

The crack of a twig stops him. He follows the sound. Sheriff Eric is to his left—the east. Deputy Will was to his south and heading southeast. This sound comes from his right.

Don't let yourself get spooked by an animal.

He's not spooked. He's being cautious. Get up, see what it is, and call to Sheriff Eric.

Max braces on a tree and pushes halfway up. Then he freezes. That is not an animal.

He sees the distinct figure of a person creeping up on him. A human shape coming his way. Someone who heard him yelp. Someone who is *not* Sheriff Eric or Deputy Will.

His whole body tenses, ready to leap up and run. Except he can't run, can he?

He slips his hand into his pocket and wraps it around the knife. Then he fake-sniffles and drops his head forward, snuffling harder and rubbing his injured ankle with his free hand.

Through the fringe of his hair, he can make out the figure. It's still nothing more than a dark shape.

What if it's not a person?

It is. There's no doubt of that. This isn't a bear sneaking up on him. It's a person, and that person realizes Max is facing his way, and they back up, deeper into shadow. They disappear to the left, out of Max's line of sight. Circling around him. Coming up from the back.

It's the bear-man. It must be.

Approaching from the rear makes things easier for the bear-man, but tougher for Max. He'd wanted to let the guy walk up, thinking Max was too hurt and scared to notice him. Then, when he was close enough, Max would have attacked.

Now he can't see or hear his former captor.

Max snuffles again, loudly, and pushes to his feet, exaggerating his twisted ankle, the toe barely touching the ground as he gives one hop and then hisses as if in pain.

In a weird way, acting like his ankle is worse than it is actually makes it feel better than it is. As if it's reminding him that things could be worse—much worse.

He hobbles another step before stopping.

"I can't," he sobs. "I just can't."

He looks up sharply, as if he heard something, and he turns.

"Is someone there?" he says, injecting as much hope into his voice as he can.

He looks from side to side, but sees only thick brush.

Max snuffles again and takes a hobbling step toward the bushes, like a killdeer luring a predator away by faking a broken wing. Except he's luring this predator in.

I'm hurt, see? Really hurt.

"Hello?" He raises his voice. "Is someone there?"

Sheriff Eric's birdcall gives him another idea. As long as he's pretending to raise his voice to lure in the bear-man . . .

"Hello!" he says, louder now. "I know I heard someone. I need help. I'm lost."

He takes another step toward the bush as he pulls the knife from his pocket. "Hello! Is someone—?"

A blur and the crackle of bushes, only it doesn't come from the ones in front of him. It's to his side. Max wheels just in time to see a figure running at him. A figure with something over his face, and all Max sees is eyes and a mouth behind a black ski mask. The figure is leaping, like he's going to tackle Max, and Max turns to run, but his ankle gives way.

His ankle gives way . . . and saves him.

When his leg folds, he topples sideways instead of lunging forward. The figure lets out a grunt as it tackles empty air.

His attacker hits the ground. Max hasn't fallen. He only stumbled out of the way. Now he sees the masked man on the ground, flat on his stomach, and he imagines leaping on him and stabbing his little knife into his back. Stabbing and stabbing and—

Max shudders.

Yes, he wants to hurt the man who captured him, who has terrorized him for days. Wants to kick and punch and pummel him and scream at him.

But stab him? Kill him? No, he doesn't want to do that, and he wishes he could be a good person and say he doesn't want to murder anyone, but mostly what he thinks is that he doesn't want to *have* murdered someone.

And he thinks something else, in that split second while he hesitates. His mind rolls the video on him jumping on the man and stabbing him . . . and then the man leaping up and grabbing him, hands going around Max's neck.

There's blood on the bear-man's leg, which must be the spot where Max stabbed him last night, and Max races over and kicks that spot as hard as he can, channeling all his rage into that kick. The man screams, and that scream might be the most satisfying thing Max has ever heard.

Then Max runs. Runs faster than he thought he could on his injured ankle. Behind Max, the bear-man bellows in pain, and that spurs him on, keeps him running.

A shout. Only it doesn't come from behind him.

It's in front of him. A woman's voice shouting, "Max!"

"Detective Casey," he says, and the name comes out as a croak as he runs faster now, tears nearly blinding him.

He doesn't swipe away the tears this time. He just blinks so he can see.

Max escaped the bear-man. Not once, not twice, but *three*

times. So who cares if he's crying when he's found? He knows what he did. He was brave and smart, and he survived. Most of all, he survived.

"Max!" Detective Casey calls again, and then Deputy Will shouts, "Max! Where are you?"

"Here!" he says, and his voice comes out as a chirp, barely audible.

It doesn't matter. It doesn't matter because they can hear him crashing through the bushes, and they are there, so close he can see them running toward him. One last burst of energy, and he claws through a bush and his ankle gives out, but it doesn't matter. Deputy Will is there to catch him, to scoop him up and hug him, and Max collapses on his shoulder, and he's sobbing like a baby, but it doesn't matter.

It doesn't matter because he is safe.

It doesn't matter because he survived.

He survived.

CHAPTER TWENTY-NINE

Casey

I catch up to Anders, who's holding Max as the boy shakes against him, his tears of relief starting my own.

"You're okay," I say as I walk over and pat his back while he clings to Anders. "We found you. You're okay."

Max stiffens, and I yank my hand away. Then he fights to get down, and Anders quickly releases him.

"He's there," Max says, the words tumbling out. "The bear-man was right there. He found me, and he fell, and I got away but he's still there."

Anders pulls Max behind him as we both lift our weapons and point them in the direction Max came. We'd heard a cry of pain, and we thought it was Max. It could have been—he's limping—but now that I replay the sound, it was more man than boy.

"Eric!" Anders shouts. "You nearby?"

"Coming!" Dalton yells back.

"We have Max! But his captor's still out there!"

"Got it!"

We stay where we are. We might yearn to go after Max's captor, but we need to let Dalton catch up.

"Max?" I whisper. "You say the man fell?"

Max nods. "I stabbed him in the leg yesterday. He was coming at me, but I got out of the way and he tripped. He fell. I kicked him in the stab wound."

Anders grins over at the boy. "Nice."

Max doesn't smile back, but his eyes glow at the praise.

"Did he chase you?" I say.

"I—I don't know. I just ran as fast as I could. I heard you, and I knew you were nearby."

"Good. Is your foot hurt? Or your leg?"

"My ankle. But I can walk."

Anders shakes his head. "You can, but you don't need to. That's what I'm here for. Piggyback duty."

Still watching the forest, Anders bends. Max hesitates, but we prod him to get on Anders's back, and he does just as Dalton appears. Seeing Max, he lets out a deep sigh of relief and then reaches up to squeeze the boy's shoulder.

"You did it," Dalton says. "You got away from him."

"More than once," I say.

Max glows now. "Three times."

"Damn," Anders says. "That is some lifelong bragging rights, kid. We're proud of you, but you know who's going to be bursting with pride? Your mom."

"She is," I say. "And we'll get you to her as soon as we can, but right now, we have a kidnapper to catch." I glance at Dalton. "Should they stay here?"

He looks around. "No, I'd rather we don't risk anyone getting lost or ambushed. Will? Fall in behind us. Stay back a bit, but close enough that we'll hear you."

"Max?" I say. "Can you guide us to where you left him?"
Max nods, and we set out.

We find the spot, and there's no sign of Max's captor. He's certain it's the right place, because he can point out the tree where he spent the night, and the mark he made to show which direction the sun had been rising when he fell asleep.

We find where his captor fell, with one clear handprint on the ground.

"Respectfully suggest we split up, boss," Anders says. "You have a hot trail for the pooch to follow, but I don't think Max should be hauled along on that."

"I can do it," Max says. "I can walk."

Dalton shakes his head. "Casey needs to process this scene, in case we can't track him. Stay with her and Will." He checks his watch. "Give me an hour. If I don't find him, I'll circle back."

"And keep in touch," I say.

"Keep giving us the bird," Anders says.

Dalton smiles. "Happy to."

I help Storm find the scent. We know that handprint belongs to Max's attacker, and she follows his scent to the spot Dalton has already identified as the man's exit point.

They set off. I photograph the handprint while Anders settles Max in with trail bars and water. As much as I want to question him, he needs that sustenance more, so I busy myself working the scene.

When Max is done eating, I lead him through the sequence of events from the time he realized his attacker had caught up with him last night.

"I couldn't see him," he says. "I know that's what you'll want to know—what he looked like. I never really saw him, even when he first took me hostage. He didn't let me. When we were walking, he had me blindfolded. When he caught me again last night, he was behind me. This time, he wore a mask."

"A bear mask?" Anders says.

Max shakes his head. "A ski mask. You know, the ones that go over your head and hide everything but your eyes and mouth? Oh, and he's not part bear." He looks a little abashed. "It was a bearskin. It took me a while to figure that out, because I was mostly blindfolded. But before I stabbed him, I saw the paw. It was a bear hide."

He shifts. "Then I remembered one time when he was holding me captive, I saw the underside of his arm, and there was pale skin, with a black line, like dirt. I thought that made sense—just skin showing through his fur—but now I realized he was wearing a brown shirt under the bear hide, and the sleeve rode up and I saw skin."

"Pale skin."

He nods. "White or really pale brown. Also, about the bear hide, this last time, he wasn't wearing it at all."

I glance over. "He wasn't?"

Max shakes his head. "He was dressed normal. Pants and a jacket. Well, plus a ski mask."

I ask him to describe the man's clothing more, but he only knows they seemed "normal."

I'll have more questions for him later. Lots more if Dalton doesn't catch up with the bear-man. But for now, Max is safe, and I need to keep gathering what I can here.

Gathering evidence as I work through what has happened. Because something tells me I have a lot to work through.

★ ★ ★

Dalton doesn't catch Max's captor. The guy went straight for the nearest body of water. He must have heard us and run.

We haven't forgotten Joe, but by the time we get there, he's gone. One of his fellow guards tacked a note to a tree, saying they found him and took him back for medical care. I only hope Joe doesn't catch too much shit from his boss. Right now, though, I'm just relieved that we don't need to escort Joe closer to the mining camp. We don't have time for that.

We return to Haven's Rock. That is the main thing. Max is safe, but he needs to get back to his mother and back to a medical examination before I can comfortably question him.

Anders carries him most of the way. Then Dalton takes over, and Anders runs ahead. Twenty minutes later, the roar of an engine sounds in the distance.

"That's your ride," Dalton says, and swings Max to the ground.

The ATV's lights hit us first. Then, before Anders can bring it to a stop, the side door is opening and Dana is flying out. She runs to Max and scoops him up.

I don't watch the rest. It feels too raw, too private, and I walk to the ATV instead, with Dalton beside me.

We quietly talk with Anders until Dana is ready to get into the ATV. Dalton insists we catch a ride with them, and we perch on the rear with our legs dangling out. I sit against Dalton, his arm around me, as I lean onto his shoulder. Over the roar of the engine, he puts his mouth to my ear and whispers, "We found him."

My eyes fill, as I nod soundlessly.

We did.

Thank God, we did.

★   ★   ★

It's nearly ten. It was dusk when we arrived in Haven's Rock, and we'd taken Max the rear way to the clinic. Yes, everyone will soon know Max is back, but Dana doesn't need the well-wishers descending just yet.

April has already been alerted, and she's waiting in the clinic. Carson is there, too. I don't see that reunion. I'm ordered to stay in the ATV while they take Max in, and then we head back home.

There's nothing we can do right now. April needs to examine Max, and then he needs to rest. Questioning will wait until morning, and it should, because my brain is in no shape to handle it. Thoughts keep poking at me, questions and riddles and all the little voices that whisper "Something's wrong with this story," but I don't have the bandwidth to puzzle it out.

Max is safe, and we can pick this up again tomorrow. For now, I desperately need to sleep, so I go home and do exactly that.

Yeah . . . that's not quite how it goes. Oh, I want to sleep, and I'm exhausted enough that I'm surprised I didn't fall asleep on the ATV ride, however bumpy it had been. But while my body screams for slumber, my brain refuses. It's not in any shape to help me unravel the case, but it's not letting me rest either.

An hour later, I'm on the sofa, with the remains of dinner scattered around me. I actually ate it all. Apparently, the trick is to wait until the sun is down and my stomach has settled.

Now I'm on the sofa watching Dalton and Anders, sprawled on the floor as they play an impressively brutal game of Scrabble. No blows have been exchanged, but insults certainly have been. I don't know who's winning. My brain isn't even working well enough to track that.

I suspect my mental condition explains why Dalton insisted on Scrabble. I don't have the energy to play anything more challenging than Snakes and Ladders. He probably hoped that if I couldn't play, I'd sleep. I'm not, but that's okay. I'm happy lying here, half dozing as I listen to them talk and argue and play and laugh and talk some more.

For this moment, life is good. Max is home. April stopped by a while ago to inform me that his condition is excellent given what he experienced. He reports no sexual interference, and there are no obvious signs of such, to my eternal relief. I'll still have to question him, but this is a start. His ankle is sprained, but that's from jumping out of a tree. Otherwise, he's dehydrated and exhausted, and there are friction burns on his wrists and ankles from being bound.

Physically, he is in better shape than we dared hope. Emotionally? That's another story. He just endured a trauma right on the heels of the trauma of his father's death. All that is for another day. Right now, what matters is that he's home with his mother and brother.

Max is home, and I am home, and I am so happy that I feel as if I've downed my usual two shots of tequila. Blame the hormones, I guess. Everything is magnified, and if that's what I'm feeling right now, I'll take it. I'm lying on a sofa that feels like a dream bed, with the fire roaring, my dog right below me, my husband and our best friend arguing over the legitimacy of the word "dawg," and I cannot remember ever being happier.

Also, I'm pregnant. I'm pregnant, and with Max found, I can stop feeling guilty every time a little thrill rises at the thought. I can take this new idea and explore it without feeling as if I'm wasting brain power better spent searching for a child who has already been born.

I want our baby. I would never deny that. I desperately want it, and I know I might not get it, and I need to be okay with that. We've made our choice. We aren't going to ignore the possibilities—the dreams—just because they might not last. We will indulge them, and if we need to mourn them later, we'll do that, too.

We told Anders. We wanted him to be the first to know, and he also *needs* to know, because as long as I'm sick, I can't take morning shifts. Also, he's going to need to cover everything for a few days, while we go south for a gynecology examination.

We'll make that appointment after we've settled the matter of Max's kidnapper. For now, it's one night to rest and recuperate and—

A loud knock sounds at the front door.

Dalton looks up, eyes narrowing.

"It might be Dana," I say, starting to rise.

"If you don't recognize that knock by now, you really are tired."

"Come in, Yolanda!" Anders calls, and the door opens.

Yolanda walks in and kicks off her boots before striding to the living room and looking at us.

"Celebrating finding Max?" Her toe nudges a cheese puff. "Wow. You guys really do know how to party."

"Hey, that's contraband right there," Anders says. "I've been saving them for a special occasion."

She reaches down to take a handful.

"Would you like some, Yolanda?" Anders asks.

"Nah, I've got enough," she says, popping one into her mouth. "You wouldn't happen to have corn chips, would you?" She peers down at the Scrabble board. "Who is trying to play 'dawg'?"

"Do you need to ask?" I say.

"Uh, yeah, I kinda do. I can't decide whether it's the white guy being cringy or the Black guy who has never used that word in his life, unless it was with his suburban buddies, trying to be cool."

"Hey!" Anders says. "I *was* cool."

Her lips twitch. "Did you call them 'bruh,' too? Or just 'bro'? Please tell me you wore baggy pants with your underwear hanging out."

He lifts his middle finger, which only makes her smile break through.

"And I suppose you never did any of that, rich girl?" he says.

"Oh, hell no. I *was* cool. The only Black billionaire at my private school. I was a novelty. Everyone wanted to be my friend. Mostly so they could say they had a Black friend."

"That one Black friend."

"That's me. You, too?"

"Hell, no. I *had* a Black friend, which meant everyone in my class could have *two*. We were very popular."

"Even if no one could tell you apart, despite there being a six-inch height difference and the other kid wore glasses?"

"Hell, yeah." He lifts his hand and Yolanda high-fives it. "But no, it was only a three-inch height difference, and I was the one wearing glasses."

She takes another handful of cheese puffs. Anders waves to the bucket filled with beer bottles. "You want some beer to wash those down?"

"Don't mind if I do. Also . . ." She leans over and takes back "dawg," replacing it with "waged." "There. More points *and* less embarrassing." She turns to me. "Why aren't you playing?"

"I'm pregnant."

I hadn't meant to say it like that, but once it's out, Anders snickers as Yolanda stares at me, as if awaiting the punch line.

"I'm pregnant," I say. "And too brain-fogged for Scrabble."

"You're . . . Shit."

"It wasn't intentional." Again, I blurt it without thinking . . . which happens when your brain is already half asleep.

"And that is none of anyone's business," Anders says with a look at me. "Even if you're just trying to be clear that you wouldn't intentionally get pregnant when the town is so new."

"Everyone on staff is going to need to know eventually," I say. "About the pregnancy at least. It just hasn't been necessary yet."

"And you've been a little busy," Yolanda says. "Well, if we're on the topic of confessions, let's add one to what I came here to say." She turns to Anders. "I have Parkinson's, and I want to be on the militia."

"Uh . . ." Anders says.

"Yes, I mostly came to say I want to be on the militia, though I needed to talk about something else, too. But Casey admitting she's pregnant made me realize I should divulge my medical status as well, if I'm applying to a position where it may be a concern. Also, I'm not really applying so much as telling you that I'm joining the militia."

"I appreciate you letting me know," Anders says dryly. "But as the person in charge of any as-yet-unformed militia, I do get to approve—or reject—applicants. Which will have nothing to do with your medical status."

"You already knew, didn't you."

"Actually, no. I just knew you were smoking pot for a medical condition. You're young for Parkinson's. Also, it's uncommon among Blacks, but your grandmother is white, so . . . ." He shrugs. "I'd say I'm sorry to hear it, but I know you don't want that."

"I don't. Parkinson's won't affect my performance for a while.

Right now I get tremors." She holds out a hand, which is shaking slightly. "Mostly in the evening, when I'm tired. They're minor, but I still wouldn't go out with a gun when I have them. I can shoot, though. Very well. With a handgun, at least. I have my own."

"All right."

"Also, I have mild prosopagnosia. Face blindness. Which could be a slight issue, mostly if you ask whether I've seen a resident who superficially resembles other residents."

"Got it." Anders stretches on the floor. "So, militia, huh? What made you decide on that?"

"While Max was out there, I discovered I felt a whole lot more useful patrolling than sitting on my ass. I'm also bored. I need a job here."

"One could argue . . ." Anders begins.

"That my job was construction, and it's done? Yes. If you mean because my job is done, I should leave?" She snorts. "I'll leave when I'm ready. For now, give me work, including but not limited to the militia."

"There's an opening on the sanitation—" I begin.

"No."

"Huh," I say, "I seem to recall you claiming a willingness to do any job here."

"Any job temporarily, to learn how it's done or to fill in during an emergency. Not any job designed to scare me off, which won't work anyway, so neither of us would get what we want." She bends over the Scrabble board and says to Anders, "You're going to want to build on that J next or Eric will."

"Do you want to play, Yolanda?" Dalton asks. "Or just tag-team with Will?"

"She can tag-team with me," Anders says, "and you can tag-team with your wife."

"Right now I think Storm would be more useful," Dalton says.

"Watch it," I say, "or when I throw up tomorrow morning, I won't bother aiming for the toilet."

"Well, there goes my appetite," Yolanda says, tossing her uneaten cheese puffs back into the bowl.

"Did you say you had something else to talk about?" Dalton says. "Or was that just an excuse to come and steal Will's cheese puffs?"

"I don't like this bear-man bullshit," she says as she plunks into a chair. "I want to talk about that."

"We all do," Anders says. "But we're waiting until morning."

"Because Scrabble is more important?"

"Because the conversation isn't necessary before morning, and Casey is too tired to participate, which doesn't mean she *won't* participate, just that she won't participate well."

"Thanks," I say.

"I got your back." Anders winks and then turns to Yolanda. "Casey is exhausted. We need to recharge her batteries and get her at full capacity for data processing."

"I'm an android now?" I say.

"Of course not. Androids can't get pregnant. Yet." Back to Yolanda. "Let Casey rest. Let us all rest. Stick around if you want to play Scrabble or just hang out. But theorizing—or anything related to the kidnapper—is off-limits until morning."

"Fine," she says. "Also, you're going to lose. I can see Eric's tiles. Call it, and deal me in to the next game."

CHAPTER THIRTY

When I finally fall asleep, I'm still on the sofa, and apparently, I'm not the only one who dozes off in place, because Dalton doesn't carry me upstairs. I wake to find our living room looking like the scene of a teen party, with empty beer bottles across the coffee table, a carpet of smushed cheese puffs, and three people sleeping on the floor.

I gingerly lift my head. My stomach rocks with the motion, and my low groan has Dalton opening his eyes. Without a word, he rises, comes over, and scoops me up over his arms.

When I struggle, he whispers, "Shh, it's still nighttime. I'm taking you to bed."

I look at the window, with sunlight streaming under the blind.

"That's an illusion," he says. "You're getting more sleep. Doctor's orders."

"You're a doctor now?"

"I can get April to write you a note, if that helps."

I shake my head. I don't argue. I'm still tired, and my stomach says I'm not ready to get up yet. I let Dalton put me into bed and then say, "You're joining me, right?"

"Course. If my detective is sleeping, there's no reason for me to be up. Unless my wife wants me to make breakfast."

"She'd rather have you in here," I say, pulling back the covers.

He strips off his shirt, and I try to stay awake for the rest of the show, but I'm gone before that shirt hits the floor.

I don't know how long Dalton stays in bed with me. Not long, I'll guess. He'll try to sleep, but then he'll be up and getting things done, and I wake to find myself alone with a thermos of tea, two fresh-baked ginger cookies, and a note.

Walking S.
< 10 m

I smile. His note writing has not grown any more eloquent since I first arrived. At least this one is clear enough. He's walking the dog and will be back in less than ten minutes.

I'm still stretching when the front door opens. Voices tell me it's not just Dalton. Anders is with him, Yolanda having presumably left.

"I'm up," I call down. "Thanks for the cookies!"

"Thank your sister," Anders calls back up. "She put in a special order, in hopes the ginger would be easy on your stomach."

Dalton jogs up the stairs and peeks around the doorway. "How *is* your stomach?"

"Better. Sleep probably helped." I struggle to uncap the thermos. "I'm going to take it slow, but I'd like to speak to Max in about ten minutes if someone can warn Dana."

"That's not taking it slow."

"In fifteen minutes then."

He rolls his eyes, but only calls down to Anders, asking him to tell Dana we'll be by in twenty minutes to talk to Max. Then he uncaps the thermos for me, pours out a cup, and says, "Tell me what you want to wear?"

I smile. "Are you offering to dress me?"

"I was offering to get out your clothing. But I can dress you, too, if it helps. Now, what do you want to wear?"

We're heading to Dana's when I spot Gunnar hovering beside one of the residences on our route. He waves me over. We head that way, and Gunnar motions again, clearly just wanting to speak to one of us. I glance at Dalton, who sighs and shakes his head before motioning for me to go.

"I heard Max is back," Gunnar says as I approach.

"He is."

"And he's okay? That's what I heard, but I wasn't sure whether that means he's really okay or he's just the 'not dead' sort of okay."

"He twisted his ankle escaping, and he's obviously traumatized, but otherwise, he's as well as we could have hoped for."

"Good, good," Gunnar murmurs, and then bites at his fingernail before shoving the hand into his pocket. "You're going to see him now?"

"We are."

"Can you tell him I said hi?"

"I'm sure you could pop by later and say so yourself."

A low laugh. "Yeah, no. His mom isn't going to want that."

I ease back on my heels. "We haven't caught his captor, but there's no way it was you. You've been in town the whole time. I can tell Dana that."

"You can, but it won't matter. Even if I didn't do this, I could do something, and she's going to be in super-Momma-Bear mode now. I don't blame her."

"You should talk to her. Later. After we figure out who did this, and Dana has had time to get some distance." I look up at him. "You've been good for Max. I understand why she's nervous, but I really think you should work something out. Whatever works for her comfort level."

"Me leaving town and never being seen again?"

I shake my head. "It's about what Max needs. Give her time to see that and then negotiate."

"If they stay."

I nod, trying hard to ignore the clench in my chest that says we've failed. That our first child residents only lasted a few months before we screwed up enough to make them leave.

"If they stay," I murmur, and then I say I'll keep Gunnar posted, and I head back to Dalton.

I love my boss. Okay, being married to him means that's a good thing. Or, maybe, it's a good thing that if I love my boss, I'm also married to him, because otherwise, things get awkward. But I love him as a boss, too, especially when he understands my process and doesn't push, however much he might want to.

I know Dalton wants to talk about the case. So does Anders. So does Yolanda. And others might want to weigh in, too. But I'm not ready for that. I've had time to recharge my batteries—as Anders says—and now my data processor needs more input to process.

I have thoughts. Many thoughts, all bubbling up now that I'm running on enough energy to open those floodgates. I've sifted through them, and I've realized I need additional data before I speak to anyone, even my boss.

I hope Max has recovered enough to provide that data. It's always asking a lot to expect someone to talk to police shortly after experiencing a trauma. But until we've interviewed them, we're spinning our wheels while the culprit is covering their tracks.

Dalton and I arrive at Dana's apartment to find her with Max. Carson is spending the day with Mathias, and Max is ready to talk. Dana will stay here to be sure he's safe and comfortable, and that I don't push too hard. I'd expect that with any case involving a minor.

I start at the beginning. His story there matches Carson's. Max had seen what looked like the bear-man, and he'd gone to his brother, wanting him to come with him for a closer look. Carson refused.

"He told me to stop telling stories," Max says. "That I was embarrassing myself."

The anguish in Dana's eyes slices through me. Carson hurt his brother, but I don't think we're dealing with a bullying older sibling. Just a kid who's going through a lot and lashing out. Unfortunately, the person he's lashing out at most is the least deserving target. Dana will deal with that.

"So you went for a closer look," I say. "To prove Carson was wrong."

"No. I was mad, but I knew better. I saw the bear-man to the west, and I went in the forest to the south. I wasn't going near him. I was just mad and wanted to get away from everyone."

"And then?"

"The bear-man grabbed me. I never even heard him coming."

"Are you sure it was the bear-man?"

He nods. "When I was grabbed, I saw claws and felt fur."

We continue talking. Max explains that the bear-man carried him wrapped in a blanket, probably to stifle his scent. He'd put him down and make him walk now and then, and then carry him again. Messing up the trail for Storm. From the time Max was grabbed, he was gagged and blindfolded with his hands and feet tied.

"At some point, he took your jacket. Can you tell me about that?"

"He took it before he tied me up."

"We found it in a clearing. He'd hung it up. Did he . . ." I struggle to word this without leading Max. "It was hung in a strange way. Do you know anything about that?"

"He took my jacket. That's all I know."

"Did he say anything about it?" I ask.

"He never talked."

"Not at all?"

Max starts to shake his head and then pauses. "He told me to stay when he left the shack. It was just that one word. Stay. Oh, and he did say something when he grabbed me the second time—after I escaped. As he was strangling me, he said, 'Sorry, kid. I hate to do this, but you're too big a risk to—' I didn't hear the rest. That's when I remembered I had a knife."

"As he *strangled* you?" Dana repeats, her own voice strangled.

"I got away," Max says matter-of-factly. "I stabbed him in the leg."

I glance at Dalton, who has been silently standing in the corner.

"I need to ask you more about that," I say. "I'm going to pretend to be you, and Eric is going to pretend to be your attacker. Can you lead me through what happened? Guide us, like you're directing actors in a scene."

Max does that. We take it step by step through the scenario. Once I have it figured out, I ask whether Max saw anything of the man during that encounter. It isn't much. He was grabbed from behind and only caught a few details—that the man was wearing a bearskin, that his hands were the size of Dalton's and that his skin was pale—like the flash of skin he'd seen when the man's sleeve rode up before.

After that, I back up to get everything I can from the time he was held captive. I take down all those details, and I add them to what we know from the initial bear-man sighting— that the man in the bearskin was tall and broad, maybe even heavyset. Strong enough to carry a ten-year-old boy a long way, too.

Male. White. At least six feet tall. Muscular and possibly heavyset.

We continue talking. I get everything I can about all three attacks—when Max was first grabbed, when he was grabbed near Lilith's cabin, and when he was nearly grabbed the last time.

Then comes the question I need to ask, as hard as it is. I have Dalton leave for that, and when I do, Max starts to fidget, as if he knows what's coming.

The moment Dalton is outside, Dana says, "The man didn't do anything, but he was going to."

I look at her, and her mouth sets in a firm line. "I know you need that information from Max, but we've already talked."

I consider. Then I ask Max to go outside with Dalton for a few minutes. This isn't going to be a court case, and even if it were, I could take Dana's statement first.

Once Max is gone, she exhales. "Thank you. That makes it easier. Max wasn't touched sexually. The man didn't undress

him. He didn't make Max touch him. But I think he was heading in that direction."

She says that and then watches, waiting for me to challenge
her, to demand proof, to ask how she could possibly know it
when she hadn't been there.

I only say, "Okay."

"He *did* touch Max. On the face. On the arm. Once on the
leg, but when Max jumped back, he didn't do it again. Max
woke up once to the man smoothing his hair, which seems innocent enough—I do it to them sometimes, when I go in to check
on them."

"You're their mother."

She exhales, as if in relief that I'm not challenging her assessment. "Yes. Family is different. If Max was scared, another
adult might touch his face or arm to calm him. But this wasn't
like that. Max thought the man was going to touch him in
other ways. That he was working up to it. That was his sense of
things, and I don't think a ten-year-old boy is going to imagine
that."

"Has Max ever had trouble like that before?"

She's quiet, and her voice drops. "A little. It never came to
anything, but he's a sweet boy who's . . ." Her voice cracks. "A
little broken. I think predators can sense that. Like chum on
the waters."

Exactly what Gunnar said.

"What happened?" I ask gently.

"It was right after his dad died, and Max might have been
vulnerable, but he was wary, too. Mistrustful. Max picked up
bad signals from someone and told me. When it was investigated, the police found that the man had a history."

"Okay. It helps to know that it's happened before and his instincts were right. That also clarifies the situation. There weren't many reasons someone would kidnap Max out here, and that was the most obvious. It's good to know what we're dealing with."

I'm not just making her feel as if this information is useful. It is, because it removes the "mountain man looking for a son" possibility. This was kidnapping a child for sexual purposes, by someone who knew what he was doing, taking it slow and putting off gratification until he had lowered Max's guard.

I don't think we're looking for a wild man of the forest at all. I think we're looking for a predator who played a mountain man . . . in hopes of playing us.

For the next step, I consult with Dalton and April. April for her brilliant mind and also her lack of inhibitions when it comes to telling me I'm wrong. I might have hated that all my life, but it has proved useful here. Oh, Dalton won't let me be wrong without saying anything. I would never want that. But he'll take more time to consider the matter before addressing his concerns. My sister has no such compunctions. If she sees a logical flaw, she'll tell me. And I need her for something else: her medical know-how.

Dalton and I proceed straight to the clinic, but my sister isn't there. A note on the door reminds patients that she is closed this morning. It's not the weekend. Oh, hell, it *might* be for all I know. At this point, if asked to stake my life's savings—double or nothing—on the simple question of what day it is, I wouldn't take the bet.

For the clinic, though, like most of Haven's Rock, there are no official weekends. If you need to observe a day off work for religious reasons, we will accommodate that, but otherwise, most people also prefer four half days off over two whole ones. It's not as if you can take a trip for the weekend. Better to have four days to sleep in or be done by lunch.

Last time I checked, my sister didn't have regular clinic hours. The clinic is open when she has appointments, and if she has several, it's open between them because closing down is inefficient.

I think I know where to find April, and I'm pleased that I'm right. We're nearing the carpentry shop when I catch her voice, murmuring interspersed with Kenny's. I smile and push open the door . . . to see Kenny with his hands on my sister's waist, one on each side, gently holding her as she looks up at him.

Hearing the door, April looks over and flails as if they've been caught naked.

"I'm sorry," I say, starting to back out. "I should have knocked."

"It's a carpentry shop, not a medical clinic," Kenny says, and he smiles, but I don't miss the wry twist to that smile, one that says he really wishes we *had* knocked.

"I was just . . ." April says. "I was . . ." When she trails off, Kenny murmurs, "Go on."

She looks at him, panic lighting her eyes. Then she takes a deep breath and turns to Dalton and me, and says, "I was upset."

"Is everything all right?" I say.

"No, everything is not all right," she snaps, turning her full attention on me. "You are pregnant, and you are sick, and you are working yourself sicker, and I know you have to, but I am still upset. You always do this. You have since you were a child. You are reckless, and you do not take care of yourself."

"And now I'm taking care of two and already doing a shit job of it?" I say, as calmly as I can.

"I didn't say that," she says. "My concern is that you did not investigate the full scope of your condition before you became involved with someone you might wish to have a child with. I know you were hardly celibate before Eric but—"

At Kenny's throat clearing, she hesitates. She glances his way, and he shakes his head. She might not understand why—that Kenny is saying my past sex life isn't a proper topic of discussion in front of my husband—but she trusts him and pauses. I almost regret that. Dalton doesn't care, and I'd rather stay on that topic than what she wants to discuss.

She plows on, "You should have been examined."

"I know—"

"And you shouldn't have needed to be examined. I don't—I don't know what those young men did to you. I don't know the details. But they nearly killed you, and they were never punished for it. You were the one who was punished for their actions. You keep on being punished, and that isn't fair. If you can't have this child, it's their fault, and that isn't fair."

I want to hug her. I know I can't. I can never force her to accept hugs or get used to them for my sake.

Kenny has been helping April navigate the neurotypical world, but he's also been helping me understand what I can and cannot ask of my sister. We need to meet in the middle where we can negotiate a healthy sibling relationship, one where I don't feel constantly berated and judged, but also one where she can be herself, without the need to mask for other people's comfort.

So I can't hug her unless she clearly wants it—and not just because she knows it'll make *me* feel better.

Instead, I say, "You're right. It's not fair. And yes, it seems careless of me not to get answers, but it's avoidance. I was afraid of those answers. If I didn't get them, I could pretend everything might be okay."

"That's what Kenny said."

"We were discussing it," Kenny says. "I'm sorry if you weren't ready for me to know. April was really upset and needed to talk."

"That's fine. I'm sorry you're upset, April. I feel better today, if that helps, and I will get that appointment as soon as I can."

"Next week," she says, straightening. "It's already been arranged."

"Okay . . ."

"You'll be seeing someone in Vancouver. She is an expert in conception and pregnancy following trauma. Émilie has made all the arrangements."

I try not to wince.

Dalton says carefully, "Émilie?"

"It was Yolanda's idea. She came to me this morning and said she had heard the news and had the sense there could be complications. I did not divulge your history, of course, but I expressed concern and suggested you had experienced trauma that could affect a pregnancy. Yolanda insisted on speaking to Émilie."

April's chin rises. "Which is correct. Émilie has even better contacts in the medical field than I do, and she can arrange for your complete privacy. You might not like accepting favors from her, but you will in this."

"I will?"

She meets my gaze. "You will."

"April's right," Dalton says. "This isn't a time to ignore what Émilie can do for us."

"I have a feeling we'll be saying that a lot," I mutter. But then I sigh. "Okay, yes. Obviously, I can't turn down superior—and private—care. Give us the details later, and we'll arrange a few days off. For now, I'd like to speak to you in the clinic, April. I want you to look at those photos I mentioned yesterday."

"Of the murdered miner whose body you would not secure for a proper autopsy."

"Could not, April. The word you want is *could* not. Now come on."

CHAPTER THIRTY-ONE

I haven't seen my sister in nearly three days. That means I wasn't the one to tell her about Sandy. Dalton had updated her—mostly so she wouldn't hear about it secondhand. Dalton gave her the basics, and then I had expected to meet with her later and go over the photos I'd taken.

My sister is understandably furious over not having access to the body. I found it, therefore it should be ours. I could say that "finders, keepers" doesn't apply to corpses, but I understand what she's saying. We have a doctor capable of performing the autopsy and a detective capable of investigating the murder. Therefore, Sandy's body should temporarily be ours.

It isn't, and I'm not sure she understands our explanation— that we don't want to give Rogers an excuse for popping by with medical issues—but she accepts it. At least I took photos, though she doesn't expect them to be as thorough as they would have been if she were there.

She also, naturally, has to tease me about stumbling over bodies. Is it really teasing? For the sake of my stress level, I've chosen to pretend it is. Sometimes I think that, deep down, she can't help but wonder whether I've developed some inner divining rod for corpses.

We're in the clinic now, and I've transferred my photos to her tablet and also to mine, so she has two screens to examine them on. I know my sister. Being able to view only one photo at a time is unacceptable. She may even requisition my phone if she needs a third for multiple comparison points.

As we go through the photos, she praises me for my thoroughness . . . while still pointing out angles I missed. There are a few shots I leave out intentionally for now, but those aren't the ones she cares about. For my sister, it's all about the wounds.

"These could have been fatal," she says, circling three. "To be sure, I would need to know how deep they were. That is why I required the body."

"Does it matter which of them was the killing blow?"

She gives me a disapproving look. "I don't know, Casey. Does it matter to you whether the murderer killed him with this one"—she points—"which would have been pure luck. Or this one"—she points—"which would indicate an intentional thrust through the ribs to the heart. Or this one." She points to one at the base of Sandy's skull.

"Shit," I say. "That last one would be the equivalent of a CNS shot. Straight to the central nervous system. Dropping him instantly. That would mean a professional— No, wait. Max reported hearing a cry. So it wasn't a silent kill. Two perfectly positioned fatal stabs, though, means something. The killer slides the first through the ribs, but Sandy has time to scream. The next comes to the top of the spine, killing him."

"And the rest?" Dalton says.

"Overkill. Literally. Wounds made after Sandy was already

dead, which I presumed proved frenzy, but I don't think so anymore. I've been compiling the evidence along with everything Max has said."

I look at them both. "Whoever took Max was a pedophile. Nothing happened, thankfully, but even Max could tell it was only a matter of time. That indicates an experienced pedophile. Could that be a wild man of the forest? Someone who escaped to the Yukon but still remembers how to hunt his victims? Yes. But nothing in the behavior of Max's captor suggests he was unbalanced. He knew what he was doing, and he was meticulous—hiding his trail, securing Max, making sure Max didn't see him or even hear his voice."

I flip through photos on my phone to the two sites we found with the hanging figures made of bones and feathers. "Then we have these. Clearings in the forest with ritualistic trappings. One of them was arranged around Max's jacket, linking the ritual to his kidnapping. Clearly the work of an unstable mind, right?"

"Or the work of someone who wanted us to think we were chasing a madman," Dalton mutters. "Making us fear he'd taken Max for a ritual. Making us look for meaning in all this."

"Like wearing a bearskin?" I say.

Dalton answers with a sigh as he rubs his temples.

"You aren't looking for a wild man, then," April says. "You're looking for someone who impersonated one to throw you off the trail? Is that enough cause to go through all that trouble?"

"There's a reason Max's captor would be desperate to mislead us," I say. "The limitations of a locked-room mystery."

April frowns.

"A locked-room—" I begin.

"Yes, I know what a locked-room mystery is. One where there is a very limited number of suspects. But there is no door on this crime scene, Casey. Anyone can get here if they wish to, and there are bound to be people out there we haven't encountered. Nomadic people, like Jacob and Nicole."

"True. We don't have a pure locked-room environment here. But the geography simulates a locked house with one window in the attic where someone could enter. Yes, the killer could be an outsider, but the most likely suspects are in here with us. Also, remember how much trouble Max's captor went through making sure Max couldn't see him or hear his voice."

"It's someone from Haven's Rock," she says. "A pedophile has his eye on Max, like Dana feared with Gunnar."

"Could be," I say. "Except for one problem."

"No resident could have been gone that long," Dalton says. "We'd have noticed."

I nod. "Also, just because the captor hid himself and his voice, that doesn't mean Max would recognize him. It could mean he was afraid that if Max escaped, his description could lead someone to recognize him—or for him to be recognized in a lineup. As for the timing, Max thought his captor was leaving for hours at a time. A man of the woods might have gone hunting. But he could also have been checking in someplace. Trying not to be missed. That wouldn't work for Haven's Rock. It's a very long walk to where he was keeping Max. Even if it had been closer, we're still too small for anyone not to be missed."

"Rule out a Haven's Rock resident," Dalton says.

"Yes, Max's captor wasn't from here, thankfully. Who else do we have in the area? Tyrone and Jen are out there, and Ty is a big man who could fit the description, but even if we didn't know that they're near Dawson City right now, this doesn't fit Ty. It sure as hell doesn't fit Jacob. Who else? Lilith. She was away—or said she was—but she'd never fit Max's description of a big, burly man. If she was working with his kidnapper, she wouldn't come to tell us she'd heard someone near her cabin."

"That eliminates everyone we know who could be in the region, leaving the most likely suspects," Dalton says.

"The miners," April says.

"We know their employees are allowed into the forest," I say. "That gave Max's captor opportunity to find a place to keep him and also to snoop over here, on a day off, and see Max himself. Then he returned wearing a bearskin, which I presume is from their camp—either an actual trophy or just rustic northern decor. He uses the bearskin to spy on Max. Grabs him. Takes him to that ruined shack."

"Which is on their side of the boundary," Dalton says. "Close enough to camp for him to go back and forth. He stashes Max there and then intends to keep going back and forth while he grooms him."

"I understand the presumed logic," April says. "But the miner won't be here forever. In fact, I doubt the camp will be here over the winter. So what would he do with Max?"

Dalton and I don't respond. There is only one answer. Max's captor could hardly release the boy to tell his story. Max was a plaything, a diversion. When the miner went south for the winter, he might kill Max . . . or he might just leave him in the wilderness to die.

It was the perfect setup for a predator. Endless empty wilderness with two tiny settlements. Take a victim from one while pretending to be a half-crazed loner. That would have everyone scouring the forest, but it's so vast that they'd never find the child, and eventually they'd give up, leaving him with his prize.

And no one would ever suspect the culprit came from one of those settlements because, duh, wild man wearing a bearskin and leaving weird ritualistic scenes? Clearly it was one of those mountain-man hermits you hear about. Maybe a serial killer who disappeared into the wilderness to avoid capture.

"There's more," Dalton says, peering at me. "Your brain has been working overtime."

"Making up for taking off early yesterday," I say. "We've met a few of the camp's security team, and even if they aren't all that memorable individually, they do fit a type."

"White, tall, physically fit. Like whoever took Max."

I nod and pick up my phone. "I'm going to read you the description Max gave. Remember that he never got a good look, but he did catch snatches and impressions."

"He's a very clever child," April says. "He pays attention."

"He does. Tell me whether this matches any of the guards we've seen." I lift the phone and read. "White male. Tall. Stocky build. Strong enough to carry Max for long distances. Gunnar said he saw the lower half of the bear-man's face and it was furred, roughly the same color as the bearskin. That suggests a beard roughly grizzly-colored. Max said the bear had brown eyes."

"So—" Dalton stops short. "Wait. Read that again."

I do. Then I say, "Does it sound like any of the guards we've seen?"

"It sounds like someone. But not a guard." He picks up my tablet and flips through to a photo. Then he looks at me. "That's why you skipped these photos. So I wouldn't be influenced. It's also why you said 'guard.' Because we've only seen one miner." He sets down the tablet, the screen filled with a picture of Sandy's dead face, his eyes opened for the photograph.

Brown eyes. Medium-brown hair. Short beard, well trimmed as if recently cut shorter. White skin. On a tall and heavyset but muscular man.

"There's one more thing," I say. "When Max was being blindfolded, he didn't see his captor's hands. He still thought the man had bear claws. But Max did see a flash of skin on the underside of his captor's arm. That made sense to him: if the creature was part bear, part human, it'd have less fur on the underside of his arms. His captor has the bear paws over his hands, tied at the wrist so he can use his fingers. He's wearing a shirt that's probably close to the color of fur. But the sleeve has ridden up, exposing pale skin. And on that skin, Max saw a black line. Like dirt, he said. A rough black line maybe an inch long, protruding from under the fur."

I flip through the photos and stop at the tattoo of a Celtic cross on the underside of Sandy's left forearm. I cover most of it with my finger. What sticks out above his wrist? The black line of the bottom bar.

"Our dead man is Max's captor," Dalton says. "Then who stabbed him? And who the hell chased Max and tried to kill *him*?"

The narrative had seemed so straightforward that I hadn't questioned it. While working in the forest, Sandy encountered the bear-man, who lunged at him with a makeshift knife. When Sandy's colleagues mocked him, Sandy took to sneaking into the forest to find evidence. He got too close to that shack—maybe he remembered seeing it on a walk—and the bear-man heard him, snuck out, and killed him.

But peel it back to the first step. Sandy reported encountering the bear-man in the forest, a crazed hermit in a bearskin who lunged at him with a makeshift knife. Sandy shouts, and the bear-man takes off before anyone arrives.

No one except Sandy saw the bear-man. Sandy, who plans to kidnap Max and is setting up his narrative—that of a crazed mountain man in a bearskin conducting shamanistic rituals.

After Sandy's traumatic encounter, he's given time off. I've gotten the impression he was a loner, so no one would be paying much attention to him. They know he's leaving camp, but the guards ignore it. Just poor bullied Sandy looking for his Bigfoot.

Sandy uses that time to kidnap Max and put him in the shack. He returns to camp often enough to be seen at meals and such.

On the second night, he's in the shack with Max when he hears a voice. Sandy goes to investigate and . . .

And here is where it gets complicated. Because Sandy isn't "poor bullied Sandy looking for his Bigfoot, murdered by the crazed mountain man." Sandy is Max's captor, checking on a noise that suggests someone is too close to his captive.

And Sandy is murdered . . . by whoever had been out there in the night.

This means Max's captor is dead, which is a relief. It's also a relief that I can stop feeling bad about the poor miner murdered in the forest.

But after Sandy died, someone pursued Max. Someone tried to strangle him. Someone dressed in a bearskin. Someone who had taken that bearskin from Sandy.

Sandy went out in the night. He wouldn't have cleaned up the shack first. He left in a hurry. But when we got there, the only traces of Max and Sandy were old blankets that had probably been there for years.

One thing that was clearly missing?

The bearskin.

Whoever took that bearskin tried to murder Max, and what comes back to haunt me is what his attacker said while strangling him.

Sorry, kid. I hate to do this, but you're too big a risk to—
Too big a risk to leave alive.

It's early afternoon when we reach the message point between Haven's Rock and the mining camp. We don't intend to stop there, but two guards are waiting.

"Sir, ma'am," one says. It's the older white guy, with the Black guard. "Our boss thought you'd come by. We've been ordered to wait for you here."

"And escort us to your camp?" Dalton says. "I hope those are the next words out of your mouth."

"Sorry, sir," the older guard says, and manages to sound sincerely respectful, despite Dalton being a good decade his junior. A real military man, accustomed to addressing younger men as "sir" and not sounding sarcastic.

The older guard continues, "Our orders are to ask you to wait here while one of us heads to camp and fetches him."

"*Ask* us to wait here?" I say. "Or order us?"

A slight smile, bordering on rueful. "I'm saying ask, and if the boss said something else, it's slipped my mind."

"Go on then," Dalton grumbles. "Bring him here."

CHAPTER THIRTY-TWO

Rogers returns in about thirty minutes. That suggests the camp is less than a fifteen-minute walk away. I also note that, while the path branches a few times within sight, they definitely approach from the south, as we suspected. Useful.

"Hello," Rogers calls as he approaches. "I thought you might be coming to speak to me. I hear you found your boy. I'm glad to hear it."

"Thank you," I say. "I'm sorry we had to leave your guard behind when he was wounded."

His mouth tightens, and I think he's angry with us, but he says, "He should have gone with you. Made the effort, if he was going to let himself get jumped in the first place. Thank you for treating him. He'll be leaving us soon."

And it's not the injury that'll win him an early ticket home. Joe had said his boss was an asshole. Yes, we knew that, but we thought he might be different to his men, in the same way that Dalton can come off as an ass to outsiders, but if you're a resident—and you haven't pissed him off—you'll see a very different side.

Apparently, Rogers doesn't have those layers. To him, Joe screwed up, and it doesn't matter if the fault ultimately lies with the guy who sent him into the forest alone, Joe "got himself" stabbed and now he's damaged goods.

"I presume you're here to talk next steps," Rogers says. "Finding the psychopathic mountain man who killed one of my men and injured another." He stops and then adds, "And stole your young man, of course."

"Who is fine, thank you for asking."

Rogers meets my gaze. "I wouldn't be fool enough to bring teenagers here. If he wasn't fine, that'd be on you."

His retort is intended to sting. To set me back on my heels. So let's do the same. "They aren't the same person."

Now he's knocked back, blinking in confusion. "Who isn't the same person?"

"You said we need to find who stabbed your guard, murdered your miner, and kidnapped our young resident. They aren't the same person."

He goes still. Then his mouth forms an expletive he doesn't utter. "We have more than one wild man? Do you think they're connected?"

"No wild men."

I'm talking riddles, like he's done, and his lips thin in annoyance.

"The wild man was a fiction," I continue. "A diversion. It was a regular guy wearing a bearskin." I pause to let that sink in. "You wouldn't happen to have any decorative bearskins in your camp, would you?"

I expect a swift denial. Instead, he goes still.

I continue, "We believe Sandy took a bearskin from your camp and used it to impersonate a wild man of the forest. We believe he was a pedophile who saw an opportunity to kidnap a ten-year-old boy."

"*Ten?*" Rogers says. "You brought children—"

"That isn't the part of this story you should be focusing on."

"Isn't it?" His eyes flash. "I was already concerned that you have women in your settlement. Do you know what sort of men give up a year or two of their lives to work at a place like this? Yes, most of them are decent people. Men willing to give up that time and do difficult physical labor in return for a substantial reward. Like those who work on oil rigs, except this is harder work, in a more difficult climate, with a much smaller crew."

"So what you're saying," Dalton drawls, "is that you have men who could be predators, and you didn't bother to warn us of that, knowing we had . . ." He waves at me. "Women."

"Good-looking women," the older guard says. Then he coughs. "Sorry. I just mean . . ." Another cough. "It makes a difference."

Does it? That depends on who you're talking about. Horny guys who might mosey in our general direction, hoping to find a lonely woman? Or predators, who don't give a shit what a woman looks like, because that's not what they care about.

"If you have sex offenders in your camp, then you should have warned us."

"I have no idea what we have," Rogers says with a snap. "My firm only investigated their backgrounds to the extent that it affects us. Not having women in the crew means a history of sexual misconduct wouldn't be an issue."

"Sexual misconduct is when a prof gives a student an A for a blow job. It's not rape, and it's not pedophilia."

"I misspoke."

"No, you gave valuable insight. What you are saying, I presume, is that you could have workers who have been accused—or even convicted—of pedophilia, because it doesn't affect their performance in a situation without children."

"Yes."

"And not knowing that we have children in town, you saw no reason to warn us."

"Yes."

"And you didn't check their pasts, even when sexual assault is not limited to female or child victims."

He only presses his lips together.

"Yet you *did* know we had women in town, and not only did you fail to warn us, but you let your damned workers wander wherever they want, with zero supervision. Knowing we have women—and realizing it was a potential problem—means you should have had your firm check who you have in town and restricted the movements of anyone who could be a threat."

"That is why we have boundaries. Our men know not to cross them."

"But they *did* cross them," I say. "You paid so little attention that one of your men was able to find and lure a child and hold him captive for two days."

"You have failed to prove it was anyone from our town, let alone Sandy."

I run through the evidence. With each piece, I watch his expression slowly turn from denial to something else, and I don't dare hope that "something else" is acceptance, but when I finish, he wheels on the two guards.

"Is there a bearskin missing?" He machine-guns questions. "Who was in charge of Sandy's work detail last week? Who was on watch this week? I want to know how the hell we missed—"

"That is a security issue for you to resolve later," I cut in.

"What matters now is that whoever killed Sandy is still out there."

Rogers goes still, and his gaze sweeps over the forest. "An actual wild man?"

I shake my head. "The kill was precise."

He frowns. "The man was stabbed in the back a dozen times."

"Nearly three dozen times, actually. One is through the ribs to the heart and one at the base of the skull, to the central nervous system. Both were intentional and fatal."

"Damn," the younger guard says, and when Rogers glowers his way, he straightens and clears his throat. "But it could still be one of these wild men, right? Besides the usual stories of serial killers, you get war veterans in Alaska, with PTSD and all that. They go into the wilderness to live on their own."

"Correct," Rogers says. "To survive out here, one requires excellent hunting skills. All it means is that Sandy didn't encounter a crazed wild man, like the one *he* was portraying, but a backwoodsman who knew what he was doing."

"Killing Sandy with brutal efficiency . . . and then stabbing him thirty more times?" I shake my head. "Whoever did that wanted us looking for Sandy's wild man. This wasn't a stranger in the forest. Sandy knew him. He heard him in the forest, possibly calling for him, and he left the boy alone to go speak to him."

I'm stretching the truth here. We have no proof that Sandy knew his killer, but this is the direction I want to pull Rogers.

I continue, "We know Sandy was costuming himself in a bearskin. Yet he didn't wear it to meet whoever he heard. He wanted to divert them away from the shack, and he wanted to do it as himself. That implies he knew his killer."

"How do you know he wasn't wearing the skin? Did you find it?"

The younger guard shifts uneasily, casting a quick look our

way that says he understands how we know . . . and it's kind of embarrassing that his boss missed the obvious.

"If he was wearing the skin, it would have been much more difficult to stab him," I say. "The pattern would have been different, and there'd have been hair in the wounds. The blade would have passed through the skin first and carried trace into the wounds."

"You're saying Sandy knew his killer, which implies . . . ?" Rogers says, though he must know full well what it implies.

I ignore that and say, "The boy that Sandy kidnapped used the opportunity to escape. Yet someone came after him. He presumed it was Sandy, not knowing he was dead. He lost his pursuer for a while, but he was grabbed the next night. Grabbed and strangled. He managed to escape by stabbing his attacker in the thigh." I meet Rogers's eyes. "Is anyone in your camp suffering from a wound like that?"

"The young man you helped," he says. "But as you know, it was a newly inflicted wound."

"Also it was in the back of his leg. This was in the front."

"You think someone from my camp killed Sandy? And then tried to kill your boy? Why not someone from your town?"

"Because no one from our town has been gone long enough to have done it. We are on a strict lockdown with round-the-clock patrols. Whoever tried to kill our boy said something to him as he was strangling him. 'Sorry, kid. I hate to do this, but you're too big a risk to—' He didn't hear the rest."

"Risk?" Rogers frowns. "What would the boy know?"

"Presumably they thought he knew they killed Sandy."

There's a long silence. I think Rogers is preparing his argument. My theory isn't bulletproof, and I've fudged facts to get where I need to be. After a moment, he yanks out a satellite phone and makes a call.

When someone answers, Rogers says, "Have you treated any leg wounds in the past two days?"

Silence from the other end, as whoever he called—doctor? medic?—must be trying to figure out where this question came from. When he answers, I can't make out more than the murmur of a male voice.

Rogers hangs up without even a goodbye and says to us, "The only leg injury was to the young man you met yesterday."

I think he's going to say that proves the man Max stabbed isn't from his camp, but he turns to the two guards. "Drop your trousers."

The older one stares at him as the younger one says, "Uh . . ."

"Just because someone was stabbed does not mean he sought medical attention. This is the easiest way to prove that. Drop your trousers."

Both men's jaws set, but before I can say I'll step aside, they do it. Neither has a stab wound on his thigh. Rogers then takes Dalton into the bushes and does the same, and the two guards don't fail to notice he took advantage of an alternative he didn't offer them.

When Rogers returns, he says to the younger guard, "Go to camp. Send two of your colleagues out. We'll start with the security staff."

Dalton glances at me. I roll my eyes slightly, conveying the pointlessness of this exercise, but I don't say anything.

Rogers is putting on a show. It seems like a surefire way to find the culprit, but he's in control here. He can summon whoever he likes and then claim he's shown us everyone. I don't think he'll even get as far as the miners, given his reluctance to let us meet them. He'll bring a few guards, pretend that's all of them, and then promise to check the miners himself.

I don't argue because I don't see the point. He's never letting us into his camp. My only hope is that he'll check everyone, and when he finds the culprit, he will deal with them.

As much as I dislike Rogers, it would be the same if he said someone from our town kidnapped one of his miners and got stabbed in the leg. We wouldn't let him into Haven's Rock. We'd find who had that wound and deal with it, and as for Rogers . . . Well, we'd feel terrible if one of our residents hurt one of his, but if he thought we were turning that person over to him, he could go fuck himself. Same principle here.

I see no reason why Rogers *wouldn't* deal with it. He won't let Sandy's murderer stick around to kill someone else.

They bring out two more guards, and I step aside and play with Storm while they're checked. Once I hear them leaving, though, I'm back in a flash to question them first. Rogers doesn't like it, but he doesn't interfere either.

One of these two had been in charge of Sandy's work detail the day Sandy apparently saw the bear-man. He confirms that he didn't see anything himself, nor did anyone else. That was why Sandy was being mocked. No one could verify his story.

The two guards are sent away, and we are back to uncomfortable waiting.

"Do we . . . ?" The remaining guard clears his throat. "Not to tell anyone how to do their job, but do we know that whoever killed Sandy is the same person who chased the boy and tried to strangle him?"

"We do not," I say. "That's the working theory because it makes sense. But if we find evidence to suggest we're dealing with separate actors, we'll pivot. The problem with that . . ."

"Is that it means we're looking for two killers," Dalton says. "One successful and one not. Add Sandy to the mix, and we'd have a pedophile and two murderers out here."

"That'd be unlikely enough in any situation," I say, "but out here, it's even more unlikely—"

One of the guards comes running down the path. "Sir? Jay's gone."

"Gone how?" Rogers snaps. "He can barely walk."

Ah, that would make Jay our G.I. Joe.

"Your wounded guard is gone?" I say.

The man nods. "Along with a bunch of his stuff. He must have packed a bag and ran."

Bolted.

Jay packed a bag and bolted because he knew we'd eventually figure out something important. That just because he'd been slashed on the back of his leg *didn't* mean he hadn't been stabbed on the front, too.

Jay hadn't wanted to drop his trousers and let me treat his leg. And as I think about it, I realize I made another critical error.

Whoever attacked Max the final time had lunged at him and fallen. His leg gave way, which made sense when Max had stabbed his leg the day before. But it made even *more* sense if he'd just been slashed. Max said he'd kicked the man in the spot where he'd been stabbed. Except Max never said where he stabbed the guy. He wouldn't know—he'd just swung his penknife down.

From reenacting it, we know that wound would be in the front. But Max saw blood on the back of his attacker's thigh. Blood through his trousers? Or through the bandage we'd just applied? He hadn't specified.

He'd kicked the man where he saw blood presuming that was the wound he inflicted. It wasn't. It was fresh.

But if Jay is the one who attacked Max, who stabbed Jay?

The answer could be that we do indeed have two culprits. The more likely one is that Jay cut himself.

We were out searching for Max. Jay had also been ordered to search. He heard Anders and me, and our conversation told him we were hot on Max's trail. He staged the stabbing. Maybe he intended to do nothing more than a slash. Just enough to bleed and support his story of being attacked from the rear by the bear-man. He cut deeper than he intended, but it did the trick.

We helped Jay, and he joined us until we were getting close to Max. He faked stumbling and being in serious pain. We insisted he stop, mostly so he didn't slow us down.

As soon as we were out of sight, he set off. The fact that he found Max first was pure luck. But he needed to get to Max before we did. That was the whole point of the self-inflicted injury. Get to Max and make sure we didn't, because he was convinced Max saw something and knew he murdered Sandy.

There's one other thing that I missed, one that came back to me before Jay bolted, already turning my mind in his direction.

When the guards brought Rogers to meet us here, he gave us shit for allowing a teenager in our town. That's because the person who mentioned our missing resident was Jay.

Except yesterday, Jay had referred to Max as a child.

"We need clothing from Jay," I say to Rogers when the initial uproar quiets. "For the dog to track. And we need to get close to your camp to find the trail."

"We cannot—"

"We know where your goddamn camp is," Dalton snaps. "We haven't gotten close out of respect, but if we need to get there, we can, and if you want to wave guns at us, then I guess we'll be waving guns at each other. We should demand to see Jay's room and talk to his roommates. He tried to murder a child. But I'm going to respect your privacy as much as I can and trust you to conduct that search. You will do that, and you will take us close enough to your goddamn camp to find this guy before we really *do* have a serial killer living in the forest." He meets Rogers's gaze. "Understood?"

Rogers turns on his heel. "Follow me."

CHAPTER THIRTY-THREE

As we walk, I convey what I need to the guard. He takes off ahead to search Jay's quarters. Jay had been sharing them with two other guards, both of whom Rogers tells him to bring back for questioning.

Rogers doesn't take us to the camp. He just gets us close enough that we can hear distant voices.

"This is the most likely area Jay would have fled through," Rogers says, his tone neutral. "There aren't any paths here where he's likely to bump into someone. There's another spot around the other side, which we can check if your dog can't find his trail."

A guard delivers the scent marker. We give it to Storm. We walk back and forth until it's actually Dalton who locates it. Hell, once I see it, I could have found it myself. There are enough broken branches and trampled undergrowth for a half dozen people.

"Guy's panicked," Dalton says. "Moose leave less conspicuous trails than this."

"Take the pup," I say. "I'll wait for news from the search of Jay's quarters."

Dalton fixes a level stare on me. Not a word. Just that stare, one that says he is not leaving me behind.

"Fine," I mutter. "Let's go."

"Sir!" a voice calls from the forest.

The guard sent to search Jay's room runs out, panting. He's holding a bundle of bloody gauze and bandages. "I found this under the floorboards. His roommates say he'd been limping even before he was stabbed. One asked what was wrong, and he said he pulled a glute muscle doing squats." The young man thrusts out the bloody mess at me, and I try not to wince, seeing he isn't even wearing gloves.

"There was something else, too, ma'am," he says. "Some, uh, pictures. I don't think it was the boy who got captured. This kid was younger. But he was . . . not dressed."

"What?" Rogers says, wheeling on the guard.

"There was, uh, photos of a, uh, boy, who, uh, wasn't wearing any—"

"I understand that," Rogers snaps. "So it was Jay who grabbed the boy?" Before I can speak, he answers his own question: "No, the tattoo means it was Sandy, who was strong enough to carry the boy."

"They were both pedos," the guard says, his lip curling. "Guys like that always find each other. When I was a cop—" He stops short, giving a furtive glance toward his boss, who doesn't even seem to have heard the slip.

"Sandy and Jay were in it together," Rogers murmurs. "And something went wrong."

"We can work out specifics later," I say. "We have a trail, and I just want to find him. Go back to camp—"

"One of my men will accompany you."

"The hell they will," Dalton says.

"What he means," I say, "is that the more people we have

out there, the more noise we make. We will find your man and bring him back alive."

"That isn't necessary," Rogers says.

I could ask him to clarify, but I don't need to. He wants Jay back. He just doesn't care whether he's alive or not. A dead body saves them a lot of trouble.

"Leave someone at the message spot," I say. "When we have Jay, we'll bring him there."

"You don't like this story," Dalton says once we're deep into the forest.

"I hate it."

He says nothing. Just keeps tracking, the path obvious enough that poor Storm looks over at me as if she's profoundly disappointed in this task I've set her on. It's like that time my eighth-grade class did Secret Santa, and mine found out I was into puzzles and gave me a book of beginner word searches. There's no challenge here.

"Sorry, girl," I say. "But you got a real one yesterday."

Yesterday had been a triumph for her, and I worry that in the chaos of finding Max, she hadn't been properly rewarded. Anders and I might have gotten to Max first, but that was only because her nose told us where to go. I must admit, though, that if I worry she didn't receive enough credit, that says more about me than her. She only cares that she eventually found him.

Yesterday she solved the *New York Times* crossword, and now I'm giving her a children's version. She can just phone it in. We all can.

"Walk me through the case," Dalton says, startling me from my thoughts. "I'm still figuring it all out, and I don't think we have the luxury of time here. Jay's wounded. He's not getting far before we need to confront him."

I explain my theory that Jay stabbed himself to piggyback on our search and then do an end run around us to get to Max.

"I think he's the guy who tried to grab Max right before we rescued him," I say. "His wounded leg gave out and he fell, and Max kicked him for good measure. The rest works, too. Hell, I even buy that he's a fellow pedophile. Sandy and Jay discovered a shared interest, and then one of them spots Max, and they hatch a plan. Sandy's plan actually does work better if there's another person involved. Sandy plays bear-man and takes Max because he's bigger and better able to handle him. Jay's job is providing Sandy with an alibi in camp so he can come and go as he pleases. But something goes wrong. Maybe Sandy doesn't want to share after all. Jay kills him and then goes after Max, who has already escaped. It works perfectly."

"Too perfectly?"

Before I can answer, Dalton waves me to silence. He peers into the forest, as if he heard something. A rustling deep in the forest has us both looking, only to see a fox fleeing, having caught Storm's scent.

Dalton stays still even after the fox is gone. He keeps looking and listening. Then he nods for us to continue.

"It's the damn photos," I say, speaking lower now, more aware that my voice is carrying.

"You send the guard to search, and he comes running back with irrefutable proof that Joe is a pedophile?"

"Except he *doesn't* come running back with it," I say. "He comes back with bloodied bandages and claims to have found photos. Still, not wanting to touch them also makes sense, so maybe I'm just . . ." I shake my head. "I don't know."

"The photos are a bit much," Dalton says. "Five minutes of searching, and they happen to notice a loose floorboard, look under it, and find child pornography?"

"Yes," I say. "But if we know Jay tricked us and went after Max, then what does it matter if they lie about finding evidence he's a pedophile? Rogers doesn't want us in his camp, so he serves us answers on a silver platter. Here's your nice and tidy solution. Jay was Sandy's partner in kidnapping a child for the purposes of pedophilia. There, now go away, please."

"He's serving us a tidy solution, not giving us a scapegoat, because we know Jay *did* go after Max. The 'why' isn't important. Which . . ." He rubs his chin. "I hate to say it, but I'd do the same damn thing to keep him out of Haven's Rock. If the culprits are caught, that's enough."

We want to see Rogers as the bad guy. We fulfilled our dream of starting our own Rockton, and this asshole is stomping all over it. He's rain on our wedding day, and it isn't ironic, it's just fucking shitty bad luck.

Except Rogers isn't the villain. He's the antagonist. The opposing force that stands in the way of our perfect happy ending. Are we going to paint him as the villain when he's doing exactly what we'd do in his place to protect our community?

I'm saved from my thoughts by Dalton's hand flying up. He tilts his head, listening, and scans the forest. Then he resumes walking, but we've barely made it five steps before Storm stops. Her head swings left, and she lifts her nose to sniff the air. Then she whines.

I glance at Dalton. He nods, meaning whatever he thought he heard came from that direction. We take out our guns. Dalton looks up into the trees. He's mentally marking this space so he can find it again, in case this isn't the shortcut it seems to be.

I ask Storm to bring up the rear. Dalton takes lead, gun at the ready. It's open enough here that even Storm can move without crashing through the forest. When Dalton stops, I look past him and catch a glimpse of a figure maybe twenty feet away.

Dalton pauses. He shifts left and then right. After a grunt, he says, "I can see you there, Jay. I know you'll have a gun so I'm not coming closer. Tell me how you want this to go down."

Silence, and Dalton sighs.

"Look, either we chase—" he begins.

Jay steps out with his hands up, gun held over his head.

"I need help," Jay says.

"Yep, I'd say you do," Dalton says. "But I'm going to need you to put that gun away."

Jay switches the gun to his left hand. "There. This has to be good enough, because I'm not lowering it. We need to talk. Whatever you think is going on here, you're wrong."

Dalton's lips tighten. He's considering whether to insist on Jay putting down the gun. I don't interfere. I'm fine either way.

"Talk," Dalton says.

Jay casts an anxious look around. "Not here. You need to take me back to your town."

"After you talk."

"Then you're going to need a séance, because if we're here for more than sixty seconds longer, I'll be dead. Did they send you to find me? Did they promise to let you handle it and bring me back?" He snorts. "They followed you, and the only reason they haven't shot me by now is that they knew you'd hear them if they got closer. They had to hang back while you were searching. Now they're sneaking up, and in sixty seconds, I'll be lying in the dirt with a bullet in my brain."

"You tried to kill a kid from our town, and now you're asking us to take you there?"

"I didn't try to kill anyone. I was trying to save him. I don't care whether you take me to your town or just take me some-place safe. Thirty seconds from now, I will be dead. They'll tell you I was dangerous, and they had to put me down like a rabid dog."

"Start walking," Dalton says. "That way."

He points. Jay turns around, hands still up. I move in behind him while Dalton and Storm bring up the rear.

We walk in silence for about fifty steps. Then Jay says, under his breath, "I am so fucked. So goddamn fucked." His voice goes a little louder, still quiet. "I just wanted a job. Pay off my student debt. Can you believe that's what I was worried about? Work up here for a year, and I'd pay it off, and they'd help me get onto a police force. That's what they promised. Good money for a temporary job."

"Don't talk," I murmur. "Voices carry."

He nods, and his voice drops again. "What they're doing out there, it's . . . it's . . . I wouldn't have believed it if you told me. That poor kid. They tried to . . ."

His voice drops so low that I pick up my pace to hear him. I can't help it, and when he spins, part of my brain screams at me for being so goddamn stupid, falling for the ruse.

Thank God for my fast reflexes, because when he lunges, my gun flies up before he can grab me. Behind me, Dalton moves fast and says something, but my entire focus is on the young man at the end of my gun barrel, his own weapon pointed at me.

"Put the gun down," I say.

He doesn't answer.

"Put the gun down or I am going to take it from you."

"I'm not the guy you're looking for. You have this all wrong. I tried to save the kid."

I kick with my bad leg, and my foot connects with the front

of his right thigh. He lets out a scream as he falls back, a scream of agony that doesn't come from my half-assed kick. It comes from that kick connecting with the spot where Max stabbed the guy who tried to strangle him.

When Jay stumbles, I go for his gun, but Dalton is already there, grabbing his arm and wrenching it to the side and then taking the gun from him.

"Tell me again how you didn't try to kill our kid," Dalton says, slamming his fist into that same spot and making Jay howl.

"Fine," Jay snarls. "But it's still not what you think. They made me do it. Promised me fifty grand for cleaning up Sandy's mess. That kid isn't going to be the only one they try to kill. You might hate my fucking guts right now, but I can tell you everything."

"For a price, right?" I say.

His lips twist. "Of course. You get me out of here and pay me what they promised me, and I'll tell you everything."

Dalton snorts. "You mean you'll concoct a very expensive line of bullshit."

"So you don't want the truth? It's your funeral. I was just trying—"

Jay wheels midsentence and tries to bolt, only to stumble. He's not getting far on that wounded leg. Dalton shakes his head as Jay tries again, his feet still twisting as he hisses in pain. He manages to get three steps. Then there's the crack of a branch snapping underfoot, and he trips, face-planting on the ground.

"How long you want to keep doing this?" Dalton says as he walks over to Jay. "We can let you run, but they're going to find you. I don't think you have anything interesting to say, but if you really don't want us turning you in—"

He stops. Then, "Fuck!"

Dalton spins, gun up. There's a dark spot of blood on Jay's shirt. It seems to be up on his shoulder, which is strange, but he's not moving, and I remember the crack that sounded like a snapped branch.

Jay is lying in the dirt and not moving, and Dalton is looking for a shooter.

"Hello!" someone calls in the forest. "We are approaching your location. Please confirm that the threat has been neutralized."

Dalton's answer is a string of profanity, but the clomp of boots means the intruder is making no attempt to hide their approach. I move to Jay. I'm lowering myself beside him when I see the blood on the back of his neck. A memory flashes of Sandy being stabbed in the back of the neck and me saying it was the knife-blade equivalent of a CNS shot.

This *is* a CNS shot. A clean sniper shot that killed him instantly.

So what the hell is that spot on his shoulder?

I touch it, but there's no hole in the fabric. It's just a dime-sized spot of blood soaking through his shirt.

"My apologies." Rogers appears, with two guards behind him, one carrying a rifle. "We shouldn't have shot when you were so close to him. I'm afraid my man misjudged the situation. We heard a cry of pain, and it looked as if Jay had attacked you." His gaze sweeps over us. "You seem unharmed."

"You followed us," Dalton says.

"At a distance, to ensure your safety. I appreciate your assistance in this matter. We will take it from here."

Dalton's mouth works. I know what he wants to say. *The hell you will.* My jaw aches from holding back the same words.

The hell you will.

We want answers.

What answers? There is nothing Rogers has said or done that we can argue against. His men apparently found evidence that

Jay was Sandy's partner in pedophilia. Jay admitted to strangling Max, and that injury on his right quadriceps proves it.

Jay said they paid him to kill Max . . . but he'd been willing to say anything to escape the fate he foresaw: the exact one that came true, leaving him dead, facedown in the dirt.

Sandy kidnapped Max. His motive was pedophilia. Someone killed him. We have no evidence that the "someone" wasn't Jay, but either way, Sandy isn't our concern. Our concern is who tried to murder Max, and that *was* Jay, whatever his motive.

Did Rogers really offer a bounty on Max?

If there is any chance that this man in front of us would order a child killed to protect his camp, then we absolutely need to know that . . . but it also means we absolutely cannot call him on it with two armed guards flanking him.

"You're going to clean this up?" Dalton says finally.

"Yes."

"And we won't have to worry about ever finding anyone from your camp on our side of the boundary line again?"

"Yes. You have my word on this." He meets Dalton's gaze. "This was a very unfortunate incident that taught me we have underestimated a potential danger. We will be locking down to ensure this never happens again. We want to be good neighbors. I think we both need that. Also, the mountain is now your territory, as requested. If we need to go there for any reason, we will consult with you."

I put my hand on Storm's head, and we walk away.

It's all we can do. For now.

CHAPTER THIRTY-FOUR

As we return to town, I mull over the bloody mark on Jay's shoulder. I mention it to Dalton, but I can tell he doesn't see the significance. Just blood spatter from the shot, right?

It wasn't blood from the shot. It was a dime-sized spot of blood that had seeped from an injury to Jay's shoulder, one inflicted before he put his shirt on. I don't point this out to Dalton. He'd see it himself if he weren't so upset over what just happened. He needs to work through that. I need to work through this, because my brain screams that it *is* significant.

And then, as we reach town, it hits me.

"Does April still have my tablet?" I say.

Dalton frowns, as if trying to understand my question in the context of what just happened.

"I need to check something," I say. "I'll meet you back at home."

He gives himself a shake and says, "No, I'll come with you. What's up?"

"Possibly just a bad case of paranoia."

He snorts as he strides along beside me. "Right now, a little paranoia feels like a damn fine idea."

We reach the clinic. April is there, pulling the blinds as the sun sets.

"I need a medical opinion," I say.

I turn on my tablet. I flip through the photos of Sandy until I come to a particular one, where I zoom in. It's the spot I'd noticed on his shoulder, where one of the stab wounds cut through a circular scar but didn't completely obliterate it.

"What's this?" I ask.

She adjusts the brightness. I grab a probe and tap the scar. "This. It looks like a smallpox vaccine mark, except it's new. They still give smallpox vaccines, right? When necessary?"

"That isn't one. I can see why you would think so. It is a scar, though smaller than those obtained through the vaccine." She peers at it and then grumbles, "It would be easier to see if it had not been nearly cut away." A frown and she starts moving the enlarged image. "The edges to this wound are different. They suggest . . ."

"More scalpel than knife?"

She looks over sharply. "Yes. A thinner blade, more precise, with signs that the flesh was pulled apart."

"As if removing something under the skin?" I turn to Dalton, who seems to figure out what I'm getting at. "The blood on Jay's shoulder was in the same spot."

"And his was still bleeding."

"I think these marks explain why they were fine with letting the miners wander. I think it also explains why they were able to find Sandy and kill him. I think they were *always* able to find him."

Dalton blinks. His lips form a curse.

"Tell me I've read too many sci-fi novels," I say.

He turns to April. "Could that mark be from someone inserting a tracking device? Like a chip?"

"A chip?" She looks at the photo again. "Yes. This is the sort of mark it would leave."

"They chipped them," I say to Dalton. "That's why they don't need to worry about them wandering. Sandy obviously didn't realize he had one."

"Jay did, and so he cut his out before he ran."

"Rogers discovers we're missing a kid while Sandy has been heading off for long walks in the woods. They track him down, kill him, and remove the tracker."

"I don't understand most of what you are saying," April says. "But from what I *do* understand, you think they're inserting tracking devices into their employees, against their will and without their knowledge?"

"Yes."

"That is highly unethical. If they were concerned about their employees getting lost in the forest, why not insist they use a wearable tracking device for their own good?"

I pause. Dalton looks at me, and I look back at him.

That's a good question.

A damn good question, and another one we can't answer right now. This case is over, however unsettling the resolution. Max is home. Sandy and Jay are dead. Such a neat and tidy solution. Such a convenient solution.

Too neat and tidy. Too convenient. And too many gaping holes that look like viper-filled pits.

Jay warned us we didn't know what we were dealing with. He'd obviously been trying to scare us into listening to him, but . . .

Had there been more to it? Is there actually something we need to know about our new neighbors?

If so, we need that answer, and it's not going to be easy—or quick—to get.

Max

When Carson comes in from seeing Mathias, he ducks past the bedroom doorway, avoiding Max as he's been doing since Max came home. Oh, Carson isn't ignoring him. He's just avoiding him.

"I'm done with the Switch," Max calls.

"You can keep it." Carson's voice comes from the living room.

"I've played enough. It's your turn."

Max sighs and swings out of bed. He walks into the living room and holds out the game console.

"Stop doing this, Car," he says.

His brother doesn't even look at him. "Doing what?"

"Giving me the Switch. Bringing me snacks. Picking out books from the library. I like all that, but I'd like it even more if you talked to me."

Carson doesn't meet his eyes. "Talked enough already, haven't I? When I said those things."

"Which things? You'll have to be specific, because it's been a lot."

Max feels a twinge of guilt when Carson's cheeks color, but he doesn't take it back. It's true.

"I didn't mean it," Carson says. "Any of it. I'm just . . ."

"Mad and taking it out on me."

"I'm not—" Carson starts, and then stops, shaking his head.

"You can't stop being mad about what happened, but you *can* stop taking it out on me. I'm not putting up with it anymore."

"You shouldn't. If I'm shitty, you should be shitty back."

"Nope. That would give you permission to be shitty."

Carson glares at him. "You planning to be a therapist now? You sound like one."

"Isabel wants us to take sessions together."

"Fuck . . ."

"And that's how you're going to make it up to me." Max pushes the console into Carson's hands. "Not by giving me all the game time. By talking to Isabel with me. About us."

"Fine. Whatever." Carson takes the Switch. "I am sorry. In case I haven't said that."

"I know. We—"

The door opens. Mom stops short.

"Oh," she says. "I . . . I think I forgot something at the store."

"Yes, we're talking," Carson says. "No, you don't need to go anywhere. We're done."

Carson flops onto the sofa and flips to his game.

"Can you put that down, Carson?" Mom says as she comes in.

"I just got it."

"We need to talk." She takes off her jacket and lays it on a chair. "Phil has asked whether we want to stay. If we don't, they'll find other arrangements for us. Under the circumstances . . ."

"I might not want to be here anymore," Max says.

"Right. So it's up to you boys."

Carson shakes his head. "Max is the one who went through all that. It's his choice."

"No, I want it to be our choice. All of ours." Max looks at his mother. "Yours, too."

"I don't want to stay anyplace you're uncomfortable, Max. Anyplace you don't feel safe."

"I felt safer here than I did down south," he says. "After what happened, maybe that should be different, but this didn't have anything to do with everything back home. It was just . . ." He shrugs. "Bad luck. I like it here, and I'd like to stay, but I'm fine with going home, too, if that's what you want."

Mom looks at Carson.

"Same," he says. "I don't love it here, but I'll survive."

"What about you, Mom?" Max says. "What do you want?"

She exhales and sinks into a chair. "Part of me wants to scoop you both up and run again, but this isn't trouble that followed us here, and that trouble is still going to be waiting for us at home. I saw how hard everyone worked to find you. The whole town pitched in, and Eric and Casey and others didn't rest until they found you. If anything, I feel safer here now than I did before. We're going to need to make a few changes, for my peace of mind, but if you're okay with that, then I'm okay with staying."

"You want me to stay away from Gunnar."

Mom exhales again. "I don't know."

"Maybe if you talked to him, you wouldn't worry so much."

"Maybe."

"Is going in the forest one of those things you want changed?" Max says tentatively. "You want me to stay out of it?" That's what he's afraid of. That after what happened, no amount of precautions will have his mother being okay with him setting foot into the woods.

"No more going in *alone*," she says. "If you need time away, we'll figure something out. Maybe ask if you can take Storm, and you tell someone where you'll be and there's a time limit." She looks at him. "Would that work?"

He grins. "Definitely."

"Okay then." She sits up. "Let's go get dinner. I hear it's pizza night."

Casey

Five Days Later

Dalton and I have come south. We'd escorted Louie, who will be looked after by Émilie, blackmailed or bribed to keep his silence about Haven's Rock.

Now, a day later, Dalton and I sit in the poshest waiting room I have ever seen. It's a private one, the two of us on a buttery-soft leather love seat. Jazz music wafts in at just the right level that we can only hear it if we're quiet. A selection of fruit and pastries covers a polished wood table. The coffee maker is the kind of fancy home espresso setup that has me wondering just how many solar panels I'd need for it and how wrong it would be to use that much power to give me the perfect cup of coffee.

"I keep wondering whether this love seat pulls out into a bed," Dalton whispers.

I arch an eyebrow.

He leans in to whisper, "A private room with coffee, bakery goodies, soft music and lighting. I feel like I'm supposed to start whispering sexy sweet nothings in your ear."

I sputter a laugh. "Well, it *is* a fertility clinic."

He takes my hand and squeezes it. I've had my examination by the specialist Émilie secured. Now we're awaiting the results in this tiny room, and I'm desperately trying to enjoy the luxury surroundings and not see the multiple boxes of tissues, poised for bad news.

The door opens, and the doctor slips in. She shakes hands with Dalton, who hasn't met her yet. I brace myself for the small talk, but thankfully, she skips that. She knows that anyone in this clinic doesn't want to discuss the weather.

"There is physical trauma," she says. "I know you've said you don't know what happened during your assault." Her lips tighten, betraying just a hint of emotion. "You were beaten into a coma, and you don't know what your attackers did while you were in that state. The attending doctor focused on your life-threatening injuries and either did not investigate the possibility of sexual assault or chose to not document it. I'd like to say I'm shocked, but that would be expressing pointless outrage."

"The choice was made," I say. "I was in no state to question it, and all things considered, honestly, knowing afterward wouldn't have done any good."

"And it will still do no good, so I'll only say that there is damage. Your concern is the chances of carrying this child to term."

My hand tightens on Dalton's. "Yes."

"First, let me say the pregnancy looks normal. Everything is as it should be."

A tremor of relief runs through me, only to be scattered by the knowledge that this is merely part of the equation.

"Can you carry to term?" she says. "I believe so. *Will* you carry to term with *this* pregnancy? That's another matter. *Can* and *will* aren't the same thing. But the 'can' is important. It means there is no health-related reason to consider ending the pregnancy. Whether you can carry to term will be up to Mother Nature."

"But is there any danger to Casey?" Dalton says.

"Beyond the usual dangers of pregnancy," I add.

"That's what we come down to," the doctor says. "The usual dangers. If you miscarry, there is always a risk. You may require a D&C to remove the fetus if it doesn't pass on its own. That goes for every woman, and there is nothing in your situation that increases the risk. The damage could mean an increased risk of miscarriage or premature birth, which means yes, an increased risk to your health, but not in a way that would have me suggesting termination unless that was what you already wanted."

"It's not," I say.

"I know you live in a remote northern community, which is always a concern, but I'm told you have access to good medical care."

"I do."

"Then I will write up your file for your doctor there. I will continue to see you, and I will be available to your doctor for long-distance consultation. Now, I know that isn't the ideal answer, but I'm hoping it's better than you feared?"

I smile. "It is. Thank you."

"Good. Now let us discuss prenatal care, and steps you can take to maximize the chances of a successful pregnancy. However . . ." She looks from me to Dalton. "If the pregnancy is not successful, that doesn't mean you did anything wrong. These are just steps that might help and will tell you what to look for. In the end, whether you can carry this baby to term isn't up to you or me or anyone."

"We understand."

The doctor walks over to the counter and begins to assemble an information package. I glance at Dalton. He's quiet, his eyes clouded with whispers of worry. To me, the doctor's news is wonderful. What Dalton hears, though, is the danger I face, and I can argue that it's the danger any woman faces in pregnancy, but that isn't the point. Any danger is, to him, too much, and that makes me feel . . .

Loved. So damn loved and more than loved, it makes me feel cherished. Important to someone in a way I've never felt important. I matter. My health matters, and he's not sure he dares risk it even for something he really wants.

"Hey," I whisper as I squeeze his hand.

He looks over.

"It'll be okay," I say.

He nods, his gaze saying he's not quite buying that.

I move closer and whisper, "We're going to take this chance together, and if it works out?" I meet his gaze. "If it works out, it'll be amazing. And if it doesn't?" I shrug. "That's the danger we face. That it doesn't work out, and we grieve. As for the rest?" I could say I face graver danger every day, but I know he doesn't want to hear that. "I have April, and I have you, and as long as no one tries to make me stay in bed for eight months . . ."

His lips twitch. "Tempting."

"But no. So we get all the information and proceed with caution, and if it works out . . ." I whisper in his ear. "I'm going to have your baby, and I could not be happier."

I watch the worry vanish into his smile. Then he leans to my ear and whispers, "Neither could I."

And there it is. This isn't our perfect ending, the answer that everything is fine and will continue to be fine. We didn't get the perfect ending to our mystery either. Both are messy and unsatisfying . . . for now. They are works in progress, just like everything else in life, and we're here to put in the work and focus on progress, however it turns out.